I0746291

TRILLIUM PRESS

 COLLUSION

H. S. J. WILLIAMS

TRILLIUM PRESS

© 2024 by H.S.J. Williams

Published by Trillium Press

All rights reserved. No part of this book may be used or reproduced in any manner whatsoever without written permission except in the case of brief quotations embodied in critical articles and reviews.

This book is a work of fiction. Any references to historical events, real people, or real places are used fictitiously. Other names, characters, places, and events are products of the author's imagination and any resemblance to actual events or places or persons is entirely coincidental.

Cover art by Kateryna Vitkovska
Map art by Noverantale
Interior illustrations by Hannah S. J. Williams
Part I, II, III art by Hannah Rogers

To Grammie

I know you and Errance would have made a splendid match,
but I promise the skinblender will take good care of him.

The Celestial Cleft
ASELVIA
Shadowshade Forest
DENJI
DORMANDY
ORIM
KORINCE
The Niar O

N
The North
TERTOREM
OOLUM
ean

Family Tree

CELESTIAL-BORN
ERRAN
RENDAR
TELVAR
ASARIE
CERENE
CERAND
CASARA
LEOREN
TRYSS
ERRANCE
ZIZAIN
COREN
TELLIE
(BY ADOPTION)
KELM
ZOREN

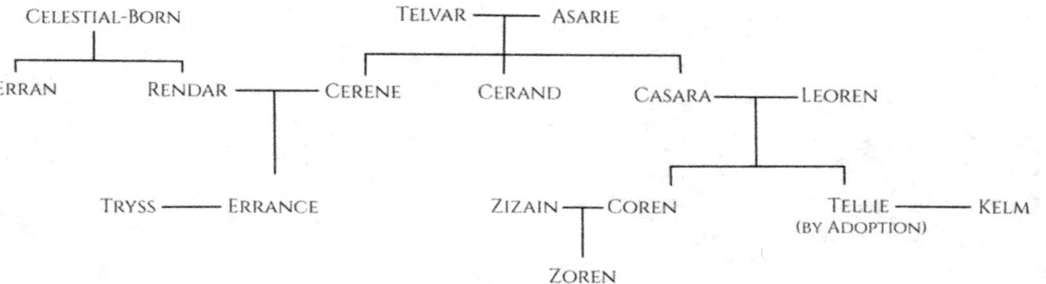

PROLOGUE

1232, Jal the 22nd

Aselvia maintains its distance. The young king's rule does not quaver, though this surely lies in the steady roots of their ancient and unchanging culture rather than the strength of his leadership. If there is any weakness within, the rest of the world cannot see it. But there must be. There always is.

The candle's flame sputtered in the draft from the opening door. If the room darkened, it could have only been the light's flickering or the presence of a new shadow amongst other shadows. The puff of the wind itself could not have been dark.

Bent over his work at the desk, the man took no notice of the approaching figure, but continued to study the papers spread before him. Reaching for the inkpot, he dipped his quill and went on writing.

The messenger cleared his throat.

"Yes?" the other replied, though he did not pause in his scribbling.

"Sir...the Elect of Oolum have agreed to the latest terms."

"Have they?" The pen went on scratching across the paper, raising the hairs on the back of the messenger's neck. "Very good, then."

Bowing, the messenger turned and made a hasty exit.

Once he was alone again, the man at the desk set aside his quill and pulled out a parchment upon which was drawn a map of Mid Orim. Beside almost every city-state shown on the sheet was a mark of success. "Dormandy, Korince, Meece, and Oolum." The man sighed as his finger traced up to an encirclement of mountains. "And yet one evades me."

Aselvia. Every city he'd taken before had been human or at least run by humans, but this was another matter altogether. This was a kingdom of elves. Elves were rarely seen, keeping almost entirely to themselves behind the mountains and magical barrier that bordered their land. Or at least until recently. Until new stories had spread like wildfire of a new king risen to the throne within the last decade. A young king who was said to have been imprisoned and forgotten for years. A young king who'd no doubt brought changes to the everlasting elf kingdom. And where there were changes…there was opportunity.

The man leaned back in his chair, his fingers pressed together under his nose, and considered long and hard. At last, he called a name, and the door opened again as a tall thin man in the clothes of a clerk pattered in.

"Send out notices to the Northern assets," the man at the desk said, quickly writing out the paper and handing it to his assistant to be copied.

"Is this about the elven city?" the clerk began. "Dormandy will try again—"

"But Dormandy has been failing," the man reminded. "We must have another plan. We need someone inside."

Revelation dawned in the clerk's eyes. "Someone to gain the king's trust and confidence. If we had his ear, we could control him—"

"No." Cold and clear the word cut. "No, there is only one way to control the king." He reached to dip his quill again, but his sleeve caught the candlestick, knocking it over.

The flame flickered out.

Part One

1

ASELVIA

It was not the sound of screaming that woke her, but rather the stillness. For a moment she lay there in the dark silence, wondering what could be wrong. Then she recognized the stillness to be one of rigid terror. She rolled off the bed before the first constrained cry came.

"Errance!" she called, but her voice was nearly drowned out by the harsh sound of his struggle, and she flinched as he threw out an arm.

"Errance."

She drew closer, though not close enough to be in reach. He was beginning to thrash around more aggressively, and she saw him start to roll to the side of the bed. Taking a deep breath, she leaned forward and called, "Errance, wake up, it's me! It's all right!" She reached out for him, but too late.

He fell off, landing hard on the floor in a tangle of sheets. "Stay back!" he shouted.

Hurrying around to the other side, she stood at a distance, heart aching as she watched him try to struggle out of the bindings of the blankets. "Errance," she said again, forcing herself to sound calm. "It's me. Your wife. Tryss."

He stopped moving. She could hear him panting like a hunted animal.

"Tryss," he said at last, his voice hoarse enough to be encrusted with gravel.

"Yes." She quietly drew closer.

Slowly, he pushed himself to his feet, pulling the sheets off, and staggered past her to the far side of the room. There he opened the glass doors and stepped out onto the balcony.

She gazed at him, haloed in moonlight, his body bent over the railing, hands gripping the edge. His shoulders shuddered with each breath. After a few moments, she stepped out onto the balcony with him, but still kept her distance. They had experienced many nights like this, and she knew to give him his space, to understand why he often shunned her comfort after a nightmare. Still, how difficult it was! How painful to watch. How impossible to comprehend the horrors her husband had suffered.

He hasn't had a nightmare this intense in a while, she thought with a troubled sigh. *I had hoped they were leaving for good.* She set a hand on the rail—not too close, but close enough for him to hold it if he chose.

He took a deep breath. "How…how long have I been king?"

"Seven years," she whispered.

"Seven." His eyes closed. "How long have we been married?"

"Two."

He said no more for many heartbeats, but at last his hand slid across the rail and slipped around hers. Though she did not move or speak, a

relieved smile blossomed across her face. Finally, he turned to face her and drew her into an embrace. "I'm sorry," he murmured.

"Don't be." She relaxed in his arms, her body feeling strangely exhausted as it always did after recovering from one of his terrors. "It's not your fault." She waited for his heartbeat to slow down, but it continued to flutter rapidly. "Are you ready to go back?"

"No." He pulled away, the shadows of the balcony closing in around him. "I…I think I'd rather sleep out here tonight."

"With or without me?"

There was a long moment of silence as he considered. "I…it's not very comfortable out here on the stone…"

"I'll be right back," she replied. Returning to the room, she lit a candle and tucked a blanket and book under her arm before stepping back out. He had sat in the corner of the balcony, staring out between the railing posts upon the darkened land below him. As she approached, he swiped a glistening tear off his cheek. He glanced up, and her breath caught at the misery in his face.

"I'm sorry," he said again. "It's just—so real." Looking away again, he swore under his breath with a shaky laugh.

Taking no notice, Tryss placed the candle on the stones near them, sat beside him, and spread the blanket over their knees. She opened the book and began to read aloud.

"The Darkness is great about me,
But Your light shines ever on.
Though I close my eyes to Your brightness,
Still You love me, even in my blindness.
One day shall I pass into Glory, where

Pain is far and gone.
I am my Lord's servant, and Ayeshune is my Lord.
Whom then shall I fear?

For a long time, nothing else was said. Setting the book aside, Tryss curled up on the stone and rested her head against her husband's shoulder. Though the breeze bit with the crisp chill of oncoming autumn, both he and the blanket were warm, and she felt herself drifting to sleep.

Errance woke with the first blush of dawn. The blanket had fallen to the side sometime in the night, and despite the warmth of his wife, he shivered in the crisp morning air. Taking care not to wake her, he slid out from under her and stood, stretching his aching limbs.

The sight of Tryss asleep on the hard stone smote his heart. He'd been selfish to allow her to stay with him through the night. It had been less than comfortable, something he often preferred, but not what she deserved. Or what was even good for her since now….

His gaze fell to her rounded stomach, and he whispered a silent curse on himself. Honestly, what had he been thinking to let her sleep out here? Thinking of himself, that's what. Caught up in his own fears, forgetting for a moment what she carried. What kind of man forgot that?

Taking a deep breath, he knelt and lifted her into his arms. She stirred, murmuring, and her fingers sweetly reached up to touch his face. He froze. After a moment, she returned to solid slumber. He carried her back inside to bed, carefully pulling the sheets over her body.

With a sigh, he turned to the wash basin across the room, rubbing his bare skin. Nearly two years of marriage, and sometimes—often—he still feared touch. Not hers. Not really hers. He *trusted* Tryss. And yet…

The water from the glass pitcher whistled softly as he poured it into the basin.

Perhaps he'd been a fool to propose marriage so soon. Perhaps she'd been a fool to accept him. From most perspectives, five years of mutual interest was not an unreasonable foundation for marriage, but as an elf he could have bided more time.

But how dared he? If he'd waited longer, would Tryss have waited for him? Perhaps he imagined the pressure and expectation from his people, but the pressure and expectation he set on himself grew heavier with each day.

He dipped the cloth into the water, then rubbed it across his face. The smoothness of the fabric seemed too perfect to be right, so he scrubbed harder than necessary.

They deserved a king who ruled with grace and confidence, who did not doubt himself. Who would marry a woman for love and who would display that love as a model and inspiration for all.

They deserved a king like his father.

The cloth dropped from his fingers, and he pressed both his hands flat on the table, staring hard into the mirror. Blue-green eyes stared out from his finely-cut face, framed by dark hair that hung to his waist. He was beautiful even for his kind. Some might have called him flawless, never mind the shadows of a difficult sleep.

And he hated that it was so.

Countless times he wished he still carried some marks of his imprisonment. Not the brands of the Darkness's ownership, no, he thanked God that those had been taken away. And if not for the healing light within him, the layers of scars upon his body would have been too numerous to carry. Yet he wished for some sign. So that when others looked upon him, they would flinch and keep walking. So that they would not say "how well he looked" and "how far he had come" since his captivity.

They saw flawless beauty. They couldn't see his ragged soul trembling inside.

He felt old. He grudgingly knew that he was considered young by elven standards, and humans often made the mistake of calling elves immortal. His eyes revealed the truth. They were not merely eyes who'd lived too long and seen too much. They were eyes that had died, died, and died again.

You're running out of time, a quiet voice inside him whispered.

Running out of time, yet these past few years seemed like the longest of his life. At first, he'd embraced the peace and protection his people offered, wrapping himself fiercely in it. But as time passed, he realized it was just a covering, and the tighter he clung to it, the swifter it slipped away. This world was so tranquil, so calm. Yet he felt like a ship trapped upon a still sea, slowly running out of food and water. He could not settle into this serenity of everyday life his people were so content in. But he panicked at the thought of it being taken away again…

His arms quivered, and a desperate urge flooded within him to seize the mirror and smash it. There was some deep, dark part of him that wanted to feel the sting of blood on broken glass. Some part of him that still whispered pain was all he was good for. But he would not. Could not. Tryss…Leoren…and all the rest. They expected better of him. They believed in him. And he couldn't let them know that after all this time, he was slowly shattering apart.

Enough of that. It did him no good to dwell on such fears. Just made it worse. Surely it would be better if he could just…just ignore it. Maybe then it wouldn't come true.

Forcing himself to step away, he tugged on a fresh set of clothing and wrapped himself up in a morning robe. He slipped through the doors that separated the bedroom from their primary living space, latching them shut behind him without a sound.

Someone had come in and left breakfast on the table by the window. Jasmine-scented steam curled up from the teacups, and the aroma of baked bread and cheese slipped out from a woven basket. He hooked his ankle around the chair, pulled it out, and sat to stare at the waiting food, but he did not touch it. Tryss wasn't awake yet, but he didn't want the food to grow cold for her. Perhaps he should bring it in and see if the smells would coax her eyes open. She could just eat in bed and then go back to sleep if she wanted. Usually she would have already been up and brought the breakfast in herself, but she needed her rest these days.

It was kind of the staff to bring them breakfast, if a bit unnerving. Honestly, ever since he'd come home, living alongside the servants felt a bit like living in somebody else's house. He remembered them from his childhood, of course, and he was fond of them, but he felt so uncertain as how to behave around them now. They certainly seemed to accept that he was not the bright-eyed boy they'd cared for in the past, which was a relief. And they certainly had practice in caring for a remote king if Rendar's last seventy years of grief and secrecy were any indication. So for the most part, they danced to their regular rhythm in life, taking pride in maintaining a large house that they lived in more than anyone else, and cooking their meals with some extra sent up to the king who happened to live in the room upstairs.

It was no wonder that Tryss had taken to them with the same grace that she embraced everything that stepped into her path. She did not accept them as servants, but rather as friends, and she was working with them more often than not—down in the kitchens, gathering out in the garden, or venturing out to the markets and even wilds for more provisions. He often went with her so it could just be the two of them. Just the two of them up on mountain heights, the cold morning wind rustling their hair, the scarves of fog trailing through the forest below them, the soil in their fingers as they dug up roots to gather in hampers...

"My Lord Errance? Your Majesty?"

The painfully polite voice finally reached through the fog of Errance's mind and he straightened, shaking his head. His eyes focused on Leoren waiting beside him with a concerned expression. It was the only expression he was used to seeing anymore, it seemed. He hadn't even heard him come in. And he was using titles, not "Errance," not "nephew," which meant it was a professional day. A day to be king. *Lovely.*

"Yes?" He forced the word out.

"Your tailor...he has been waiting in the dressing room these past ten minutes."

Ten minutes? How long had he just been sitting here? Now that he looked about, the light in the room had increased significantly, suggesting it had at least been an hour since he'd awoken. His untouched tea sat in a vapid pool inside its cup, no longer sending up wisps of warmth.

"Of course," he murmured, rising. It was childish to wait for Tryss to wake up and join him. There was nothing he wished more than to sweep into the room and tell the tailor he was taking a holiday, meaning he would dress himself and fly on The Daisha all day. Except that was childish as well. For though it was true that affairs in Aselvia were hardly ever so important as to demand immediate notice, it would be only flippant of him to ignore them. His father had ever been a worthy king, and Errance would not shame him by being anything less.

And if being a worthy king required him to let the tailors dress him in finery so that he might sit on a throne and listen to the report of his people, then he would be man enough to do it, God help him!

It was only once a week, after all.

He strode into his dressing room, shrugging off his robe. He already wore the leggings and tunic that would be base for the royal attire. Without a word, he stood in the light before the window and posed with arms held out lightly from his sides.

Murmuring some morning greeting, the tailor shook out various coats and sashes and whole capes of shining fabric, pulling across Errance's shoulder here, tucking in there, and tugging tight in the middle. For occasions like this, his tailor also served as a valet since he always liked to build his creations on his subject, altering and adding as needed to complete the overall look. It was a great deal too much effort, in Errance's opinion, for something as simple as sitting on a fancy chair all day, but the Aselvians took pride in their attention to detail and effort in elegance.

For the first few months, he had been altogether adamant against the tailor, even with Leoren watching in the same room. No amount of sense had been able to stifle his anxiety. Bare skin, narrow tape, sharp scissors and pins…what could *possibly* go wrong? The endless scenarios were never far from his mind, but it was of course best to keep such thoughts quiet, since he'd nearly made his tailor weep the first time he sardonically spoke them aloud.

He waited silently for the end, staring across the room at a shining disc ornament from which came a constant tick. He watched the delicate little spears upon the disc's face twitch down their circular path, small step by small step. It was a clock, he had been told long ago. A human invention that had become popular sometime during his imprisonment. When Leoren became ambassador, relations with Dormandy greatly improved, and soon Leoren was bringing back all sorts of far-fetched ideas for the elven craftsmen.

A tool to tell time was one of the worst things Errance could have possibly imagined. An hourglass was bad enough, but that at least had to end and time would go on without it. This never-ending device clicked on and on and counted each and every second of his life. If it never stopped—and indeed, it showed no sign of stopping—then it would continue to tick after his death. The rhythmic beat recalled another sound he'd heard eternally tap against his ear—the drip of water in a deep dungeon grotto.

"I asked Ahspen to see you this morning before you head to the throne." Leoren's voice broke through the dark sediment of his thoughts.

Errance started. "What? Why?"

Looking a little exasperated, Leoren sighed. "Errance, you haven't been sleeping well."

Perhaps he shouldn't have asked while the tailor was in the room. Oh well, what did the tailor not know already? What did the whole of Aselvia not know already? The elves did so love to gossip, and he wouldn't be surprised if his meek and quiet tailor was actually a wealth of information on the subject of their king. Not to mention he already knew Ahspen had told some things to his wife who had told practically everyone else. So much for privacy.

"I never sleep well," he said, difficult as always.

"But you've been sleeping worse than usual, I can tell. Have you been keeping up with the teas and oils he's given you? The exercises and meditation?"

"Yes, yes, I am a model patient," he said. So, that wasn't the total truth. There were many nights he didn't even see a point in trying to drive the misery away. Besides, Tryss was a better comfort than all those chamomile drinks and lavender lotions.

"I already have him waiting in the willow room."

"Of course you do."

"Please go, Errance, there's no harm in trying to help. He is already here; it would be ungracious to waste his time."

Because clearly he had a very busy schedule. There were times Errance wondered what exactly Ahspen even did to keep his job. He was all about "wellness" in mind and body. And as far as Errance knew, most elves were already well enough, so did that make the king his special patient? An interesting subject of study? What did other elves go to him for anyway? Probably massage and body alignment. Ahspen swore it was a wonderful way to relieve stress. Errance assured him his body had been manhandled and his bones rearranged well enough to last a lifetime. Ahspen hadn't smiled. Or even flinched. He must have been tired of the cynicism.

All right, he would go. It was the least he could do for Tryss.

But it wasn't Ahspen who waited in the willow room. The moment Errance stepped through the double doors, he recognized the tall figure standing in the open windows across the way. A tall figure with black hair past his waist, streaks of white running through it.

Damarik. Head healer of Aselvia, the father of Ahspen.

Errance halted, knowing he'd already been sensed and that it was too late to turn around. Had Leoren set this up? No, his uncle wasn't sly. Besides…Damarik didn't bite. He just had that way of looking at you until every one of your problems was laid bare before him. When Errance had been a child, the head healer had frightened him. He was kind enough, just hardly spoke, and the mystery of his scarred face and missing eye was terrible enough that Errance had never pried into it. A remnant of the Dark Days, a history that had been kept veiled from his young mind, and now…now he was too daunted with his own troubles to add knowledge of tragedies past.

"I asked Ahspen if I could speak with you today, but he sent me along with a new tea he brewed. It contains kava, some root imported from the islands, I hear."

"Thank you," Errance murmured, taking that as an invitation to sit in the white woven chair and take the cup of steaming tea from the nearby table. He took a sip, noting the warm, rich flavor. If it was supposed to be calming, he'd definitely need it for this conversation.

"Do you know why Ahspen took up this work?"

Because it was the family trade? Literally everyone in Damarik's household practiced some form of healing. He took care of illness and wounds, his wife tended all the animals, and his daughter Dahlya was a midwife. But instead he answered, "I guess I never really thought about it."

"He was a boy during the Dark Days. Anyone who lived during that time came away with deep scars and had to find their own path of healing. Ahspen had a particular difficulty with night terrors; they clung to him for years afterward. He started searching for which plants benefited him, took time for prayer and meditation, dedicated himself to making the world around him beautiful. But it wasn't until he started trying to help others that he began to feel real change within himself. In truth, it was much the same for me." He reached up and touched the scarf bound across half his face, concealing his missing eye and the scars puckering the flesh. "I was wounded, so I sought how to heal others."

"So you're saying I should take up medicine and nursing?"

Damarik's brow rose. "I'm saying I think you are drowning in a sense of lost purpose. Would you disagree?"

Of course he was right, he was always right. He saw everything with that one dark brown eye. Stars, it was unnerving.

When he thought about it, the first few years coming back from imprisonment had been a climb uphill, but still, he'd been going uphill. There had been so much to do. He'd thrown himself back into life, taking the challenge between his teeth. It hadn't been as full of humiliation as he'd feared, because Tellie and Kelm and Tryss were there. They'd joined him in studies of elvish culture and language. Tellie had needed to be taught basic skills such as reading and math, and Leoren had seen to it that Errance checked her work as a way to freshen his own memory on the subjects. All four of them had learned dancing together, and Casara often saw to it that Tryss was his partner. She'd been so graceful in his stiff arms, somehow always easing the tension away, and the children had pranced about them, laughing over themselves.

Yes, the pain of Tertorem had been near in those days, but yet he remembered that time as a happy time, and now…well now, Tellie and Kelm were grown up, married, and traveling about Orim on business.

The Daisha grew fat up in the frosted forests on the mountain borders. The old miner and the former prisoners of Tertorem whom he'd brought back on his return either had peacefully passed away or lived quiet and content out in the woods.

"Have you taken up any trade?" Damarik asked gently. "It is important for even a king to find some pastime to ease his duties. What about art? I know excellent masters, and painting is especially relaxing."

Relaxing was not a word he would have used to describe the recollections of his childhood art endeavors. He'd been far too impatient and distracted, and would hardly be any better now.

Damarik's gaze had turned to Errance's restless fingers. Drawing in a breath, the young king slipped his nervous thumb under his fingers and held tight.

"Ahspen can give you some herbs to help you sleep at night. I know you don't want him to examine and adjust your body, but he can teach you some exercises that will help loosen your muscles before you push them so hard in training...but I believe the source of your anxiety will remain."

"And you can't really do anything for that," he said, unsurprised and trying not to sound bitter.

"Some scars never heal." He eased into the chair opposite Errance, his robes and slippers rustling. "But you learn to live with them, live through them, live abundantly. It takes time and patience and pain, but eventually you notice less and less that they are there."

There was that word again. *Time.* Time he didn't have. "Is that it then? Just keep living?"

A slight smile softened Damarik's face. "The key," he said, "is in the living. Find purpose. Take Ahspen's help. But there is hurt that lies in your spirit, not your body or your mind. That is something only God can truly help you repair."

"I am saved, aren't I?" The words came out far too sharp. Far too questioning. Ashamed, he unclenched his hand and hid his face behind it.

Damarik's hand was on his shoulder, firm but encouraging. "Being saved is one thing. Understanding and living according to that salvation is another. Go to the Elder Priest. He will help you find your way."

The Elder Priest. Oriah. He liked Oriah. The man had the warmest smile in all of Aselvia, one that could coax a fawn into his lap. But he usually said the same things, the things everyone said.

Love. Learn. Live.

It should have been simple. It never should have been so hard.

2

DORMANDY

As far as the guards of the governor's gate were concerned, mornings were always the same. Now that the sun had risen, the people of the city sprang to life. Fog began to creep away from the tall brick buildings, leaving only the typical smog that skulked in corners and alleys.

The guard, leaning upon his pike, watched the usual processions with glazed eyes that bespoke he'd have been better off not drinking with his cronies at the brew the night before. But then, there wasn't much need to be alert—the only people passing were newspaper boys, bakers with tempting treats, and businessmen in sedan chairs and carriages hurrying off to their work.

"I wonder what he'll look like," the guard at the opposite side of the gate said suddenly.

"Eh? Wuss that?" the first guard said.

"The wood carver. The wood-carving specialist the governor called in. An elf and all that."

The guard blinked, trying to clear the haze in his head. Yes, now that did sound vaguely familiar. Bother it. Why did something unusual have to disturb a perfectly good and lazy morning? Worst of all, it was even rather interesting, maybe even exciting. Elves didn't simply walk about Orim, not in Dormandy anyway. He wondered if it was true that the men were just as pretty as the women. That just didn't seem natural.

Thoroughly awake now, the guard straightened and began eyeing the streets with more interest. A simple wagon, driven by a young man and woman, escaped his notice altogether, and it was with great annoyance that he had to acknowledge them when they stopped right in front of his gate.

"Hear now, move on then," he said. "We don't give directions."

The young man upon the wagon seat handed the reins to the young lady and leaned forward, a friendly smile on his freckled face. "Actually, I think I've reached my destination. This is the governor's estate, is it not?"

"What business is it of yours?"

"It's business entirely," the stranger said, grin ever widening. "I do believe I was hired by Governor Dolfen to work my magic, as it were, on his wooden walls."

The other guard coughed and stepped forward. "Now then, that's not right. He's expectin' a Lord Kelmthrander."

"That's right," the young man said cheerfully. "Except it's Kelm Thrander. First and last name. You mashed it all into one," he added in assistance to the guard's confused expression.

"You can't be 'im!" the first guard exclaimed. "If you're an elf, I'm a daisha!"

"Happily, we are both human," the proclaimed Kelm said. "Here are my papers certifying my position. I was trained by the elves, but I am not of their race. I was even acknowledged as a master artisan by the Korince business guild."

The guard scanned the documents with the severity of a man determined to prove fault. But his face became ever more anxious,s and at last he looked up in desperation. "You're sure you're the real thing?"

"He could give you a demonstration if you like," the young lady said. She gave the guards a very pretty smile, and they both had the sense to blush.

"Go on in, then," the guard said unhappily, handing the papers back. He felt quite cheated. Elves, indeed. So much for that.

The entrance to the governor's house towered twice as tall as any man, with two wooden doors carved in concave, layered squares. Once upon a time, it would have overawed the young woman. After all, she had been raised as a poor orphan in this city, and when she'd passed by this house, she'd wondered what glories hid inside. Now, it was simply beautiful to look at, but not astonishing, because she'd seen better things. Being adopted by royal elves tended to do that to one's perspective.

"Kelm Thrander as requested," her husband told the doorman. "And my lovely wife and assistant, Tellie."

The doorman looked down his astute nose, but if he held the same misgivings as the guards at the gate, he did not voice them. With a small bow, he stepped aside, opening the way to an enormous chamber of cherry-wood floor, tapestries and portraits hung on papered walls, and mirrors reflecting the castles of candlelight from above.

A maid came to greet them, her black dress a stark contrast to the surrounding colors. "I will take you to your work, if it please you," she said, dipping a quick curtsy.

Tellie gave her the warmest smile she had to offer, but the maid's face remained passive and polite, a professional from the inside out. So they followed her up the wide wood stair that curved both to the right and left and took the left corridor. The floor turned to carpet, which while soft and luxuriously silent, must have been a nightmare to clean. Tellie hoped she wasn't dragging stains across the material that a poor servant would have to scrub out later.

After passing several closed doors, they came to a study at the end of the hall. Every bit of furniture had been taken from this room and the floor was covered in thick paper. The heady scent of cedar poured from every corner and just for a second, Tellie felt light-headed with homesickness. The entrance to this study and the corners of the room were reinforced with freshly hewn cedar posts. Wood just waiting to be carved into intricate detail.

"Is there anything you need before you begin, Master Thrander?" the maid asked.

"No, no, I've brought my tools with me and I shall start at once."

She touched a small bell hung at the wall. "Please ring this if you have any questions or wish to be brought to the guest hall for food and drink."

As soon as she'd left, Kelm laid down his case and unbuckled the locks, opening it wide to reveal the rows of sharp knives, chisels, and hammers all strapped into place. While he selected his tools, Tellie sat cross-legged in a corner and opened her own bag of things, pulling out a sewing kit and a bundle of fabric. She shook out the tiny dress, pressing the creases smooth against her knee. A casual observer would have considered the dress complete, and she had to admit if she just left it simple, then she could make more clothes. But she also remembered how much having nice things had meant to her as an orphan child, and she could only imagine what an impoverished mother might wish for her baby.

So she threaded a needle with shining green thread and began stitching delicate vines across the blouse. Later, she would add little flowers and drops of sparkling dew. Painstaking, lengthy work, but she'd learned it all from the elves who were nothing if not patient with detail. When she was done, she would add it to her collection of clothes that she donated to orphanages or carehouses for the sick and destitute. It wasn't much, but it was something.

Perhaps an hour passed spent in soft scraping of wood and low humming, when a new sound came from down the hall. Approaching footsteps and voices. Tellie bent her head and listened as they came closer.

"—should have arrived this very day. He came highly recommended by the Korince Carving Guild, and I have asked him to fashion the wood in the likeness of Aselvian forests. Of course, as few have ever seen your forests, we can only imagine the splendor—"

Two figures came through the door. One was the governor of Dormandy, a stout man with a rich red beard, and the other was a tall and slim male elf with pale yellow hair reaching halfway down his waist.

Tellie didn't even spare a glance for the governor. "Daava!" she exclaimed in delight. Without a thought for etiquette, she flew forward and threw her arms around the elf's neck. He embraced her in turn, smoothing down her curls. When they pulled away again, he turned to address the perplexed governor.

"This is my daughter, Tellie Thrander," he explained.

"I did not know you had a daughter, Lord Leoren," the governor said, kissing Tellie's hand. But all his politeness could not hide the confusion on his face, for Tellie, though a pretty young woman, was clearly human.

She laughed gaily. "I am adopted, Governor, if that was what you're wondering."

"Ah," the man said, his brow clearing. "Well, that does explain things. I did not know that the acclaimed Kelm Thrander was son-in-law to the Steward of Aselvia."

"Well," Kelm said with a cough. "I do try to be modest."

"I must say I am delighted," the governor went on. "The woodwork will have genuine inspiration from the very heart of Aselvia. Is it really as lovely as they say?"

"It is," Tellie said, but only got that much out before the man was talking again. He apparently loved to talk.

"Is the castle as grand as my house? Of course, you need not answer, how could I compare to the castle of a king? But I wish you to be as content as you can in my humble abode, so feel free to look about and partake in what we have to offer. I am always eager to improve our friendship with the great realm of Aselvia in any way. You know, Lady Thrander, I was just talking with your father about possibly visiting someday. If not I, then a representative!"

Tellie could always tell when Leoren was annoyed. She saw the signs now—the slight straightening of his mouth, the pucker in his brow. She curtsied in return to the governor's comment, but it was all she could do to keep from grinning.

"Governor Dolfen," Leoren said carefully, "our relations have been steady and agreeable for generations. We export and import goods with reasonable tariff rates, and have established communication between our two houses of office. You might excuse us if we choose to remain cloistered given the history of my people."

The man gave a wave of his hand as if blowing away dust. "But that is history, my lord, the suppression of Aselvia was at the beginning of the age. You have a new king, after all, and it was so very long ago!"

There was a heavy moment of silence. Then Leoren said in a cold voice, "There are some who yet remember it."

After an awkward pause, the governor gave an apologetic cough. "Ah. Of course. Do pardon me, lord." He bowed to Tellie and Kelm. "And I beg your pardon for interrupting your fine work. Please continue and let me know if there is anything that can make your stay more comfortable. Now, Ambassador Leoren, if I could show you to my office, we can discuss the new imports."

Not even an hour had passed before Leoren returned to the room on his own.

"Lovely meeting?" Tellie inquired innocently, glancing up from her needlework.

"Satisfactory," Leoren replied. "Though I am not sure he would give you the same answer. Either way, we struck a deal and I am returning home." He reached out to clasp Kelm's hand in farewell, and then hesitated as he looked to Tellie. "I would offer to take you with me, but..."

"My place is with Kelm," she answered.

"Well, hang on a moment, Tel," Kelm said. "This was the last job I was taking before we headed home anyway. Traveling from place to place is swell and all, but sitting here can't be the greatest fun for you. How about you head back now? It will take a few weeks for me to finish, and if you-know-who arrived before we were home, you would be awfully disappointed."

A glow had brightened her face, held in check only by hesitation. "Are you sure?"

"I wouldn't have said it if I wasn't."

She tossed her stitching to the side and sprung at him, whirling them both around the room, nearly bumping into Leoren who had to step out of the way. "You are the very best, Kelm," she exclaimed. "You really are! All right, Daava. I'll head home with you."

OOLUM

The boy perched on the edge of the flat roof, as much at home there as the seagulls surrounding him. The heat of the sun did not inflame his brown skin, only bronzed it to shine with nearly the same copper as his red hair. He watched the bustle below him with the same idle curiosity as the birds, both relaxed and ready to leap at once.

"Eh, Spark, where'd you run off to?"

At the sound of that voice, the boy hopped down to the nearest crate, then to the ground, startling the gulls in a blur of white feathers. He darted between clusters of people until he reached the man who had called him.

"Here, Da."

His da's mouth curled into a smile at the sight of him, the anxious gleam in his green eyes fading. "There you are, lad. Don't wander off from me or your mum, you're not old enough for that."

The day he was "old enough" was taking its sweet time in coming. All six years of his life he had known adventure. These sandstone walls, trampled streets, and kaleidoscope markets were as familiar and dear a home to him as any place could be. Oh, sure, he knew the streets held danger. He'd seen and heard plenty of that, for his da was none other than Captain Coren, a sailor to most, a savior to many. Only the trusted few knew about his operation of smuggling slaves to safety. The rest of the city would have paid a fortune to have his head for that.

So yes, the boy knew it was dangerous to wander far. That's why he'd taken to the roof. So he could see everything—where his da went, what the people around him were doing. The street they stood in could not be considered one of the many wonders of Oolum. Bodies bent on straw mats, hunched frames heaved with coughing. The clothes were ragged, belongings few. This was one of the beggars' alleys, kept out of sight of the social elite and excited travelers. At dawn and dusk, these people would move (or be moved if too ill) to the gates of the city and beg for money or food. It provided them with some things. But it could not heal them.

And so the boy's parents would come here with food and medicine to treat the folk as best they could. It was a large city, not everyone could be reached, and certainly not every day. But that never stopped his da from trying.

He studied the person his da tended to now—a woman curled up on a mat, shivering every few moments. He'd never seen anyone so pale, not even on his visits back to Aselvia. Her skin was almost pure white with greyish tints and blue veins. He might have thought it was because of sickness, but— "Why is her hair blue, Da?"

Perhaps it was more silver, but there was definitely a bluish sheen.

"She's a chema from up North," Coren replied. He looked over at the man kneeling at the head of the mat. A man who was equally pale but whose hair was a dark grey, save for a few frosty white tips. "Although it is pretty rare for Northern folk to come here."

The man ducked his head in acknowledgement. "We were traveling when she took ill. I brought her to our sister tribe in the jungle just east of here, but they couldn't heal her. So they told me to come find Captain Coren in Oolum."

"I provide relief and medicine, but I'm no expert healer," Coren said with a shake of his head.

"I know that, but—" the man's voice lowered and he glanced around as if to make sure the commotion around them would be enough to drown out his words. "—I know who you really are."

The boy watched his father stiffen, even though his expression remained neutral. "Aye, and who's that?"

"They told me the story, because, well…I'm one of Tryss's brothers. My name is Taersidel, though they call me Taers."

Coren looked at him blankly, the stiffness easing from his shoulders. "I'm sorry, have I already met you? She has so many brothers."

The chema man gave a small laugh. "That she does. But no, we haven't met, I've been living up North, and I haven't seen her since she moved to Aselvia. I actually was hoping to head that way and visit, but then Allu started coughing and now…I'm frightened for her. I've never seen a sickness this terrible. If my tribe couldn't help, her only savior might be the elves. Please."

Coren stood, wiping his hands on his trousers. "One moment, friend. Come on, Zoren, let's talk with your mam for a moment."

The boy trotted after his father, having enough good sense to wait until they had turned the street corner and were out of hearing. "Well, Da, can you make his friend better?"

Instead of answering, Coren lifted a hand to his mouth and hollered, "Zi? Could you come here for a bit?"

A woman further down the street, dishing out soup to a cluster of small children, lifted her head. Her wide smile stretched from ear to ear, and she handed the kettle and spoon to an older girl, then hurried over to meet them.

Zoren considered his mother a spectacular beauty, as all little boys ought to consider their mothers. He'd inherited his cocoa-colored skin from her, but her hair was brown, thick and straight. Her wide mouth and nose suited smiling which was perfect because she smiled all the time, brown eyes dancing. She was small, but strong and cushy, perfect for cuddling though he was rather too old for that now.

"Eh, love?" she called.

"Those chemas who came in this morning. The man is claiming to be one of Tryss's brothers, and he's asking that we bring them to Aselvia for aid." Coren glanced down at the boy by his side. "Not a word of this to those folks, all right, lad?"

"Yessir."

He turned back to Zizain. "She's ice cold, even in this city, barely breathing. It's almost like she's gone into hibernation because of her illness, but I don't know if that's common among chemas. I'm not sure I want to bring sickness to Aselvia, let alone from Northern chema folk…if he's not her brother, like he claims, it could very likely be sabotage trying to start a war again..." He trailed off, hand rubbing the beard glued onto his chin.

"Thinking is that much work?" Zizain prompted after a few moments of waiting.

"Daava will have a fit if I don't think about it carefully," he said with a wry smirk. "I suppose we can bring them as far as the border, and then I can bring his story inside to Tryss. If it checks out, then we'll keep them at the healer's house to contain the illness." He nodded, a final stamp to his decision. "Better wrap up here and pack what you need for a visit back to Aselvia."

"It's about time we visit again anyway," Zizain agreed. "Zoren will have forgotten."

"I have not!" Zoren protested. "I want to ride the horses!"

"Then you certainly shall," Coren said with a smile. "You certainly shall."

3

ASELVIA

The day brought a certain sense of stability as it usually did. It was in the afternoon that Errance felt best, farther from the previous troubles of the night and not immediately pressed by the oncoming darkness.

He and Tryss took their lunch together in the shade of the castle gardens, close by the tinkling creek. He absently picked at the layers of watercress, thin apple slices, and cheese on his sandwich. Regular meals were still a peculiarity to him, for after being frequently starved in the seventy years where his life relied on his inner light, he often forgot to eat until someone sat him down.

Flyfar bounced from branch to branch above their heads, sometimes flitting down to steal a crumb from their meal. Tryss laughed at the magpie's antics and tossed it another piece of bread from her plate.

Sometimes, it was hard to believe that his parents must have shared moments so very much like this one. Flyfar would have been here, exactly the same.

He was no ordinary magpie; one could hardly even label him as a bird. At the beginning of time, the chosen rulers had been given a divine gift from Ayeshune. To Aselvia's first king and queen, this bird was presented. This bird that was soft to the touch, that could eat and drink and carry things in its beak, and yet had no true physical form. It could flit through the Unseen itself, crossing vast distances in moments. And so long as it well knew the soul of the person it sought, it could sense them anywhere. Such an amazing power, and yet Errance's own parents had most often used it to write letters to each other. A habit he had picked up himself. Although, now that he thought about it, it had been some time since he had sent Tryss a letter through Flyfar.

He glanced up at Tryss, hand lowering his forgotten sandwich back to the plate. She looked as if the very sunrays had spun themselves into the form of a woman. The sheer folds of her dress, gently sifting around her, were as yellow as her loose hair, and the soft brightness of the day cast a halo about her body. It never ceased to amaze him that she could take his breath away so suddenly, and that it was a good sort of breathlessness.

Yet shadows did drape under her eyes, and her smile, no matter how content, was more worn than usual. He felt a sudden surge of fear, seeing her so transparent, so ethereal, as if she might vanish in a breath of wind.

She needed enough rest for the days to come; he could not keep waking her in the forsaken hours of the night. And lack of sleep was the least of the harms he could cause her. His dreams were taking new directions, feeding off new fears. What if, one night—

No, he would not risk it. He had been a fool to risk it so long already.

He stared back down at the table, his finger tracing the silver etched vines on the rim of his plate, without really seeing anything. "I've been thinking," he began. "You are looking very tired—"

"Thank you," Tryss said, smirking.

"—and perhaps I should sleep somewhere else for a time."

Like a cloud covering the sun, her smile vanished. "But—what?" Concern widened her ever large eyes. "No. No, I'm fine. I don't mind."

"I can't keep waking you."

"You must! I must be there for you when the dreams—"

"The dreams are the problem, Tryss," he interrupted, hand clenching the tablecloth.

The ferocity in her eyes dimmed.

"They've been getting worse. Again. I need to be alone." *Alone.* The word stung.

"But I can help!"

That only makes it worse. He almost said it. He almost lied. What kind of coward did that make him? As if she was the problem, when the truth was—

"What if I hurt you or the baby?"

Tryss opened her mouth, but said nothing. Her hand reached to touch her rounded belly.

His heart sank as he watched her consider the reality of the words. *Please don't look at me with fear and regret*, he thought. *Please, please. I don't want to be a monster.*

"If…if that's what you really want," she managed at last.

It wasn't. Stars above, it wasn't. But it was the only thing he could think of to keep her safe.

After a moment, she cleared her throat. "I don't think you should be the one to sleep somewhere else though. Actually, there was something I've been meaning to ask you. I've wanted to visit home and my mother again before the baby comes. I didn't know if you wanted to come…"

A shiver skittered across his skin. Outside the border of Aselvia. He hadn't crossed over once since coming back home. As if the same monsters who had snatched him the first time were still out there, waiting. "I don't think…I'm ready for traveling."

She gave a small nod, no doubt expecting that answer. "So if I'm gone for a few weeks, it could just be what's needed to give you time and space. Perhaps this is only a short attack and you will feel better soon."

"One would hope." He managed a smile, trying to ease off the weight of the conversation and bring peace back to her face. A peace he always seemed to take away.

Only a few in Orim had seen this northwestern land hidden inside a circle of mountains and forest. The far-rolling meadows, the ribbons of sparkling rivers, the lavender blue peaks draped with snow. This land, this realm of the elves, long protected by their past celestial king.

Her home.

Even now, Tellie sometimes feared she would wake and find it all a dream. Discover that she was still a child in the stone-cold orphanage of Dormandy or a young woman in the narrow attic of her uncaring, distant relatives. That she would again have no parents, no home, no real hope for the future.

How it happened that she, a regular human girl, had been chosen to aid the elves in rescuing their long-lost prince was still a mystery of providence to her. She'd been just barely fifteen at the time, still starving for the care and affection of a family that had been taken from her all too young. And Leoren and Casara, steward and princess of Aselvia, had chosen to bring her into their home not only for guardianship in her final few years of youth, but as a daughter.

Seven years ago that was now, and still, she wondered at the miracle of it all. But she never questioned it so far as to doubt that this land was where she had belonged. No, Aselvia was the land she had been meant for, and she loved everything and everyone in it. Aselvia had adopted her and she had adopted it in return.

She didn't look much like a typical elf maid, true, but that hardly mattered. Once she'd assumed that an elvish diet and lifestyle would have given her a figure similar to theirs, but as she'd grown, she'd only filled out more. It wasn't as if there weren't any curvy elf women, there was the midwife Dahlya, for example. But Tellie was short and plump and…well, eventually, she'd accepted that as its own beauty. Once she'd even asked Kelm if he minded, and he'd stared at her so incredulously that she decided to never ask again.

She loved traveling with Kelm, but coming back home always kindled a special light in her soul. It had been three months since she'd ridden across the green valleys, three months since she'd seen the white spires of the royal city, Telvar—three months since she had seen Errance and Tryss. Her eagerness to see Tryss in particular was buzzing in her ears.

A few elves noticed her as she rode by, calling out a greeting as her horse clattered up the stone street. She cheerfully waved in return but didn't stop to say hello. She had one destination at the moment and that was the palace, the center of the city. The street led her up the three tiers, the sunlight whisking overhead between stones arches covered with vines woven into a macramé of green and gold.

Whether by word on the wind or just plain elf intuition, a few servants were waiting by the time Tellie and the rest of the riders came cantering up to the glade before the palace stairs. Tellie swung off, handing her reins off with a smile to the waiting stableman.

The palace was rather large, housing not just the king and his family, but also quarters for servants, the throne room, and the council chambers for the lords to discuss their duties, but she knew it well enough to have a pretty good guess as to where she could find Tryss. So rather than heading up to the great doors, she darted off down a pathway into the surrounding gardens. The air was sweet here, heavy with the perfume of nectar. It seemed something was always coming to fruit in Aselvia no matter the time of year, each season bearing its own form of life. Right now she could smell the apples and hear the buzzing bees and chattering birds among the foliage. She knew that Tryss often came here because it reminded her of home.

"Tryss?" she hollered. Casara had once tried to impress that elves didn't holler or run about, but Tellie had been rather too ingrained in her ways by the time such manners were taught. Anyway, it wasn't true. She'd seen plenty of elves both holler and run.

"Tellie? Tellie, is that you?" Tryss appeared around a tangle of honeysuckle, her long hair a golden waterfall down her shoulders. One hand held a book, the other supported her belly. A belly that rounded fully underneath her pale yellow gown.

Tellie squealed. "Oh stars, you've gotten so big!"

Tryss laughed, staggering under Tellie's enthusiastic embrace. "That's a way to greet someone…"

Pulling back again, Tellie took another look, her eyes wide and sparkling. "You were barely showing when I left. How much longer, a month?"

"She's due in four weeks."

"*She*, is it?"

"Call it a mother's intuition."

"And Errance? How is Errance? Is he excited?"

Just for a moment the happy glow on Tryss's face dimmed. Only a little, but it was enough for Tellie to notice, and she felt her own heart sag.

Covering up her slip with another happy smile, Tryss shrugged. "Oh, he's nervous, but what can you expect?"

"I suppose that's true. Errance gets nervous about everything."

"Thanks," he said, just behind her.

Tellie gasped. She spun and seized Errance in a hug, which he awkwardly returned with half his arm. He never seemed used to the concept of hugs, even from her, a self-proclaimed expert in hugging. "What are you doing, sneaking around like that!" she exclaimed.

"Sneaking," he repeated. "That's nice. A king walks about in his castle, and you call it sneaking."

"I'll never get used to the silent way you elves move," Tellie said. "Or you, Tryss. Chemas are even worse at that."

"Yes," Errance agreed. "If anybody could sneak, it would be her."

"Not right now." Tryss shook her head, patting her belly. "Definitely not right now."

"So where is that husband of yours?" Errance asked. "Did he wander off again?"

"He's back in Dormandy. Should be home before the baby comes. And then we'll all be together again, just like we ought to be. With a new little one soon to arrive."

"Mmhm." Errance smiled, but it didn't quite reach his eyes. He gave a little cough into his hand and took a step back. "I was just on my way to meet up with Leoren and discuss how the meeting went. I'll leave you two to talk." And then he was already headed off.

Tellie could have moved on then, changed the subject to something cheery and contrived. But she'd never been one to shirk from honest conversation. "He looks tired," she said. *You both look tired.*

"I suppose we are getting a head-start on parenting," Tryss said with a weak laugh. When Tellie didn't laugh along, her shoulders drooped. Taking a glance to make sure Errance had left, she lowered her voice and admitted, "I know he's troubled about this. I…I don't know. When we first—" She paused, rose color blossoming across her cheeks.

"You can talk to me about it; I've caught up with you," Tellie said with a grin.

"I don't know that you've caught up, but you are an adult," Tryss allowed, smiling in return. That smile slipped away again as she went on. "When we agreed to have a child, he seemed happy. I felt like a normal wife, that a bridge had been crossed that would lead us to a better relationship. But lately, as I've progressed in pregnancy, he's started to pull back. I thought it would draw us closer together and instead…I just hope he will love the baby when she comes." Hugging her arms around her middle, she stared off into the thickets of wisteria.

"Of course he will love Baby," Tellie said. "He's just afraid right now, Tryss."

"He's always afraid," she said, then bit her lip as if realizing that came out far too bitter. "I mean, he has been showing incredible improvement, but this relapse was unexpected."

"It's because he has new reasons to fear. He loved his father so much, and he's not sure he can live up to that glorified role. He's worried his child won't love him the same way. That he won't be able to keep them safe, just as he, despite being loved, could not be kept from harm."

Shaking her head with a smile, Tryss paused and faced her friend. "You always make it sound so understandable."

Well, at least she could speak encouragement. She had other, less generous thoughts on the matter, but it wasn't any use sharing those aloud.

"Oh," Tryss said, fingers pressing to her mouth. "I am going to visit home again within the week! I guess I should mention that now since you just came back. I wanted to speak to my mother for any last tips and see if she wants to come back with me for the delivery."

"I say, what a perfect idea! They must miss you. You haven't seen your parents since the wedding, yes?"

"Yes…did you want to come with me? I shall be traveling with my midwife Dahlya and others, but since you are here now, I do not want you to be left out."

"It would be nice to see the jungle again," Tellie said, not sure if she really meant it. She remembered a lot of sweat, bugs, and frightening noises in the thick, green tangle of trees and vines. "But since Kelm might not be back yet, I really should stay and wait for him." Not to mention she was ready to be home. Life on the road was exciting and all, but sometimes, she just wanted to be still. "You shan't be gone long though, right? Aren't you cutting it rather close?"

"Dahlya has been watching my development and says there are no signs of an early birth. So I should be fine. I'd rather do something than just wait in suspense. The waiting is getting harder every day."

Tellie threw her head back with a laugh. "You impress me! I hope I'm as active as you when I…when I…" Her smile flickered, then faded, a bright candle blowing out in a breeze.

"Tellie?"

Forcing the smile back on, Tellie reached out and squeezed her arm. "You know, I think I shall go find Casara. Let her know I'm back home and all that."

Tryss's yellow-green eyes studied her for a moment, before she nodded and returned her embrace. "Of course. We will catch up more later. You must be tired from the journey."

Tellie found Casara where she could usually be found—keeping care of the queen mother of Aselvia.

Although there were many elves counted among the Firstborn, none seemed quite as old as their first queen looked now. It wasn't entirely because of her features, although these were thin and had more lines than most elves, or even because of the grey hair that threaded the dark brown. No, perhaps it wasn't even a matter of age, but of health, because the woman hardly ever moved of her own accord or focused or even spoke. An invalid who had lost interest in life, she simply followed directions without question, eyes often empty and face pale. It was said her mind had broken from solitude and grief during the Dark Days, though there were still times she recognized those around her.

Times such as now.

She saw Tellie come through the door first, and her head lifted and a smile curved her flat expression. The sight of that smile warmed Tellie straight through.

Following the direction of her mother's suddenly snagged attention, Casara paused in washing the old queen's feet and started at the sight of the girl standing in the door.

"Tellie!" She dropped the cloth, leapt up, and ran to catch her close.

"Maava." Tellie snuggled into the embrace, soaking up every bit of warmth and comfort found there. Once it had been strange to say that word. Strange, because it was elvish, stranger, because of what it meant. After all, she had been fifteen when she was adopted—too old, according to some opinions. She was fortunate Leoren and Casara had not shared those views but instead drew her into their fold. It hadn't been without awkward transitions, certainly, but she had never doubted that she was wanted by them, loved by them, and it was because of this that she could now call them Maava and Daava with complete belief.

"We were not expecting you back so soon!"

"I came back with Daava. Kelm will be following in a few weeks or sooner." She bent down to kiss the old queen, the woman she now thought of as grandmother. She picked up the cloth Casara had dropped and continued wiping down the elder woman's feet with the scented water from a nearby bowl. "I can help you while we talk."

It had become one of her favorite duties, a duty Casara had never shared with anyone else before. She took the care of her invalid queen mother as her own role, not that of the servants, and making Tellie a part of it only sealed her into the family.

"I saw Tryss, she is looking wonderful," she said, before any questions could be asked about her. Sometimes she preferred to wade into the subject on her mind, other days she just dived right in.

"Dahlya says she is in excellent health," Casara agreed. "Which shouldn't be a surprise, given her lineage of large families."

"I saw Errance too."

"Ah? Yes."

Was that all she was going to say? Tellie's hand tightened on the cloth. Heaven help her, elves were gossips, she knew Casara was one too. She didn't have to pretend to be evasive. "He looks stressed. Frankly, I think they're both stressed."

"That is quite common for new parents," Casara said softly.

She'd said something similar, hadn't she? And Errance had even more reasons to be anxious. But it wasn't exactly what she really thought. "I wouldn't be," she groused. "I would be ecstatic."

Casara sat next to her, hands folded in her lap, violet eyes soft and sad. "It…has only been a few years, Tellie dear. Too soon for you to worry yet."

She dropped the cloth back into the bowl with a forceful splash and watched the ripples splash against the rim. "I know that. But I can't help but worry anyway. Kelm and I already want to adopt, of course, but I just thought I'd have my own baby by now. I want one. And…and…and Errance goes into marriage not sure if he ever wants one and then he decides that he does, and now he has one and he is *stressed* about it. And poor Tryss, who I am sure is otherwise very happy, knows he is stressed and she is trying to figure out why. Don't get me wrong, I'm happy for them and I'm sure it will all turn out wonderfully, but I just want to know why they got their baby first, when I already knew I wanted one and I wanted to name her Sharlitte."

Casara only looked at her.

"Litty for short," Tellie concluded, fishing the wet cloth back out again.

"I'm sorry, darling."

"I know you're the last person I should be complaining to," she sighed.

"On the contrary, I am the first person. I understand." She certainly did. She'd had Coren, yes, but she had wanted more children, and the midwife had advised against it due to the extreme difficulty of the birth, a difficulty that had taken her sister's life in the birth of Errance.

"I don't know how you elven women do it, having only a chance every ten years." Discovering this had in fact been the first time Tellie was ever completely glad to have been born human.

A hand touched the top of her head, and she looked up at her elvish grandmother. "Do keep that all a secret between us girls, won't you?" Tellie said with a wry smile, imagining the old queen suddenly deciding to break her usual silence in front of Errance or Tryss with the latest bit of juicy gossip. "I just needed to get it off my chest."

A soft smile curved the old queen's lips, almost as if she had understood.

4

Tryss was asleep on his lap. Probably asleep. She'd curled up on the bench, which wasn't exactly comfortable, even with the padding, but her head was resting on Errance's thigh, and his fingers were running rhythmic circles across her scalp. A head massage wasn't something he found particularly enjoyable himself, but she seemed to like it. His other hand propped open a book, which he was only vaguely aware of. Rather than reading, he wanted to breathe it all in—this moment when he felt peaceful. Calm. Assured that everything would be all right.

"Your Majesty!"

Errance muttered a silent curse as Tryss jolted awake under his hand. So much for that. He pinned the approaching guard with a peeved glare, pinned him right through to the stone wall beyond.

"Yes?" He didn't bother to thaw the frost from his tone. They could have declared themselves with a much quieter method; so much for the legendary grace of the elves—

"I don't need an announcement or a guard escort, stars." That voice only belonged to a redhead, and sure enough, a redhead was what came through the garden arch behind the guard. Not just any ginger, but his cousin.

"I believe my guards are to keep people from disturbing me," Errance said, setting the book aside. Tryss rubbed her eyes and attempted to sit up. He eased one arm under her and helped her straighten. "But I suppose it's a little late for that."

"Sorry, cuz," Coren said, dipping a bow. "I would have hung back, only the matter is rather urgent."

"Gracious." Tryss rubbed her face again, as if she could smooth out the pattern of fabric pressed into her skin. "Everyone is coming back at once, and it's not even harvest yet. Are Zizain and Zoren with you?"

"Yeees," Coren said, shifting from one foot to another, his arms folded behind his back. "And they're not the only ones."

Errance narrowed his eyes, trying to guess what sort of bad news could bring Coren back so suddenly. What other guest besides his family would he have brought to Aselvia? It wasn't as if the kingdom had open borders.

"I met someone in Oolum," Coren began, and the whole time his attention was fixed on Tryss's face. "Someone who claimed to be your brother…but from up North."

There was only a moment's pause in which Tryss's brow wrinkled and then cleared in an image of incredulity. "*Taers?* Taers is back in Mid Orim?"

"So you do know him." Coren's tense posture eased and the usual brightness returned to his eyes. "He is with a chema woman who is very sick, and he said your home tribe couldn't help them. So I brought them to the border until I verified their story with you. I do realize he could be stealing a name you recognize, and we won't know if he's legitimate until you see him. And also, if the sickness of the woman with him is contagious, we wouldn't want to endanger you." His gaze slid to Errance, knowing that the final say rested with him.

Errance looked away, fingers tightening around his arms. A northern chema. The skirmishes with them had ended mainly when he was born. The reason why his father had been away at his birth was to search for any survivors from the chemas' attack on the last family of daishas. He'd brought back only a small, mewling daisha kit. And then there had been no more reason to keep fighting up in the cold and snow…they had no allies up there who needed their help. So while he hadn't any personal experience with their age-old war, the stories that were passed down did nothing to warm his heart.

And of course, bringing strangers into Aselvia was not practiced, but he'd already broken that unspoken rule extensively when he'd first returned to Aselvia, bringing several strangers with him.

But this…this wasn't about tension with the North. Or about border security. This was about Tryss's family. Granted, he also didn't have any good history with them, but that didn't mean he couldn't try.

He returned Coren's questioning stare. "Bring him and the sick woman to the healing house. Just take a guard escort with you until we can identify him for certain."

Flourishing a cavalier bow, Coren turned on his heel and left them.

Tryss reached across and squeezed his hand. "Thank you, Errance."

"Have I met him?" He tried thinking back to the first time he'd encountered her family, then again at the wedding. Mainly, he remembered glares, not names.

"No, he is—" she paused, biting her lip. "He is my older brother."

"Hang on, I thought you were the eldest."

"Eldest daughter…eldest…still at home…still…part of the family."

He waited, raising a brow.

She sighed. "Taers is a year older than me, and he had some…serious conflicts with our way of life. When he was seventeen, he left for the North and whatever…ideals he agreed with there."

"Were you close?"

She cleared her throat, covering her mouth with the side of her hand. "Actually, no. We didn't get along at all. I thought him irresponsible and troublesome. But who knows. Time changes many things. Maybe he found what he was looking for up North."

The ash trees surrounding the healer's house were beginning to turn yellow, casting color across the forest like strokes of paint, mixing with shades the hue of wine. A few leaves, fallen too early, crunched underneath the horse's hooves as Errance and Tryss rode to the clearing before the veranda.

It probably was late in term to be riding a horse, Tryss speculated, but she wasn't going to take the time of a carriage ride to find out whether this newcomer was her brother or not. Still, she did wait for Errance to dismount and come to help her, grabbing onto his shoulder for balance as she slid down.

His muscles were tense, his face set in a frown as he glanced towards their destination. Not exactly the first impression she wanted made on her estranged brother. She stood on her tiptoes and kissed his chin. It worked. His mouth twitched in a smile and his shoulders eased just a bit.

The guards who had escorted the strangers waited just outside the healer's house, drawing into a salute at the sight of their king. A moment later, the latticed doors opened wide and Damarik swept out, arms folded in his long robes. With a respectful bow of his own, he announced, "I have studied the patient, Your Majesties, and the woman is not sick with any disease. She seems to be poisoned, though by what I have not decided."

"Poisoned!" Errance's mouth twisted. "What sort of enemies does your brother have for her to be poisoned?"

"Well, they did come from the North," she said, a bit shakily. "May I see him then?"

"He is just inside," Damarik said, stepping away from the door. "I requested he wait for your permission. Come now, my friend, she is ready to greet you."

The door opened slowly. Tryss drew in her breath, almost afraid to hope. She sensed rather than saw the guards reach for their weapons, and Errance stiffened beside her.

"Taers," she breathed.

It was him. Oh, but he'd changed. Gone was the lanky and awkward youth of her childhood with shoulder-length yellow hair and fuzz on his chin. The young man standing on the porch now was pure North chema. Tall, strong, slim, with silver hair shorn short at the sides of his head, finger-length strands tousled on top and slashing across his eyes.

He stared down at her, face wrinkling. Something almost like a scowl flitted across his mouth.

But of course, she would be a shock to see too. Hair and clothing all elvish, and there was no missing the baby curving her front.

"Taers, I can't believe it." She stumbled a step forward, arms opening to catch him in a hug. The confusion on his face faded, replaced by a smile as he crossed the final distance and caught her embrace. She'd forgotten he'd been the tall one in the family, his chin resting on her head.

A chuckle rumbled in his chest. "Didn't ever expect to find you here, Tryss," he said. "What's this about them calling you things like 'Your Majesty' and all that?"

She pulled back with a shaky laugh. "It's been a long time. I don't even know how to explain it all." She was aware of the stares from the surrounding elves, one pair of eyes more important than the rest. "I guess to start with, you need to meet my husband." Still holding her brother's arm with one hand, she stretched out the other to Errance. "Taers, this is Errance, the king of Aselvia."

Errance remained where he was, but he pressed a hand to his heart in elvish greeting. His expression could have stood to be warmer and a little less suspicious. When she glanced back at Taers, his face was much the same. And yes, she might have just declared them brothers- in-law, but she'd tacked the 'king' on there too. Taers should have known a courtesy called bowing, if only for being hosted. Really. Did they have to be this difficult?

After a moment, Taers cleared his throat. "Taersidel is my Northern name. It is a pleasure to finally meet you, King Errance. The stories that circle Orim about you are legendary indeed." He spoke with a new accent, sharp and cold, tilting into fine edges like the shape of a snowflake. When he looked back to Tryss, worry dug lines into his brow. "Tryss, you kept up your skills as a healer, didn't you? Maybe you could help my friend."

"If Master Hathon was at a loss, then I'm not sure what I could do. But you are with the best healers to be had, so I'm sure we will find a cure soon. Did—" She swung a glance to Damarik. "—you discuss your conclusion, Master Damarik?"

"Not yet." Damarik remained poised, expression unreadable. "Taersidel, it appears the young woman in your company was poisoned. Do you have any explanation for why this is so?" In any other tone, it might have sounded accusatory, but the elf's voice was deep and mild as ever.

"Poisoned!" His mouth dropped open. "Why would she be poisoned?"

"What do you do for a living? That could be a start." Errance was not at all managing the same peaceful nature as Damarik. His arms had folded over his chest, but when Tryss looked at him in exasperation, he tried to relax the stance. "Does she have any enemies? Or was she in a situation where she might have intercepted something meant for someone else?"

"No!" He whirled back to Damarik. "She isn't going to die, is she? You have a cure, yes?"

"To have a cure, it is preferred to know the cause. But until we determine it, I shall give her what medicines we can. We have not had dealings with the North for years now, but there may be some who are familiar with the symptoms." He glanced sideways at Errance, but if he was trying to send a message, then he needed to work on communication in that one eye of his.

The Daisha. Tryss almost said it out loud.

Years ago, when she'd been inflicted with an injury from a creature up North, it had been The Daisha with the answer for a cure.

But as much as she wanted to say it, Errance's silence echoed in her ears. In that silence, she remembered the strife that once existed between

The Daisha and herself, merely because of her chema blood. A bitterness reasoned by the slaughter of the daishas at the hands of the northern chemas. And while her brother had not been a part of it, had not even been born, she couldn't help but wonder where the loyalty to his newfound people ranged. As for this girl with him, she knew nothing of her origins. So perhaps it would be best to speak with The Daisha privately rather than risk any bad blood or contention by declaring her presence.

"I'll look into it," Errance said. "If you will excuse me." He took a step back, then hesitated, looking her way as if asking for permission. Which was sweet, if not silly.

"Please," she answered. The sooner they could find answers, the better. Once Errance had disappeared, no doubt to find The Daisha, she turned back to her brother. "Take me to her," she said. "There may not be much I can do, but we can watch her together while Damarik prepares his medicines."

With a weary nod, Taersidel led the way. The healing rooms always felt like forest groves to Tryss. The coned ceilings were built of glass, reinforced with cedar beams. Actual vines grew up the walls and hung from the rafters. Little fires burned in small hearths inset into the wall, with kettles steaming on the racks. In a way it reminded her of back home, but the light was purer and the air was still crisp in that way of the mountain forests.

The bed, centered in the room, was covered in thick blankets, the mattress narrow enough so that the patient could be easily reached in the middle. The slightest rail at the edge discouraged anyone from rolling off.

A chair sat by the bedside, and Tryss dragged another one up so she could sit with her brother. She pulled back the covers, looking over the pale, still body with a critical eye. A touch to her cheek confirmed her body was ice cold, even underneath all those blankets and with the warmth of the fires. She took her hand in between both of hers and began rubbing, but even the friction didn't seem to break through the frigid layer encasing the young woman.

"What is her name?" she asked.

"Allu. Well. Alludium, but Allu is what I call her."

A slight smile twitched across her mouth. She'd noticed Taers introduce himself with a Northern name, a name more intricate than the one he'd been given, but if he'd given his Northern friend a nickname, perhaps he hadn't completely snubbed the culture he'd grown up in.

"How long have you known her?"

"Some years now."

"Good friend?"

"Mmm."

She eyed him. She could never have said she was good at reading his mind and distance had done nothing to improve that, but still, there were basic things one might assume in any case. There was a certain fierceness in his eyes, a desperation when he looked at this pale creature.

"Allu…is she your fiancée, perhaps?" she asked, soft as could be.

"My lover," he said firmly. "Not everyone up North binds themselves with such antiquated vows."

She blinked. "Oh." Well. There was a certain challenge in his voice, the tone he used when he was trying to egg her into an argument. But there was no point to that, so she chose to move on. "I can't believe you're actually here, Taers."

"I could say the same," he muttered. "*Here* was definitely not where I ever planned on meeting."

"It's quite shocking, isn't it? We've both changed. Do you want to share your story first?"

"Not now, Tryss." A heavy sigh deflated his chest. "It's been an exhausting time running about, trying to find someone who could help her. And I still don't know if she'll be saved."

"They'll do everything they can. This is the best place you could have brought her." She spared one hand to squeeze his, then rose and gave a gentle kiss to the top of his head. "I will go find Damarik or Ahspen and ask that a cot be brought in here so you can sleep next to her."

"Tryss!"

Before Tryss had even taken a step away from her brother, a dark-haired elf woman swept into the room, the remnants of flower petals drifting from her braid.

The woman shook a finger in her direction. "I move to the castle to keep an eye on you, and now I find you've moved to my home! You're too pregnant to move around this fast. It isn't fair, I say!"

Tryss caught her in a soft hug and then turned to her brother. "Taersidel, this is my dear friend and my midwife, Dahlya, daughter of Damarik."

"We met at the wedding, did we not?" Dahlya asked, extending her hand in a graceful curve.

He took her hand with the barest tip of his fingers and bent in a slight bow. "We did not," he said. "I have lived in the North and I did not hear of the wedding till much later."

"Oh, then it is wonderful to meet you!"

"I wish only that it was under better circumstances." His gaze flickered to the sleeping woman in bed.

"As do I," Tryss said, resting a hand upon his arm with what little comfort she could give. "We shall leave you to rest and talk more later. You've colored out the shadows from under your eyes, but I am certain they are there."

"Clever girl," he said, a ghost of a smile whisking past his lips. "Thank you."

The ground was still damp in the heights of the forest. If Errance climbed much higher, the dew decorating every leaf and blade of grass would turn to a white frost. As it was, it was cold enough to turn his breath into a fog in front of his face.

A perfect, beautiful mountainside. And upon that fresh air, he could smell blood. He could smell death.

He climbed over a ridge, looking up a small cliff in the mountainside.

A great, winged beast crouched upon the rocks, the freshly slain carcass of a deer beneath her front paws.

"It's a good thing I know you and you know me, otherwise, this could be seen as a very dangerous encounter," he said, crossing his arms.

The Daisha stared down at him, looking as guilty as a child caught with their hand in the cookie jar, although this scene was far more bloody than that.

She let out a light, tinkling laugh, which might have been considered unsettling due to the flash of her enormous teeth. "Erre, dear, you do like dropping in on me in the middle of dinner. Makes me feel quite the savage." She carefully ran a paw along her elegant snout, her finger-long toes brushing at her whiskers and trim little beard hanging from under her jaw.

"And then you call me things like "Erre, dear" which is far more appalling," Errance said, shaking his head as he leapt up onto the log alongside her and sat, legs dangling over the edge. "I do believe I told you I'd rather that name *not* catch on."

"It could be worse," she insisted. "It could be Erre Berry."

"Stars, no."

"It could be," she went on, voice dropping to a whisper, "even worse than that."

"I actually came about something important and time-sensitive," Errance interrupted, lest she come up with anything worse. "Tryss's brother came to visit."

"Oh?" She frowned, no doubt in mixed disinterest and annoyance that she'd been interrupted over only that.

"From the North."

Her features morphed from a frown to a terrifying scowl. "And what," she said, acidly, "was he doing there? And better yet, what is he doing *here?*"

It was much the reaction he expected. If he was honest with himself, it was much the reaction he felt, even if he already knew some of the justifications. "He has a sick friend, a young woman who is poisoned. Damarik does not yet recognize the cause, so we don't know the cure. We thought that…." He trailed off, eyeing her with hesitation.

"You thought I might know a thing or two about chema poisons," she finished, prickly as the spines trailing down her back. "Well, as it is, I actually tried to avoid chemas while I was up North, believe it or not. I kept to the alith villages and strongholds or kept to myself altogether."

"But you have heard of chema sickness and other ailments." He folded his arms, waiting her out.

Heaving a sigh from the depths of her mighty chest, she leaned back on her haunches. "Tell me the symptoms."

"Unconscious, cold as ice, pale, barely breathing."

The Daisha ran a tongue over her teeth, considering. "It doesn't sound unlike one of the drugs they use to kidnap and spirit a person away. We should have something like the cure for that up in our mountains, but if it's a more powerful strain of the drug, it may not work."

"Our mountains?" He squinted up through the trees.

"Your father had many plants from the North transplanted in the snowy heights of Aselvia. Kept under watch and control so as not to take over, of course, but useful for study and practice. The chemas did so love their poisonous warfare." She turned a flat expression his way. "Don't tell me you didn't know."

"I forgot," Errance said, which was not untrue. There was no doubt at some point he'd heard about this, but there were so many things to keep in his mind, and his mind tended to let things slip out of its many cracks.

"Come on," she said, nodding to her back. "I'll take you higher up the mountain and see if we can't find a bush or two."

5

"Taers?" Tryss hurried through the halls of the healing house. She'd spent the night in her old room here, both to be close to her brother and to give Errance that space he wanted. It had not been the most pleasant of nights, first because the empty space beside her felt increasingly cold, second due to her worry for her brother's friend, and third, because the baby made her nauseous for several hours. Dahlya had been kind enough to notice the candlelight in her room and brought up soothing tea and small talk.

Now pushing open the door to Allu's room, she found her brother sitting beside the invalid young woman. And the young woman herself sat up in bed, propped against several pillows, her face still wan, but her eyes open.

"Ohhh," Tryss breathed. "Dahlya told me the medicines had taken effect, but I didn't realize…"

Damarik and Ahspen had spent all night taking the plants that The Daisha and Errance had gathered and mixing them together in various tinctures. It was, they admitted, not the most effective way to know exactly which was the cure if her symptoms were to be relieved, but the point was to relieve them rather than know by what and why.

As Tryss came alongside the bed, Allu turned her head with great effort and reached out a hand to her. Tryss took it and laid it back down on the blankets before she could exhaust herself further.

"Taersidel told me," she whispered, voice thin and fragile as a butterfly's wing. "He told me you are his sister."

"And it is wonderful to meet you and see you awake, but please, do nothing to tire yourself. You still have much to mend."

"That's healer's orders, my love," Taers said, bending over Allu and kissing her pale brow. "Rest some more, I'll talk to Tryss."

He stood and gestured to Tryss to join him outside of the bedroom, softly drawing the door shut behind him. He let out a thick, haggard breath. The shadows under his eyes were not invisible now.

"I told you Damarik could help her," Tryss said, a smile stealing across her face.

"Never thought I'd have to be coming to the elves for aid," he groaned, rubbing a hand down his temple. His silvery blue eyes swept to her, a gentleness softening their glint. "But were it not for you, I would never have been given entrance here. So, ultimately, it is you who saved her life."

"You will find that the elves are far more gracious than you believe. I'd like to repair the gap between our peoples, and I'll start with you."

His mouth quirked. "I suppose you can try. Though you'll have better luck with our kin in the jungle than any up North."

"I'll go to our cooks and fetch Allu some warm broth, how about that? And I'll bring some food too. There's no better way to build good feelings than with good food." Stifling a smile under the back of her hand, she hurried off down the hall and to the kitchens.

On the third day, there was no doubt that whatever poison had plagued their chema guest, it was no longer a threat to her life. She still would need much rest until her body recovered, the healers informed, but the danger was past, even if its origin still remained a mystery.

Allu's hands trembled with fatigue if she tried to hold her own bowl of broth, so whenever Tryss came by, she would hold the bowl herself and feed her by the spoonful, dabbing away the trickles of broth from her chin with a cloth.

"Taers told me you were always a caretaker," Allu said weakly, "but I admit I didn't realize how much of one. Are you sure you should be doing all this when you're..." She flopped her arm out in a loose shape of a round belly.

"Never mind that. I've still got a few weeks to go. I have the constitution of my mother, I guess."

"Speaking of which," Taers interrupted, leaning on the bedpost. "If you are this close to giving birth, I'm surprised our mother isn't here. She was always very fond of you, and she'd be sorry to miss helping you deliver her grandchild." His eyes narrowed. "Unless your husband has estranged you from them."

"Actually, I was about to travel to the jungle and say hello to the family for a few days and then return with her," Tryss said, rubbing her hand across her wrist, trying not to let her disappointment at missing that chance show on her face.

"Wait, you were planning to visit?" Taers straightened, mouth agape.

"Well, I was—"

"Don't let us stop you," Allu said, gathering up a little strength in her posture. "You would need to leave soon if you want to travel before your baby comes."

Tryss waved a hand at her. "No, of course not, you are also my family and my guests."

Allu raised a brow, the most definitive movement she'd managed, and then turned her head towards Taers. "Taersidel," she said, voice thin and yet firm. "Go with her. I'll be bed-ridden for some time yet. There is no point in just staring at me till I recover. Go to your family together. I will be taken care of here."

A moment of hesitation. And then, Taers murmured, "That's not a bad idea."

"Oh, but we couldn't," Tryss began, then paused at her brother's expectant stare, and a thousand reasons why she wished they could paraded across her mind. Allu was right, she was on the road to recovery from here. If Taersidel was willing to trust the elves for keeping his love safe, then who was she to argue if he wanted to go? "Well, I mean. Perhaps. If you were quite sure, and Errance still didn't mind...."

"You'd be traveling with family to visit family, what could he possibly object to?"

"Well, I suppose...he wouldn't...."

"It's decided then! Allu, you are a queen to think of this." He bent over and kissed her brow. "You know, Tryss, our mother and father were so worried about you. Perhaps they will finally stop being angry with me when I bring you back to visit them!" He laughed at that.

She joined with a weak little laugh of her own, mind still uneasy. There wasn't anything wrong with it, was there? She hadn't even officially canceled the plans of leaving, not with how busy she had been.

Dahlya would still go with her, and Coren and his family would probably accompany her now. In a way, such a group would be less suspicious than the elven guard she had first planned on taking. So…Errance would be all right with it, wouldn't he?

Errance was not all right.

He didn't say so, and he even managed to keep that information off his face. That was one good thing about seventy years of imprisonment; you learned how to hide what you were really thinking.

First, he was not all right with her leaving. He despised himself for that. Aselvia was not a prison. She'd given up so much to be with him, so of course, she wanted to visit her family, and of course, she should, and of course, he should go with her, and of course, he was too…too afraid.

That's what it came down to really.

Cowardice.

About everything.

And then her prodigal brother who she hadn't seen in how many years had come along from who-knows-which-ice-ridge and volunteered himself as her traveling companion. Perfect. Just perfect.

The training court was empty, which was no surprise since no one else thought to come down in the dark hours of the morning to swing at a target they could barely see. Errance usually liked the emptiness, the sounds of nothing but the waterfall rushing down the high surrounding wall, but this time he felt a bit lonely and wished that Leoren had arranged that foreign instructor to come by. At the very least, it would have provided a challenge to focus his mind on. Instead, he stepped through the paces, hit the marks, heard the thunk of metal into wood, and he thought of nothing but the anxieties churning within him.

What game was he playing at in wearing a crown? He did his duties at minimum and kept distance from his people. In the beginning, he'd been afraid of what they would think of him, and he was still afraid.

The sword twisted in his hand, and he let the blade arc and whistle through the air, unimpeded by any target.

And somehow, getting married was supposed to have fixed that. To appear as a normal man in the eyes of his people so that they would be happy…so that he would be happy. Of course, he should have realized that if he wasn't enough of a man to be a king, he certainly wasn't fit to be anyone's husband. Leoren had tried to hint that, he realized now.

Thunk. His arms shivered at the impact with which his sword sank into a wooden mock-man. He wasn't supposed to be using a real sword on the mannequins. It damaged both the blade and the prop. But he usually didn't care. He wanted to feel the harm. Although the mannequin was without a face, it seemed to stare at him reproachfully as he wrested the blade free again.

Once upon a time, when he was young and innocent, he'd been full of the right kind of love. It was broken now, hanging in useless tatters from his heart. He still knew he would lay down his life for Tryss in a breath, that if suffering was the answer to save her, he could bear it. But he didn't have the special sort of everyday magic that brightened someone's day, that tended gently to small hurts, and that gave supporting strength when the other was low. She was all that to him, but he could hardly repay the gift.

So he'd thought he would go and swallow his pain and be a normal husband to her, and they could have a child, and perhaps then they would be happy....

Idiot, *idiot*, IDIOT!

If he was not enough as a king or a husband, what had possessed him to think he could be a FATHER?

The mannequin was shuddering on its post now, hewn with cuts deep enough to cause concern for his blade breaking. He had a passing thought he would ruin both sword and wood model before the sun was up, but he didn't slow down.

Having a child sounded somewhat pleasant in imaginative fancy. It brought to mind the happy days of him and his own father. Glorious, precious days full of sunshine and laughter.

But what could he promise a son or daughter when he could barely lift his eyes to the blue sky anymore? He'd drag them all—kingdom, wife, and child—into the depths of his misery and they would despise him.

The head of the wooden figure flew off under the force of his next blow and soared through the air, landing and rolling across the stone. Its frantic flight was stopped under a finely buckled boot.

Panting, Errance stared across the courtyard where he could see, in the gradual light of sunrise, the silhouette of his dueling instructor. Oh. So Leoren had called the man for another visit. Just when had he arrived exactly? Last night? Errance didn't remember being told, but then again, he probably hadn't paid attention. Leoren insisted he did warn him of these things.

With a quick spin, Errance turned his back to the man for a moment as he wiped the sweat and hair from his face and hoped the haunted look in his eyes would recede as well, or at least not be noticed in the dim lighting.

"Another dummy dead," the man said, tossing the wooden head from hand to hand. "Well done."

Please. The last thing he needed was more guilt, especially guilt over an inanimate object. Though he did feel sorry for the carpenters who would be receiving yet another order for the models. What was the use in pretending he was normal to his people when all the craftsmen knew he ruined things?

He began to tuck his sword back into its scabbard, but the man said, "Sunrise is the traditional way to begin, not to end. Finished already?"

Errance paused, considering. On one hand, he wanted to be alone and left to ache as he pleased, but on the other, demolishing a dummy was not very satisfying and the tension in his shoulders had only double-knotted. Besides, there was something calming about dueling this trainer. Leoren had called him the best, and Errance had been cynical about that, but it was true. It was also true that Errance had disarmed him once in a flash of rage, but somehow the man had calmly talked him out of the red haze that had taken over his vision. So all in all, this tutor was someone he could rely on. It was comforting to not be so destructive that someone couldn't stop you....

After a moment, he nodded and lifted his blade.

Most days, these bouts helped him release the last of his pent-up frustration. He'd grown to trust his trainer enough that he could relax in the art and energy of the fight without being drawn into memories of other, more desperate battles.

Today, he wasn't sure what it had accomplished besides running him out of breath and drenching his shirt in sweat. His trainer had suggested they go find a river to wash off in, but that suggestion seemed to hold a hidden message that he'd be willing to talk or listen if Errance had something on his mind. And Errance most definitely did not want to share what was on his mind.

So instead, he excused himself and headed for his rooms to wash by himself.

Funny thing, he was still out of breath. He paused a moment in the shade of an aspen tree, pressing a hand to his side at the sharp pain stabbing between his ribs. Had he overdone it, pulled something while training? That would be a laugh, considering what his body used to put up with.

He winced. Don't think about that. Not now. It sent a coldness straight to his bones, dispelling the touch of the summer sun. The pain pinched again, sharper, in his ribs. Like a snake's bite.

Don't.

A silver sheen began to glisten on his skin, his breathing quickened to a pace his heart wasn't prepared to keep up with.

Good lord, it was the middle of the day, there was *daylight*, he had no good reason to be panicking, there was nothing to be afrai—

The next stab of pain sent him to one knee. He caught himself on the ground with a gasp as the pressure around him constricted. He couldn't breathe, his mouth was open, and he wasn't getting any air. He could feel the grip around his throat like a noose, around his chest like the coils of a serpent, drawing tighter, till his ribs began to splinter like matchsticks—

"It's not real!" His voice came out strangled, unfamiliar over the thunder in his ears. "I know it's not real." It didn't matter how real it had been, it wasn't happening now. It wasn't.

He stayed on the ground, fighting for control, one breath after the next. It could have been a few seconds, it could have been hours, he didn't know. All he knew was that eventually he could hear the sound of a nearby stream again and the flitter of a few birds passing by. His heart was sore, but back to a manageable pace. Out of breath, but breathing.

Heaven help him. A panic attack in mid-afternoon. At least no one had been around to witness it.

Ah, yes. Solitude. He had *that* to look forward to for however long Tryss would be gone. Oh. And probably longer if she agreed to sleeping separately afterwards for safety's sake.

He stared at his own shadow stretched out on the path before him. He'd managed nights alone the first few years coming back to Aselvia.

But now.

Now it sounded unbearable.

6

"*A*re you sure this is all right with you?" Tryss asked again. She held his arms, looking deep into his face, and he didn't let his assuring smile slip.

"Of course it is, Tryss. A visit back home for you has been overdue."

"And you're sure you won't come with us?" Her eyes were so very large. Those bright green eyes woven with threads of gold and canary yellow.

Errance hesitated, glancing at the flurry around them. Horses being saddled, Coren calling out orders, Zizain and Dahlya laughing about something, Zoren bouncing on the baggage already atop the packhorse. Somewhere, there was Taersidel, but he played no part in the commotion.

It didn't feel like the official entourage he'd left with when he was only twenty. Somehow, that almost made it feel safer. Just friends and family having a good time. But his gaze lifted to the east horizon, where the mountains marked the Aselvian border, and an unwanted shudder passed through his body.

He kept the smile in place, regret shadowing its brightness. "I think I'll stay…this time, anyway. But bring your mother back and whoever else so that they can be with you when the baby comes."

Lifting his chin, he gave a sharp whistle through his teeth. A moment later, Flyfar came swooping down from some nearby tree and perched upon his shoulder. "Flyfar knows you as well as me now. Wherever you are, he can go through the Unseen and bring you word from me. So at least, then, we won't be completely apart."

"Yes, now that you mention it, I do rather miss those letters you used to send. I suppose you should be the one to hold onto him, because otherwise you might be drowning in mail," she said with a twitch of a grin.

A small laugh fluttered in his chest. He reached out, hesitated, but she caught his hand and held it to her rounded stomach.

"Be safe," he whispered.

And then they were gone.

It seemed strange to him that with so much preparation, the moment of departure was so swift. One instant she was giving him a final hug after he'd helped her into the covered carriage, the next the carriage and accompanying horsemen were out the gate and down the street and out of sight.

It was too sudden. He should have taken a horse and gone to the border with them at least. He could take a horse and gallop after them even now. But would that make the moment of parting any easier?

So he stood on top of one of the high porches of his castle and stared out across the rolling green hills as if he could still spot the company somewhere in the distance.

"Perhaps you should have gone with her," Leoren said, quite suddenly. He hadn't been there a moment ago; he had this habit of appearing at hand with barely a sound.

Errance threw him a look of disbelief. "You say that now? You're the one always reminding me how unsafe it is."

A pained frown wrinkled his usually mild expression. "I know. It's just that I…that perhaps you are stifling yourself. You used to be—"

"What I *used to be*? You did *not* just say that."

"I know," Leoren said again, even more strained. "But I think the core of who you are is still the same, Errance. And that central part of you loves people. Loves adventure. Craved to see the world."

"Look where that got me."

"The desire was not wrong. You were just vulnerable and with powerful enemies. You are stronger now."

Was he? He didn't care to test it.

There was one room in the palace where Errance felt truly safe. A room guarded by his father's light that only bade those with Celestial light to enter. The door softly clicked shut behind him, and he was alone. The serenity of his surroundings always rooted him to the floor for a moment, afraid to breathe or move in the profound silence. A glass window in the domed ceiling let a little light in, but the very air seemed touched with the former presence of Rendar's glow. There was no other place in the castle he could go and feel that his father was still living.

In the center of the room stood a pedestal and upon it rested a book—the Moonscript.

The inheritance that had both blessed and cursed his life. A connection to the Higher World that the Darkness so craved that Errance had spent seventy years in imprisonment and torture for the purpose of making him reveal whatever was written within.

In a way, he was surprised he did not resent the book for the trouble it had caused him. He'd read that his own father had attempted to burn it to be rid of the threat it posed, but that the book had remained unscathed, unable to be destroyed by mortal means. But he could not hate it, could not even bring himself to blame any of his pain upon it. For the Moonscript held the writings of his father and uncle, brothers sundered since the ruin of the world. And now it was his, this connection to the Celestials and to an uncle he had never known.

Uncle Erran.

He picked the book up off its pedestal and sat on the nearby couch, pulling his legs up to nestle in the cushions. While the book looked deceptively heavy, it really was quite light. The whole thing smelled of magic, infinite in pages and intricate in design. It was crafted by celestial light, same as the moon medallion that always hung around his neck, and both these gifts had powers that no other object in the Lower World possessed.

He flipped open to the most recent page and spotted Erran's handwriting. A wave of relief and comfort washed over him. Erran had been his father's older brother, so he was used to giving counsel. Somehow, having someone both so far and so near helped Errance spill out all his troubles on paper. Yes, his uncle was perfect—actually perfect—but it didn't stop him from sharing his struggle. True perfection was less judgmental and ignorant than one would assume. Erran didn't have all the answers, but he listened, and sometimes that was all that was needed.

He briefly read over the letter that had been left for him—an eloquent, poetic study of the stars that probably held some hidden wisdom—and then scratched his own message on the page opposite.

Tryss left for Oolum this morning.

For all he knew it could be the next day before any response. But Erran must have been nearby, because not a few moments had passed when a reply scrolled into bright letters. *How are you doing?*

He snatched the pen back up and scribbled in answer. *Already feel horrible. I keep thinking I should have gone with her, but that just seems like it would have added more potential problems. I don't know. I don't know what I should have done or should be doing now.*

Did you ask Ayeshune about it?

Errance stared at the page. It always unsettled him when Erran referred to God—the Creator of the very world—so casually. Like he could just drop by for a chat.

The lack of his reply brought another question from his uncle. *Errance, are you speaking with him? Or are you just coming to me for advice?*

"Well, at least with you I get an answer," Errance muttered aloud. He didn't write such words, of course. He tried a more diplomatic response. *His presence was so clear when I was first saved, but it's faded now, and I don't really think I would recognize it if he was trying to tell me something.*

There was a long pause. When his uncle wrote back, he could almost hear the sadness in his tone. *Sometimes I fear you come only to the*

Moonscript seeking guidance, but you must remember that it was an exchange between your father and I. Yes, there is counsel and experience in it, yes, there is great wisdom. But do not neglect the teaching of Ayeshune as chronicled by the priests of your people. You don't build relationships with people by ignoring them. The same goes with God.

Errance frowned at the answer, but it didn't fade no matter how sour his stare. At last, he closed the book, folded his arms across it, and nestled his head down into his own embrace. "Couldn't you just get rid of all of it?" he murmured. "You took away the physical scars. Why must the rest of it stay?"

DORMANDY

"Do you have a moment, sir?" Kelm knocked on the edge of the doorframe and then peeked his head inside the office. The governor was nowhere to be seen. Perhaps he was in another part of the house or perhaps he had gone out for the day. Either way, Kelm planned to dine in town and couldn't wait long for him. He walked to the desk, found a loose pen and paper, and wrote out a quick question about some of the carving details. He laid it out on the table in front of the chair where he would be sure to see it and—

Aselvia.

The word caught his eye, even though he hadn't intended to look at the many open letters upon the desk. But he saw it anyway, and by reflex, he looked again. It wasn't Leoren's handwriting. It wasn't the governor's. For a second, he kept his eyes pulled away, telling himself that to read it would be a dreadful breach of propriety.

He read it anyway.

As he read, his brow furrowed deeper and deeper. He grabbed another piece of paper, wrote a few notes from the letter, and then folded it into his breast pocket. Then he snatched the other note with his question about the wood carving and folded it away too.

He'd changed his mind. He wasn't going to eat out. He was going to tell the servants the carving project was on momentary pause until he could fetch a few important tools from Aselvia. It wasn't a very good excuse, one that was unlikely to please the Governor, despite his assurances that there was no timeframe for the project. But at this exact moment, he didn't care if the man was pleased or not.

He needed to return to Aselvia. Now.

7

ASELVIA

Papers and books covered the cherry-wood desk, but Errance wasn't reading them. Ink stained his fingers, but he wasn't writing. Instead the king of Aselvia was folding the papers into various shapes of birds and animals. Juvenile, he knew. He'd have to smooth them out later so he could properly look them over. Leoren insisted that reports were important.

"Errance!"

Speaking of Leoren.

Swiping the paper figures into his lap and out of sight, he assumed an interrupted, scholarly expression as his uncle rushed into the room. But one look at the worry on Leoren's face wiped all other concerns away. All he could think of was Tryss, only a few days departed on her journey. "What is it, Uncle?"

Kelm came right behind his uncle, smiling instead of fretting. The sight of his good-natured face soothed the worries that had sprung to mind. He rose from his desk, scattering his paper creations everywhere, and reached out his hand to clasp Kelm's arm. "We weren't expecting you home this soon. Is everything all right?"

"Oh, I'm sure it is," Kelm replied. "But just in case it isn't, I wanted you and Leoren to double-check something." He moved to the desk, pulling a slip of paper from his pocket. "I was dropping something off for the Dormandy Governor, and I happened to see an open letter addressed to him concerning Aselvia."

"Funny how you just 'happened' to see it," Errance remarked.

Kelm pulled a face at him and went on. "I didn't touch the letter, but I took some notes. Whoever wrote the letter was pressing the matter of establishing contact within Aselvia. See, I quote, that *we are very disappointed with your efforts to enter Aselvia.* They went on to mention a few other things and then stamped it only with this." He held out the paper to show a hasty copy of a complicated symbol.

Leoren took the paper and studied it for a bit. "Well," he said slowly. "It is not necessarily a malicious thing that other governments or establishments want presence within Aselvia. It has long been a desired goal for many people to have better access to our riches and mysteries. Dormandy has indeed been trying for years without my suspecting any foul motive. But what bothers me is that whoever is writing this orders the governor about like a puppet."

"Yes," Errance murmured. "Nothing worse than a puppet ruler."

Not seeming to notice, Leoren folded the paper back up. "Thank you for bringing us this message, Kelm. Better safe than sorry, especially in these matters. I do not recognize the signature, but I'll review files tonight to make sure I haven't forgotten something. I'm afraid it would be suspicious if I returned with you to Dormandy at once and began questioning the matter, but I will find a way to get to the bottom of this, I promise."

"Good," Kelm said, a barely noticeable tension in his shoulders finally easing. "And I think I shall stay the night before I head back."

Visit the Priest, he will help you find your way, Damarik had told him.

Somehow, Errance didn't think it would help, but he had to keep trying. He had to get rid of these dreams before Tryss came back, and for heaven's sake, definitely before the baby came.

Oriah lived out in the wooded foothills near the palace city. He rarely could be found inside his little house, instead far more likely to be seen out in the wild.

But it was Errance's luck he was at home that morning, judging from the curl of smoke drifting up from the pipe in his roof. It was a quaint, unassuming little house built of wood and inviting all manner of moss, vine, and animal into its structure till it looked like a natural part of the forest. Pressing open the front door in a gentle jingle of bells, Errance stepped inside.

The priest perched atop a stool beside a long wooden table in the center of the room, surrounded by shallow baskets filled with the grey withered leaves of tea, dried fruit, and bright, freshly plucked petals of late autumn flowers. The room was filled with what seemed like a thousand scents—honeysuckle, rose, and lavender—yet each one complimented another.

"There you are, Errance," Oriah said, without lifting his head as he chose handfuls from each basket and set them in layers in smaller baskets before him. "I was wondering when you would come to visit me again."

Errance hovered in the door, scuffing one foot against the threshold. There was always something so welcoming about the priest's little home, even in its simplicity. The man brought the same aura with him wherever he went, so perhaps it was his presence itself that made the difference. And yet no matter how peaceful Errance felt here, he always found it hard to come back. As if that peace shouldn't belong to him. As if he was too distracted to remember it existed.

"I've been busy," he said at last, the excuse sounding lame as a lost sheep.

"Busy being stressed?" Slight amusement colored Oriah's tone, and still not looking around, he flapped a hand in the direction of one of the furthest baskets. "Could you hand me the honeysuckle? I was fortunate to find a little still blooming even this late in the year."

It was surely just a tactic to pull him in, after all, Oriah had been doing this by himself just moments before, but it was effective. He picked up the small tray and brought it near so that Oriah could pluck the petals and mix them with the tea.

"So what is the matter?" Oriah asked.

"I'm trying to figure out what I'm doing wrong."

"I suppose I should first know what you're doing and how you're doing it?"

"Living!" Errance threw up a hand in frustration, fortunately not the one still holding the basket. "Living without constantly feeling like I'm about to get crushed by something. I have been given everything they say a man needs to be happy, and I don't feel happy at all. I feel lost, Oriah.

They say God helps those who seek him, but I do seek. At least, I think I do. I'm reading the chronicles of the Sacred Texts that you and others wrote down. All right, so maybe I haven't been reading them as often as when I first came back home, but if they're supposed to bring peace, how come I get so restless and frustrated while studying? If I am called to be a king, a husband, and a father, how come I feel so inadequate to do it? WHAT am I *missing*?"

"When shadows gather across the sun and the foundations of the earth are shaken, remember me and my promises, O children," Oriah said, the verse flowing from his tongue as naturally as his breath.

Words he'd heard, words he'd read. "Annnnd that is supposed to help me…how?"

"These words were written *before* the Fall. We did not know what they meant when we recorded them. All the texts were burned in the Dark Days, so the memory of them faded from many minds. I was one of the original writers, and I remembered, and I clung to their promise. But it was twelve long years of hardship before I saw anything to give me hope that they would be fulfilled. Sometimes, Errance, it is a matter of believing without seeing and waiting for your next step to be given to you. Don't be discouraged, keep reading, keep seeking, keep listening, and when the time comes for change, you will be prepared."

"Everyone keeps telling me it's about the *time*. It's getting quite annoying."

He chuckled softly. "I am sure it is. And yet time is the nature of this world. We are eternally bound and set free by it. God is the only one who exists beyond such confines. To everything its time." He rolled the withered leaves between his hands, cupping them to his nose with a deep breath. "This harvest is the last I shall make before winter comes. These leaves and petals that I have gathered did not come to my door, but I spent days collecting each and every one. Then by hand I panned them over a fire until they withered, and this too took its time. And now the petals I add shall also have to wither and let the flavors of the flowers marry with the tea till I remove each petal. Every step with purpose and with patience."

"How will I know the next step when it comes?" If he didn't return the subject to the matter at hand, who knew how long Oriah could talk about tea?

"I cannot say for certain. But often it will be only the first part, not the full thing. Go for it anyway." He smiled as if some memory amused him.

Unsure of what to think or feel, Errance decided to remain standing there, watching the priest's fingers weave his blends of tea together and set them aside after covering them with lids. As hard as it had been to visit, now that he was here, he wasn't in a hurry to leave.

"Oh, and Errance?" Oriah peeked over his shoulder, that smile still tickling the corners of his mouth.

"Yes?"

"Just be aware that sometimes the will of God looks like a very bad idea."

"Thanks, Oriah," Errance sighed. "Thanks."

OOLUM

Yes, Tryss reflected, Oolum was just a stressful city to pass through, no matter the circumstance. In many ways, it should have been fascinating, what with all the colorful sights, sounds, and smells. But considering her first visit had been while on the run from dark forces, the city never did much for her nerves. And her nerves were already shot these days.

They had left the carriage behind in Dormandy, boarded Coren's ship, and passed across the narrow band of sea in little time thanks to the currents and fine weather. Even so, she had not cared for the voyage and her already sensitive stomach had lost everything in it. Now back on solid land, she tried to stay steady on two feet. Coren had offered to hire a carriage or palanquin immediately, but she had refused it, wanting to walk at least a little on her own without the constant feeling of sitting in something that swayed back and forth in its own motion. Flyfar nibbled on the edge of her ear as if to remind her he subjected himself to the swaying of sitting on her shoulder rather than charting his own course through the air, and she reached up to tickle his feathered breast.

She wondered how Dahlya saw the city of Oolum. While hundreds of years her elder, the healer's daughter had never stepped outside of Aselvia at all, content with the safety and beauty within the mountains. Really, it was quite kind of her to come along. So what did she see? The vivid hues of the fruits in the stalls and the silk scarves wrapped around the merchants? Or did she notice the whirl of flies and the constant shouting? Hard to say, her eyes were large as saucers either way.

"It's something, isn't it?" Tryss said, all but shouting to be heard. Even with being raised in a small and noisy village with constant attention from children, the energy in this city exhausted her.

Dahlya nodded. "Truly. It is quite…quite interesting. But I cannot imagine living here." She reddened and glanced Coren's way as he led the way through the crowd, wife and son by his side, but they had no chance of overhearing her.

"Human cities for you," Taers said, from just behind them. "Filth clings to filth."

"Taers." Tryss threw him a frown. She'd hoped he'd matured from those prejudiced views he used to carry, but apparently not.

Without warning, Taers reached out, grabbed her wrist, and began to pull her away into the crowd. "What—!" she began, but he threw her a wide-eyed expression of pleading. "What are you doing?" she hissed, looking back over her shoulder to see that they'd already lost sight of Coren.

"I saw an old enemy of mine. I didn't want to be spotted," he said, ducking them both into the shadows of a nearby passage between two buildings.

"You could have just told Coren!" she said. How come every time she came to this city, she was playing hide-and-seek in it? She peered through the rattling carts and swirling robes in an attempt to see if any of their company was coming back to notice their sudden departure. Surely Dahlya had noticed, she'd been right there. "Or, you know, not dragged me along. What sort of old enemy? What have you been up to?" She turned to face him and blinked as she looked at nothing but air. Her heart skipped one beat. "Taers?"

The next moment, a damp cloth was pressed against her mouth and she felt a strong arm wrap around her waist, pinning both her arms to her sides, dragging her deeper into the shadows of the alley. Flyfar bolted from her shoulder, squawking in furious protest. She struck out with her feet and head but connected with nothing. The pungent scent of the cloth sent rolls of yellowed fog through her head, clouding her vision and mind, darkening the light from view.

She caught one last glimpse of the bright market street and saw someone standing there, almost as if coming after her. She was not sure if she wanted them to come or if she wanted them to run. Before she could make up her mind, her mind was swallowed up by the consuming dark, and she knew no more.

Part Two

8

The smell of rosehip, vanilla, salt, and clay drifted up to Tryss as she ground the mixture together with a mortar and pestle. She lifted up the bowl to sniff deeper, but not too deep, lest she inhale a whole whiff of the powder, sneeze, and cause a natural disaster. Once the final ingredients were properly mixed, she would pour it carefully into a glass bottle so that it could later be used as a paste elf women liked to scrub their skin with.

The women at her chema village had taught her to mix such things before with silt and jungle flowers, but the pace had always been so rushed and to the point. With Dahlya, it had become a favorite pastime. Her best friend always had tea brewing over a small fire in a room where dried flowers hung from the latticed windows and old books towered in stacks on the tables and shelves.

Tryss reached over to a plate full of fresh almond cookies and popped one into her mouth, taking care not to let the crumbs sprinkle into the mortar....though it would not have made a huge difference with such natural ingredients.

"So I probably shouldn't mention this," Dahlya said, a sudden teasing smile twisting her lips. "But one of my friend's cousins mentioned to me how very fine you looked the other day out by the lake." She raised her hands quickly as Tryss glanced up. "It could have just been a nice compliment—you do know how easily we praise beauty—but still, I thought he said it in a particular way."

Shaking her head, Tryss tried to bite back a rueful grin. "Well, that is kind of him."

"Yes, very kind, I'm sure." Dahlya rolled her eyes. "Has anyone caught your eye though? I mean, not that anyone has to, but I know one of the reasons you're here is so you aren't under that kind of pressure. Still, we do have a large number of attractive and single gentlemen as opposed to other places."

It was hard not to laugh, because it was true, though Tryss had to wonder if the amount of options was one reason many elf women chose to abstain unless they were won heart and soul. Her cheeks warmed as she thought of the one whom had negated the chances of any other suitor...someone who probably barely thought about her existence. It didn't matter. She could be happy on her own. She could be happy just watching him from afar. Unless of course....he chose to marry someone else...she wasn't sure what she would do then.

The sudden turn of her thoughts apparently reddened the color in her cheeks enough to be noticed by Dahlya's searching eyes. "Ah-ha," the healer said smugly. "One doesn't blush over nothing. Come now, do tell."

"There's nothing to tell," Tryss said, grinding more salt in with a little too much force.

"Has he not noticed you then? You must forgive our nature. We can get so content with our life we don't consider change, but I'm sure he could be coaxed...."

"I doubt it," Tryss said, reddening even more. She ducked her head to her chest in an attempt to hide under her hair. Just then the tea kettle began to whistle, and she jumped to fetch it before Dahlya could.

Dahlya remained sitting and staring at her, and when Tryss glanced back she saw that her friend had taken on a pensive and mystified expression.

"Is it the age difference bothering you? That can take some getting used to for those not of our kind. I cannot think of anyone who would truly be so intimidating, unless—" She stopped mid-sentence and a very peculiar look came over her face. Tryss wasn't sure whether to translate it as dismay or shock, and she barely carried the kettle over without spilling it in her trembling hands.

"Oh, Tryss," Dahlya said, and the pure sympathy in her voice was completely transparent.

"I know!" Tryss snapped. "I know it's stupid."

"Well, I don't know that I would call it stupid," Dahlya said. "It's just that...well..." She hesitated then added a bit dubiously, "We are talking about King Errance, right?"

She would tack the King on there, Tryss thought miserably. Elves didn't seem to give too much mind to keeping classes separate, but the word King did nevertheless ring as something lofty and unattainable. Though if she was honest with herself, that wasn't the real reason why Errance would never consider her. "Ye-e-s, it's Errance," she bit out.

Dahlya changed expressions as quickly as the sky changed clouds, and she now adopted a look of bemused and somewhat concerned *intrigue. "Well, I do think he looks upon you better than he looks upon most...but as prospects go, do you think he would make a very good husband? I mean, I don't wish to presume to know him, but that's just the thing, he comes across a bit...unknowable..." She winced.*

"I know," Tryss said again and sighed hard. "I just have this unreasonable want to know him anyway, and if I can't, to just be there. And...and I feel like an idiot."

"Stop calling my friend things like 'stupid' and 'idiot." Dahlya pelted her with a rose petal. "I happen to think my friend is quite intelligent and deep-thinking, so this is something more than shallow attraction. No one can deny he is attractive, but after a while, he gets a bit off-putting, and I'm guessing you've felt this way for some time?"

"It just gets stronger."

"Well then, there's commitment on your side, at least," Dahlya said. "So talk to me about it."

"Well," Tryss began slowly. "I began thinking about it after he started sending letters through Flyfar and—"

"Letters! Through Flyfar?" Dahlya all but shrieked.

"Yes, don't get excited. He does that for business when he's busy in his rooms or the receiver is too far for him to reach."

"I'm sure the letters were very business-oriented." Dahlya rolled her eyes. "Whatever did he say in them?"

"It was just small talk, really. Things about his day, occasionally something on his mind. Usually, it was asking about me and Tellie and Kelm and anything interesting I saw. I figured it was his way of getting to know the world slowly without having to be present for everything himself when he'd rather hide. But he kept it up even after his life became busier, and I started wondering...well, maybe if his interest was

in me too. I didn't see Tellie and Kelm get any letters from Flyfar, when I'd assumed they had been. I could be mistaken, of course."

Dahlya set her chin upon the palm of her hand and gazed hard out into nowhere. "Hmm. Hmm. Do the letters come often?"

"Not every day. Once or twice a week, I'd say, though not every week. We see each other quite often, or at least we do when there is something involving the kids or something Casara needs my help with."

"Do you write him back?"

"Of course!"

"That's promising," Dahlya muttered, almost to herself. "That's very promising."

Tryss's eyes slowly opened. The ceiling above her was rough sandstone, poorly lit by candles instead of by natural light. She shifted on the hard cot, pulling free of the last few fibers of the dream.

A small scraping sound drew her attention, and she turned her aching head to see Taers propped against a crate, sharpening his knife on a whetstone.

"Taers," she murmured. "What happened?"

He looked up, eyes cool. "Oh, good. You're awake. Nothing to worry about, Tryss. I just rescued you, that's all."

"Rescued me from what? What happened? Who attacked us?"

"I needed to talk to you, Tryss. Somewhere away from those elves."

That made no sense. Even if her head were clearer, she was pretty sure that made no sense. And her head was aching, abominably. "Didn't…didn't you say something about spotting an old enemy?" she murmured, her voice coming out slurred. She smelled something pungent and it seemed to be coming from the skin on her face. "Taers, hold on, somebody…did somebody drug me?"

"Ah," he said, ducking his head. "Yes, sorry about that, but I needed you to come quietly."

She stared. Blankly. Because none of this made any sense. Maybe it was a dream. If drugs had been involved in some kind of attack, maybe this all was just in her head. But one question stood out in her mind, important to know even if it was a nightmare. "What kind of drug did you use?" Tryss's hands immediately went to her stomach as if she could sense trouble inside. "It would not have harmed the baby, would it?"

"No, not as if that thing matters." Venom laced his words and an actual look of disgust coiled his face.

She wrapped her arms around her stomach, eyes narrowing. "Thing?"

"The elf king's whelp."

"It's called a baby," she snapped. "And it's *our* baby, thank you very much."

"How did they make you do it? What bribe or threat did they use?"

It was as if the very air was being pulled out of reach. Her heart hammered so hard in her chest, it hurt. "What are you going on about! What is with these questions? I'm not answering a thing until you explain yourself!"

The fierce gleam in his eye faded and he gave her cornered stance a swift appraisal. A second later, the tension in his own posture relaxed and he adopted a soft, wheedling tone. "You needn't get all defensive, Tryss. I was only upset."

He was upset? *He was upset?* She was so upset, she was shaking! His change in tune did nothing to ease her mind. It was the sort of voice he'd used when wiggling his way out of responsibility or blame.

"Taers, if you don't tell me what is going on right now—!"

"All right, fine. Fine, I'll tell you. I rescued you from that elvish web is what I did. And I'm hoping you'll tell me you actually had a good reason for mixing with the enemy."

"The…" She leaned back against the wall. It was solid. She needed that. She needed something that wasn't falling apart underneath her. "Enemy?" Not once growing up in their jungle village had the elves been referred to as the enemy. Yes, her family might not have been on a first name-basis with them, but her grandfather had always been respectful when speaking of their history, often noting the North chemas were on the wrong side of the war. Had Taers really become loyal to the North? And why would there still be animosity? Conflict had ceased between them years ago.

"So you've kidnapped me," she said at last.

"If you want to put it that way."

"This has all been a lie."

"That really shouldn't surprise you. We are chemas, after all."

The "we" brought another thought to mind, and she gave a sharp inhale. "Alludium…was she even sick?"

His mouth quirked, as if amused by the whole thing. "She was. But by now the antidote I gave her should have finished her miraculous recovery."

"What—what is she doing there? Why did you leave her behind?"

"She will strike at the heart of the kingdom."

"You can't possibly mean—" Her heart thudded against the confines of her chest. "You do not intend to kill my husband?"

"She intends to kill the king of Aselvia. That he is your husband is your fault, not mine."

Her heart plummeted, even as fire in her soul raged upwards. "You are no match for him! Neither is she!"

His eyes narrowed, and she took a deep breath. She had to be better than this. Calmer. Was there a way to be calm when your brother betrayed you and your kingdom was endangered by an invisible assassin?

There was no use in blending into her surroundings and trying to escape. Any chema with a stronger ability could still see you. And he had always been stronger.

"What about..." She pressed her hands to her head, trying to remember everything of the last few days. "Wait. Dahlya. I thought I saw her coming after us. Did you harm her?"

He rubbed the tip of his boot into the dirt, not forthcoming with an answer. She glared, waiting him out. "No," he said finally. "In fact, you might be glad to hear I brought her along." He knocked his hand against the frame of the door, and it swung open, two figures stepping through.

Tryss's first thought was that the door was open, followed by the reality she was in no condition to attempt an escape. Second, one figure coming through the door was another north chema male, which meant Taers wasn't working alone. This was a whole operation. Third, the figure being dragged in by the new male was Dahlya.

"Dah!"

Her friend wrenched free of the chema holding her arm and hurried over to her side. She didn't say a word, but she took Tryss's hands as she sat beside her and then sent a glare back the way of their captors.

"She followed us into the alley," Taers said. "She is alive right now because she insisted you needed a nursemaid, and I decided to agree. That is the only reason. I expect you both to remember that." He flicked his fingers together, prompting his henchman through the door and then went to follow. Pausing at the exit, he looked back. "I'll give you some time to absorb everything, since you seem on the verge of hysteria. We can talk later." The door slammed shut, followed by the clack of a bolt sliding into place.

Breath shattering from her lungs, Tryss bent double and raised a shaking hand to her head.

"Oh, Tryss," Dahlya said gently, rubbing a hand across her shoulders. "I'm so sorry."

The sweet ludicrousness of such a statement was the only thing that made Tryss laugh instead of cry, although the difference between the two was very slim just then. "*You're* sorry? Dah, I've got you kidnapped by my brother, who, by the way, is some northern zealot who has declared war on your country."

"Our country," Dahlya corrected. "You're the queen. Quite the bold move for the North to make. I'm just so sorry your brother is involved. That must be absolutely heart-rending."

"More in concept, I think," she said faintly. "There is a part of me that isn't surprised. I always did hate him." She sputtered a laugh again. "I didn't mean to say that. Not even now. I'm just so…so…"

"You're tired, pregnant, and quite betrayed," Dahlya said smoothly, looking none the worse for wear about this whole turn of events. "Now just breathe. I'll look around this room a bit, see if there isn't a weakness."

"It's solid stone, Dah," Tryss muttered. As far as she could see there, was one skylight too high to reach, one water closet without a door or curtain, and one locked door leading out. But she obeyed the command

and focused on breathing. Deep in, deep out. Pressing her fingers into her temple, focusing pain and then releasing.

Flyfar.

He'd flown from her shoulder when she'd been grabbed, but what had happened to him after that? Surely he had escaped; Taers hadn't said anything about killing her bird. After all, he would just think the magpie was an ordinary pet. So Flyfar would go to Coren, and Coren would be looking for them. He could find them before the end of the night. How many chemas were here anyway? No, none of that. He would find them and he would know what to do. And if he didn't and wrote Errance…

Oh, Errance.

Errance was going to bring the world down.

9

ASELVIA

A sharp chirp and flutter of wings caught his attention, the very sound he'd been waiting for since Tryss had left. Throwing the book he held aside, Errance rushed to the railing where Flyfar now perched, a small note tucked in beak. "Good bird," he murmured, taking the note in hand. His fingers shook a little as he unfolded the paper.

The handwriting did not belong to Tryss.

It took a confused moment of blinking to recognize the penmanship as Coren's. After a longer blink, he could discern words. Fragments of sentences. Puncturing his chest, stealing the air from his lungs.

Tryss is missing, along with Dahlya and Taersidel.

Missing.

For all I know and hope, they will be found before you read this letter. But I know you'd want to know as soon as possible. I'm doing as much as I can. Please send Flyfar back so I can update you quickly.

The paper crumbled in his fist.

Missing.

He should have never let her go—

—No, he should not have let her go *without him.*

Who had taken her? Why? Was the Darkness up to his tricks again? No, no, no, there had to be some mistake. Tryss could not have been taken; some confusion must have just separated her from Coren. There had to be an explanation.

He flung open the door, taking two steps at a time as he ran down to his uncle's study. Leoren sat amid the towers of books and papers like usual, his spectacles perched at the end of his nose. His expression suggested annoyance as Errance's violent entrance sent a few of the precarious book towers tumbling over. The annoyance shifted to alarm when he looked up.

"Dear heaven, Errance, what is it?" Fear edged his voice.

"It's Tryss," Errance stuttered. "Coren's lost her." He shoved the note into Leoren's hand.

His uncle read it with swift precision, brow wrinkling.

Before he could give a response, Errance blurted, "I'm going. I'm going tonight."

"Going where?" Tellie and Casara stood in the entrance just behind him, perhaps already on their way in or perhaps having noticed his charge down the hall.

"Hold on," Leoren said, turning a shade white. "If this is a dangerous situation, you can't go charging in without any intelligence. We don't want you also taken."

"Like I care? Tryss needs me."

Casara, having slipped the note from her husband's hand, gave a small gasp as she read the contents. Tellie's hand reached up to cover her mouth as she read over her mother's shoulder.

"Listen to your uncle, Errance," Casara pleaded. "Send Flyfar to Coren first and see if he has more information now. We can't lose you too. It is never wise to have all the royals leave the kingdom. That's why you stayed in the first place."

"Yes, because that worked so well last time," Errance snapped.

She flinched, retreated, and Leoren took up the argument again. "We will set out first thing tomorrow morning. It is too late to head out now, but we can send word to Commander Maril to gather an elite search party and guard. We'll do whatever it takes to find Tryss, I promise. In the meantime, use Flyfar like Casara said. Doesn't he have a connection to Tryss? Could you send him looking for her? If she can send a message back, then—"

That was quite a big *if.* If she was being held captive, it was very unlikely she would have the free hands to write anything, let alone have paper or quill on hand. For all he knew, Coren had already tried it, even if he had not made the mention of that in his curt letter. But it was still worth the attempt.

Drawing in a deep breath to steady himself, Errance clucked his tongue and reached a hand out to Flyfar. The bird hopped to his wrist and cocked his head, bright black eye staring up at him in question. Waiting for a command from his king.

"Go find Tryss." The words cut out between his teeth, sharp-edged and brittle.

Without hesitation, the bird gave a flap of his wings and then was gone. No sparkle of magic, no sound of a shift. Just gone. Often Errance had wondered why he could feel the bird on his hand at all, feel the flutter of its warm little heartbeat beneath its soft feathers, when it ignored physical rules just like that.

He could be back in a few minutes. Or not at all. There was a chance that, if Tryss was in a certain sort of danger, Flyfar would never return.

"Do you think Errance is going to wait till tomorrow or sneak out during the night?" Tellie ripped the brush through her brown curls, for the moment ignoring all of the counsel for hair care that Casara had given her. All she could think of was Tryss frightened somewhere, in darkness and alone.

Kelm shuffled through the closet. "Come on, Tellie, it's Errance, of course he's going to sneak away."

True. If Leoren didn't know it, it was because he'd missed out on the recklessness Errance displayed during their first adventure together escaping Tertorem. In that case, they should probably be watching his rooms about now. Or rather the wall he'd have to climb down if he was taking the escape through the window.

A sensation like a cold wind shivered across her soul. She dropped the brush, clutching at her heart. Not a single candle had flickered, but the room seemed to darken all the same.

"Errance!" she gasped.

"Hm?" Kelm peered out of the closet, squinting. "Wuh?"

Without answering, Tellie leapt up but her foot tangled in the skirt of her gown, and she fell with a thump on the floor. "He's dreaming—

hurry!" she shouted as she staggered back upright and flung open the door to the hall.

She raced down the dark corridors, beams of shadows and starlight blurring past her vision, and she little cared that her footsteps did not fall with silent elven grace. Somewhere behind her, she could hear Kelm complaining for an explanation, but she couldn't wait for him to catch up. Just as she reached the top of the last stairway, the first scream came.

There were guards stationed just outside the door. Normally, there were no guards in his personal quarters—Aselvia was too safe for that— but Leoren must have had his own inkling that Errance might try to leave on his own.

"Open the door! Open the door!" she called to the guards, but they were already wrenching fruitlessly at the door handles that would not open. Stars save him, Errance had not actually locked himself in, had he?

Before she reached them, one of the guards took a step back, whirled once, and kicked the door in. The wood around the handle splintered as the lock broke, and the door swung swiftly open.

Tellie dashed between the two guards as they stepped into the room. She took in everything with one glance. The bed was empty, and the curtains and balcony doors were open wide, the cool air sweeping in soft light. For one moment her heart froze as she stared at the empty balcony, but then her eyes dropped down to the floor. A long lamp lay fallen across the tiles, the candle snuffed, and all the glass shattered across the tiles, twinkling with reflections of starlight and the other lamps in the room. In the eye of the glittering galaxy sat Errance, his arms pressed to his chest.

Tellie waved the guards back when they were certain no one else was in the room. She went to the closet and found two pairs of boots, one belonging to Tryss and the other to Errance. Stepping into the queen's, she hugged the other pair under her arm and headed out into the ocean of shattered glass.

A pattering of footsteps sounded behind her, and she looked over her shoulder to see that Kelm had arrived, his face still rumpled with confusion. He started to follow her, but she shook her head, and he remained by the hovering guards.

Since they'd entered, Errance had not moved or made a single sound. He did not lift his head as she came beside him and scuffed aside the glass with her boot enough to crouch down.

"Errance?" she whispered. "Are you all right?"

He did not answer, but now she noticed the light catching in red blood streaming down his cradled arm. A few shards of glass were still embedded in the skin. She carefully set a hand under his elbow, pulling upwards ever so gently.

"Let's get you out of this glass, yes?"

He gave into her gentle prodding and slowly rose. When she put his boots in front of his feet, he stepped into them, but without lifting his face from behind the curtain of his long hair. She led him out of the glass and to the side of the bed, but when he reached it, he dropped to the floor instead of the mattress and sat with one knee pulled to his chest.

"Send them away," he whispered.

The guards heard him themselves and they slipped out of the room without a word from her. She was not sure if he also meant Kelm, but she had no intention of sending him off. Sometimes, he could connect with Errance when she couldn't.

"Could you bring me the washing bowl and cloth, Kelm?" she called. "And a candle too."

He handed them to her and stood aside, staring down with large, sorrowful eyes. Tellie held Errance's arm up and shifted it this way and that so the candlelight caught in the embedded glass. She picked out the shards one by one, then dipped the washing cloth in the water and rinsed away the blood from his skin.

When at last she finished, she let his arm drop back to his chest and sat back on her heels. "Errance," she said firmly. "Look at me."

After a long stretch of painful silence, he lifted his head. For one second, she thought more glass was stuck in his face, but it was the glimmer of tears. Her heart thudded inside her chest as she remembered the last and only time she'd seen him cry.

"Were you dreaming?" she asked.

"No."

"No?" Tellie blinked. The sensation that had come upon her was much like when she had been a girl, called into the realm of the Unseen to battle against the darkness that would plague Errance's dreams. "You mean you did this while you were awake?" She gestured to the shattered glass. "You screamed."

He groaned and buried his face in his hands. "I was angry." His words were muffled.

She gently squeezed his arm in understanding, and her eyes bade him continue.

"She's gone," he whispered, lifting his chin. "He's taken her away, and he won't tell me why. He answers nothing."

She stilled. "Oh."

"I'm going after her tonight. On The Daisha."

Naturally. Perhaps the news should have made her stomach drop, but it was such an Errance thing to do, the heroic Errance that she'd adopted as a brother, that instead her heart lifted up on wings. "Of course you are. We're coming too!"

"No, you're not," he said and held up a hand to her oncoming protest. "First of all, carrying three adults will be too difficult for The Daisha. Second, I need you to be here and smooth things over with Uncle and Aunt."

She opened her mouth, then closed it again. Unfortunately, that made sense. Dash it all, why did it make sense! She should argue anyway, insist on having her way. She might have gotten away with it as a child, and she was fairly certain she could still bend Errance around her little finger if she wanted to. But…she could also imagine the frustration and fear from her chosen parents and she couldn't…couldn't do that to them.

So she said nothing and neither did Kelm as Errance stepped out onto the balcony. He leaned against the rail and raised a whistle to his mouth, bursting out a short, almost silent blast. Though it was but a faint whisper of sound to them, the pitch would carry up to the mountains above the city. To the forested heights where a certain creature slept.

And within minutes, they could hear her coming. One would think her gripes could be heard a mile away.

"…middle of the night…better be a good reason. Who invented…whistle anyway? I demand restitution!"

The Daisha dove in, a magnificent dark shadow against the stars, the gust of her wings knocking them back as she swept in to cling against the side of the balcony. "Do you remember that remark you once made about me becoming fat, Erre dear? Well, I am beginning to agree with you. I am much too well-endowed to be flitting about at your whim like a giant bat." She broke off, staring at him. "What is it, pet?" Her tone turned anxious and she slid her bulk up onto the landing and nuzzled her nose against his shoulder. "What's wrong?"

"It's Tryss—" he began.

"Oh, I know, you miss her. Don't worry, she will be back soon, you'll see."

"Daisha, she's missing!" he blurted.

The worthy beast blinked at him for a few seconds, not even bothering to correct his neglect to use the proper 'The' in her title. "What do you mean *missing?*"

"Coren sent us word a few hours ago that Tryss, her brother, and Dahlya all disappeared while they were in Oolum. I need to get there now. Will you fly me?"

The Daisha didn't answer immediately, the fur about her neck fanning out in a slow ruffle. "For heaven's sake," she said, a shrill growl hovering in her tone. "Can't any of you take two steps beyond the border without getting kidnapped? Yes, yes, dear, we shall go this very moment."

"Hold on, don't you need to pack?" Tellie asked in alarm.

The look Errance sent her confirmed he hadn't even thought about such a thing and found the suggestion unnecessary. How typical of him to think he could do without, well, basically everything.

Shaking his head, Kelm turned to the wardrobe and started digging through it. "At least take a flask of water. And a sword. And maybe a couple of knives. I'll get you a warm cloak; it will be a cold flight."

"I did already grab the weapons I'd need," Errance said, flicking his chin to where his sword, several knives, and a coil of wire sat on the bed. Apparently his life motto ran something like *danger first, self-care optional.* He belted the sword to his waist and tucked the knives away into their own scabbards, some hidden, some visible. He accepted the water flask that Tellie had filled and then took the cloak from Kelm and swung it over his shoulders.

Errance hesitated, hand reaching to his neck, and then he slipped the moon medallion over his head. "Could you keep this on you until I get back?" he asked Tellie.

"Of course." She could not help but feel a little thrilled to have the necklace once more, even if only for a little while.

Be careful, she wanted to say. Instead, she took a deep breath and said, "Be smart." She stepped forward and wrapped her arms around him in a fierce hug. She could feel Kelm join the embrace from alongside and knew from Errance's stiff posture that he wasn't really thrilled to be hugged by multiple people at once. But after a moment, he relaxed and gave their backs an awkward pat.

"I'll be back with her soon," he said, even though his eyes were glittering with the fear that such a promise was impossible. A shudder shaking his shoulders, he turned to where The Daisha waited and climbed atop her back, secured right in front of the wings.

"Don't do anything I wouldn't do," Kelm said, far too cheerfully.

"Can't promise that." The ghost of a smile flickered across Errance's face, and then The Daisha leapt from the balcony. The awful silence of her drop hung in the air for a moment, followed by the gust of her powerful wings lifting her up into the sky.

Kelm wrapped an arm around Tellie, tucking his chin upon her head, as they watched them fade into the night.

"They better come back," Tellie whispered, turning her face into the warmth of his shirt.

"They will, Tellie-girl," he murmured. "They will."

Errance hunkered against The Daisha's neck, her fur soft against his cheek. The landscape of Aselvia sped by below them, dark forests blurring, bright lakes glittering for an instant, moonlit fields shimmering in the wind.

But he couldn't see the beauty. He could only see vision after vision of whatever horror could have happened to Tryss. To his wife. His wife and child. Who had even taken them, and why?

One answer was obvious, but he couldn't even look at it straight on.

Tertorem was gone. Even the mountains had faded into nothing but foothills. But the Darkness was not gone. He wandered to and fro upon the world, sunk deep into mortal hearts. Who knew what other strongholds he possessed, what other influences he wielded.

He could not find her fast enough. He couldn't reach her in time.

He leaned forward, yelling to be heard above the wind. "I want you to take the high roads of the sky where the wind currents are swiftest."

"It's a bit thin to breathe up there for your tiny lungs."

"I've breathed in less," he retorted.

"Aren't you kind to yourself," The Daisha muttered, words barely audible above the whistling air. But her wings beat in heavy strokes, lifting them higher and higher into the sky until a thick wind caught her wings and sent her soaring on its wake.

Tea. Tea helped soothe any soul. Might be a small comfort, but if you stirred enough comforts together, it could have healing magic. Ahspen had chosen a gentle chamomile with a taste of lavender and honey woven into the golden waters.

He'd already brewed two pots, one for drinking and one just to have the scented steam nearby. Anything to calm the rapid beat of his heart and get him through the sleepless night ever since the news had come that Dahlya, his sister, had gone missing in the city of Oolum, along with the queen. The tea hadn't done much to help the pain and fear, but it had reined in the anxious racing of his mind long enough to consider that he had a patient to attend. And if he could keep busy and care for the chema woman's sickness at the same time, so much the better.

The brightness of morning had bathed the Aselvian healing rooms for over an hour, so there was a good chance that dawn had already woken his patient. He softly knocked against the wooden door of the room where Alludium slept. "May I come in?" he called. There was no answer. A deep sleeper, no doubt from the exhaustion of her sickness.

Balancing the tray of tea on one arm, he pushed open the door and stepped inside.

The bed was empty.

He glanced around, looking for his patient. She hadn't been well enough to stand on her own. Perhaps she had fallen to the floor?

The window had been closed before, of that he was certain. It now swung open, curtain fluttering in the wind.

And there was no sign of Alludium.

10

OOLUM

Deep aches and sharp threads of pain spread out across Tryss's body like a web. She shifted on her bed again, grabbing the pillow and shaking it out before tucking it between her neck and her elbow. A few moments later, she yanked the pillow back out and let her shoulders rest straight on the thin mattress, squishing the pillow over her head. The pillow sheet was made of coarse cotton, and the padding was poor. The mattress was worse.

If she could focus on what was so terrible about her physical discomfort, maybe, just maybe, that would hold back the overwhelming urge to weep and rage over the stabbing outrage and fear in her heart.

Dashing the pillow to the floor, she sat up and stared out into the empty little room where Taersidel kept her and Dahlya. The only furniture was their two cots, a chair, and a crate with a wash basin. A round skylight let in the starlight from overhead, but the glass covering that was thick and warped, dimming what little light existed.

The pain blooming from her abdomen was normal, wasn't it? She'd experienced plenty of discomfort in this pregnancy so far, although thankfully not so much nausea as some women whom she'd witnessed. But it was different to be feeling ill in one's own home than to be experiencing pain in a place like this. It felt less safe, less certain, all the more likely to cause some problem inside that she couldn't prevent or predict or....

Pressing her hands to her face, she took one deep breath in and let it out in a rattling swell. Panicking would not help. Talking to Dahlya might help, but she could hear her sleeping breath from across the room and didn't want to disturb her after their stressful day. She'd pray, that's what she'd do. Pray for her baby's safety, for her own sanity, for some way of escape, for Errance to come quickly, and—

Flyfar bounced out of the empty shadows, landing on the narrow bed rail just beside her arm. Sucking in a gasp, she reached for him, but not as quickly as the hand that also appeared from nothing.

The magpie squawked in Taersidel's grip.

"Don't!" Tryss shouted, struggling to stand up on her swollen feet. "Don't you dare! Don't you dare kill him!"

"Tryss," Taersidel said, even and cool as polished marble. "This bird just appeared out of thin air. I would never kill it. It's practically kindred."

Her fingernails bit into her palms as she clenched her shaking hands. She wasn't sure what to be angrier about, the sight of her husband's bird in danger or the fact that Taersidel had been in here, keeping guard, when she'd thought herself alone with her thoughts.

Dahlya had woken at her shout and softly stole to her side, eyes fixed on Flyfar.

"So," her brother said, softly and more to himself than to them, as he turned the bird this way and that to get a better look at it. "What exactly is it? I've never heard of any bird species that can camouflage itself to such a degree. Or is that what it was doing? After all, it seems like it only just got here, which is of course impossible." He stopped muttering and looked directly at her, eyes narrowing. "Does it explain how the elves always seemed to exchange information so quickly between battles up North and their home kingdom? You know, records always did question the efficiency of their message system. Not even the Wraith of Aselvia had that kind of speed or skill."

Like she was going to tell him anything! But in the time that it took for him to finish his monologue, the pulse in her head calmed enough to remember one important detail.

Flyfar couldn't be held captive.

It was possible he couldn't even be killed, though she wasn't ready to see that theory tested.

"It's Aselvia's royal gift, isn't it?" Taersidel said, startling her back to attention. "Don't look so surprised. I'm not that jungle bumpkin anymore, only learning what our elders told us. Up North, we *know* things. There are libraries of stone carved deep into the roots of the mountains. Some of the clans still possess their original gifts as well, mystical things that can't be explained by any other pattern in this world."

He glanced down at Flyfar again, and the bird looked indignantly back, then plucked at his hand with his beak. "I don't suppose there is a way to keep it from going off again, is there?" He didn't seem to expect her to answer any of his questions, which was relieving as it was offensive. "No weakness, nothing to exploit? I suppose if I put it in a cage it will be gone by morning. But—" Tilting his head, he considered and then gave a sharp nod. "—but I think I shall put it in a cage regardless. It will help me keep track of its movement. After all, it might stick around if it was sent to find you. And don't get any ideas about sending messages back. I'm not the only one here, Tryss. You will be watched at all times."

She opened her mouth, but she had no response. She couldn't possibly speak. The most she might manage would be a scream of rage and she wasn't about to concede that.

"Anyway, try to get back to sleep," he went on, as if she could. "You'll need rest as we will be departing for Dormandy shortly."

"What! Why? We just came from there!"

"Believe me, I know it," he said, rubbing his finger on the ridge of his brow. "I would have much preferred to steal you away in Dormandy while we were there. But you were never a moment away from that redhead and his family, and I had no opening. I was prepared to take drastic measures in Oolum if it came to that."

She stayed silent for a moment, trying not to imagine Coren, Zizain, and their sweet child meeting some horrible end at her brother's hand.

"What's in Dormandy?" she asked at last. "I thought you planned to take me North."

"The client who hired me to kidnap you."

Dahlya gasped.

Tryss sputtered. "Hired. SAINTS, Taers, I thought you were doing this by some twisted sense of righteousness! You're selling me out? How dare you pretend to be family!"

"Calm down and let me finish," he said, not the least bit ruffled. "Yes, I took the job when I heard of it. You should be glad it was me and not somebody else. Somebody else would actually give you over for the bounty. I intend to collect the bounty and *then* take you North. It will damage, if not destroy, my reputation as a reliable mercenary, but that's the thing about chemas, I can always put on a new coat and a new identity."

He really had no shame.

"When are we leaving?" she asked, strength draining. She did not wish to be on a ship again this soon. Even the short trip on the *Solitary Star* had rendered her seasick. But at least afterwards they would be on the right side of the sea, and maybe, just maybe, they would have a chance to escape during the transition from ship to building. That is, if Taers didn't drug them again. He probably would.

"Soon," Taersidel said, and that was all.

11

OOLUM

The candle wick lay drowned in its own wax, so Coren wearily paused in scanning the reports to exchange it for a new one. With the brightness of a fresh flame, he returned to the papers, but the words remained the same. There was no news from any of his contacts of a person matching Tryss's likeness. Painfully, it made sense. If they were smart, whoever they were, they would keep her hidden in the first few panicked days of searching. And she could have left the city by now. He had someone to watch the ships and wagons, friends among inspectors to check large crates. But they couldn't cover it all, and she might slip by. Forever.

At least Dahlya was still with her. And her brother. Hopefully. Maybe together they could save themselves. A heavy groan exhaled from his gut, and he rubbed his sore neck. He couldn't sleep. He just couldn't lose any chance or clue of finding them.

Someone knocked loudly on his back door.

A contact? Information perhaps? He bolted up and hurried over, opening the door with a snap.

Errance stood on the front step.

Even in the poor lantern light, his face shadowed underneath the hood, it was undeniably him.

"Oh brights," Coren swore, then reached out and yanked him inside. He slammed the door shut and leaned against it with a pant. "You're already here. Where are your guards?"

Errance remained hunched in his cloak, not fully facing him. "I'm alone," he said quietly. "I came on The Daisha."

"Then where's she?" He almost yelled it, panic coating his throat.

"Hiding in the hills outside the city. I didn't want anyone to realize I was here."

Coren stared at him, appalled. He couldn't think, couldn't believe this was happening. He'd known Errance would come, but he'd hoped to have Tryss back by then or at least have a trail to follow.

Neither of them said anything for a few moments.

Swallowing hard, Coren spoke first. "I...I am so sorry." His voice cracked and he had to clear it before trying again. "I'm so sorry for losing her."

"It's not your fault," Errance said, quieter than ever. "I should have been here. With her." He let his hood fall back onto his shoulders, and Coren sucked in a sharp breath at his appearance. The shadows in his cheeks might as well have been bruises and the raw guilt in his eyes was completely unmasked.

"Come sit down and have a drink," Coren urged, stepping away from the door and leading the way down the hall. "I'll catch you up on what I've gathered so far."

"You can catch me up while we search the city."

"But—" No, he couldn't argue with him. The man had lost his wife, of course he was going to set out like a madman and not listen to any reason or strategy. "All right, but let me get Zizain. She'll want to know you are here."

"Wouldn't she be staying with Zoren?"

So Errance had enough presence of mind to remember his cousin had a kid to take care of. Coren hadn't given him enough credit. "We have Zoren staying with some friends for the night," he said. "We wanted to be ready to leave at a moment's notice if any news came up, and anyway, we already had plans to head out and gather information tonight."

Errance looked at him as if it was strange he should have trustworthy friends in a city like this, but made no further comment. Good. The fewer questions, the sooner they could set out.

It took more than a moment to fetch Zizain.

There also had to be costumes, because of course, it was Coren. Clearly the man couldn't walk out in the street as himself, now could he? So when he came out with Zizain, both of them were dressed in the tunics and head-wraps common to Oolum, Coren's skin a bit darker than normal and the patch on his chin having grown to a small red braid.

Zizain's smile was bright as always, but sorrow edged its corners and her usual chatter was absent. "I am glad you are here, Errance," she said, reaching out and wrapping him up in a hug. "We will find her."

"Thanks," he murmured, trying not to wiggle free of the said hug. "So what exactly is the plan?"

"I already have my spies and contacts searching for word of her," Coren assured, ushering them out into the streets. "But we'll do some investigating of our own. All three of them disappeared soon after we arrived in the city. I had been leading the way and Taersidel had the rear guard. I didn't notice they'd fallen behind or anything, just one moment they were there and the next, they were gone. Flyfar came to me a few minutes later, screeching an alarm. Too bad the bird can't talk or write, I'm sure he knows what happened. Pull that hood up, eh? The dark and mysterious stranger look will suit the mood tonight. Just keep quiet and hang back as an intimidating presence. Zi and I will do the talking."

And an hour later, Errance discovered that what Coren did not mention about his plan, costumes and all, was that it revolved completely on the bit about talking.

Lots and lots of talking.

Terrible plan.

Sometimes when they encountered strangers in dark alleys, Coren spoke in hushed, conspiring tones, and sometimes he laughed and slurred as if dead-drunk. It took forever to actually get to any questioning about Tryss and her whereabouts, and when it finally did, nobody had any information.

Errance shifted his weight from one foot to another while he waited for the latest conversation with the latest stranger to end. At some point they had switched from the common tongue to some kind of Oolum native tongue, which was a language he hadn't much studied in the last few years, so there wasn't much point in trying to listen. Instead, he watched their surroundings, never one to trust the dark.

And yes, there was somebody watching them. Someone peering around a nearby building. They straightened as if they'd realized they'd been caught and disappeared around the corner.

Errance took one glance at Coren and Zizain, both of them laughing at whatever the man was saying, and then he set out after their observer. He could imagine Coren telling him not to go off alone and he didn't much care. He was used to handling things alone.

But when he rounded the corner, he only stared into a dead end between shop walls. He looked up because one should always look up when an alley turns up empty.

A soft hand curled around his arm. "Looking for me, *adorante?*" an even softer voice murmured. He found himself staring down into the face of a complete stranger. A young woman in rags, eyes gleaming out of the hooded shadows of her face. She gave his arm a gentle tug.

His blood turned to ice water. For a moment, he could not move, could not speak, could not even think. Everything stripped away and he was falling back into a dark void, the shadows clawing up to grab him—

"Get away from me!" he shouted, seized her shoulders, and threw her from him as hard as he could. She tripped over her skirt, landing hard on the ground with a shrill scream. Without bothering to stand, she scrambled away, hunkering in the corner of the wall.

"What's going on?" Coren came skidding into view, a knife drawn in his hand. He took one look at them, both backed as far from each other as possible in the narrow alley. His eyes widened. "Oh, saints," he said, staring from the young woman to Errance. "Oh, saints."

Zizain arrived behind him, taking the situation in just as quickly. Stepping forward, she held out a hand to the woman. "Sorry, dear, I could have told you to leave this one alone. He's a bit wrong in the head, you see. But he wouldn't have harmed you. Are ya hurt?"

The woman spat, then skittered past them like a crab, vanishing into the darkness. A long moment of silence passed. Zizain stared down at the ground as if the woman still sat there, and she did not bother to wipe the spittle from her hand.

Errance shuddered, skin still crawling. He opened his mouth to speak but shut it again when he saw how Coren was looking at him.

"What," Coren said, "did you do?"

He blinked. "What did *I* do? Don't you know what that woman was?"

"I know perfectly well what she was. I also know she was a woman and a great deal smaller than you. Brights, Errance, you could have hurt her!"

Errance laughed, sharp and short. "Ha. As if. The witch."

With a harsh breath, Zizain spun towards him. He stepped back, surprised to see her face so savage. But before she could speak, Coren caught her arm. "Not here," he said. "We'll talk about it back at the house."

When neither moved, Coren took Errance's arm and pulled him along. They fell into a sharp pace through the city, passing a few patrolmen who paid them no mind. Merchants, sleeping in intervals to guard their wares, stiffened as they passed by. Though the city was a maze, even worse at night, Coren led them without hesitation until they reached their destination. He sent Errance in ahead of him and left the door open to let in the light of the moon.

"Now sit," he said, pressing a hand down on the king's shoulder.

Errance sat with a thud, legs crossed underneath him. The chill in his blood had changed to heat, but now it just swirled in an irritated state of confusion. His cousin sat across from him, and Zizain leaned against the doorframe. He supposed they were expecting him to be guilty about something, but he had no idea what. "She attacked me," he said, not liking how defensive he sounded. "What was I supposed to do?"

Coren raised a brow. "Attacked you, did she? Sure it wasn't just a proposition? You could always excuse yourself with dignity in that case. Anything other than flinging her away like she's some sort of viper."

Wrong word to use. The woman's touch crawled across his arm, turning to snake skin. "She and her kind *are* vipers," he bit out.

Zizain went rigid. Her lips, just bordered by the light, pressed together and went down.

Coren braced his hands against his knees, frowning. "You have no idea," he muttered.

"I have no idea?" Errance jerked his hand to his chest with incredulous force. "You're telling me I have no idea?"

"No!" Coren thundered. "You don't!" Shadows rolled across his face like storm clouds, so that even Errance drew back. But the storm passed, leaving weariness in its wake.

Sagging, he sighed. "Look. Errance, you have always lived in extremes. If it wasn't the perfection of Aselvia, it was the sadism of Tertorem. The only evil you've encountered is that which was designed to hurt you merely for the pleasure of it. But the world is more complicated than that. Out here, not everything is about you. That woman wasn't trying to be frightening or offensive. She expected you to snap up the offer. She probably just saw you as another way to survive a day, presuming you were a paying sort. You don't know her. You don't know why she was there." His words lingered in a heavy, uncomfortable silence.

Errance glanced at Zizain uneasily. From a time long past, he remembered Coren saying that she'd been betrayed and sold…and he'd never really thought about it further. "Surely not all of them are forced into it?"

"Forced?" Coren's voice was one with the surrounding dark. "No, not all are forced. There are those by desire. But most believe they have no other choice."

Errance's mouth twisted. "There's always a choice."

"Not for them!" Zizain's foot slammed to the floor in a harsh slap as she turned, the light swept across her face, edging the anger and pain. "Many women here have no real way to support themselves if they have no talent or learned trade! There is no safe place for them on the street! Many have no other place to turn! And even if they desire it, why do you think they do? What sort of life might they have grown up in to think that is where their value lies?"

Whitening, Errance lowered his head. "But…"

"No one's a victim besides you, eh, Errance?" Coren said.

Errance sent him a dire look, but his hands gripped his arms so tight that he could feel the veins rise from the skin. "I…I did not mean to hurt her," he said at last.

The remnant of Coren's anger melted in his tone. "I don't think you did. Scared her, that's all."

"Do you think we could find her again? Offer an alternative—"

"Unlikely. If she was shaken up bad, she'll probably hunker down somewhere for the night. As for later, who knows? We can hope. We do try to help these people, even better if it's ahead of time, but the claws of the sensual slave trade are sunk deep into this city. They'll prey on anyone they can."

Errance considered that for a few painful moments. The thought that had already been on his mind since he'd heard the news, the thought that had grown increasingly strong, was now unavoidable at the forefront of his mind. "You think they took Tryss and Dahlya, don't you?" he said. "That's your best guess, isn't it?"

Coren rubbed a hand over his face, stretching the skin into unnatural shapes. "Could be another reason. But it's a pretty common outcome for young women here."

"But she's pregnant," Errance said weakly, and then winced at the immediate thought that they would raise his child in captivity. "What about Taersidal, what happened to him?"

"Could be the same fate, or they could have killed him, or they could sell him for another trade. Plenty of things a talented chema could be wanted for. Look, let's not jump to that conclusion quite yet. No use making yourself sicker." Coren rose, flicked a match against his heel and held it to a wall sconce. "Get yourself washed down and head to bed. We'll search more in the morning."

12

ASELVIA

Boneblight.

The curse hovered on the edges of Alludium's lips, unspoken, but intended with every fiber of her being. She lay flush upon the white roof tiles of Aselvia's palace, perfectly blended into her background. Occasionally, she could hear guards trot past on the pathways beneath her, but their steps were not alert enough to suggest they were looking for her. Not yet.

She'd *told* Taersidel that she needed to strike before any news of Tryss's disappearance came back, but *no*, he had insisted that she wait so that no suspicion would be cast upon him before he could steal his sister away.

Due to the midwife's disappearance with the queen, the healers were some of the first people to be alerted. She overheard the news the moment it came, and set out immediately afterwards. Even so, it had not been soon enough.

The king was already gone.

His chambers were the first she visited, and if he'd been there, he would have been dead well before anyone noticed she'd left her bed. But his rooms were completely empty, and she gathered from eavesdropping that he left perhaps only a few hours before she'd slipped in through a window.

He won't come after her, Taersidel had said with a terse laugh. *He's too shattered.*

Idiot. When glass hit the floor, it scattered to the furthest corners that could be found. Didn't he know shattered things had the sharpest edges?

A hissing breath slid through her clenched teeth. Reaching into the folds of her wrapped tunic, she pulled out a few papers and pressed them out against the roof. While in the king's chambers, she'd swiped some papers from his desk. Not something that would aid her particular mission, but something she could sell to Aselvia's other enemies. Only, as she found out now while rifling through them, it all contained very useless information, Wraith take it. There were no reports to suggest the amount of gold circulating the kingdom because most costs were covered by trade. If there were any disputes about fair trade, they seemed to be handled by local courts, rarely making their way to the hearing of the king. There was nothing from the papers she had grabbed that anyone would pay money for. If Aselvia had any dirty or dark secrets, they probably kept it under the same protection as they kept their infamous Moonscript.

She eyed the eastern mountain border. There was one blessing about the king leaving, and that was that he'd taken the daisha with him. The daisha who could most assuredly track her down by scent instead of sight. When the king's death had been the goal, Alludium hadn't much cared what happened to her afterwards. But now that the goal had shifted, survival and escape were key. There was no telling when the creature would return, so she could not tarry long before making the trek to the border. Only then would she find out for certain if the shield had any sort of intelligence that kept enemies from leaving as it kept them from entering.

But not yet.

Taersidel's part of the plan may have succeeded, but it had thwarted hers. She had not infiltrated Aselvia for paltry notes; she had come to make a name for herself in Glory.

She could not leave without tossing at least one stone to ripple these placid waters.

The room was not small enough for Tellie's comfort.

A strange thing to think considering that the room she was standing in was not only small, but overcrowded.

They were all gathered here in the steward's study—Kelm, Leoren, Casara, Damarik, Ahspen, Commander Maril, and herself—and yet there were still empty spaces in the book-strewn and undersized room that could possibly hold a person.

An invisible person.

Upon waking the morning after Errance's flight, she'd thought she'd have to spend the day explaining to her daava why they thought it was a necessary risk.

But instead, she'd found Leoren in another kind of panic.

Allu, their chema patient, was no longer in her room.

"Do you think someone could have come in and taken her?" Maril was saying. She stood at the study door, her back flanked by the guards standing watch at the entrance.

"Our house of healing is sacred ground for the sick," Damarik said. "I do not believe that any elf, no matter their personal hatred for chema kind, would have violated my home in such a manner. Besides, there was no sign of any kind of struggle."

"Since both you and Ahspen have confirmed that it should not have been possible for her to be wandering far, sick as she was…" Leoren had not ceased sorting through the papers and books piled on his desk. He normally kept a very orderly study, but now he tore through it with the discretion of a hurricane. "…And since no one has seen her for hours now, we must presume that Allu has tricked us and is an enemy of Aselvia."

"Do you think she acted on her own?" Tellie asked. "Or that Taers was also involved?" She thought she already knew the answer, but she hated it and wanted another opinion. It didn't seem possible that Tryss's own brother would have betrayed her like that.

"She was poisoned, there was no lie about that," Damarik said. "But I do not believe that anything I administered was what helped her heal. Recovery this quick suggests that not only was she self-poisoned, but that she also had the antidote. It is possible she gave it to herself, and Taersidel had no knowledge of the deception, but…"

"…But unlikely." Leoren's grim expression hardened further. "And in that case, I think it is safe to assume he has a hand in Tryss's disappearance. We do not know what her goal is, if she is here to kill or steal, but it's probable Errance would have been the first target, so at least that is one blessing in his departure." He paused a moment, sending a pointed look Tellie and Kelm's way, before continuing, "Unfortunately, that also means we are without The Daisha for the moment, and she would have been invaluable in scenting this enemy out."

"She could have also been the target," Maril pointed out. "If the chemas desired to finish what they started."

"True. We must send a messenger to Errance; he needs to know the most likely cause for Tryss's capture and the danger that is posed to himself. If we only had Flyfar, he could know already, but the bird has not returned to us. I can only hope Errance has him and will send a message to us that way. But what we need to do now is protect ourselves the best we can. If you would please explain, Commander."

Maril dipped her head before facing the small company. "Chemas are a terrifying enemy on the battlefield. We had to get creative in how we fought them, and we are going to have to apply those same tactics here. First, nobody is ever to be alone. If she is here to assassinate, she is less likely to attack large numbers. All food and water cannot be touched unless it has been under lock and key. Any kingdom secrets or treasures are also to be locked safely away."

"What sort of things would she be looking for?" Kelm asked.

Leoren pulled books and scrolls off the shelves, armfuls at a time, and stacked them into a trunk. A puff of dust blossomed in the air, and he waved it aside with a cough. "Records of the war. The known casualties on both sides, the chema leaders who are still alive today and could still cause problems. Accounts of known strength and locations. Most of this information is outdated, but we still have it. Not to mention there are the records of the soldiers we have enlisted in our own army. There are too many things she might be after."

He stiffened, spinning slightly on his heel and frowning at the far wall. The guards tensed, hands tightening on their weapons.

"Wouldn't we be able to see her if we were looking straight at her?" Tellie whispered. She was certain she had seen shimmers of movement when Tryss had blended into backgrounds.

"Not necessarily," Leoren answered, still frowning. "Some are very skilled."

She shivered. The war with the chemas had not been brought up much in her life here. For one, there had not been a skirmish in years, for another, it was not a popular subject with a chema queen on their king's arm, even if she was innocent of her colder cousins' actions.

"How...how do you defend yourself against an enemy you can't see?" She was afraid to hear him answer that it was quite impossible.

"You make ways to see them," Maril answered. "They can't hide the effect they have on the world around them. They cast shadows, leave footprints, cause sound. When entering rooms or passages, it is useful to spray the area with a strong perfume or dust. It can not only flush out the hidden shape of a body, but it might cause her to cough or otherwise give herself away."

"I say, that's sharp." Kelm nodded to himself, fingers tapping on chin. "What about some sort of wax or dust on the floor where we can see the footprints?"

"Assuming she stays in the palace, that's a good idea."

"And that brings us to the next threat," Leoren said, drawing in his breath with steely resolve. "We must ensure she stays in the palace. If she goes out into the wilderness and targets the civilians of Aselvia…the results would be disastrous."

A heavy silence fell over the gathering as they considered this possible turn of events, a cold shiver running through each of them.

"Messengers are already being sent in groups of three across the country to alert our citizens to the danger," Leoren continued. "I wish that they did not have to be alarmed like this, but it is the best way to protect them until we have her in custody."

"Does everyone know Errance has gone after Tryss?" Kelm asked.

"Not yet," Leoren admitted. "I'm going to have to break that news soon, but one panic at a time. We must have all energies set on capturing Allu. Until then we have to live very, very carefully. The queen mother has already been moved to a room deemed secure and under close guard, and Casara will join them shortly. If any of you desire to join them, then—"

"Oh no, Daava," Tellie said, gripping Kelm's hand. "We'll stay and help." They could get through this together, as they had overcome all other perils in the past.

A small, grateful smile fluttered across Leoren's face, almost as if he were surprised to not be standing alone in such a crisis. His eyes closed for a moment, and when they opened again, their green shone sharper than ever through his gold-rimmed glasses.

"Commander Maril will instruct her soldiers to lay the traps we've prepared for times of war. But I suspect this will take even more unconventional means. Alludium came for something. Which means we must lay the bait."

"What sort of bait?" Tellie asked, a nervous prickle pattering across the back of her neck. It wasn't cold in the room, but she found herself wrapping her arms around herself anyway. Kelm noticed and tucked her under his own arm, which was even better.

"Obviously, we can't risk a person, so it will have to be information. And it will have to be legitimate, or she won't take the bait. But what kind of information she'd want that I'd be willing to risk her seeing…I'm not sure…" He paused, swaying where he stood.

Tellie waited for him to continue, and when he didn't, she took a closer look at him. "Daava?"

"Never mind," he said. "It's just the shock that's catching up to me. Hang on a moment, I'm sure it will pass." His voice was thin, a slight wheeze rattling the sound. He reached out to the nearby table for support, his arm gripping the stack of documents closer to his chest. He coughed again, harder this time, till his face reddened. "Oh, *brights*."

"What is it?"

"She was already here," Leoren said faintly. The next moment his legs crumbled beneath him, and he toppled to the floor, papers scattering out like a moth swarm around him.

"Daava!"

13

OOLUM

With a flick of his wrist, Coren cracked an egg on the pan's edge and let the yolk drop onto the sizzling iron. The yellow aroma, mixed with the bright red of peppers and earthy greens, wafted through the room, melting into the brightness of morning light. Even with such heavenly smells, he did not find himself particularly hungry, not with everything that was happening. But the chaos was all the more reason to eat. They needed the fuel for whatever lay ahead.

"Can I have some of that bacon, Da?" Zoren was hovering by the stone oven, eyes fixed on the second skillet that simmered with slabs of pork fat.

"Aye, just don't burn yourself."

Zoren, heedless of all burns, snatched some up, stuffed it into his mouth and then looked back towards the stair with a curious tilt of his head. Coren followed his gaze and heard the telltale stamp of approaching footsteps.

Errance descended the stairs. He didn't merely walk down the steps, he came with energy and force. Crossing the room in two strides, he swept out an arm and stabbed a finger forward as if it was his sword. "I will see it destroyed."

"I'm sorry, what?" Coren asked.

"The sensual slave trade. I want it razed to the ground. I want every captive freed and every life restored. I refuse to let it continue while I draw breath."

Coren quickly turned his back so that Errance could not see the smile that washed across his face. Of course, a million reasons why such an evil could never be completely erased from an imperfect world sprang to mind, but those reasons really didn't matter. What mattered was that there were people with a passion to act against it. And saints, he'd waited so long for Errance to wake up and see the brokenness around him and to realize he could do something about it. By all the lights, he could! He had fire within him, and it was a fire not meant to smoke and smolder in sodden misery, but to consume the world in brilliant whiteness.

Still, he kept his tone calm and reasonable. "It's a never-ending fight, you know. But I always say that even one life saved is a victory worth all the struggle."

"Whether Tryss is there or not," Errance growled. "I hate it, I hate the monsters who run it, the demons who inspire it, and I want it gone."

"Well, good!" Coren said, far too cheerfully. "After we find Tryss, I would love to join forces with you! Now, how about—hold it, where are you going?"

Errance was already halfway out the door. "We have to continue the search!"

"Not before you eat something!"

"There is no time for eating!"

"What, you plan to just run on your celestial light?" Coren knew as soon as he said it that was exactly what his cousin planned. Did he remember to eat in regular times? Probably only if Tryss was around to remind him. His inner light would evaporate into thin air with that kind of behavior. "Spark, give your uncle some bacon, will you?"

Zoren hopped off his stool and bounced over to Errance, holding out a few sticks of bacon in his grubby hands. "Da has told me lots about you!" he proclaimed cheerfully.

Errance accepted the offering with a dazed look. "Oh…I didn't realize you were here. Coren, I'm sorry, I shouldn't have brought up the subject—"

"This is the kid I'm raising in Oolum whom we're talking about," Coren said, sliding the cooked eggs off onto a clay plate. "He knows a thing or two. Anyway, why don't you tell him hello."

"Hello," Errance said, still blinking.

"Hi!" Zoren grinned. "Da says you're not really my uncle but that I get to call you that anyway."

"Morning, darlings!" Zizain trooped in through the door, throwing a bag to the floor. "They have the cart all loaded for us, husband mine."

"Perfect. I'll wrap up breakfast and we can eat it on the way."

"Wait, where are we going?" Errance asked. "What do we have a cart for?"

"Some of my crew brought in provisions that we're bringing to the homeless and sick in Oolum's alleys."

Errance stared in consternation. "But…Tryss…?"

"Don't worry, this is part of finding Tryss. People on the street hear things and see things, but they aren't just going to tell you for free. We bring food and medicine to the poor districts as often as we can and while we're there, we can ask if they've heard anything that might lead us to her. But just one thing, Errance. I need you to promise me that if an old woman pinches your bum and calls you 'sweetheart,' you will not smack her across the street."

"Um. Is that likely to happen?"

Coren gave him a swift look up and down, a wicked smile curving his mouth. "Oh, yes."

The cart wheels rattled like a bucket of rocks, catching every single bump in the road. Errance was fairly certain it invented bumps of its own, as he hadn't noticed uneven ground while walking in the sand-paved streets. He sat in the back along with Zoren, steadying the clay pots every time the cart jerked.

The sun was not visible above the buildings yet, but it was already hot. Errance tugged at the loose collar of the white shirt he'd borrowed from Coren. He had thought it too thin when he'd first pulled it on, but now he was glad for the papery fabric. He didn't usually notice his elvish smell of evergreen, but he noticed it now as he reached to tie his hair back into a tail.

Most of the streets were still cast in shadow, yet the cloth banners stretching overhead shone vividly in the rising light. Every color of the rainbow, brightest of every hue. As the cart drove on, however, he began to notice the dye in the cloth fade till the streets were overhung with dirty rags or dusty boards.

The ox bellowed, the cart jerked to a stop, and he just managed to stop the tallest pot from tipping over.

A smell, hidden only by the dust, wafted under his nose. No, not a smell, because that suggested something temporary, but a stench baked into the ground. A smell he had once been so accustomed to that he'd stopped noticing it altogether, but it slammed back into his memory with vicious force. Filth. Sickness. Death.

Zoren was already unlatching the backdoor of the cart and hopping to the ground. Coren came around, reaching in and pulling out a few crates. "Mind helping, Errance?"

Errance grabbed a hefty sack and stepped down, taking a swift study of their surroundings. Last time he'd been in the back alleys of Oolum, he'd been running for his life and had little chance to observe his surroundings. The shanties back here were so brittle he suspected a gust of wind would send them all toppling, assuming any wind made it down between the tall buildings on either side. Sand-eaten cloth hung across doorways, ghostly shrouds of some former glory. Overall, this place felt like a graveyard, and the thought of anyone living in it turned his stomach.

But people did live here. They came pouring out of tipped over crates and flimsy tents at the sight of the cart, crowding about and shouting in fevered excitement. A few bodies lay on mats, but even they raised their heads and watched in expectation.

"Wait, why are they here?" Errance managed to say it in Elvish, though he wasn't sure anybody spoke the common tongue, their Oolum accents were so thick.

"Either they can't afford a good house, or they are sick and forbidden from the main streets, or they are injured and can't work, or they have been excluded for any other reason. Take your pick," Coren said with a shrug. He turned a bright smile to the skinny child tugging on his arm and answered their question in flawless Oolumeese.

Clearly, of the languages Errance had studied in the past few years, it had been a mistake to neglect this one. He just never saw himself coming back...

Too many people grabbed at his arms, too many voices rang in his ear, too many eyes looked at him in curiosity or expectation. The moment he unloaded the last pot, he squirmed his way free of the crowd and stepped back into the shadows.

He watched his cousin's family bustle about, completely at ease. Smiles flashed, strange against the backdrop of extreme poverty. Somehow, it made his heart ache and his eyes sting, and so he looked down at his boots instead, scuffing a toe through the dust. There was no use in trying to ask questions right now. He would just have to wait for Coren to take the lead.

Zizain's ceaseless chatter drew near him and something bumped his folded arms. He looked up just in time to see Zizain shove a thinly swaddled baby towards him. More out of reflex than thought, he caught the little bundle, and then choked on a horrified gasp as she turned back to the mother huddled on the ground, leaving him to cradle the child. In a panic, he tightened his hold, then loosened when the baby squirmed, then tightened again at the thought of dropping it. It took several moments of

readjusting before he decided he had it in a decently safe position. By then his heart was hammering so loud that he was sure the small creature would raise a fuss.

Have I ever held a baby before? He hadn't as of the last seven years because elven babies did not come by often, and while there had been one or two shown to him, he'd let Tryss or the parents do all the holding. As for before, he vaguely recalled that Rendar had once given him a baby to hold. It had been stressful then, but it was so much more stressful now.

How did one handle looking after something so helpless and fragile? So—he paused, peering closer—so perfect? Were they really born with such tiny and flawless little fingernails? Each wrinkle and swirl already imprinted in their hand? Lashes full, eyebrows in, eyes intelligent and already judgmental?

He swallowed hard. This was what Tryss was carrying inside her. It hadn't really struck him until now. Babies…well, he'd really thought of them more in a conceptual sort of way than as a little person. But he had one of these little miracles of his own somewhere, just waiting to blink their eyes at the sky. Did they look more like him or Tryss? Did they already have all their perfect tiny nails?

Hands reached out to pull the baby away from him, and he pulled back on instinct.

Zizain looked at him in surprise. "The mama would like her baby back, yes?"

Flushing, he handed the baby over, but not without some reluctance.

As soon as his arms returned to his sides, a little hand grabbed his fingers and tugged hard. He looked down to find a small child staring eagerly at him, eyes and smile bright as stars in a midnight sky. Like most of the children here, their clothing was ragged, their dark hair shorn short and clustered in tight curls over their head. They were too small to determine whether they were a girl or boy. When he didn't move, they tugged again and chirped a word he didn't understand, but the hope behind it was recognizable.

"I'm sorry, I can't—" He took a step forward in answer to the child's insistent tugging, but when the child pointed off down the streets, he paused again. "Coren, I don't know what they want?"

Coren weaved his way out of the crowd and crouched down beside the child, asking a question in a friendly and open manner.

The moment Tryss and I are back home, I am learning this language.

Errance blinked, a little surprised the thought had come in so confidently. As if there was no other ending to this story except a happy one. Normally, hope was not the first thing his mind chose. But for now he'd cling to every shred of hope in his heart.

14

ASELVIA

Damarik took one look at Leoren's reddened face as they brought him into the palace's medical room and dropped the stack of recipes and ingredient guides he'd been packing into a trunk.

"I know what it is," he said in answer to Tellie's tearful plea, his manner short and swift, altogether unlike him. "I have to treat it very quickly, or he won't be able to breathe much longer."

Maril and Kelm laid Leoren's limp form onto the nearby cot, the commander massaging his swollen throat.

"How?" Tellie tore at the roots of her hair, pacing between the bed and the table where Damarik worked. She hated feeling so helpless. She hated the impending loss of another parent. This couldn't be happening. Daava could *not* die. "How did she even poison him?"

"It is typically a fine powder that one breathes in or gets on one's fingers. Once ingested, it acts within a few minutes, swelling the airways." Damarik did not slow down or stumble as he spoke, grinding dry leaves from a jar into a fine powder. There was a pot of water boiling over the hearth, and he ladled a large amount of it into a bowl. He poured the powder into that, dissolving it completely with a few sharp swipes of a whisk. "Lift him up please," he commanded, taking the deep bowl over to Leoren. Kelm propped him up in his arms, and Damarik held the bowl under Leoren's chin, letting the hot steam billow up into his nostrils and parted mouth.

"It might burn him a bit," Damarik told them, as if things were so normal that it would matter. "I just need him to breathe it in as much and as quickly as possible to calm the swelling. After that, I'll get him to drink a bit, once it cools enough."

"Then…then…he will be all right?" Tellie's voice trembled. She sat down on the other side of her daava, staring closely at his face. His skin seemed no less red nor did the terrifying wheeze leaking from his throat seem to lessen.

"He will be," the healer said. "The wheeze is a good thing, Tellie. It means he's still breathing, which means he can inhale this. He will be well. Just give it a few minutes, and he might even wake."

The wheeze grew stronger as time wore on, but as Damarik said, this was a good thing, and within a little while, he coughed again, and his eyes fluttered.

"Da!" Tellie leaned forward, gripping his hand between both of hers.

"Tellie—"

"Everyone is safe," Damarik said warmly. "Please drink this." He took a spoon to the bowl, blew on the small scoop of water, and slipped it into Leoren's mouth. "Tuck his chin down, will you, Tellie? The last thing we need is him choking on it."

After Leoren took a few more sips this way, he coughed again and straightened, pulling away from Kelm's support. "It was in the books," he said. "I thought it was just dust, but that was foolish of me. I never let my books get that dusty." He rubbed his hand against his throat, wincing at the lingering pain. "I'm sorry to have caused everyone distress…thank you."

A small sob escaped Tellie, and she leaned forward to hug him with all her might, but Damarik's hand caught her shoulder and pulled her back.

"He may still have some of the powder on him," he warned. "You were holding his hand a moment ago; please go and wash your hands thoroughly. Best find a new pair of clothes too. Whatever you do, just don't put your hands near your face until you have everything clean."

He turned his attention back to Leoren as Tellie and Kelm both hastened to the wash basin. "Now then, after I make sure you are purged of any remnant powder, I suggest you stay in bed."

"What?"

"I must make sure you recover fully, and you will not be strong enough to lead us for days yet," Damarik said, stern as he was gentle to his patient. "You must let yourself rest."

"Rest?" A small hysterical sound, somewhere between a laugh and a sob, rattled in Leoren's chest. "You expect me to rest while a spy, a killer, prowls around my country? You are telling me I just have to wait in a locked room until somebody else takes care of it?"

"Yes," Maril said, arms crossed from where she'd taken guard by the door. "You are not the only one who can lead in times of crisis." She glanced at Tellie with a smile. "Isn't that right, Princess?"

Tellie froze in the middle of reaching for a towel, water still dripping from her hands. Wait. Wait. The pounding of her heart threatened to burst through her chest. Princess was just supposed to be a pretty decoration to her name, another badge to remind her that she was a part of this family. It wasn't supposed to include *leadership*. She was certain—fairly certain—she was not good at leadership.

Her fingers latched around Kelm's arm in a vise-like grip. "This is my husband!" she yelped, as if nobody knew. "Any title I have, he shares with me."

"I rather think Princess doesn't suit me, Tel," Kelm told her with a small chuckle.

"Both you and Kelm have fresh minds that look at things differently than we do," Maril went on, ignoring the panic she'd incited. "I would love your input as we decide how to move forward from here."

"All right," Leoren's shoulders drooped. "All right, I know you all can handle it. But please, please be more careful than ever, and I still want to help, even if I'm resting. I'll be thinking. I'll decide what bait we could use."

"You do that," Damarik said soothingly. "Now, about changing you into some new clothes. These ones should be buried. Can the rest of you step out for a moment?"

The three of them stepped out as required, closing the door behind them. Tellie didn't look Maril's way, still not sure what to think of being the only royal currently available in Aselvia. Did they really expect that level of responsibility from her when they were far more capable of leading themselves? Before she could ask anything, the soft swish of footsteps caught her ear, and she looked up to see Oriah coming towards them, a few guards cautiously shadowing him.

"The guards told me! How is he?" Fear edged the priest's voice, probably the first negative emotion Tellie could recall hearing from the man.

"Damarik says he will be well," Maril assured. "But it was a bad scare for all of us. And so long as that woman is still loose, we are all in danger."

"If we can catch her," Tellie said carefully, "how can we make sure she doesn't escape again? I know you can use chains or ropes or all that, but won't we constantly have to check she's still in them if she goes invisible? And can't some chemas turn things they are touching invisible? I swear Tryss told me that."

"You are right. However, I wager Tryss never told you about manifix ore, nor am I sure she even knew of it. It is, after all, one of the chema's most guarded secrets. You see, there is an ore in the north that directly resists their power. It can interfere so badly that they cannot turn invisible while it is touching them."

"Golly, that's handy! And we have some of that, right?" Kelm exclaimed.

"We do." Maril drew the word out, biting the edge of her lip at the end. "But only enough was taken during our wars in the north to make a few shackles. You see, all the mines for this ore are deep in the mountains, and they are under intense protection by the chema courts."

"Ahhh, so nobody can use it against them."

"That. That, and so they can use it against themselves. The infighting there is atrocious, I assure you. But anyway, even one pair of shackles will be enough once we have this assassin, so that's all that matters."

"Speaking of catching her," Kelm began. "Well, I did think of something, shortly before Leoren started coughing. It's about how Tellie explained the Unseen to me—how the colors of the souls can be seen and how one's spirit can travel vast distances in moments. Tellie, if you could go into the Unseen, don't you think you might be able to spot her and see where she's hiding?"

From his perspective, it was logical, but there were so many things wrong with it, that Tellie flinched. "I can't just go into the Unseen," she said. "It's only when Ayeshune calls me as I sleep, but it doesn't happen very often. I could pray he'd call me tonight, but there's no guarantee."

Besides, even if she did cross into the plain where souls, feelings, prayers, and haunts became visible, she wasn't sure finding Alludium would be so simple. It would not merely be picking out one shadowed soul amid a thousand bright ones. No, in her rare ventures into the Unseen since coming to Aselvia, Tellie had been troubled to discover darkness under the surface. In waking, she found her community happy, healthy, and thriving, but she knew that not all the citizens of Aselvia were as carefree and blissful as they seemed, nor did they all hold to the faith they professed.

When she looked up, she saw Oriah watching her with that knowing expression. He'd helped her understand more about the Unseen, often visiting it himself.

"It is as she said," the priest said. "I will watch for her as well if the opportunity is given, but it is not simple to find anyone in the Unseen. Usually identity is only clear if you have a strong connection with the target of focus already."

"Drat it," Kelm muttered.

"I like the innovation though," Maril said with a wave of her hand. "As I said, you look at things differently. Let's keep tossing ideas back and forth, and we'll have to figure out something that will work."

"But what if..." Tellie hesitated, afraid to even speak it out loud. "What if she just leaves? Will we ever even know if we can't find her? Or are we just going to have to forever live with the fear that maybe she's around the corner?"

Kelm looked at her, aghast, and Oriah winced.

"Using their power requires a certain amount of stamina," Maril said, firm and gentle in her assurance. "Even if she hides while recovering her strength, she still needs food and water and basic ways to survive. Her footsteps cannot be hidden forever. We'll know. We'll find her."

15

NIAR SEA

Taersidel had drugged her again. Of course he had.

This time, Tryss couldn't even remember it happening. She just woke from a dense, uncomfortable sleep to find herself lying on a new cot in a small wooden room. She knew the sway beneath her body was that of the sea, not just of sickness. They were already on a ship, on their way to Dormandy.

Dahlya was still asleep on another cot across from her, breathing heavily.

In the opposite corner, Flyfar perched in a wooden birdcage, looking very much like an ordinary bird and not something that could disappear any moment. It was both a comfort that he had decided to stay and a concern that Errance would be fearful over his disappearance on top of everything else.

The door to their narrow cabin opened, and Taersidel strolled in. He carried a tray of food, and he shut the door behind him with a flick of his foot. "Good morning, sister."

"Taers, we need to talk." Her voice came out scratchy from little use.

"Do we?"

The tray of food held bread and grapes, and he set it on the small table bolted down next to the bed before taking a seat on the stool beside it. She didn't hesitate to tuck into the food; her stomach had been growling for the past few hours. Like her surrounding quarters, the fare was simple, but at least the bread was soft and the grapes were sweet. Hopefully that was a sign that her brother was in there somewhere.

"I've tried looking at this from your point of view," she began carefully.

"Ah, good!" The flash of his smile shone obnoxiously bright.

She bit her tongue from saying anything that would raise tension and tried again. "I can see how if you'd heard only parts of the story, it would seem quite alarming that I would be married to the new king of Aselvia. And maybe it would cause you to think you needed to interfere. But I need you to know my side of the story."

"I've heard about it, Tryss," he said with a wave of his hand. "The man was imprisoned in Tertorem for years and years, and you helped with his escape and recovery. You know, I would be impressed if you told me the entire time you had a plan to infiltrate and take control of Aselvia, I really would be."

"That's not it at all. I may be queen, but I do not have a hand in the ruling affairs."

"Sounds like your husband is as stuck up and prejudiced as I thought."

"I asked for it," she said coldly. "I didn't want to take part in rule because I wasn't comfortable making decisions for a country I barely knew. Errance offered to return the queen's throne to the side of the king's as it had been for the previous two generations. It was I who said no."

"You missed a golden opportunity."

She shook her head in exasperation. "Taers, you need to listen to my story, I mean it. Sit down, it will take a while."

With a longsuffering sigh, he settled himself more comfortably on his chair and raised his brows. "Fine, fine. Go ahead, if the specifics are that important."

Swallowing another bite of food, she sat back and pressed her hands over stomach. All she needed to do was stay strong and talk clearly. It wouldn't help to have nausea now from either the baby or her anxiety.

She just needed to be as calm as on the day that Errance had proposed to her.

Strangely calm. That's how she felt.

In her head, Tryss wondered why. If she was on her way to speak with Errance about marriage of all things, she should be the exact opposite of calm. And yet, why not? They were just discussing it. She'd wanted clarity on this matter for some time and now she would have it.

The balcony prepared for them was on the east wing of the palace rooms, set just so that the morning light would warm the stones and table. The table was already set with cloth, tea, and an assortment of treats. A planted tree stood nearby, its dangling leaves a natural chandelier above their seats.

Errance was already there, and he rose when he saw her. As she came close, he pulled her chair out and inclined his head. "Thank you for coming," he said. His formal tone was rather laughable.

"What were you expecting me to do?" she inquired, brushing aside her dress as she sat.

"Tell Casara no and then awkwardly avoid me until your sudden announcement to return home?" he said, voice a little too high.

"That's detailed."

"Yes, I thought it all out." He hadn't looked straight at her yet, and his movements to pour the tea were too concentrated.

She folded her hands. "You always do." It was better to get straight to it. At this rate, she could feel the tension rolling off him in waves, and one of them needed to start. She knew what she was about to say would come off a bit ruthless, but she needed the truth, even if she didn't like it. "So, what's your strategy?"

Errance froze and stared at her. At the last second, he pulled up the teapot before it overflowed the cup. "My...strategy?"

Her mouth was dry, and she licked her lips before plunging ahead. "It's all right. You see, I know elves here only marry if they truly love someone, but back in my home, marriage is less about romance and more about the advantage. How two families can best benefit each other. My original future in marriage would have involved my father speaking with some young man's father and deciding what would be best. So I understand reasoning. And I'm sure you have some. Let's start with that."

Slowly, he lowered the teapot then sat down. He wasn't looking at her again, and a pained expression was pulling on his face. "Well.....you see....you know that I'm always trying to improve myself. To heal from the past and get beyond its power. I'm trying...to prove...to everyone...that I can be the king they expect. And I thought marriage would be a good answer. Maybe it's not expected of every elf, but since the two kings before me were shining examples in marriage, I feel the eyes of the people on me. I wonder if they question why I haven't. I know it's only been a few years yet, but...I don't want them to think I'm broken. I don't want to be broken. In the stories, Daava and Maava's marriage was a great comfort to them and an inspiration to others. So..." His voice trailed away.

As reasons went, they made sense in a sad way. They were perhaps not the right reasons. She didn't believe marriage was supposed to be a bandage or cover, but she couldn't blame him for hoping for some solace and normalcy. But as she sat there, her heart sinking, one glaring error in it stood out. "There's a problem with that, though," she said carefully. "If those are your sole motivations, I'm not the right answer. If you want to be normal and fulfilling of expectations, then you'd marry some nice elf maiden here. So...why me?"

His cyan eyes lifted up to meet hers. "I...trust you. In some ways, the idea of marriage terrifies me, and I know it shouldn't. I know the Darkness corrupted the concept for me. But...I want to overcome that, and I couldn't do that with anyone but someone who I know I could depend on. Who I care for. I...I wake up at night sometimes, and I'm afraid and alone...and you're the one I wish was by my side." Red flooded his face. "Brights. That sounded awful."

The stiff, calm wall inside her chest broke. She could feel her heart beating. She could hear it in her ears. A faint smile softened her lips. "Hm. Not from you."

"I'm not asking you to be some nursemaid," he blurted. "But at the same time, I don't know if I can offer you everything a husband should. It's not that I don't want a family, I do. I just…I don't know how long and hard it will be for me to get past my fears. And yet I'll never know until I'm married. It's…it's risky."

"After twelve younger siblings, I'm not in a huge rush to start a family if that's what you're suggesting. Quite honestly, I always thought…" it was her turn to blush, "…that after your imprisonment, adoption would be the only option."

"The Darkness wouldn't have missed the opportunity for heirs if I had ever been turned," Errance said flatly.

"Oh."

He blew out a breath. "Anyway. That's about it. I want to move on and not by myself. I have friends and family and…maybe I don't need marriage. Maybe my people don't require it. And yet…you. You make me be honest with myself, even as you're doing now. I need that. You're patient, kind, and caring, and I…"

"All right," she said.

He blinked. "All right, what?"

"All right, I'll marry you."

He blinked again. Sat back. And then he said, "Wait. Hold on. You weren't supposed to say yes, not just like that!"

Her brows shot up. "You'd rather I say no?"

"No! It's just that…" Even with little movement, he appeared to be scrambling, like a man dropped in the middle of the ocean and told to swim. "Shouldn't you think about it? Pray, that sort of thing? I don't want you making a decision you'd regret."

"How long do you want me to think about it?"

He stared at her, helpless, clearly having not thought this through.

"How about this," she said, pushing back from the table and standing. "I'll think it over today and you come back tonight and propose again."

After a moment, he gave a slow nod and also rose to his feet.

"I already know my answer," she continued, "so if you're really serious about this, then I suggest you work on your second delivery." And with that, she flashed him a smile, turned, and swept from the room, not waiting to see his expression.

It was only after she was out and down the hall did she realize she had not eaten or drunk a thing.

She wore a dress of blue. Soft blue, pale enough to be nearly white, floating from her figure like waterfall mist. Delicate stitches of green laced the edges of the outer, transparent layer like tiny vines and lichen. She knew Errance liked the color, and she was fairly certain she'd seen him blush when she'd worn this very dress to a dance.

A more difficult choice had been what to do with her hair, but she'd finally chosen a loose side braid that suited the sylphish atmosphere of the dress.

She sat in front of her vanity, peering into the mirror as she scrolled delicate flowers of silver across her cheekbones. Years of tradition had given her a steady, sure hand, and yet it quavered now.

It would have been much more fun if she'd invited Dahlya and Tellie over and they'd helped her dress up. She could imagine the laughter and chatter ringing in the empty room. But although her heart had been near bursting throughout the day with her secret, she hadn't told a soul.

There was, after all, a chance that Errance had spent the day thinking about it and had decided that it was a bad idea. If he didn't show...she wasn't sure what she would do. How she would be able to look at him the next morning. Maybe that would be her sign that it was better if she just went back home.

A knock.

The brush dropped from her hand, knocking over the bottle of facepaint in a shimmer of silver. She didn't notice, only stared at the door, trying to assure herself she hadn't imagined it.

There it was again.

But not from her door.

From the window.

Really?

Unsure of whether the laugh bubbling in her chest was from amusement or hysterics, Tryss hurried for the window and unlatched it, pulling both doors inward so as not to knock into whoever waited on the other side. The warm light from her room cast across the slope of the roof just below her window, lighting up the figure of both Errance and The Daisha.

"Why, hello!" she exclaimed, leaning out.

"Hello," Errance answered automatically and then paused. "Is this...is this too forward? I thought this was a good idea, but now—"

"Unexpected," she said. "But not unwelcome. Good evening, The Daisha."

The Daisha made some sort of sniffing noise. "I am not sure I would call it either 'good' or 'evening,' gallivanting about in these unholy hours of the night."

"Um." Errance rubbed the back of his neck, stirring the silver-twined braids running down his shoulders. "I thought we could fly somewhere to talk. Do you want to sit up front or behind me?"

"Front," she said, a little selfishly. After all, she had not grabbed a coat and the thought of being nestled between his arms was already making her warm. He scooted back, giving her ample room to huddle on The Daisha's neck.

"Now there are rules for this," The Daisha said. "Rule one is absolutely no kissing. I'm not going to put up with that just because I've agreed to be some sort of romantic flight service."

Tryss was already climbing up and couldn't see what reaction this earned from Errance. As for herself, the warmth that flooded through her was enough to stave off the cold night air.

"Hold on, lovelies," The Daisha said, shoving off with a thrust of her wings. She banked to the right so severely that her riders hung parallel to the ground far below and then straightened with another flap.

The night sky of Aselvia shone stunningly clear, only a few white wisps bright with moonglow. Forests and streams sparkled below, coming closer as The Daisha dipped nearer to the earth. In the stillness suspended between each thunderous thrust of her wings, the rush of the wind could be heard through the leaves and the ripples of the river.

She did not ask where they were going, she only waited, each breath burning with cold and excitement. Their path led to the foothills of the mountains, where the forests reached fingers up to the snow-laden slopes. When the first pale glade gleamed below, The Daisha circled thrice, then swooped to the ground.

Errance swung easily down, then held out a hand for Tryss to lightly balance against as she sprang off.

"Thank you," Errance said solemnly to his winged friend.

"Oh, by all means," The Daisha said with an airy sniff. "I'm always ready for an impulsive midnight flight that doesn't concern me at all. No, no, don't apologize, I can tell when I'm not wanted." Tossing her head, she leapt back to air and spiraled high into the sky.

Tryss laughed nervously. "Impulsive? Didn't you ask her at all?"

"I did," he said. "Twice, actually, but she kept claiming it slipped her mind."

Their fingers were still slightly clasped, and instead of letting go, he adjusted his grip and led her down a path through the trees towards the rocky face of a cliff-side. He paused at a fissure between the rocks and beckoned her forward. Reluctantly letting go, she stepped ahead of him, through the narrow entrance and into a hidden alcove of heaven. A silver ribbon of water fell far from a ledge above and pooled into a carved bowl at the foot of the mountain. Long lacy ferns peered down from the cliff face and willows crept along the banks. The pool was deep and blue, forever swirling under the waterfall's stream. Everything sparkled under the moonlight—the starlit water, the thousands of droplets hanging from every leaf and frond, the shimmering branches, the mica in the shore, and the crystals in the cliffs.

Hardly breathing, Tryss sat on a mossy stone, and she turned to look at Errance where he stood at the water's edge, hand slightly reaching out to catch the misty spray. "Daava told me this was one of his favorite spots to come with my mother," he said.

"Oh," she managed, amazed at how silly she sounded. Then she said, "I can see why. It's very beautiful," and winced even harder at her lack of original responses.

He turned, hands folded behind his back, and looked at her, pale eyes bright even in the night. "You told me yes earlier today," he said. "And if that answer hasn't changed, I should like to know why."

"Why?"

"Yes, why. I consider you a smart person, Tryss, and so therefore, I want to know why you think that this—" he gestured at himself, "—is a good idea."

Drawing in a long breath to support what she needed to say, she folded her hands and looked him straight on. "I've stayed here for mainly one reason, Errance. Yes, I love this land, and I've made good friends. But I do miss my family and feel guilty for not returning to them. Yet I can't. Because I've watched you. I watched you change from the day we met. And it's...breath-taking. God has some magnificent plan for you, and for some time now, I've wished I could be part of it. So I stay and I watch and I wish."

He considered her for a moment, and then his mouth twitched. "And here I thought it was because I was pretty."

She laughed. Except it was more of a snort. If that was his idea of flirting, it needed work. "Please don't tell me you think that is your only good quality."

"No, I just...thank you...your words are kind. Too kind, probably."

His gaze broke from hers, staring off into the waterfall, and it gave her a moment to gather her senses. Various thoughts had troubled her today since his proposal; in fact, they had troubled her ever since she'd first realized she loved him. If she held her tongue now, she would feel guilt forever, even if she hated to speak these words.

Prying her dry tongue from the roof of her mouth, she began, "While we are on the subject, I should tell you that I am not sure you have thought this through. I know you trust me and like me, and that means more to me than I can say, but are you sure you should just propose marriage? In years to come, you may find a more suitable wife in an elven maid who you could also trust. I mean, you are the king after all, and while the elves have always been very gracious to me, I'm not sure what they would think of a chema queen. On top of that, even though I will live hundreds of years, that's nothing compared to your thousands, if indeed you die at all. So I really think you should consid—"

"Tryss, none of that matters," he interrupted.

"Why shouldn't it matter? It—"

"None of it matters because I love you."

The air swept from her lungs, stirring the soft strands of hair framing her face. He said that. He really just said that. So easily. "You...you mean that?"

His hand reached back to tug at his braids again. "I do. I have for some time. I'm not sure when it changed from just a friend. Maybe I always thought of you as more than that. Maybe that's why I was scared of you in the beginning. But the more of a friend you became...the less frightened I felt. And now...." He trailed off, seeming unable to find more words.

Her heart might have grown hummingbird wings, it fluttered so fast. She stood, hands clasped to keep them from shaking. "Well then. I don't see any reason we shouldn't get married. Because I love you too." A smile curved her mouth. "For some time. Not sure when it changed."

"Then you will have me?" he asked softly. "For wherever that takes us?"

"It will be an adventure." Stepping forward, she reached her hands out. He took them, and a shiver pattered across her shoulders at his

touch. "Fortunately, I like going on adventures with you." She drew his hands up, almost to her mouth, and she found that he had stepped near as well, his breath on her fingers. "So yes. Yes, with all my heart."

Her wedding day came faster than she could have dreamed.

In reality, it took months to arrange.

She would have preferred a small wedding with just family and friends, but this was the marriage of the king. A king's wedding couldn't happen at the drop of a hat. The planning and preparation required many minds and many hands.

All of Aselvia was invited. It was a small enough kingdom that this was possible. So it was being held in an enormous outdoor amphitheater that usually hosted public celebrations. The hillside was lined with tall trees and rows of seats built into the slopes. Spread out below was another large seating area in the grassy dell. At the forefront stood a stage built of the earth, reinforced with stone and wood, and trees grew upon it to make a natural arch. Streams had been redirected over the theater to trickle down the front in little waterfalls and gather in pools glittering with silver fish.

Having that many thousands of eyes on her was most unnerving, but it helped that they would be some distance away. And she would not have to look at them.

For now, she just had to bide her time in the white tents built in the forest behind the dais. She and Errance each had one where they would receive the blessings of their families. For her that meant her father, mother and the Ancient, who had resolutely made the journey to see Aselvia and the wedding.

For Errance, that meant Leoren and Casara.

She had been told that normally when they arrived together on the dais, they would receive the blessing of the king before the people, but as Errance was the king, that role too would belong to Leoren. And then the priest, Oriah, would bless them before God.

She wasn't sure why she was repeating the steps in her head over and over when they were fairly simple and she already knew them by heart. Taking a deep breath, she ran her hands again over the folds of her skirt.

Ah yes, this dress. She'd spent weeks alone on the gown. Not so much the designing and sewing, no, she'd left that to the professionals, but she, Tellie, and Dahlya stitched thousands of flowers and stars into the frothy white fabric. Simply practicing that technique took time, and the pressure of not ruining the yards of material was yet another hurdle, but the three of them enjoyed the challenge.

It hung from her now, the inner silk smooth against her skin and the outer layers sheer and sparkling with silver and rainbow thread. The skirt fell like a waterfall, even pooling behind her in waves. The sleeves draped open at the shoulder and then split at the elbow into a long trailing ribbon. Her hair too hung loose, caught in places with invisible pins that fastened small flowers.

"You are a vision of beauty," her mother said, even though Tryss knew this was not the vision she'd ever had in mind.

Nothing about this was easy on her family. Originally, they'd hoped her stay in Aselvia would be temporary, but as the years passed, they'd realized it wasn't. Talk of some elf man catching her eye had been the word around, but nobody planned on it being that unpleasant prince person who'd insulted everyone in the village on their first meeting.

Her father was the most difficult to convince into giving his blessing. He'd only done it at all because of her earnest pleading and the Ancient's approval.

As for her brothers, they were skeptical, but compliant.

At least her sisters approved. "He's very handsome," said one of them, adjusting the flowers threaded through her hair. "Probably the finest man I've ever seen, even here."

"So brooding and mysterious," another sister said with a dramatic sigh.

Tryss didn't bother trying to explain again that she wasn't marrying him for any of those reasons.

"At least he will make beautiful children," her mother said grudgingly.

Tryss most certainly held her tongue then, not daring to mention that children were not guaranteed in this marriage, lest her mother be fully convinced she'd lost her mind.

"Out, out," one of the older sisters said, waving the younger ones from the white tent in which they waited for the ceremony to begin. "We must find our seats up front and give Tryss time with our parents."

While they'd surrounded her, Tryss had thought the tent would be more peaceful once it was less full, but now that they'd gone, she wished them back. She wished to wrap herself in their warm, golden laughter and gentle jokes. It would be better than the solemn looks on her parents' faces and this unbearable wait before she could be joined hand in hand with Errance.

She could hear the sibilant music out in the forests, soft and gentle as a morning breeze. Now and then, she thought she could hear voices and laughter.

The curtain door swayed open, and the Ancient hobbled in on his staff. "It is time," he said. "It is time to give our blessing."

Drawing in a deep breath, she knelt before her parents, a soft tapestry beneath her knees. The strong hand of her father touched the crown of her hair, followed by the gentle caress of her mother. She listened to their prayer for her blessed future with bated breath, smiling a little past the tears that were beginning to sting her eyes.

Lastly, the Ancient came to her, but he tugged her to her feet with a smile. "You have done well, my child," he said. "You are a gracious young woman who always seeks to care for everyone around you. You are wise, and you are strong. I pray for your happiness with this great man, but also for your courage. For great courage is needed to be a wife. To be a mother. To be a queen."

She bent and kissed him on the cheek, and then gave a kiss to her father and mother in turn, the latter of whom was now weeping, though if from pride or regret, who could say.

And then she was walking from the tent and down the trail scattered with petals to lead her to the wedding dais. The petals passed through an arched tunnel of vines and flowers, the pathway becoming a small wooden flight of steps. And when the tunnel ended and she stood atop the stair, she looked out across the dais to see an archway on the far side and Errance coming through it.

Stars, he was regal in silver that glittered like a galaxy. Their eyes met across the distance, and she was quite certain his cheeks colored at the sight of her. They started towards each other until they met in the center of the dais where the petals swirled about the ground in a circle.

Leoren was there.

Either he'd been there the whole time and she hadn't noticed or he had come up from the back.

He was speaking to the people about the very first king and queen and then he went on to speak of Rendar and Cerene. Some vague part of her was listening. But the rest of her was focused on breathing.

When Leoren's speech ended, he acclaimed them to the people, and then the elder priest was there.

"Errance Celestrum, son of Rendar and Cerene Celestrum, child of the forests and streams, offer your hands to the woman you have chosen," Oriah said, that contagious warmth in his voice.

It was all Tryss could do not to immediately grab the hands held out before her. Long-fingered, strong, elegant, lined with vein, muscle, bone, and ever so slightly shaking. But she waited for Oriah to speak again, as was proper.

"Tryss, daughter of Ilyrin and Felisii, child of the sunlight and trees, will you accept the hands that have been offered?"

She slipped her fingers over Errance's, drawing them closed against her palms.

"In the beginning of time, when we were created, we were given a king and a queen. Ayeshune himself gave them to each other in marriage. An eternal commitment not to be broken, but strengthened by whatever lay ahead. May you honor him first and then each other. Will you make this promise to one another?"

"Yes," Errance said, quiet, but determined.

"Yes," Tryss answered.

Oriah held a glass pitcher and he raised it high to let it pour down in a glittering trickle upon their clasped hands. "This is the water from the purest spring in Aselvia. It begins small, but it grows to the greatest of our rivers, sending out many streams from it, and everywhere it goes, it brings life. Its flow never ends. By the grace of Ayeshune, so too shall be your love for one another." He paused pouring the water long enough for them to unclasp their fingers and cup their hands before pouring a bit of water in each palm.

Fighting hard to keep her hands steady, Tryss lifted the trembling pool of water to Errance's mouth. Fire spread across her cheeks at the touch of his lips as he drank it dry.

The water had somehow stayed in his hands. Whereas they'd been shaking before, they were steady now. Somehow, she didn't think it was from a lack of nerves, but by that insane inner strength he possessed. She closed her eyes and drank when he offered it, the water clear and cool.

"Then I present you before Ayeshune, before your loved ones, before all the people of Aselvia, as husband and wife," Oriah said, beaming with joy.

She could hear the elation of the crowd somewhere beyond the thundering of her own heart. This was real. Actually real. No more dreaming, no more hoping.

It was true.

And then before she even realized what was happening, he bent down his head and kissed her. Swift, soft, and sweet. The lightest touch against her lips and yet it sent a thousand butterfly wings fluttering through her.

She had not expected it.

Perhaps he'd kissed her to prove to himself that he could. Perhaps it had been assurance for the people. But when she opened her eyes and found herself reflected in those cyan depths, she knew the kiss had been for her and her alone.

She'd prepared herself for a slow journey of restoring touch, and yet here he was, taking the first step. Perhaps it was not the most romantic kiss, but it was a kiss of courage, and that in and of itself was an act of love.

She gave him a dizzy smile and he returned it with one of his own. After a few long seconds, the sound of the cheering crowd returned to her hearing, and Errance tucked his arm into hers as they turned to face the celebration, together.

After Tryss finished her tale, Taers did nothing but stare at the far wall for a long while. At last he drew his hands down his knees and straightened. "I see," he said, words clipped and cool. "So you really do love him."

"I do. And this child is more precious to me than all the stars of the heavens."

"And he feels the same way, does he?"

"I—what? Of…of course."

"Does he?" He stood, arms crossed, the corner of his mouth twisted up in a smirk. "Sounded to me like he was trying too hard to make you happy. Get you to think that he's committed. But come on, Tryss. He was a prisoner too long to ever be normal. He had many masters in Tertorem—I know their names, I know their methods. Was a baby really *his* idea? Seems to me like the last thing he'd want. It was probably all your provocation."

His words struck from one side of her heart to the other, a hollow, echoing ring in the depth of her soul. Shadows of grey eddied through her mind, her throat closed tight. It was as if every fear devils had ever spoken in silence now voiced themselves aloud.

And that was what it was. Voices of darkness.

"You really have become something poisonous, you know that?" she said quietly. "First you insult my child, then my husband, and now me. Well, let me tell you this. You might try to make me doubt my marriage, but I chose him and I will go on choosing him, and neither you nor anyone else can stop me."

"Very well," he said coldly. "I had planned on taking you to the North as my sister and guest. But I can bring you as a prisoner instead."

She sat back, nails digging into the side of her chair. She wanted to say something, but nothing more was coming to mind. It didn't shock her, it just hurt. A dull, throbbing ache.

He stood, a bit of remorse brushing across his face. "I didn't want it to be this way either, Tryss. But it's clear you've taken their side."

"Side?" Burning tears filled her eyes, and she blinked them away in frustration. "You're the one making this about sides. You could have told me you didn't care for my choice of a husband, and I could have told you I didn't much care about your opinion, and then we could have agreed to disagree like a normal family. It doesn't have to be about some war that's been over for years."

"Over? You think it's over?" He shook his head and headed for the door.

"Wait! What is that supposed to mean?"

He paused, hand resting on the frame. "You might think I'm completely selfish to take you out of Aselvia. But I think soon enough you'll see it was for your own good."

16

OOLUM

The world swam red. Errance could not breathe and that had nothing to do with the scarlet silk wrapped around his face or the tight shackle encircling his neck. A hand like a talon grabbed his arm, and the red silk was torn off his head as he was thrust forward.

He stood on a balcony overlooking a chamber of stone, fire, and molten rock. Dark figures cavorted in the shadows far below him. He saw himself as if he was one of the spectators, held upright by a man in scarlet.

"Behold," his captor cried. "The prince of Aselvia!"

The man struck him, and his breath returned in a terrified gasp as he fell off the platform. The golden chains caught him, jerking him to a halt out over the edge. His feet scrambled against the side of the slick stone to prevent his own weight from strangling him. The acrid stench of smoke burned his throat and stung his eyes. Even with the fire far beneath him, the heat still lapped against his bare shoulders.

One length of chain pulled back, twisting him towards his captor. The man who was not a man leered in his face, breath stirring his hair. "Beg for mercy, Highness," he whispered. His eyes glowed with a spirit not belonging to the body he wore.

"You have none to give," Errance whispered in return, shuddering. The waves of heat caught his hair, tossing it across his wide eyes where it clung to his sweaty skin.

The demon grinned, gathering the chains in his hand, drawing him in even closer. "You know me so well." His hand opened, the severed chains slid free, and Errance fell backwards, down, down to the fires below—

Errance jerked upright with a scream. He tore off the blanket that had wrapped around him and threw it across the room. Panting, he pressed his back against the wall. The sensation of falling still coursed through his body.

"Errance?" Coren burst through the door, an oil lamp aloft in his hand. His face hardened in the dancing light as he looked upon his cousin. "A nightmare?"

He nodded, not trusting himself to respond. He stared straight ahead into the darkness, refusing to look anywhere else, even as Coren set the lamp aside and sat on the edge of the cot.

"I should have known better than to sleep tonight," Errance rasped. "Not after…the slave market today…and the girl…in red and gold. Ajahliesh…every one of the Red Three…had a thing for those colors." He dropped his head onto his drawn up knees, pushing his damp hair back from his face.

Coren watched him grimly, arms folding across his chest. "How long has this been happening?"

After a long moment of hesitation, he admitted, "It's grown worse this last year." He straightened with a deep sigh, tilting his head up to stare at the ceiling. "It's like I was given a respite only to destroy my defenses before being thrown back into it. I feel as weak and afraid as I did the first few decades. I...I can't control it." Gritting his teeth, he glared down at his trembling body. "I can't even stop shaking!"

Coren reached out, took him by the arms, and drew him into an embrace. Errance stiffened with a strangled cry and fought to pull away.

"No," Coren said firmly, hanging on. "Let me. I will not hurt you. I am your cousin, I am your brother, I love you, and I will not hurt you."

Errance sat like stone, and then he slowly, very slowly, sank his head against Coren's shoulder. They remained thus for some time, the warm night air still about them before Errance spoke again. "Sometimes," he said, his voice muffled, "I wake and feel as bruised and exhausted as if I'd really come back from *there*. I thought I was free of them."

"You are free of them," Coren said. A weary breath puffed from his lips. "But the fear? Not so easy to shake, I guess. It's the fear they will use to steal your joy, to fool you into thinking you belong with them." He pushed away and held Errance out at arm's length. "You don't belong to them," he growled. "Don't ever let them deceive you."

Coren rose and crossed the room to the window, swinging himself up onto the ledge and staring up at the night sky. "This feels sort of familiar," he said with a laugh. "I should have learned sooner to drag you back to a room in Oolum in the middle of the night if I wanted you to talk. Do you have anything more to say or would you rather I just shut up?"

Errance shrugged his shoulders, a gesture lost in the darkness, and leaned back against the wall. Slight warmth still resided in the stone from the hot day. Various sounds of distress or surprise drifted through the open window where Coren perched like a guard. Somewhere far away, he thought he heard a child's cry.

"How did you feel about becoming a father?" he asked softly, his voice nearly lost in the heavy air.

"A mess," Coren replied brightly. "Terribly excited, but oh, so nervous." He crossed his legs on the ledge, and his shadowed face turned back towards his cousin. "I wouldn't mind having a dozen children, but Zizain says she has her hands full with one, and—" he faltered "—I don't suppose my work is exactly ideal for children." The starlight glinted in the return of his smile. "Still, Spark is a smart little fellow, and he is doing well enough."

There was a long moment's pause, and then he asked, "How about you?"

Errance lifted his face towards the window, and the little light drifting through cast a ghostly pallor upon his cheeks. "I was a miracle child," he said quietly. "Did you know that, Coren?"

"I did. But tell me again."

"My father and mother thought they could never have one. And yet after a thousand years, I came. But I came too early, and Mother did not have enough life to save us both."

Coren, far more able to see Errance than Errance could see him, watched how his king's hands clenched till the nails drove into his palms. "Tryss is hardy, Errance, and in good health."

"She was. I don't know what this stress is doing to her. What conditions she's being kept in."

"Dahlya and her brother are both going to do their best to keep care of her. It will be all right. You'll see. But back to my original question, how are you feeling about being a father? Hoping for a boy or girl?"

"That doesn't matter. It will be enough for me if I can raise them without them coming to hate me," Errance said weakly.

"You give yourself so little credit! Tellie and Kelm adored you as children, and you had a fine example of fatherly love in Rendar."

"It's just that…I can barely take care of myself. So how am I supposed to take care of a child? And once they are grown, then what? What will I do then?"

"Have another baby?"

"Coren, I'm serious."

"So am I!"

"I'd rather just see how I do with one, all right?"

"Who says you have just one? Tryss could be carrying twins! Or triplets!"

"Coren!" Errance choked on a laugh and shook his head. After a breath, his smile faded. "I don't know. I can't think about that while she's in danger—"

"I want you to think about it! You are always dreaming up the worst possible outcome. Why not try picturing a future you *want*, and then hold onto that!"

"I…" He stared down at his folded hands. Voice small, unsure. "That's terrifying."

"It is." He reached out and squeezed his cousin's shoulder. "But it's better."

"How do you do it, Coren?" His voice was soft, almost unable to be heard, even in a quiet room at night.

"Hm?"

"How do you keep living, keep loving? I get so tired looking at the tragedy in this world. If I can't even help myself, how am I to help my wife? Help others? I'm trying, but—"

"How do you try?" Coren tilted his head. "Errance."

His cousin spoke his name like a command. Errance looked up at him, askance.

Was it possible for eyes to be soft and sharp at once? Perhaps only stars understood that impossible pairing and they seemed to shine in Coren's gaze. "You're really going to try to do everything by your own strength again?"

His mind stuttered. He was strong. He knew that. Not strong enough. He knew that too. He knew better than anyone his limits, his breaking points. But Coren was right; he immediately, repeatedly, kept turning to his strength as if that was all he had. Honestly, the further back he considered, he'd been doing almost everything on his own.

Accepting Ayeshune as his Lord, *the whole point*, was to acknowledge he needed strength beyond what he had.

And to add to his blessings, he'd been given a family so he never had to do things alone.

Coren's hand patted his shoulder, and he blinked, broken momentarily from the spinning inside his head. "How about you go sit up on the roof for a bit?" his cousin suggested. "I always find that a good place to think and pray. I'll be downstairs if you need me."

With a creak of the door, he was gone, footsteps fading down the steps. Errance's gaze lifted to the hatch in the ceiling. He would listen. He wouldn't just shrug away the council of those who loved him with excuses that it wouldn't help, wouldn't work, because he'd already tried. He would keep trying, keep seeking.

He climbed up the rope ladder, took a seat at the edge of the flat roof, and breathed in the night air. Oolum was far too crowded a city to ever feel peaceful, but even with the distant clamor of the night, a sense of solitude calmed his aching nerves.

"All right," he said, staring up into the vault of the dark sky, sparkling with a myriad of stars. "This would be easier if you would just sweep me into the Unseen. If I could hear you there would be no room for doubt in my mind. But seeing as that isn't happening, I'll just talk here, and I don't care if I sound like a lunatic."

His knuckles tightened around his elbows. "I admit it. I've been living with my eyes turned inwards. I've made it all about me and my problems. And I'm tired of it. I'm tired of fearing my past, my future, fear itself. I'm sick of all of it. I am a husband and a father, I am a king, and somehow I've turned all this into a problem. I'm not enough. But you are. So I'm going for it with my heart open. Help me see the world the way you do. You somehow loved me, so help me love others. Please just bring Tryss back and—" he paused. "Not trying to make that sound like a bargain. Just…please let me have a second chance with everything you gave me. Please help me trust you. I can't do this on my own."

There was no answer. Not one that he could hear.

But somehow, he felt a little calmer. A little more at peace.

He did not sleep much the rest of the night, so the moment the window suggested even the faintest hint of dawn, he dressed himself and hurried out the door. A bit of light from the floor below suggested Coren was already up.

He clambered down the stairs, already chewing on a stick of salted beef left over from the day before. If his cousin had strict rules about eating before a quest, then he wouldn't be accused of forgetting today. "Where are we headed?" he asked before his feet even touched the final floor. "What's the plan?"

"Hold your horses, I haven't finished getting ready for the day yet." Coren sat in front of a small table, peering at the smudgy bronze mirror propped up on the surface.

Errance sighed dramatically. "A disguise? Really? Couldn't you just go out as Captain Coren today?"

"Aye, that's the plan," he said, snapping open a case filled with a palette of powders and several small jars. He rubbed a creamy silver paste over the teeth of a comb and then began brushing it through the roots of his hair.

Coming to terms with the fact that they were not heading out the door any time soon, Errance sat on the nearest chair, arms crossed over the back of it. He watched as Coren rubbed in some darker shadows about his face and then began applying a sticky substance that pinched his skin in tiny wrinkles about his eyes and mouth. About the time he was applying the grey-sprinkled red bristles to his chin and jaw, Errance spoke up. "You're making yourself look older."

"Well, you know, I have been here for several years, and if I don't start aging, people will begin to talk. After all, plans are for Zizain and I to become an old married couple. I'm surprised you haven't noticed— I've been wearing these alterations when I'm Captain Coren in public. But you have been distracted, so can't say I blame you."

"Zizain...she..." The words faltered and fell from Errance's tongue. Now that he thought about it, there had been something niggling at the back of his mind, something he couldn't quite figure out. It had happened so subtly over the past seven years, he hadn't much noticed. But Zizain had begun to show age. There was no silver in her hair yet, but something in her soft, warm features had grown a little more tired, a little more mature. He'd guessed it just came from having a child and living in such a city, which was no doubt a part of it, but Zizain was human, and therefore....

He stared at Coren wordlessly. Until now, he'd never really thought it through. Not at their wedding. Not when their baby was born. Time was such a terrible thing. It had been passing so slowly for him these past seven years, but how quickly it must have passed for his cousin. This time eating away the life he would share with his wife.

Coren gave a low chuckle. "Don't look at me like that, Errance. What, did it just occur to you she's mortal? Well, so am I. We're both going to the same place eventually, and there really is no certain way to know who goes first. We're happy with what time we have. You needn't look so sad."

"Sorry," Errance stammered, trying to keep both sadness and guilt from overwhelming his expression. Not easy when his mind was already moving from Zizain to Tryss, which was selfish, but he couldn't help it. Presumably, his own wife would live hundreds of years, but she was not likely to live as long as he would. When such a time came, would he be able to smile about it as bravely as Coren?

Time to turn away from such a depressing spiral of thought. He cleared his throat. "You really take the time every morning to do this?"

"You know, women all over the world paint their face each morning," Zizain said, suddenly appearing behind him. "Though I suppose elves wouldn't know about that with all their *natural* beauty."

"Chemas either," Coren added with a laugh. "They can color themselves however they want. Come along, Errance, while the day is young!" He was out the door in one bounce and Errance was left standing in the house, blinking at Zizain's smug smile.

"Hey!" he shouted, spinning and running after him. "That's not fair, I was the one waiting on you!"

Nothing. No word.

A pregnant woman with golden hair, most likely accompanied? Sure, there were a few leads, but all were quickly dismissed.

It was such a large city, it really shouldn't have been a surprise that a few women could be lost in it with nary a trace, but it still drove him mad that there was no trail to follow, not even the slightest crumb.

He dragged an arm over his face, cursing the intense heat of the long day. Of course, he'd survived in much worse conditions, but still, this constant press of the sun was overwhelming after years back home in the lush lands of Aselvia. If it was any consolation, his skin wasn't burning and flaking, just turning a rich shade of gold. Even so, he was feeling absolutely parched. Just so long as Tryss was not suffering in this oppressive temperature.

"It's a long walk back home," Coren said, eyeing his lagging stride. "You know, we can just take a cab."

Errance had seen several such cabs since he'd been in the city, though he didn't recall them from his last visit seven years ago. They seemed more western in nature, a small enclosed box upon wheels driven by a swift horse. He much preferred the open wagons where one could jump out if one needed to or even the palanquins which, while still enclosed, were at least not being hurtled down the street.

"Cab driver!" Coren called, not seeming to notice the disapproval on his cousin's face. He waved his arm at one driver passing by, and the carriage paused at the corner. "North Quarter, Merchant Road," Coren addressed the driver, catching the door open and motioning Errance inside.

Errance frowned at the small dark chamber, disliking the way the shades were pulled. But there was nothing for it, Coren was expecting him to step inside, and he really did need to stop being so paranoid. So he stepped in, his cousin just behind him, and the door closed with a click. They settled into the seat as the carriage began rattling again.

With the curtains down, the interior was dark, but as their eyes slowly adjusted to the warm shadows they could see a man sitting across from them. A man from West Orim, by the look of his black tailcoat, fine vest, and neatly tied cravat. He blinked at them through his small spectacles. Coren gave an easy smile back, Errance sat stiff.

The man set both his hands upon the small case he carried in his lap. "Good evening, Captain Coren," he said. "My name is Remrant Cole."

17

Coren's smile slipped. He reached for the door, but whether it was jammed or locked from the outside, it didn't so much as budge.

Errance didn't even bother to try his door; he already knew it wouldn't open. His eyes narrowed. "Should we know that name?"

"Not at all, not at all. And I'm afraid I do not know yours either, I only had heard you were in the city. I was hoping we would have a chance to talk."

"And you just happened to know we would climb into this cab?" Coren said in disbelief.

"It is not a regular travel cab, good sir, though I can understand why you thought so. I did have it refurbished from an old travel cab, after all. You are not the first to have made that mistake, not even today. Of course, I always correct the misunderstanding, but since I was waiting for a private moment to speak with you, it seemed prudent to allow you inside. It was more fortunate than I had hoped."

"Yes, truly a stroke of fate," Coren snapped, the edge of every word sharp as a blade. "You've said who you are, but what are you and what do you want with us and who do you think we are, anyway?"

The gentleman gave a delicate cough into his fist. "Ah, forgive me, forgive me. I am an intelligence officer of the All Nations Bank of Orim, and I have heard that the queen of Aselvia has gone missing and that you are looking for her. I am here to offer my services."

There was a moment of blank silence. Errance shifted on the seat, glad to feel the knife rubbing against his hip. Mention of Tryss sent his heart racing, but there was one word in the man's announcement that had him stalling. "Did you say bank?"

"I did."

"Since when do banks have spies?"

"Since when have they not? Money is a very tricky business, even when multiple governments are not investing their gold in it. We seek to protect our affairs and the affairs of our patrons. Aselvia is not a patron, but since your queen has been taken, I thought we could begin an alliance by offering my knowledge of hostage situations. Ransoms demanded from the rich are common situations, so we have a network of spies for this sort of thing to protect our clients from losing money."

"And you heard the queen was missing how?" Coren growled.

"The same network, friend. Also, it hasn't been quiet that an elf appeared in the city very recently and started working with the charitable Captain Coren. It has also not been a secret that they have been looking for a young woman. So I put two and two together." He turned to Errance and gave a little bow of his head. "Your name has not been mentioned in the information my contacts have gathered."

Errance drew in his breath and held it. This man did not know he was king. At least that. So he had to come up with another name. Fast. "I am Reyi—I am Reyid," he said. Forcing more confidence into his voice, he coolly added, "Officer of intelligence for Aselvia."

Coren sat very still next to him. Perhaps because he'd noticed he'd almost said Reyin, name of Aselvia's former general. Perhaps because he was trying to figure out if this man also knew he was an elf or simply thought him a friend of the elves.

"I am glad to hear Aselvia has its own spies," Remrant said with a smile. "I was beginning to wonder. But of course, elves are too clever to leave any trace of their footsteps."

There was no mocking lilt to that statement, but Errance didn't miss the irony that if Aselvia really did have spies that excellent, Tryss probably would have never gone missing to begin with. "What is this service you offer?"

"Our spies heard of the bounty that went out for the elf queen. We know who took it. With further investigation we can track down who sent it out and where they are taking her."

"Who *did* take her?"

The carriage rattled again, coming to a stiff stop and jolting them all in their seats. "I do believe we have reached your destination, gentlemen," Remrant Cole said. "Let us continue this conversation at another place. There is an office for the All Nations Bank in the guild quarter of the city. I will have tea ready at nine o'clock in the morning. I'm sure the good Captain knows where it is. Of course, you cannot enter the guild quarter without an invitation, so here, my card."

The door clicked, swung open, and the cabman bowed as he waited for them to exit.

"I'd rather that door shut and you tell me now," Errance said acidly, not taking the card that was being held out to him.

"Would you really take everything I say at face value?" Remrant asked, raising a brow. "If so, you would be a fool, and I know you aren't a fool. Meeting me at the bank office will authenticate my claim, and I will have the reports of investigation ready. For now, that is simply impossible. I was, after all, not prepared to have you step into my carriage just now." He pressed the card into Errance's hand, and then waved to the door. "Good day, gentlemen."

"Not *prepared?*" Coren raged, pacing from one end of the room to the other. "Not prepared, my hat! I called for a cab, and his carriage was the one that came! What was he doing, following us around?"

"I'd say so," Errance said. They'd returned to the house for the night to rest, but he doubted he would find any sleep. He sat on the edge of his cot, holding the card between his fingers and turning it this way and that. "Nine o'clock tomorrow."

"I don't trust him one bit," Coren said. "He was far too smug about the whole situation."

"But he potentially has our first lead on who took Tryss and where they're keeping her," Errance said, for once the patient one. "So as for me, I am going."

"You aren't suspicious?"

"Of course I'm suspicious. I'm always suspicious. What does that have to do with anything? If I have a chance to save her, I'm taking it."

"Fair." Coren groaned, running fingers through his hair. "All Nations Bank of Orim. Huh. Wonder if there's any truth to that. I've heard of them. It's not a common bank, you know. It's a privately owned bank for the governments of Mid Orim. Quite an old establishment. I guess it is plausible they could have one ear to Aselvian affairs and heard about Tryss. They won't be doing this for free, however. I'm sure they're in it for a benefit."

"I'm sure," Errance said, waving away such concerns. "Leoren's taught me about bargains and Tertorem taught me long before that."

"Try to get some sleep then," Coren said with a sigh. "I'll take us to the merchant quarter tomorrow."

They took a cab the next morning. A real cab.

A tall wall and gate partitioned off the guild quarter from the rest of the city, guards wandering the parapet and standing before the entrance. The cab paused to give Coren the chance to hand Remrant's card through the window to the guard that halted them, and after a moment of inspection, the man handed the card back and called for the gates to open.

The carriage rolled on, passing through clean and relatively quiet streets that looked more like rich villas than places of business. When it arrived at their destination, Errance peered out. The building for the All Nations Bank looked much like the other buildings around it. Two-story house built of sandstone, colorful domed roofs, latticed windows.

"I'm surprised there aren't more guards," he muttered.

"Money is not kept here, it's just a place to discuss business," Coren said. "And this quarter is well protected, as you just saw. I wasn't sure Remrant was telling the truth or not until the guard accepted our invitation. They are trained to recognize fake passes. So then, shall we go in together?"

"I think I should do this one alone," Errance began, raising a hand to halt his cousin's protest. "Look, this is an internal matter of Aselvia, and we don't need him wondering why you are so closely involved. It would be better if you appear to be my help and contact, but not someone so personally connected to the royal affairs."

"I suppose you're right," Coren grumbled. "He already seemed to know too much by half. Just…just be sharp."

"When am I ever not?"

He stepped out and ascended the stair. The door was open before he reached it, a servant ushering him in with a bow so well maintained one could suppose he was permanently bent at the waist. Another manservant led him through the open courtyard into a glass-domed tearoom filled with sharp-edged plants, pillowed seats, and even a small fountain. The green flora, the bubble of water, and the birdsong was welcome in such a dry, hot city, and he wondered at the expense it took to maintain it. So different from anything he'd encountered in Oolum, even if it had been a short distance away.

"There you are," Remrant said, not raising his eyes, but raising his teacup as he waited by a small glass table. "I was beginning to wonder if you'd arrive. Ten minutes late, you know." He tapped the gold-rimmed clock pinned to the lapel of his coat.

Ah, another reason to hate those horrid little ticking things. Now those people who complained about others being late could know *exactly* how late you were.

Not deigning to answer, Errance took his seat and crossed his arms. "I am here. What is the information?"

"First, refreshment and a proper introduction." He gestured to the tea, but Errance ignored it. "It is a true pleasure to meet you, Reyid. Aselvia's ambassador only ever visits Dormandy, and while that is my base of operation, the queen went missing here, and therefore I needed to be on the scene of the incident. I had planned to speak to Captain Coren because there were rumors of his friendship with Aselvia, but I was unsure…" he paused, eyes narrowing, "…how deep that connection ran."

"Coren is but a friend of Aselvia. I alone am representative of the king and his queen." Best to shut down that trail of thought before the man could run with it. "So, the kidnappers. Who are they?"

Remrant reached into the little case set upon a nearby chair and passed him a paper, a bounty paper. "This letter was sent to the best guilds across Orim. An elite team of chema thieves took the job."

Errance stilled. For a moment, he couldn't breathe. "Chemas."

"Yes. I understand the queen is in fact a chema. Do you think it is not a coincidence?"

"Do we know the names of these chemas?"

"Ah, that took quite a bit of digging, but we discovered their leader is named Taersidel."

There it was. The small fear that he'd never quite acknowledged, had never let speak. It had all been a ruse. The snake. The cold-blooded, hissing snake. He knew he hadn't liked him; he just hadn't expected to be given such a good reason. Poor Tryss. Poor Tryss. What would that betrayal have done to her?

Remrant was studying him, and he could only imagine how many emotions were ranging across his face and body. With great effort, he unclenched his hands and jaw.

"I see the name means something to you," the man observed.

He couldn't think of a reason not to tell him, but he still kept the whole truth. "We…the king allowed him into the country believing him to be a friend. We had thought him also lost to the capture."

"Yes, the creatures are quite devious. Excluding, of course, your queen." He hesitated, teacup poised in midair. "Unless she has gone with them on purpose?"

"No," he growled.

"I was merely wondering. I do not know details of your royals or their lives."

The truth was still somersaulting in his mind, but for one instant it hung still with crystal clarity. Taersidel, vile liar that he was, would not hurt her. It wasn't slavers who had taken her. It wasn't that, at least. She was safe as she could be in this situation. She would be safe until he could reach her. He could hold onto that.

"Who sent the bounty out?"

"That is the tricky bit. They have so far proved untraceable. Very clever, that. But we do know where they are meeting up with the chemas for the exchange. For that information, I have one request."

Errance set his teeth. Just briefly, he imagined himself pouncing onto the table and grabbing the man by the collar, telling him there would be no requests, only answers. But he pushed the thought aside. There was politics involved in this. Of course there would be a request.

"I would like to accompany you on this rescue mission. I have a small company of mercenaries in Dormandy I can contribute, along with continued information. I will be very clear, Reyid." He leaned forward, clasping his slim fingers together as if in reverent prayer. "It is my intention to begin an alliance of goodwill between my company and your country. Do we have an agreement?"

Blinking long and slow, Errance let the man wait for an answer. The fellow was bold, no mistake. His silver hair and steely eyes shone with an experience and expertise that few men possessed. "Very well," he said finally. "You may accompany me. But as for the alliance, that is up to the king. And I will tell you now, he is in an ill humor."

"I would imagine so," the man said, amused. "Now then, as you will see from this report—here—the mercenaries were hired to bring the queen to Drywater Street in Dormandy. It is not an actual address, unless one works in the shadows. A quiet, backwater housing quarter for the disreputable. They would have already left by now to reach the agreed date, which, by the way, is tomorrow night. We will have to take a fast ship to catch them in time."

"I'll tell Core—"

"Allow me to provide a ship," Remrant interrupted. "As I take it that your queen and her kidnappers first traveled on Captain Coren's ship— the *Solitary Star*, is it not—then they will be alerted you are pursuing them if the ship takes port in Dormandy. It is a rather unique ship."

Errance folded his arms. "You know a lot of things."

"I should hope so. It is my job." He glanced down at the table, dabbing at his mouth with a napkin. "Now are you going to take your tea, Reyid? There are many things I am willing to overlook in an alliance, but I could not forgive a cup of tea going cold."

18

DORMANDY

The ship Taersidel had boarded reached the port of Dormandy while it was still dark. A few lanterns were lit above the deck when Tryss and Dahlya were taken from confinement, but the light was low to conceal any details of the passengers. Even so, Taersidel ordered they wear cloaks and hoods over their heads.

The commotion of the port was not lively as lively as it might have been during the day, but there were enough people milling about that somebody could notice them—or perhaps the opposite was true, and there was just enough activity that their presence would not be considered strange.

A hazy fog drifted through the masts of ships and the chimneys of the buildings, ghostly pale in the light cast from the ships and the dock.

Tryss swallowed as she clutched the cloak around her to keep off the chill. She glanced about for the ship captain that had agreed to take on such suspicious customers. Perhaps he wasn't a criminal, but merely deceived. There was no telling what web of lies Taersidel had spun to the man. But he was nowhere in sight.

"Come on." Taersidel's hand pressed lightly against the small of her back, and she started down the gangplank, one of the other chemas carrying Flyfar in his cage just ahead of her.

"I can't..."

Tryss turned at the sound of her friend's voice, and saw Dahlya sag, her teetering footsteps almost taking her off the gangplank.

"I can't walk. I..." Dahlya clapped her hands over her mouth and lurched to the edge as if about to be sick, breaking through the chemas on her either side. They lunged for her, but couldn't reach before she toppled off the gangplank into the waters below.

Taersidel shouted a command, and her chema guards jumped into the water after her. Dahlya's yelps of terror could barely be heard over her violent splashing.

Now.

Now, Tryss had her chance.

She slipped forward to the side of the chema who was holding the birdcage with Flyfar in it, and stuck her fingers through the bar. She held a thin ribbon she'd torn from her dress, and Flyfar took it from her without hesitation.

The chema noticed her by his side and spat out an alarm, dropping the cage to grab her.

The light wooden frame crunched on the ground, springing the latch open. Flyfar darted into the air with a sweep of his black and white wings.

Taersidel turned just in time to see him fly, and he lunged, fingers closing about the magpie's body.

His hand fisted on nothing but air.

Flyfar and the ribbon were gone.

Taersidel staggered upright and stood very still.

Dahlya had been hauled up onto the pier by her captors and they stood there, the water pouring from them to form small lakes on the stone.

It might have only been a few seconds, but it felt like an eternity before Taersidel turned around to face Tryss. "All right, sister. You won that time. I won't even punish your friend for that trick. Don't look innocent; I know you two planned this. Go ahead. Send your message to your king. Send him false hope. See what he does about it."

Taersidel gave his men a disgusted look, then pivoted on his heel and continued walking down the plank. "Bring them."

OOLUM

Later that morning, Errance went to the dunes outside of Oolum to find The Daisha. Coren came with him, bringing along Zizain and Zoren, who were excited to see the great winged creature again.

When Errance told The Daisha about Taersidel and Alludium, he expected a string of curses and complaints. Instead, she listened very silently as he explained the whole thing. Only when he neared the end did she make a sound, and that was a very low growl starting at the pit of her stomach and working its way up her throat.

"So you need to go back to Aselvia," he finished. "You need to warn them. And catch Alludium, if you can. Coren and I will be traveling to Dormandy with our new ally by ship. I'll try to send a message from there."

"Very well," she said.

"Is that it?" he said, rather faint.

"Is there something more I should say?"

"I thought you'd say 'I told you so' or some other such assurance."

"Not even I was expecting this kind of treachery from someone related to your sweet wife," The Daisha said magnanimously. "Anyway, there is no time for curses and laments. I must go at once if I am to stop this mischief." Her stern gaze softened as she looked from him to Coren and his family standing a small distance off. "The little one can pat me good-bye if he likes."

Zoren's eyes lit up even brighter at this offer. He rushed forward and gave the soft shoulder of The Daisha a hearty pat and then a gentler one on her nose when she offered it.

"All right, now stand back," she said, spreading her wings. "This kicks up quite a bit of sand."

They hurried a distance away, but the wind buffeted them even so when she rose from the ground and circled upwards. If anyone passing along the roads or in the city saw her rise from the dunes, they might have blamed sunstroke, for soon she was no larger than a bird wheeling high in the sky.

The ship that Remrant provided was not owned by the bank, but was a vessel designed for quick passage across the strait, quite expensive on short notice. And the notice was indeed short, for Remrant arranged for them to depart that very evening.

The sooner the better, as far as Errance was concerned. To think that they'd been combing Oolum and she was already back in Dormandy. What if they were too late? Would it even be possible to track her from there? If they could catch Taersidel or any of his company, they might discover who had hired them, but odds were slim to nothing for catching a chema who did not want to be caught.

Coren still seemed nervous about the whole thing. He knew the ship they were taking, grudgingly admitting that it was fast and well built. But he kept asking questions and throwing side glances at Remrant every chance he got.

"You can stay," Errance said again while they waited to board the ship, some distance away from the other travelers who had previously booked their passage. "You have Zizain and Zoren to watch over." He still felt wretched about watching his cousin say goodbye to his family.

"Oh, just stop," Coren muttered, stuffing his thumbs into the waist of his sash. "They are well adjusted to taking care of themselves. Better than you, I bet. I wouldn't let you do this alone, even if I weren't responsible for the mess in the first place."

Errance didn't answer, partially because arguing was useless, partially because he was glad not to go alone, and completely because Remrant was waving them forward.

"Come, come," Remrant said. "We are the first to board."

"Even though we were the last to book?" Errance noted dryly.

"I don't know if Aselvia is different, Reyid, but here there is very little you cannot get if you just throw enough money at it."

"Master Remrant Cole!" the captain declared, doffing his hat as he waited for them by the gangplank. "Quite an honor to serve you, quite the honor, I say." He took a glance at Errance and Coren, and then a second glance, brow creasing in question. But he was professional enough not to ask questions, and so led them aboard. "The best two cabins have been prepared. I'll have a man escort you there, and your belongings shall be kept safe and clean."

"The two best cabins just happened to still be available?" Errance whispered at Coren, raising a skeptical brow.

"Pretty sure your fancy friend probably threw enough money to bump someone else out," Coren whispered back.

"He's not my friend."

"Tell *him* that."

Somewhere from the rigging above, somebody made a distinct wolf whistle as they stepped up the gangplank. It might have been drowned out by the seagulls had the seagulls not decided to be quiet at that exact moment. Errance's eyes narrowed, but he pretended not to have heard anything.

Remrant, on the other hand, stopped in his tracks and spun to the captain. "If any of your sailors think harassment of my distinguished affiliate is amusing, I will see them in court."

The captain turned an uncomfortable color. "As you say, sir." He threw an anxious glance Errance's way and stammered, "They don't mean any harm by it, sir, you have nothing to worry about."

"Captain," Errance said coolly. "It is not *me* whom you should be worried for."

The captain stared at him a bit longer and then seemed to finally decide he should be moving on. With an awkward tip of his hat to both of them, he tramped off down the deck.

"Like I said," Coren muttered, nodding at Remrant's departing back. "Pretty sure he thinks you're friends."

Errance had been on a ship before on the way back to Aselvia after his imprisonment. But it wasn't like he had memories of the voyage; he'd been far too rapt in the wonder, the shock, of being free, of going home. Of beginning to understand he wouldn't spend another second in Tertorem again.

So the sensation of standing on a large boat that floated on top of a deep ocean was entirely new. No surprise, but he did not like it. It wasn't just the constant feeling of movement—vast, uncontrollable movement—but also the way one had to descend into the hold as if entering the mouth of a beast. The halls and cabins below were narrow, poorly lit, and smelled strongly of salt.

"You and Coren shall share a cabin. I am right next door," Remrant said. "If you wanted your own, I am sorry, but we are fortunate to have two cabins at all rather than bunk with the rabble. You may think this ship small, but it is larger than most vessels of its kind. Not only that, but I made certain this ship had a fine cook. We should arrive in Dormandy by tomorrow morning, so if you join me for dinner tonight, we can discuss more details of the road ahead."

Eating on this floating, bobbing death-trap? No, thank you. But he couldn't pass the opportunity to learn more about this inscrutable man.

"Fine," he said.

"Settle into your quarters," Remrant said. "Dinner is in an hour." He tapped the tiny clock clasped to his coat and stepped into his own room, closing the door behind him.

"Can't say I'm hungry," Coren muttered as they entered their own cramped cabin.

"Aren't you the one with the sea-hardened stomach?"

"It's not the sea that unsettles me, it's him." Coren kept his voice low, throwing a glance to the thin wood walls separating the cabins. He yawned loudly, and threw himself across the lowest bunk. "Besides, I think he'd share more with just you around. He keeps giving me as many sideways glances as I give him. It results in us both pretending we didn't notice. I don't think he has me entirely figured out, but he is well on his way, and like you said earlier, I'd rather he didn't reach any conclusions."

"So you want me to go eat dinner with him by myself?"

Coren opened one eye, arms crossed behind his head. "You had tea with him this morning. Do you have a problem now?"

Yes. "No," Errance said.

Dining with strangers?

No problem.

He did it *all* the time.

Heady aromas of sizzling pork and thyme curled up in wisps from the pie's flaky crust, and Remrant cut it straight down the middle to reveal a quail's egg cooked perfectly in the center. "By gods, that is *quite* scrummy," the man remarked. "I did check to see that there would be proper provisions on this short voyage. Even if these circumstances are less than ideal, I would hate your experience out here to be void of good food. I can only assume you eat like kings back home."

"Mm," Errance agreed, taking a moment to taste the mulled berry cider rolling across his tongue.

"Speaking of kings," Remrant continued, knife and fork clinking against his plate. "I had a few questions about yours. What is your impression of his rule?"

Errance set the mug down, the back of the chair suddenly hard against his spine. "The king. Ah. Well." He stared at the table for a few seconds and then snapped, "I find him incompetent."

Remrant tossed his head back and laughed. "So blunt! I suppose that must have felt good to get off your chest if that's how you feel. Go on then, tell all."

It *did* feel good. For once he could say it without a sad sigh or retort. "Errance is weak," he said, stabbing his fork into the pork and waving it for emphasis. "He comes back from imprisonment and begins to recover, but then he just nosedives into depression. He's an adornment for the throne more than anything else. Not like his father, now *there* was a leader."

"And his queen?"

"She's incredible."

Remrant paused mid-bite and eyed him. "That was emphatically said. Quite the contrast to your opinion of the king. What is so special about her?"

"She...is immensely graceful and patient. She may not involve herself much in the way of ruling, but she leads by example."

"Your thoughts on her marriage to the king?"

"He doesn't deserve her," he spat.

An amused gleam sharpened Remrant's eyes. "If I didn't know better, Reyid, I would say that smells strongly of jealousy."

Errance hesitated, a bit off balance. "Well. He isn't the one out here trying to rescue her, is he? Just goes to show you what I mean."

"Indeed," Remrant said with a smile. "Indeed."

By the time Errance finished dinner and stepped back out into the ship's hall, the shadow of night had settled into the hull. Glass lamps were fastened to the wooden walls at intervals, casting a dull orange halo, but the spaces in between were utterly black. It was only a few short lengths to the next door, but he found himself short on breath before he reached it. Somehow this dark narrow hall looked like other, endless passages, and the sensation of the ship moving beneath his feet reminded him far too much of times he'd been so injured he could not see or walk straight.

He closed the door behind him with a hasty thud and all but staggered to the bottom bunk, which Coren had graciously left open for him. His cousin was sitting cross-legged on the top bunk, looking over some documents by lamplight.

"There you are," Coren said, peeking his head over the edge of the bunk to look at him below. "How did it go?"

Errance ran a hand through his hair, heaving out a hard breath. "Remrant might now assume that…Reyid…is in love with Tryss."

Coren stared at him for a few moments longer, then slowly pulled back out of view. An exasperated smirk colored every word. "Saints spare us, Errance, having an affair with your own wife? Scandalizing Aselvia already."

Errance groaned, hands sliding down to cover his face.

A breath of air brushed against his skin, followed by a slight flutter of wings. He was just processing the sound when something sharp nipped his fingers. He jolted upright with a hiss.

Flyfar stared back at him, black eyes bright and innocent.

"Flyfar," he breathed. "Coren, Flyfar's back."

"Finally!" Papers fluttered into the air as Coren leapt to the floor. "Does he have something?"

Errance held out a shaking hand, and Flyfar bounced to his wrist. He saw then the ribbon held in the narrow talons. Taking it between his thumb and forefinger, he pressed it tight. "It definitely came from Tryss's dress," he said after a choked moment of silence.

She was alive. *Alive.*

He hung there for an eternity in that suspended moment between one breath and the next.

While he had never allowed himself to consider that he wouldn't see her again, that he would have no way to rescue her, this confirmation of her existence solidified the ground on which he stood. While a ribbon alone didn't give any promise of her safety, it was some sign she could interact with Flyfar.

"She might be able to get a better message out next time," Coren said, gripping his shoulder. "For now, she's alive, thank God. I suppose we shall just keep sending Flyfar back until she figures out some way to write?"

"Yes." Errance's knuckles whitened as he clutched the ribbon to his chest. His eyes were burning to the point he could barely see, but still he stood and strode to the writing desk in the cabin's corner. His free hand wrenched out a piece of paper, and ink splattered from the quill across the white parchment as he began ruthlessly scratching out letters. "But first, I must send Flyfar to Aselvia. He'll still get there before The Daisha. If for whatever reason Alludium hasn't struck yet, every moment matters. Either way, I need to know what's happening back home. It won't take long."

"Good," Coren said. It was a quiet, pained word that sounded anything but good. "I won't…I won't lie…I've been thinking non-stop about what might be happening with a chema spy on the loose in Aselvia. Daava. Maava. Tellie…if anything happens to them…it will be my fault for bringing the danger. Just as it is my fault for letting Tryss out of my sight."

"Hush," Errance growled, folding the finished letter up and setting it in Flyfar's beak. "If you're going to play at who's to blame, I will win every time. And I'm not in the mood for competition just now."

Flyfar gave one beat of his wings and then was gone.

For now, all they could do was wait.

19

ASELVIA

Leoren was not recovering as Damarik had hoped. The healer had not said as much yet, but Tellie could guess the truth. Damarik's constant checking on his breathing and attendance to the herbal steam was proof enough that something was still wrong.

"The poison isn't leaving his system," Damarik said at last, running a strained hand through his thick hair. "I'm only keeping it at bay. It might work its way out eventually. I don't know. I thought I recognized the symptoms of the poison, but if this isn't working, they could have developed a stronger variant."

Tellie nodded, not trusting herself to speak. All that she could think of at that point was the history she had read on Errance's mother, Queen Cerene. She'd once been poisoned, and there had been no cure. There was only Rendar's light keeping it restrained, keeping her alive, up to the day she gave all the light away to Errance.

Swallowing a groan, Tellie rubbed the heel of her hand against her temple. What was it about long nights that presented such dark and gloomy thoughts? She needed sleep. But how could she sleep when all she wanted to do was stay and listen to her father's raspy breath?

Leoren's eyes suddenly sprang open. "I've got it."

Tellie startled, almost falling out of her chair. "Daava, you should be resting—"

"No, hear me out." Leoren struggled to sit upright even as Tellie and Damarik moved in to help him. "If this is the last thing I can do for my country, I will see it through."

"Daava!"

"It's about Cerand."

Tellie's protest fell unfinished from her mouth, and her face scrunched in confusion. "Cerand…you mean, Maava's lost brother?" It always felt strange for Tellie to consider that somewhere in this world, she had another relative. Casara's elder brother, the original prince of Aselvia, though he had not inherited the crown due to being second-born. Nobody really spoke about him. She remembered seeing a picture once in the king's study behind the throne, but that was about as far as recognition went. That, and dear grandmother would sometimes murmur her son's name.

"Cerand was known as the Wraith in the North. The chemas hated and feared him above all others. Any information on him would be very important to them."

"And that information is not sensitive?" Damarik questioned, his spine stiffening and his one eye narrowing.

"Cerand is gone!" Leoren's voice broke harshly from his stressed throat. He winced and passed a hand over his eyes, taking a deep breath.

When he spoke again, his usual soft tones had returned. "Cerand is gone. It's the least damaging information she'd still be interested in."

Tellie folded her hands in her lap, chilled by the anger and hurt she'd heard in her father's voice. He'd almost sounded…bitter? But she didn't dare ask for details now. "How do we get her to take the bait? And what sort of trap would she not see coming?"

"I would suggest a trade," Damarik said. "It is no lie that I need further details on how she poisoned Leoren if I'm going to save him completely. She'll believe us desperate enough to trade secrets to save him. I will inform Commander Maril to send heralds announcing the time and place for the exchange, and to prepare our best soldiers and spies for the ambush."

It sounded a bit dishonorable for Tellie's taste, but honor be dashed with this many lives on the line.

Flyfar nestled his downy head into her cheek, and she reached up a finger to stroke his feathery breast.

"Flyfar!" she shrieked, causing the poor bird, her father, and Damarik all to jump about a foot into the air. She snatched the letter from the bird's beak and unfolded it with enough vigor to risk tearing the paper.

"What does it say?" Leoren asked, leaning over as far as he could, then scowling when Damarik pushed him back.

"It's from Errance. He…he confirmed that Taersidel is the one behind Tryss's kidnapping. He's warning us about Alludium. And he still hasn't found Tryss, but he has a lead to Dormandy, so he's headed there with Coren."

"Write back right away," Leoren urged. "He is no doubt worried sick we have all been murdered in our sleep."

"Shall I tell him what happened to you?" Tellie asked hesitantly.

"Stars, no," Leoren said with a cough. "He has enough on his mind. But tell him to send Flyfar back to us if he can. And that we have a plan to catch Alludium, and if we do, we can send something of hers as proof. Maybe it will help him in any encounter with Taersidel."

Tellie found a loose sheet of paper and tore off a piece that was small enough for Flyfar to carry and hopefully large enough to write all that. Really, it had been impressive how much information Errance had sent with concise wording. She just had to try and write tiny.

After she finished writing on both the front and back, she folded it up and glanced Flyfar's way. "Poor thing. I wonder if he ever gets tired of playing messenger. I remember Rendar could cross great distances in the Unseen in a few seconds when he knew where he was going, but still."

But Flyfar did not look at all discontent when Tellie handed him the paper. Finished preening, he took it in his shining black beak and vanished into the Unseen.

Tellie stared at the empty space almost jealously. Obviously, the bird had been created just for that purpose, but she still wished her visits to that otherworldly dimension were more frequent.

It really didn't take long. Flyfar was back within a few minutes, new message ready.

"Errance is relieved we already knew about Alludium, and he'll wait for our next reply. Oh! The Daisha should be arriving soon! Do you think we should wait to capture Alludium till then?"

"No," Leoren said. "If the chema sees or hears of The Daisha's arrival, she will flee at once. Best we move now, and if we fail, we can hope The Daisha will be able to track her down anyway."

"Then I will send for Maril and explain our plan." Damarik sounded tired. Tired beyond these many days and nights of caring for Leoren and Alludium. Tired beyond his years.

It was not often that Tellie thought about just how old the elves around her were, but she saw it now clear as day. Pity twisted her gut and she reached over to hug the ancient healer. He accepted the embrace without a word, resting a hand against her curls.

They would get through this. Somehow.

"Alludium of the North! Alludium of the North, take heed! At the second hour after dawn, the court offers you a trade! A secret in exchange for a secret! We bring word of the Wraith! Bring the cure for the poison you have laid! Alludium of the North, heed our call! Meet at the crescent courtyard at dawn, the second hour!"

A glint of water flew through the air as Alludium flicked the droplet from her finger. She lounged in the shadows of a fountain in the palace garden, listening to the heralds walk up and down the city streets. Surely their voices were getting worn by now. Surely everyone in the city must have heard them. What a scandal this would cause, especially if anyone knew who was meant by the Wraith. But then, perhaps that was a secret kept from the common people. Royals did so love their dark little secrets.

The Wraith.

The mere mention set her teeth on edge and summoned saliva into her mouth the same way as a wolf when it smelled prey.

Of course it could be a lie.

But this was one of the reasons she'd lingered here. Waiting for that moment, that desperation, when they'd be willing to give up secrets they'd been so careful to hide.

It was worth the risk.

Everything she did, every breath she took was for Glory, and if she did not lay it all on the table, then she did not deserve to live. But in Glory she would live forever.

At dawn, on the second hour, the elves waited. The crescent courtyard was so named for the pattern inlaid into the stone. While the walls of the city were white, the ground was a mix of grey stone, grass, and earth. But here, a giant perfect white moon of polished gems curved upon the floor. The rays of dawn were beginning to peek over the walls, turning the moon into shining brightness.

Tellie waited on the borders of the courtyard with Maril and Kelm beside her. A few guards stood near them as a pretense of caution, but the rest of the ambush was well hidden in the bushes and trees encircling the yard.

It was so quiet. Birdsong usually filled the courts of Aselvia. But perhaps they knew. Perhaps Alludium was already here.

"Let me be the one who does the exchange," Tellie suddenly whispered.

"Your Highness, that is far too dangerous," Maril began, but Tellie interrupted her with a raise of her hand.

"I am aware of the dangers, Commander, but as you said, I am the princess, and I think Alludium might be less on guard if I'm the one at the exchange. She might even suspect this was all my idea to save my father. I…I want to do it. I will do it."

After a moment's pause, Maril gave a slight nod. "Very well, Princess."

Tellie took the enveloped document from the commander, only to find herself staring at Kelm's chin, so close had he been behind her. She looked up into his blue eyes, a bit breathless to find them so soft and serious.

"What was it you said earlier?" he asked, a little smile playing on his lips as he took the hand that held the document. "About sharing any title with me?"

"Yes, and you said Princess didn't suit you," Tellie replied, trying hard not to smile in return and giving an insincere tug of her wrist.

"The title doesn't but the responsibility is just fine by me. If you're confronting Alludium, we're confronting her together."

"But what if she finds that suspicious—"

"I hope she would find it more suspicious if you were there without me," he said, giving a kiss to her nose.

"All right, all right, fair enough." She didn't know why she argued in the first place, because she wanted him by her side more than anything. Her free hand slipped into his and together they walked out onto the center of the moon mural.

Alludium appeared with the suddenness of someone stepping through thick fog.

Tellie's teeth clenched together with the same force that her fingers tightened around the paper. A flicker of memory slipped into her mind of the first time she'd seen Tryss appear out of thin air. It had been so frightening, it had felt so wrong. And while she'd quickly adjusted and Tryss had never given her the same feeling again, she felt it now. That same wrongness.

"Hello, mortal girl," Alludium said, and she smiled.

Oh, how Tellie despised that smile.

She did not honor the woman with a greeting, instead going straight to business. "You poisoned my Daava. I'm here for the cure."

"And I am here," Alludium said, carefree as a floating feather, "because you promised information that is of interest to me. So hand it here, and let us see if it's worth your father's life."

"Oh no," Tellie said, her hand squeezing Kelm's palm in anger rather than fear. "Oh no, not just so you can spirit it away. I will open it and you may read it, but you shall not touch it."

"And how will I know this information is real?" Alludium tilted her head, mouth pursed. "How will I know you didn't make something up just to interest me while causing no harm to your kingdom?"

"Well, if you weren't willing to take that risk, you wouldn't be here, would you?" Tellie glared, letting go of Kelm's hand long enough to open the envelope and pull the sheet out. The paper was yellowed with age and the ink had faded. Hopefully, that would be enough to convince the chema of its authenticity.

Alludium took a step forward, eyes squinting as she perused the contents with practiced swiftness. Her expression was guarded, but even so, Tellie saw the tightening of her jaw and the hunger that colored her eyes. She looked from the paper to Tellie, and their gazes locked.

And then Tellie knew.

Alludium didn't need the paper. The information was enough.

Tellie opened her mouth to yell for the waiting guards to jump *now*, before it was too late, before she was gone—

—when the sun darkened.

Alludium's head jerked up towards the sky, a venomous curse spitting from her lips. She was out of sight, but before Tellie could even begin to panic, the trees around them bent under the pressure of wind, and The Daisha dove to earth.

She pounced upon the ground with a snarl, her wings still pumping the air from the violence of her landing. As the sound of the wind died down, another sound of spitting and hissing could be heard under The Daisha's claws.

A moment later, and Alludium reappeared, captive in The Daisha's grasp. She'd stopped struggling, and her face had become passively quiet.

Kelm hollered, punching a fist into the air. "That's right, that's how it's done, you big, beautiful beast!"

The Daisha gave him a withering look, but turned it back towards the chema in her claws. "The culprit is caught. Now, may I ask why you were having a nice chat out in the sunshine?"

"We were trying an exchange," Tellie explained. Ah, her chest hurt, so badly had her heart wanted to leap from its confines. "But she was about to run. She promised us a cure for Leoren. He's…poisoned."

"Poisoned," The Daisha repeated flatly.

Damarik and Maril hurried forward, flanked by the guards that appeared from the hidden depths of the trees and foliage. "I've tried administering *iisveth*," Damarik said. "But it has not had the usual effect."

"WHAT IS THE CURE, YOU SMIRKING LITTLE WENCH!" The Daisha's roar blew everyone's hair back from the pure force of her breath.

Yes, Alludium's smile had returned to her lips, windswept though she was. "I see you were planning to ambush me even before The Daisha arrived. How amusing that we both aimed to dishonor the exchange." She sighed, leaning her head back against the hard ground. "I suppose now that the show is over, I can play nice. You are correct, *iisveth* is the cure. But the poison has been developed to be more potent, and it will require a more potent remedy. Only fresh *iisveth* will help this, and that only grows in the northern mountains."

Tellie's mouth dropped open and she didn't know if she was going to speak, shout, or cry. It wasn't nice, it was cruel. If the cure was that rare, how long would it be till they could acquire some? And by then, would it be too late?

Damarik tugged her aside before she could decide on any kind of reaction.

"She made an arrogant mistake. We actually do have *iisveth* growing in our mountains," he whispered. "It was extremely difficult to grow, but we managed. I'll need to take The Daisha, and I'll be back as soon as possible."

"Oh, manifix ore!" Alludium said it in the same way she cursed, bringing their attention back to her. The guards had pulled her out from under The Daisha, and Maril was locking the shackles onto her wrists. "I should have known you'd have some of these precious things lurking about," she went on, a dangerous brightness to her tone. "I'm honored you'd use them on *me*." She looked up at the commander and cocked her head. "Hold on. You aren't related to the infamous General Reyin, by any chance? You resemble him strongly. I noticed he hasn't been here all this time. Could it be that he met his fate in that tragic attack so long ago—?"

"Silence," Maril said, a dangerous edge to her voice. Her countenance was calm, but there was something roiling underneath it, like the deep currents of the river. She lifted the chema's bound hands together, inspecting them closely, then grabbed one finger between hers and ripped a ring off it. She held it out and Tellie hastened forward to take it. "This should serve as proof, Princess. You know what to do with it."

Maril and the guards marched Alludium away, leaving the rest of them to try and piece together their shattered nerves.

"That was too close," Kelm said, wiping his brow. "The Daisha, I can't even begin to say how wonderful you are."

"You can begin saying it and you can keep at it," she replied. "Now, Damarik, my dear, please tell me we have some of that cure she mentioned."

"We do. Do you still have the strength to fly me to the mountains? I know you have come a long way already—"

"Never mind that," The Daisha growled. "This is for Leoren. I daresay I consider you all family. I'll fly until my wings fall off if that's what it takes to keep you safe."

At that, Tellie wrapped her arms around The Daisha's neck and buried her face into her soft fur, inhaling the scent of the clover fields still present even after so long away from home. The creature's head nestled down behind her shoulders, a purr trembling in her throat. By the time she'd let go, Damarik was waiting to climb atop the Daisha's shoulders, so she stepped back and into Kelm's arms.

They hurried to the corner of the court to avoid the buffet of wind from The Daisha's wings, then watched her spiral up into the sky.

"They'll be back real soon, Tel," Kelm assured, kissing the top of her head. "They'll cure Daava. And then everything will be right as spring rain, you'll see."

Tellie opened her clenched fist to stare at Alludium's silver ring. Even if this was so, everything would not be right. Not yet. Not until Errance and Tryss were home.

20

DORMANDY

Errance woke to Flyfar poking a rolled up piece of parchment into his face. He startled upright, jolting the bird from his chest. Something heavier than paper fell from the bird's claws, and he fumbled for it before it was lost in the blankets. When he lifted it up to his face, squinting in the poor light, he beheld a peculiar silver ring. It was engraved with some marking that meant nothing to him.

"Thanks," he muttered to Flyfar as he took the parchment for explanation.

The note was brief to fit on the small slip of paper.

Errance, we've captured Alludium. This is her ring if you need proof for Taersidel. The kingdom is safe.

A long, shaky breath rattled from his lungs. Honestly, he didn't know what he would have done if the note had brought only more terrible news. Now he could loosen his grip on the fear of what was happening back home and focus solely on the mission before him.

Sliding off the bed, he made his way to the desk and lit the candle there, then took the ring and sealed it inside a small envelope for safe keeping.

He grabbed a fresh sheet of paper and stared down at its blank surface waiting to be met by ink.

What kind of message should he send Tryss? He couldn't give away anything about his plans to save her, because Taersidel would likely intercept it. He might even catch the bird, which was no doubt why Flyfar had taken so long to return the first time.

At last, he scrawled a few words across the paper and rolled it up with a deep breath.

He held out his wrist, and Flyfar fluttered to it, shifting up and down his arm in impatience.

"Go to Tryss," he said. "Stay hidden until you can reach her safely." He honestly wasn't sure how much the bird understood besides names and basic commands, but Flyfar's intelligence wasn't to be underestimated.

No sooner had the magpie flown to the Unseen did a knock sound at the door.

"Good morning, gentlemen." Remrant's voice came through the wood. "Best wake now, we are coming into Dormandy's port."

Once, Dormandy had been a name of much wonder, excitement, and intrigue to Errance. As a boy, he'd dreamed of the day he could accompany the embassy to their nearest human neighbor and see their tall stone towers, grand university, and enormous harbor where boats sailed east to Oolum or south to Korince and the islands beyond. He'd wanted to see the bearded men with their stovepipe hats and the women with piles of hair on their head almost as wide as their skirts. He'd wanted to taste the coffee brought in from the islands or try the famous chowders on the wharf.

But he'd never gone further than one of the many small villages in the country surrounding Dormandy. And as for the journey on the way back from Tertorem, well, like most places, it had all been in a haze to him.

If he was completely honest, his impression now of Dormandy was not all that favorable. Could have just been the fog that was drifting between the boats, shrouding the buildings ahead. Could have just been the reason he was here. But whichever, he didn't see why anyone had settled down in this spot, let alone built a city. Or maybe it had been a fine area before everyone and their distant relatives moved in.

"The fog will lift within the hour," Remrant said, coming up alongside him to look over the ship's edge. "You won't be able to see much of Dormandy in the carriage we'll be taking, but perhaps when all the trouble is over, I could take you on a tour of this fine city."

"Where are we going from here?" Errance asked, ignoring the fact that his disapproval for the city must have been written all over his face.

"My house."

"Your house?"

"I did say Dormandy was my base of operations."

"Yes, but—" House suggested home, base of operations did not. "Is it the building for the All Nations Banks as it was in Oolum?"

"By gods, no. I do try to keep my work separate from my life, at least for a few hours of the day. No, we are simply going there to prepare for tonight. Come along now, the captain is about to dismiss the passengers."

Remrant Cole lived in a fine townhouse on Albine Avenue, deep within the apartment blocks of the city. The roof had two peaks, one windowed tower, and several chimneys. It was three stories and built mostly of brick. Several houses of similar structure lined the street on either side. There was no wall, no gate, just a short stoop leading up to the door that had a double lock, and that was the only form of apparent security. The man didn't seem to fear enemies, despite working for such an important bank.

"Good day, Master Cole!" A young lady, probably no more than sixteen, opened the door for them as they came up the stairs. She was very neat in a dark blue dress and starched apron, and wore a genuine smile. "It is good to have you back, sir!"

"Indeed, dear girl, indeed." Remrant doffed his coat, handed it to her, and waved his hand between the girl and his guests. "This is Beki, my housemaid. She will show you up to your rooms and you can rest till we head out."

"Good evening, sirs," the maid said, bowing.

"I'm not sure I can rest—" Errance began even while bobbing a distracted bow to Beki in return who looked astonished by the gesture.

"The meeting on Drywater Street will not be till midnight," Remrant said with a wave of his hand. "I will be going out to finish preparations. I've already hired my own mercenaries for this mission, but I should like to check over them a final time. Also, I must go to the court office and pick up our curfew passes."

"Our what?" Errance paused with one foot on the stair.

"Curfew. Dormandy has a curfew now to cut down on illegal activity. Obviously, it is not working as well as it should since operations in Drywater Street and the like are still active, but it's a way for officers to question anybody wandering out after dark. With a pass, we will be free to go about our business."

"I've heard about the curfew," Coren said, a slight frown on his face. "It wasn't active when I—" he paused, remembering his age, and finished, "—was younger."

"The Governor has been making great strides towards the safety of this city," Remrant replied. "I only hope I'm still alive to see it become a beacon to the rest of the world."

There didn't seem to be anything to say to that, so Errance and Coren retreated to their room.

As evening approached, the maid brought them up a package containing outfits for the night.

Like Coren, Remrant seemed to believe in a wardrobe for whatever situation. It was exactly the sort of thing you'd expect to wear on a midnight robbery—fitted black trousers, fitted black shirt reaching high up the neck, long black jacket to conceal weapons. The clothes were not a perfect fit, but close enough that Errance felt a prickle of unease that he'd already been measured and tailored by eye.

"It needs one more thing," Coren said once they'd assembled their attire. "Fortunately, I brought it with me as I saw the need in the future." He dug into his belongings and tossed a tubular black cloth Errance's way.

Errance frowned as he inspected the mask. "What do I need it for? Tryss needs to see me."

"Taersidel cannot be allowed to recognize you," Coren muttered. "If he does, you will become target number one. And anyway, if Tryss saw you, she'd probably call out your name, and then Remrant will also find out who you really are and then we have more of a mess on our hands."

"So what if Remrant knows?"

"He knows too much, that's what. I'd rather keep an edge on him."

"Fine." He couldn't argue with that. He slipped the black cloth over his head, pulling it up over his nose so that just his eyes glinted over the edge. His hair he pulled back in a messy knot at the nape of his neck. If he'd kept it down, that in and of itself could be a giveaway that elves were involved, and if the chemas thought they were only dealing with humans, they might underestimate them.

Taersidel. That reminded him of Alludium's ring. He found the envelope he'd hidden it in and stashed it away in the deepest pocket of his coat.

He looked up to see Coren carefully peeling off the patch of beard on his chin and combing his hair back into a different style. He didn't appear to have any intention of donning the eye patch he usually wore in public.

"I haven't been running around Dormandy for a while," Coren explained at Errance's look of curiosity. "So I don't think anyone but Taersidel would recognize me if I'm not looking exactly like Captain Coren. And I think it would be best if I didn't carry that identity while we search for Tryss."

"And you're all right with Remrant knowing that your eye patch is a total fake?"

"Somehow, I wouldn't be surprised if he knows. I think he knows my other secret as well, though I can hope to keep that unclear."

No sooner had they finished than a knock came at the door. Coren opened it, expecting the maid again, but found Remrant there instead. He wore dark clothes like them, but he gave off the impression of being dressed for business rather than dressed for a scrap.

He gave Coren's altered appearance one glance, but indeed did not seem very surprised.

"Your passes, my good sirs," he said, handing them each a sturdy waxed card. "If you would follow me, I have our transportation ready."

The maid smiled and waved as they went down the stairs, eyes widening a bit in excited curiosity, but not total shock. Errance wondered what sort of life Remrant led so that his housemaid would be used to such comings and goings.

On the curb of Albine Avenue, three black carriages waited, very much like the one he'd driven in Oolum. One, Remrant explained, was for the three of them, and the other two were for the hired mercenaries who already waited inside.

"Won't we be considered suspicious heading out like this?" Errance asked, imagining being checked for curfew passes on every street corner.

"Our carriages will head out one at a time," Remrant replied. "Anyway, we have a little time to reach our destination before curfew hits, and then we can lay low until our attack where we can rescue your lady and fade back into the darkness."

"About that," Errance said, reluctantly climbing into the carriage and waiting until Remrant had taken the seat across from him. "You haven't clearly explained how we are going to rescue Tryss. With your mercenaries involved, I feel we ought to be let in on the exact plan."

"Of course. It was already my intent to explain on our way. We shall take places of hiding on Drywater Street, and at the moment of transaction, I shall give a signal, the mercenaries will launch smoke bombs into their midst, and you shall be the first forward to try and reach your lady."

"Won't the smoke bombs make it difficult for me to find her?" Errance asked, ignoring the repeated use of "your lady."

"It might, but the confusion it will cause for your enemies should work in your favor. We must already expect to not see the chemas once we attack, but the smoke might give us a clue to their movement. At the very least, our best hope is to make it as difficult for them to see us."

"What's this signal then?"

Instead of answering, Remrant reached under his coat and brought forth a weighty tool, elegantly barreled with iron and its wooden handle embossed with patterns of gold.

"Brights!" Coren started forward, eyes flaring in appreciation. "A flintlock pistol! And a beautiful one at that."

Something else Errance was behind on, apparently. Besides the invention of ticking clocks and a thousand other things, parts of Orim had been developing firearms. He remembered when he was a youth hearing rumors of early attempts brought in to his father, but recent study as king had informed him those clumsy efforts had paid off. They were still rare enough, found mainly in Dormandy or Korince and usually for law enforcement. Most of the rest of Orim had not taken to the fashion yet, considering it an awkward and inelegant weapon.

"Some of the guards in Oolum are carrying these now," Coren said, continuing to appraise the weapon. "And occasionally I run into a ship captain that has one. The first captain I ever served carried an earlier model, though I never saw him use it. I've heard they're not very dependable."

"They are dependable to cause a very loud noise," Remrant said with a wry twist of his lips. "Which is exactly why it will work as our signal. It should startle our enemies enough to add to the necessary confusion."

"All right." Errance gave a firm nod, fingers tightening into fists.

He was more than ready.

21

DORMANDY

The shudders that coursed through his body every other breath shook the bed. No doubt that was what had awoken her. Reaching across to the bedside table, Tryss found a box of matches and struck a flame, the bit of light bursting into the darkness. Once the candle was lit and the match dropped into a tiny bowl of water, she turned back to her husband. "Errance, wake up," she said, trying to sound calm.

His eyes snapped open, but it took several moments before she could be certain he was seeing reality. The glaze of terror and confusion that shone in their depths smote her heart. Finally, his gaze flickered over to her with recognition, but the erratic breath rattling from his lungs was not showing any signs of settling. She sat back as far on the edge of the bed as possible, knees scrunched to her pounding chest. This was the hardest part...staying away, only able to watch as he lurched with each waking breath. Everything within her wanted to hold him, to shield, to protect. But it only did more damage. Soon enough he would ease and then she could come...sometimes.

"You're safe," she whispered, keeping her gaze locked with his. "You're safe now."

Without answering, he shoved himself upright and stumbled out of bed. He'd almost made it to the wash basin when his knees buckled. His hand flailed for the edge of the table before he hit the floor, catching the bowl and sending the water splattering across the tile.

She was at his side the next moment, grabbing the neatly folded hand cloth and spreading it across the puddle. But she hadn't touched him yet. She wasn't sure she should.

The soft sound of a muffled sob jerked her attention to where he sat curled up on the floor, fist pressed into his brow. She had never seen him cry during or after one of his terrors. He rarely screamed. It was as if those years of training himself to hold it in had become his natural response. But he was crying now, even if it was hidden in his gasping breath.

"Errance...?"

"Please..." he whispered. "Please hold me."

He asked her for the very thing she ached to give? Without waiting a moment more, she crawled to his side and wrapped her arms around his shoulders.

The moment she touched him, he recoiled. Not the opposite direction, but inwards. As if that was his only escape, to hide away inside himself. She blanched, snatching her hands back.

"No—" His voice broke, but he tried again, forcing it out. "N-no, don't stop. Stay with me. Prove them wrong. P-please prove them wrong."

Slowly, she reached out again, fingers resting on his back. He flinched again, but she didn't withdraw. Instead, she drew him closer. Carefully. Gently. Scooting a bit closer so she could support him better, she guided his hunched form to rest against her own, nestling his cheek against her heart and resting her chin upon his head. His words and tears told her this was what he needed, but he was shivering from her touch. It was too terrible a contrast. Her mind screamed for her to stop, insistent that she was hurting him, but her heart fought to remain pressed against the pounding beat of his own heart.

Help him, God. Help me. Help us...

She wasn't sure if she said it aloud or not, but she ran her fingers through the roots of his hair in rhythmic strokes, a tremoring hum in her throat, until eventually, finally, his shaking began to cease.

Perhaps an hour passed, perhaps more, but certainly enough to make her stiff and numb. Then she felt a wheezing, warm breath against her arm, accompanied by a small, rustling sigh. The tension in his body was gone, his weight sinking more heavily against her.

What? Was he sleeping? He had actually fallen asleep in her arms...? She blinked several times.

Then she was shaking. Stars, she hoped it wouldn't wake him. Maybe it was the shock and horror finally catching up with her or maybe it was the overwhelming thankfulness. But whatever demons had plagued him tonight, they were gone, gone, and they'd fought it together...he had let her help him fight.

And in that moment, she knew. They would be all right.

"Errance," Tryss murmured, reaching across the pillows to wrap her arm around her husband's shoulders. Only he wasn't there. Fear stiffened her body even before she opened her eyes, even before she was certain what she was afraid of. "Errance?" She sat up in a jolt, looking about the bare, melancholy room with confusion. The blank walls stared back, completely unsympathetic.

"Tryss?" Dahlya sat up in her narrow bed and hurried over, dragging the blanket with her. "Tryss, it's all right, it was just a dream."

Her heartbeat was slowing down, her mind was catching up with the situation, and if there was one thing that remained clear, it was that everything was *not* all right. She wrapped her arms around her stomach, a wave of nausea coloring her mood into an even more unpleasant shade.

"This is so stupid." Hardly the most elegant words to ever leave her mouth, but she had zero interest in prose at the moment.

Fighting back a small laugh, Dahlya fetched a candle and struck it for light. "I don't think we've been asleep for very long." The mattress creaked as she sat back down, and she poked her hand into it with a frown. "This is hardly the most comfortable thing for you to sleep on anyway."

"I don't want to sleep," Tryss grumbled. "I keep dreaming about him. About us. And then I wake up and he's not here." Stars, was it the pregnancy or just the awfulness of everything that made her switch from wanting to scream to wanting to cry at a moment's notice?

Perhaps noticing her crumbling face, even in the low light, Dahlya let out a wide yawn and arched her arms over her head in a stretch. "Then don't dream, just talk. Tell me about the proposal."

"You've heard that story."

"Well, I could ask about the wedding night." Dahlya said, the innocent expression on her face not quite hiding the impish edge.

Tryss let out a snort. "Oh, that? That one's easy. He slept on one side of the bed, I slept on the other, end of story."

"That changed at some point, apparently," her friend remarked, reaching over to pat her belly.

Tryss narrowed her eyes. "Are you *trying* to make me blush?"

"I'm trying to distract you, dearie, is it working?" Her eyes twinkled, lively and bright as fireflies.

"In that case, why don't you tell me about yourself? I've always tried to be polite and not pry, but I'm tired, very pregnant, prone to be hysterical, and just now a bit bored. Was there ever anyone, Dah? Anyone at all?"

Dahlya leaned back, a pensive line furrowing her brow. "There was."

"And?"

"And he married someone else."

"Oh." Then, after a pause. "Who?"

With a cheerless laugh, Dahlya shook her head. "Tryss, I'm not going to tell you just so you can see him and go 'oh, there is the man my friend would have liked to marry, only now he's with someone else.'"

"I suppose that's fair." She considered in silent regret, and then jolted at the intrusion of a worrisome thought. "Um. Do I know him?"

"Actually, you don't. It's all right, Tryss, you needn't pity me. He changed in character anyway, so it all worked out for the best." She gave a swift shake of her head, then smiled again. "Best to turn to another subject. As it is, I'm a little dull on chema knowledge, and I'm curious how coloring works. I know most of the north chemas are all cold shades while your tribe tends to be flaxen-haired, so how does that work? The girl brought to the healer's house had hair that looked rather blue, and I've wanted to ask you about that."

"Our colors are crafted by our mothers in the womb. A chema with a strong ability can later take on a new look as long as they like. Generally, it is chosen to reflect something in our environment."

"Ohhh, does that mean you get to pick colors for Baby? How exciting! What are your ideas?"

"I…I don't know that it will take since Baby is only half chema…but if it does, I am thinking of silver hair to honor Errance's heritage, and I want the eye color to be like his."

"Heavens, that would be gorgeous."

They did not say anything more for some time, the silence stretching out into a painful reminder of their captivity. Tryss sighed and pulled her knees up onto the mattress as best as she could. "This is dreadfully selfish of me, Dah, but I'm glad you're here."

"Is it so very selfish?" Dahlya returned. "I would have been worried sick back in Aselvia hearing that you were stolen away to who knows where. I am glad to be here too."

Footsteps. Very light, but insistent. They approached the door, followed by the sound of the locks turning. Tryss straightened, legs sliding over the side of the bed to brace against the floor, and Dahlya laid one hand on her knee, a reassuring arm to stand between her and whatever was coming in.

The door opened and closed, and Taersidel stood before it.

Tryss drew in a shallow breath and held it, waiting for some new snide remark.

But he only said, "Good, you are already awake. It's time to go."

"It is the middle of the night," Dahlya growled. "You really just expect her to be able to jump about to your every whim? You're about as dense as they come."

"I did not set up the time," Taers replied with a shrug. "Anyway, you won't have to do much. We'll take a taxi carriage and then walk a short way and wait."

"Wait for what?" Dahlya still had not removed her hand from Tryss's knee, as if she planned on keeping her there no matter how many foes assailed them.

"Never mind," Tryss said with a terse toss of her head. Waving Dahlya aside, she pushed to her feet with only a bit of a wobble and looked her brother straight on. "I have decided to be quite calm. It doesn't matter where we go, My Majesty will come for me."

Taers blinked. "I'm sorry, your what?"

"My Majesty. It's my pet name for my husband. I just came up with it on the spot. Doesn't it make you gag?" Her eyes shone alarmingly innocent and challenging at once.

"Yes, it does!" Taers said, raising his brows. He shook his head with an uncertain laugh. "I'll tell you this, sister. You always annoyed me for being the only sibling who didn't worship the ground upon which I walked. But now I am halfway to admiring you for it."

"Halfway isn't far enough."

"No," he agreed, moving for the door. "It is not."

When they stepped forth to the coach waiting outside their confinement, the night hung heavy with the dark and cold of autumn's passing. There was moisture in the air, but not that of damp earth—a sickly sort of fog clinging to stone and grime.

Another chema stood beside the carriage, but where the rest were, who could say? The coach driver did not look their way; he only hunched over his reins like an old crow.

Taersidel pressed a small card into both Tryss and Dahlya's hands.

"What's this?" Dahlya squinted at it, but the script was impossible to make out when the only light came from a street lamp some distance away.

"A curfew pass, just in case we're stopped."

"And you somehow managed to obtain them for us despite never showing any official our faces?" Tryss rolled her eyes.

"They're forged, obviously, but I doubt the officials will be checking too closely."

"Then what is even the point?" she muttered, climbing into the carriage with a deathlike grip on the side of the door. She wondered what the chances were of receiving help if they were stopped by officials and if she yelled that she was being kidnapped. Most likely it would just end up getting the men killed by her brother.

The door shut behind them, leaving only her, Dahlya, Taers, and the second chema in the seats. As they rattled down the street, she guessed the rest of his men had already gone ahead to their destination.

Not much time had passed before the coach came to a halt again, and Taersidel leapt lightly out onto the pavestones. He held out his hands to help her down, but she very pointedly ignored that and climbed down herself, even though it was difficult.

"It's not far," he reassured, as the coach clattered away.

"It had better not be," Dahlya said. Whatever whimsy colored her voice when she spoke to Tryss was utterly absent when she spoke to Taersidel. A delicate frost sharpened her words instead.

It was as he promised. They had not gone more than a block when more chema figures stepped into sight, hidden by shadow and smog. They stood at a cross section of streets, but the streets were not wide enough for any carriages. It was the back alleys of a low-class housing district, Tryss guessed. There were a few lamps set into the walls, but this wasn't the sort of place to be visited by a lamplighter. The oil here burned low and wouldn't last long. No, this place was meant for a brief, discreet moment.

She heard footsteps before she saw the men coming down the street across the way. Human men, bundled up in coats, scarves, and knitted caps pulled low over their eyes. One held a small wooden chest.

"There you are," Taersidel said, as bored as if he'd been waiting for hours rather than arriving only moments before them. "It's been a lot of trouble getting her here, I'll have you know. I'll need to check that payment to be sure I receive every coin I'm owed."

"The woman is exchanged at the same time as the payment," the man barked. "You bounty hunters should know how this is done."

Her brother's voice was soft next to her ear. "Don't be afraid, Tryss. I would never betray you like this. The moment we have our payment, we will be gone like smoke on the wind."

Oh yes, he would never betray her *this* way. How good of him. Perhaps he should get a medal. Gritting her teeth, she moved forward at the slight gentle press of his hand on her back.

She was already bracing herself. Bracing for the moment when his power would surge through her, hiding the both of them from all other eyes, and she'd be dragged away from the ensuing chaos.

From the corner of her vision, she saw the reward chest held out to the receiving chema, even as her awaiting captor reached out for her. And then the man paused, his eyes widening, a grunt slipping from his mouth as he staggered beneath some unseen chema knife.

Thunder cracked through the air.

Blue smoke exploded from the ground with a sharp crack and hiss. Dark figures came hurtling through the smoke towards them.

In that moment of utter confusion and panic, one thing stood clear. Nobody was touching her. Not the man, not her brother. She lunged forward into a run, not sure of any direction other than away.

But there! There was Dahlya! The chema holding her was backing away, both still visible, so perhaps the one guarding her didn't have enough skill to focus his power in a moment of bewilderment.

She didn't even slow down. She barreled straight into them, catching Dahlya by the arms, yanking her away from them with the same momentum that sent them tumbling towards the ground. She planted her foot against the stone, refusing to fall. If she was right, this chema was the weakest member of the team. Which meant she might have just enough skill to best him. She poured her power through her body, feeling the change ripple across her skin, and let it spread from her fingertips to Dahlya. She knew she couldn't make her friend disappear. She couldn't. But if she could change just enough to create some confusion, maybe...

Dahlya had gained her footing beside her. Now she was the one leading the way as the faster of the two. They dodged between one of the human men and one of their new attackers, heading for the alley and the darkness beyond.

The gunshot was still echoing in the streets as Errance launched from the roof, hit the stone pavement with a roll, and came up running. The smoke bombs peppered the ground around him, but he didn't turn his eyes from where Tryss was standing even as she vanished from view.

He hated that moment of being blind, but they would be blind anyway against this enemy and the smoke would give them a chance to see—movement. He dodged, watching the smoke part inches from his face from the stroke of an invisible knife. His hand snaked out, connecting with a body, and he sunk his fingers into the fabric of a tunic. It wasn't Tryss. He'd know the moment she was in his arms, visible or not. Yanking them forward with one arm, he drove his knife out into empty space and was rewarded with a grunt of pain.

Someone else was leaping at him. From behind, where he couldn't even see the smoke move, but he felt it coming. He spun, throwing the body he held towards the attacker.

Tryss. Where was she? He couldn't waste any more time fighting. They couldn't have already grabbed her and spirited her out of sight. He hoped she'd taken the chance to run, but how far could she get?

One man in front of him—ally or foe, he didn't know—fell with a cry, and he leapt over the body, cutting a path through the smoke and struggling figures. As he broke free of the smoke, he found nothing but the empty street on the other side. She wasn't there. She wasn't there.

"Tryss!" He didn't care if Taersidel heard and recognized him. Tryss answering was the only thing that was important. But no response came.

Other than the distortion of stone to his left.

He flipped backwards, landing in a stance ready for battle, but no further attack followed. Instead, the distortions rippled away, soft footsteps vanishing into the distance.

"Errance!"

He turned to see that the smoke was clearing, revealing the bodies lying on the ground. Coren had one struggling man pinned. "The chemas killed the other brokers, but I've got this one. They might have taken off with her again."

No, no, *no*. They had been so close. She'd been *right there*.

He could not have found her just to lose her again.

Every part of Tryss's mind screamed at her to keep running, but every inch of her body screamed for her to stop. The stabbing pains shooting from her abdomen and back slowed her pace, and by the fourth stumble, she lost her footing completely, caught only by Dahlya's quick hand.

"We need to hide." The words broke from between ragged gasps. She barely heard Dahlya's response over the thunder of her own heartbeat in her ears, but she felt herself being tugged from the street. The closest thing to a shelter on that street was a stairway leading down into the ground next to one of the old houses, an overhang built above it to keep out the rain. They took the first few steps down, Dahlya holding her in a death-grip to stop her poor balance from hurtling her headlong, and then they crouched upon the stairs in the darkness, breath echoing on the stones.

No sound of pursuit, just a distant clatter of the chaos they had fled.

She didn't trust that her brother and company wouldn't have seen them leave, and even if they had somehow slipped away in the confusion, it would be hard to get anywhere without being spotted. She needed to think, but right now, thinking felt like the most impossible feat in the world.

A scrape of leather on cobblestone.

Light dropped down upon them. Biting back a cry, Tryss squinted up into the intense brightness of a lantern and the figure who bore it.

"Evening, misses," a voice said, male, middle-aged, and thick with Dormandy's seaside accent.

It was Dahlya who had the presence of mind to answer back, the tremor of her voice barely noticeable. "Good evening," she returned. "Did we trespass on the stairs of your basement? Do forgive us. If you could point us in the direc—"

"Not my stairs, not my basement," he said. The contrast of light against the darkness had balanced a bit in Tryss's vision and she could see the man give a polite tip of his hat as he said, "But I was looking for you, misses. If you could just follow me, we'll see what we can do to get you out of this mess."

Her heart flipped, unsure if she should feel hope or terror. Run, that was what she would normally do. Run right after a flying kick to his face or a jab into his ribs. But she couldn't hope for those kinds of reflexes in her current state, and any disappearing wouldn't help Dahlya.

"Thank you," Dahlya said, voice stiff as her posture as she slowly rose, pulling Tryss up along with her. "But before we follow you anywhere, first I must ask exactly who you are."

"Just a messenger, ma'am, just a messenger. But the man in charge wants you both safe, make no mistake about that."

22

As prisons went, it was a very nice prison. Yellow floral paper patterned the walls and a soft carpet hugged the wooden floor. There were two couches and a seat filled with round pillows and soft blankets. The hearth was merry with a fresh, crackling fire, and even the chandelier and sconces had new candles flickering inside their glass coverings.

But it was still a prison. Tryss was certain of that. She turned and glared at the man who had brought them in. At least he had the courtesy to stay outside the doorway, even if his hand on the knob suggested he was about to close it and leave them inside.

"You work for whoever hired Taersidel, don't you?" she said. "So who wanted me captured in the first place? For what purpose?"

"Never you mind that, missus," the man said with another tip of his cap. She had half a mind to dart over and knock the cap off. "I'm paid to guard, not to answer questions."

And then he stepped back, closed the door, and the sounds of a lock and bolt rattled into place.

"We should have made a break for it," Tryss muttered.

"You know we couldn't have outrun him," Dahlya replied. "Anyway, I had hoped he was involved with Errance or Coren somehow."

"He would have said so," she snapped. "He had "stooge" written all over him."

"I'm sorry," Dahlya said quietly. "If I could have thought of another idea in time, perhaps we wouldn't be here. But, I mean, we were not getting anywhere with your brother, and I feel we have a better chance of being found in Dormandy than up North."

A shudder coursed through Tryss as if just the mention of the North had brought its icy winds into the house. "Don't blame yourself," she said. "We at least have more assets here than the bare room Taers kept us in." Not that the assets were very useful. There was no fire poker or ash shovel, more the pity. The pillows and blankets might be used in strangulation and suffocation, but only if the said person using them was very strong or had their target already unconscious. Instead, the pillows and blankets seemed to be coaxing her over to collapse in their depths. She shoved back against that temptation. "We'll just have to breathe a little and look for our next chance of escape…"

"Tryss." Her name was spoken sharply, far sharper than any tone Dahlya had ever used. "I don't want you to be thinking about escapes right now."

Tryss blinked and took a step back.

Dahlya looked her dead in the eyes as she said, "What I want you to think about is how all of this is affecting your body and the little body that is inside you. This whole thing is exhausting you, and I need you healthy for delivery, which by the way—" Her voice rose in pitch. "—could be any day now. We are with strangers and we can't afford to anger them with escape attempts. So far their treatment is not malicious. From what I've seen, this feels like a ransom situation."

"Ransom? Why pay people to kidnap me if they just want ransom money?"

"The king of Aselvia is wealthy by any standard. Rendar made many smart deals and left Errance quite an inheritance. They could easily ask a price that would cover whatever the capture cost and still be left with a nice fortune. So either Errance will pay the ransom or he will soon show up here and make them regret they ever asked. Whichever the case, I know you will see him soon. Please, Tryss. I'll keep you and Baby safe here, I promise, until he comes. You just can't keep straining yourself like this, it's too risky, it's too—" Her voice broke, and Tryss stared, appalled, as her dear friend's soft sage eyes filled with tears. "I already lost one queen in childbirth. She too was a very good friend. I can't let that happen again. For now, we should just rest. Rest and keep you well."

For a moment, Tryss continued to stare at her as if preparing to argue. But she couldn't really argue against that last bit and against those tears. Her shoulders sagged and she stared down at her hands in her lap. All the energy in her body drained like wind leaving sails. "I…I don't want to rest. The last thing I want is to bear this child in captivity. But you're right…I am tired."

"Then prop your feet up and take a nap," Dahlya said. The brightness was already returning to her face, that miraculous optimism that was always so contagious. She led Tryss over to the couch and eased her down onto it, sliding a pillow underneath her heels.

It did feel marvelous just to lie still and breathe and not think about what to do next. Maybe sleep was the best thing.

Her eyes were beginning to close when Flyfar hopped into her vision, and she raised a weak hand to tickle the feathers of his breast.

Wait.

Flyfar.

"Dah!" Tryss struggled to sit upright. "He's back! Flyfar is back!"

"Then Errance has your message." Relief spread over Dahlya's face. "Do you think he was the one that interfered with the exchange tonight?"

Tryss felt her stomach drop. Had she done the wrong thing by running away? Had she missed her husband by the narrowest of threads? "I don't know. I wish I could write him."

Flyfar dropped a small piece of paper in her lap, and she seized it with the ferocity of a wildcat. The ink was smudged but the words were still legible. A single line.

I love you.

The words blurred in her vision, and she folded the paper up with much more care than she'd ripped it open.

"He sends his love," she said softly. It was more than enough to fill and burst her heart, leaving it empty all over again. "I wish I knew where he was."

"He probably thinks any information would be dangerous until we can update him of our surroundings and captors," Dahlya reminded.

"I suppose all I can do is send another ribbon," she said with sinking shoulders.

"Wait a moment. I will say this for our mysterious captors—so far, they are actually better hosts than your own brother. I think I shall see if I can ask for paper and ink. While I'm at it, I'll order some food."

"Food?" Tryss's chin jerked up just as it was lulling down towards her chest. "Do we dare take food from them?"

"It's either that or starve," Dahlya said in that practical tone of hers. "I'll take small bites first, and we'll see how it affects me." She strode towards the door and gave a sharp rap upon the wood. When there was no answer, she knocked again, more insistent.

After a few seconds, the door cracked cautiously open and a man peered through. It was not the same man who had brought them. Tryss had thought that man's politeness infuriating, but she found she actually preferred it to this one's scowl and the way his eyes kept darting around as if expecting to be attacked. "What is it?" he grumbled.

"We're awfully bored," Dahlya said, tilting her head. "Do you think we might have some pen and paper to draw? I'm an artist, you see, and we would—"

"No paper. No pens."

"But—"

"No buts."

"Then I would like two cups of hot water with some lemon and any soft bread you might have on hand," Dahlya said, sweet as honey. "Scrambled eggs, fully cooked. In fact, I would like a list of what you carry in your larder so I know what to order and what to request that you have on hand."

The man stared at her, his jaw going slack as if he could not believe what he was hearing.

"What?" Dahlya set her hand on her hip. "You're holding a pregnant woman captive. Don't tell me you didn't see this coming."

It took some time before Errance could be pulled away from searching the streets and calling for Tryss. Coren looked sorry to stop him at all, but he made it clear that Tryss would not be found in such a way.

Errance knew that, deep inside. Even if the rest of him couldn't accept it.

Remrant and the mercenaries were waiting back by the carriages, guarding the broker that Coren had caught during the fight. The man was trussed hand and foot and a grimy gag bound his mouth.

Errance started towards him, but Remrant held out an arm.

"Not here," the man said. "Patrol officers should be coming after this ruckus, and while we have our curfew passes, I'd just as soon not try to explain all of this to them. Let's get back to the house, and we can question him there. Ban, Garis, load the prisoner in the second carriage and keep a tight hold on him."

That drive back was one of the longest spans of minutes in Errance's life, at least outside of Tertorem. He said nothing, so neither did Coren or Remrant.

When they pulled up to Albine Avenue, the street was quiet as one might expect in a city where civilians were not supposed to just wander about. The second carriage with the prisoner was already parked in front of Remrant's house, but they did not unload him until Remrant Cole had unlocked his front door and gestured for them to bring the man inside.

Only two of the hired mercenaries, the ones he'd called by name, climbed out of the carriage, dragging their captive along. The carriage drove off after that, dismissed by some prior agreement and payment.

"Garis and Ban." Remrant said again, but this time as an introduction to Errance and Coren. "Two hired brutes who have served me on multiple occasions. They can question him about the queen's whereabouts in the basement, if you like."

"Oh, so you have your own thugs too?" Coren said, raising a sharp brow. "I really shouldn't be surprised."

"No, you shouldn't," Remrant agreed lightly. "The matter of money has started wars many a time, so of course banks should have their own resources for protection."

"I don't need anyone to do the questioning for me, I'll question him myself," Errance growled. "And I don't need a basement, the parlor will suffice."

"I don't want blood, spittle, or vomit on my rug."

"It won't need to go that far." Errance's eyes were narrowed into slits, zeroed in on the approaching captive. Baris and Gan barely reached the threshold of the door before he reached out, yanked the man out of their grip, and dragged him into the parlor himself.

The maid, Beki, was nowhere to be seen, which was all the better. A few wall sconces were still lit, and the moon had cast a glow through the windows onto the floor. Errance shoved the man down to his knees in one of those frames of moonlight and ripped the gag from his mouth.

"Who hired you?" he snarled, eyes burning with the bluest of fires.

"I—I—" The man sputtered and choked, his gaze spinning to everything in the room but the elf standing right in front of him. "I don't know. I wasn't in charge, I was just told to be there."

"Why were you there? For what reason did the chemas bring those women to you?"

"Gore, I didn't know skinblenders were even involved in this! It was just supposed to be a hostage exchange, cut and dry. We're not the ones who wanted them; we were just bringing the girls to a different location."

"And where was that?"

"The captain had those orders, not me!"

"You know more than you're saying," Errance said, taking a step forward and catching the man by the collar. "And believe me, I know methods on how to make a man talk."

"I don't know!" The man was practically blubbering, his skin turning a shade grey. "I'm not paid enough to know things! I'm just some muscle!"

"Muscle, eh?" Errance's other hand slipped around the man's arm, squeezing at the socket of the shoulder. "Doesn't feel like muscle. Feels more like bones and ligaments to me."

"Reyid." The name came out forced, as if Coren had only just remembered to use the alias as opposed to his real name. When Errance looked back, he found his cousin standing in the doorway, arms crossed.

Reluctantly, Errance released his hold on the prisoner and followed his cousin out to the hall. Garis and Ban moved past him into the parlor to secure the hostage.

"Calm down," Coren said, the moment they'd walked down the hall far enough to not be heard. "He doesn't know, that much is obvious, and you don't need to be doing anything you'll regret."

"Sure that I'll regret it?"

Coren gave him a look, and Errance turned away from him with a huff.

Remrant came down the hall just then, a lit chamberstick in his hand, and looked them both over with a critical eye. "No luck?" he said. "As I said before, my men can press for answers."

"Coren is right, the man doesn't know a thing," Errance bit out. He hadn't wanted to admit it, but the clueless terror in the man's eyes had been no lie. "Which means we are once again without a lead." How could this have happened? She'd been right there. He'd *seen* her.

"Taersidel is an infamous asset in business done by shadow. When he appears again, I will hear of it," Remrant said.

"You will hear of it too late," Errance snapped. He ran a finger against the ridge of his brow, fighting the pounding headache that had taken root.

It really had seemed that Taersidel was just going to sell Tryss off to those men, but there was still a part of him that struggled believing it. He didn't know why. It wasn't like he hadn't seen enough betrayal. But still. Taers had been her older brother. His very role should have been of protection.

Now that the deal had fallen through, would they head straight to the North? Or would they try to find their contacts again? And if they were staying in the city, could they even be found now that they knew someone was seeking to stop them?

His finger paused in its relentless rubbing. They knew someone was seeking to stop them. And while Coren had taken the precaution to disguise them, Errance had not bothered to disguise his voice. There was a possibility—a very high possibility—that Taers had recognized his call.

His hand reached down into his pocket, finding the letter from Aselvia there and Alludium's ring inside.

"I just need a moment alone," he muttered, shoving through a nearby door to the next room over. Fortunately, neither Coren nor Remrant attempted to follow him. Their voices, thick with tension, murmured through the wall like drain water in the pipes.

Errance took a quick look around the office he'd retreated into. Ah, good. Plenty of blank paper on that desk and a quill next to an inkpot. He grabbed a parchment and scribbled, *If I'm not back by morning, assume things have gone wrong.*

Coren was just going to love that.

Slapping the paper on top of the stack at the desk, he unlocked the nearest window and slipped out into the night's embrace.

23

Blessed were the few who walked the rooftops of Dormandy. Perhaps only the birds, the chimney-sweeps, and the occasional thief caught such a view as the endless terrain of shingled peaks and sharp-pointed towers.

The stars hung above, veiled by the passing cloud and plume of smoke. Though they did not feel so near or bright as they did from the towers of Aselvia, seeing them still brought to Errance's mind the tales that Tellie described of her travels in the Unseen and how his celestial kin walked among the constellations. He wondered if they watched him even now.

The stars were mirrored dimly below him by the thousands of amber lights scattered from the city windows.

In Errance's perspective, it was pure insanity to pack so many people so tightly together, no better than a prison. But it was unexpectedly convenient when it came to finding a pathway high above the city streets. So he walked through the stars upon the rooftop spines, only having to make the occasional leap from building to building. His light footsteps hardly stirred the roosting birds, his form barely noticed by the fluttering bat. His silhouette cast not a care in the world as it meandered from university steeple to church bell tower.

But he knew up here against the dark sky, he would be watched.

Watched by a particular sort of people.

A soft sound, no more than a brush against the wooden surface of the roof ridge. Nothing but his elvish hearing and ready expectation would have noticed it.

He waited a breath more and then dropped. He spun in a low crouch, left hand snaking out into the air. His forearm clashed with an incoming strike, and that positioning gave him his target. His right hand struck at the center, catching in fabric and quickly scrambling up to find the throat. He threw his weight forward, driving the unseen body down, pressed against the ridge under his knee. His blow shook the chema's concentration and they flickered into focus enough for him to find the knife and pry it from their hand.

"Come any closer and this one dies," he snarled, flipping the knife against the chema's neck.

A moment of hesitation and then two more chema appeared. One just in his peripheral vision behind him, one perched on the chimney just ahead, bow drawn and ready to fire. They could have already fired and knocked him off their friend. But they hadn't. Which meant they wanted him alive.

"Taersidel wishes to speak with you," the archer said.

"What a coincidence. I also wish to speak with him. So since we're on the same page, how about you put that bow down, I'll let this one live, and you can lead me to him without unpleasantries." He eased off his captive's body, and they scrambled backwards, off-balance from the hard hit.

The archer lowered his bow but kept the arrow nocked. He flicked his head, striding south along the rooftop ridge. Errance followed, the other chemas melting into the path behind him. They were far too comfortable with constant camouflage. Tryss said it took stamina to maintain it, but they wore it like a favorite coat.

No other words were exchanged as they led him from the shops and living quarters to the university grounds. There, marked by the tallest bell-tower in the city, stood the university's magnificent cathedral, set apart from the other buildings. He wondered if they intended to drop down to earth and walk in like civilized folk before he noticed the thin black line cutting across the sky. Someone might have seen it during the day, maybe, if they'd happened to look up, but at night no one in the streets could possibly spot it this high.

The chema sprang onto it, an elf's only equal when it came to balance, and started nimbly running across the considerable distance from the apartment roof to the cathedral's parapet.

Errance chose not to question how long it had been since he'd walked across anything so narrow and trusted on instinct alone. A few moments of held breath and then he was over.

He followed his guide's path up one of the buttresses to the second roof and scaled the slope to the tower. The stone wall was rough with enough edges and cracks to provide a ladder up to one of the tower's enormous windows. It was already unlatched, and when Errance slipped inside, he found wooden steps just below his feet. The creaking above him suggested the chema had already started up the stair and he followed all the way to the bell chamber.

A cold wind blew through the open arches, threading through the thick ropes that hung from the giant bells above. The room he stood in appeared empty, the ropes dangling their ends on the wooden floor. Another small ladder was in the shadows to his left, leading up to a walkway just below the open arches. He watched the darkness there, waiting.

The flame appeared first. With a sharp hiss, it snapped to life in the darkness, then steadied into a persistent ember suspended in air followed by smoke that spiraled forth on an exhaled breath.

Taersidel materialized from shadow up on the ledge, the slim cigarette poised between his fingers. "So. Look who finally crawled out of his gilded castle. I guess Tryss wasn't wrong about that. At least."

"What do you want, Taersidel?" Errance folded his arms, tilting his head to the side. "What is it going to take for me to see her again?"

"Now that's an interesting question. How much would you be willing to give?"

"Quite a lot." He cast another look over the man's pose, breathed in another dose of the tension surrounding him. "That is, if you actually had her."

Even in the dark, Taersidel couldn't hide the flash of surprise that stiffened his body. So much for master of disguise. After a few moments, he softly chuckled, the echoes of the sound stirring the tower like tiny bells. "And here I thought that you were the ones who had taken her. That is, until my men reported you just walking across Dormandy's upper rooftops like some lost pigeon."

"So if neither of us has her…" Errance's heart clenched as the rest of his mind caught up with his conclusion. "…then the men you were dealing with must have taken her." He watched as Taersidel came to the same conclusion, snuffing the end of his cigarette against the wall, arms also folding across his chest as if to tightly contain his rage.

"I was never planning to give her over to them, you know," Taersidel growled. "If you hadn't interfered, she'd still be safe."

"Funny. I was just thinking how if you hadn't kidnapped her, she definitely would be." He shook his head like that could shake the growing sense of anger and terror that was clawing up his spine. "Who are they, Taersidel? Who hired you? And why?"

"We didn't ask. Not a mercenary's business. But if they think they can just take her without payment, their treachery runs deeper than I thought."

"Oh," Errance said, flaring his eyes. "You mean you were backstabbed by the people you were planning to backstab? How tragic for you."

If chemas had the ability to turn their surroundings cold as ice, Taersidel was definitely using it. "I could have you killed here and now, Errance." Thin. Brittle.

He shrugged. Bold claim. Probably legitimate. But he didn't feel like dying yet. "You could try. But then you'd be cutting Tryss's chances of rescue in half. For all your pride, I'm sure even you can see the reason in that. If not, I have no more time to waste with you. But if you want, we can meet up again and exchange what information we've gathered in a few days. It could help us find her faster."

"As if I would help you?" The sneer was back to his voice. "All I see is benefit for you, but you have nothing I want."

"Don't I?" Errance folded his arms in reflection of the figure facing him down. "You left Alludium in Aselvia. And she is our prisoner now.

Didn't you say something about her being your lover? Unless of course that was also part of the lie."

That smug self-assurance faltered. "Liar," he said. "She'd never be caught."

"Really." Errance reached into his coat pocket and found the small envelope inside. He tore it open and held the ring aloft.

Taersidel stared, but even he couldn't see detail from that distance. After a moment, he stepped out onto the thick rafters, grabbed one of the bell ropes, and came sliding down. His boots hit the wooden planks with a crack, and the next instant, his hand was flashing out to catch the ring from Errance's grasp.

Errance sidestepped, pulling the ring back into the cavity of his fist. "Don't even think about it."

"It could be any ring." Anger gleamed in Taersidel's eyes now, but concern as well, as evidenced by the way he did not immediately just disappear and attack.

"It isn't." He held up the ring again, ready to snatch it away.

But Taersidel only stared, the line of his jaw hardening into a ridge. A breath, still smelling of smoke, hissed from between his teeth. "What do you plan to do with her?" he asked at length.

"She will remain our prisoner as long as Tryss remains missing. If you will search for Tryss with the intention of returning her to me, then once my wife and I are back home, I will release Alludium back to you."

Taersidel's cheek constricted, and he turned to walk a few steps away. When he looked back, the starry shine of his eyes had hardened to lead. "Well played, elf king, well played." He sighed and stuffed his hands into his pockets. "I suppose at this point my interest in keeping both Alludium and Tryss unharmed hangs in your favor. Very well. I'll be your spy in this. But mind you, you have to play fair. Whatever information you find of Tryss comes to me as well, because I might be able to follow it places you won't. And you will return Alludium to me once this is done, or I will haunt every dream until the nightmare kills you in your sleep."

For all that, Errance didn't know if he could believe him. It all depended on the hope that Taersidel truly did care for his lover more than his own ends. He cared for her a little, Errance guessed, but possibly not enough.

Still, the bargain was the best he could do for now.

Maybe, just maybe, it meant something.

"Istallir," Taersidel called out to one of the chemas lurking in the shadows. "See the king back to Albine Avenue." He smiled at Errance, proud to flaunt how he already knew his address of residence within a few hours of knowing he was even in the city. "We wouldn't want him getting lost, now would we?"

"No," Errance said, mouth curling. "I suppose we would not."

24

Warmth began to color the pale morning light inside Remrant Cole's parlor. The teakettle was whistling over the fire and the smell of freshly baked scones drifted out from the covered platter that the maid, Beki, had brought out from the kitchen.

A strip of pale cloth huddled in the center of Errance's clenched hand. Another ribbon brought from Flyfar, another promise that he had made contact with Tryss, that she was still alive. But still unable to give him any information or lead to her whereabouts. He'd sent the bird back again, hoping against hope that something in her situation would change so that she could write him with every detail he so desperately needed.

"Nothing," he muttered aloud. "All this and we are left with nothing. Not even Taersidel knows where to go next."

Coren shot him a sour little look at the mention of that name, still not over the fact that he'd been left behind, even if Errance had returned well before morning and without a single scratch. It had taken some time to get him to stop scolding long enough to share the details about the meeting with the chemas.

Remrant, on the other hand, had been very calm, hands folded under his chin as he listened first and asked questions second, taking down small notes here and there. There were various files and reports spread out upon the table beneath his hands, but they might as well have been scribbles for all the usefulness they contained.

"None of that pessimism, Reyid. We can still find a lead, even before the chema creature," Remrant said, shuffling through the papers on the desk he bent over. "Until someone comes forward to negotiate with a hostage contract, we can dig deeper into who is behind it all. It is unlikely at this point that the queen has been taken by common traffickers, but still, those rings very well might have heard who wanted her and why. We can start there."

Errance breathed in. Held it. Breathed out. He could do this. He would do it. Tryss would be fine. He had to believe that. "Good. I've wanted to pay a visit to that kind of scum anyway."

"Of course we can't do it without permission, not in this city. We'll need clearance with the Governor. I shall get us an appointment with him this afternoon."

"You think he'll agree?"

Remrant gave him a look as pointed as the quill pen he poked in his direction. "Do remember who you're talking to. If you're going to come with me, however, you will need a new outfit." The feather of the quill gave a flourish as if it was some magic wand that would produce the new clothes then and there.

Errance pinched the bridge of his nose, ignoring the smug look that was forming on his cousin's face. "Great," he muttered. "Not this again."

So long as it wasn't anything purple and strung with bling.

When setting out to save his wife, Errance hadn't pictured spending any time wondering what to wear.

Not that he was the one doing the wondering. He left that mostly up to Coren and Remrant when they visited the high-end gentlemen's boutique in Dormandy's upper class ring. They would grab things off the shelves or rack and send him off to a closet to try it on. The only time he really paid attention to anything was when Remrant tried to hand him a red waistcoat embroidered in gold. He'd refused it flatly.

In the end, after far more debate than he considered necessary, he found himself sitting in a carriage on its way to the Governor's House, wearing a seal-blue tailcoat with ivory embroidery over a light gold waist-coat, white trousers, and dark knee-high boots. The ivory froth of an ascot felt far too tight around his neck, but whenever he reached up to tug at it, Coren would reach over and slap his hand away. Errance might have slapped him back if Remrant hadn't been watching them from the other side.

The black iron gates spread wide to let them in, and several servants came hurrying out to line the walkway, bent in a bow, grand door already opened.

"You would think they were welcoming a king," Coren murmured to Errance, with a brief chuckle at the irony.

Remrant stepped out of the carriage the very moment it ground to a halt, his cane clicking on stone with ringing authority. The servant waiting at the door bowed lower as the three of them ascended the stairs and then led them through the mansion to an enormous parlor.

"Please make yourself comfortable," the distinguished servant intoned. "I shall inform the governor of your arrival."

Remrant was holding one of those little hand clocks, the sound of its ticking quite loud in the otherwise silent chamber. "Indeed," he said only, snapping the gold case shut and taking a seat on the nearest sofa.

Errance remained standing, pivoting in a slow circle as he glanced about the room. Everything was ornate, from the ceiling to the carvings, the statues, the potted greenery, the upholstered seats. The entire wall encircling them was a painting, which might have made the room dark, except the tiles and ceiling were white, and there were quite a few mirrors which reflected the light shining in from the tall windows and the candles ensconced in a chandelier.

"What is with the nude people painted all over the walls?" Errance muttered.

"Nude elves, you mean," Coren whispered back.

"What?" Errance spun back to look at the paintings he'd avoided observing directly and found pointy ears on each of the figures dancing through the woods.

"Yes, it is quite popular in the upper class to portray the fantastical lives of elves as we clearly all prance about in nothing but transparent scarves."

Amazing. Even more amazing that Leoren had never mentioned it. Apparently, he didn't see it worth starting a war over.

"Master Remrant Cole, what an unexpected surprise!" A stout man came bustling through the entryway, his smile both gracious and nervous at once. "I do hope nothing serious is the matter for such a sudden visit."

"Not for me or for you, good governor," Remrant said smoothly, not bothering to rise from his chair. "But I wish to introduce you to an acquaintance and friend who is in need of your assistance. Governor Dolfen, please meet the distinguished Lord Reyid of Aselvia."

The man's mouth opened and closed several times as he turned startled eyes to Errance. After looking him up and down once or thrice, he managed, "Of Aselvia? Reyid, you said? I don't believe I've ever had the pleasure of meeting you! You know, I always tell Ambassador Leoren how we would love to visit your homeland."

"I am sure," Errance replied, "But you know, you must understand that we prefer to maintain—" he flared a hand towards the painted walls "—the privacy of our lifestyle."

The governor's cheeks colored just a bit, and he pressed a small cough into his hand. "Do you come on behalf of Ambassador Leoren?" he managed.

"I come on behalf of the king."

That took him back a step. "What…what can we do for Aselvia, my lord? As your longest running ally, we gladly will provide whatever assistance you need."

Big promises for knowing nothing about the situation. "A citizen of Aselvia has gone missing," Errance said, tapping his finger against the wooden ledge of a sofa. "We believe it to be a case of kidnapping, and they might be held even within this very city."

"What! I've not heard even a whisper of this! Although one of your artisans in my employment was suddenly called away with very little explanation. Is this perhaps the reason?"

"Partly," Errance said, not bothering to explain Kelm's departure was triggered by a completely different reason. He had not forgotten that report about this governor. This governor who was far, far too eager to enter Aselvia, on another's prompting no less.

He paused, considering that. Perhaps the two things were connected. They still didn't know who had written the letter to the governor or why. Was it possible that Governor Dolfen was in league with the chemas who had kidnapped her? Or perhaps the actual instigator of the kidnapping?

With his mind spinning, he had not continued, so Remrant cleared his throat and went on instead.

"Governor Dolfen, we understand there are laws in your city against human slavery and prostitution, but in every city, such underground rings exist. We would like to question any prisoners of this trade your police have taken."

"Oh." The man looked uncomfortable. "Well, I don't know who my chief of police has incarcerated, but I'm not sure you'll find many of that sort in our prisons."

"Don't you bother to stop crime?" Errance snapped, coming out of his daze.

"Of course, lord, of course! It is just that prostitution can be a very messy business, very hard to dig up and stop, and my law officers have had their hands full of so many other matters, and—"

"I believe you told me that great efforts were being made to improve your police force," Remrant interrupted, eyes narrowing. Those eyes were somehow intimidating even set in such a studious face. The gold rimmed glasses only added a sharp glint to the overall effect.

If the man had looked uncomfortable before, he looked downright pale now. "I did, and there is! It's just that with the new laws and curfews, we have been spread thin."

"In that case," Remrant said. "Since you are understaffed and underfunded, I have an alternative solution. A license. A license granting Lord Reyid and myself the clearance to search out and arrest the criminals in this trade and question them in pursuit of the missing citizen."

"I—" Governor Dolfen blinked, but whatever arguments he had about this faded as quickly as they came. "As you say, Master Cole. I will have one drawn up immediately. Let me provide a raid force to accompany you. I shall have a message sent to one of my captains to prepare a squad."

Errance shifted in his seat, spine stiffening to a rod. There were still things he did not understand about human society, but he was quite sure that most governments did not just hand out licenses to foreign and private agents to enforce their own domestic law, even when trying to establish good relations.

He was missing something here, something he felt certain should be obvious.

"We thank you for your assistance," Remrant said, tipping in a slight bow.

"Not at all, any favor for our Aselvian allies and the master of our bank," the governor said, waving his hand.

There. There it was.

Pulling his lower lip in with a slow breath, Errance flicked a glance in Coren's direction, and guessed from his cousin's blank expression that he had not heard of this either. In a way, they probably should have looked into it already. Finding out such information couldn't have been hard, but there just hadn't been time.

He knew Remrant's position had to be high, but for whatever reason he hadn't expected him to be at the head. He hadn't even thought of one man holding mastery over a bank, it wasn't as if the Cole name was attached to it.

Good lord, no wonder the governor was falling over himself in an effort to please the person who kept his city's fortune secure.

The rest of Remrant's negotiations with the governor passed by in a fog for Errance. He knew that a lawyer had come in and then later a captain of the Dormandy guard and between them a license and agreement was made. The whole thing felt like it took hours, and his throat was dry by the end of it even despite being given drinks and refreshments by the staff.

The sun was beginning to sink behind the stone towers of the city when they boarded the carriage for the return to Cole's residence.

"Tomorrow," Remrant said, as if knowing he would have to summarize everything that had been agreed. "The guard has kept watch on a particular brothel, and we will meet them early morning at the police headquarters to accompany the raid from there. So I suggest we rest well tonight. Now, about dinner—"

"Coren and I will take our meal in our quarters," Errance said shortly.

Remrant gave him a look of surprise, almost disappointment, but nodded. "Very well, to each their own respite."

Beki had the door open to greet them when the carriage pulled up. Coren bounded inside with a smile and a tip of his hat to her, but Errance paused to wait for Remrant. It was not often that the man showed any age beyond the silver of his hair, but he was a bit slower to climb in and out of carriages and took the steps with a careful grasp on his cane.

Errance stood before the door, his hands stuffed into the pockets of his tailcoat. "You failed to mention you were the owner of the bank," he said as Remrant reached him.

"Yes, well, I try to live as a humble businessman, nothing more. What difference does my position make?" he said, forced to come to a halt now that his way forward was blocked.

"I don't like being lied to."

"To be fair, it wasn't a lie, just not the total truth. You could have noticed if you were paying attention."

Errance opened his mouth, then shut it again. Fair point. He had no business getting offended over this when *he* was the one lying about identity. "You carry a great deal of weight with the governor," he said instead.

"I suppose that is natural since the bank holds most of his wealth," Remrant replied with a chuckle. "Why does this interest you?"

"There was a letter," Errance said. "An intercepted letter to the governor of Dormandy. Insisting that they reach a stronger alliance with Aselvia. It was marked only with a strange symbol. Was that you?"

The man's face was almost always neutral, making it hard to tell if his expression now was surprise or amusement. "It was."

"You were that insistent to reach us?"

"Businessmen are always insistent, Reyid, please remember that. Why bring this up now? Did you think the letter could have been a clue to the queen's disappearance?"

"I did."

"I am sorry to be a disappointment then. I do not think we will find any foul play on the governor's part. He is a fairly simple man." He drummed his fingers upon his knuckles. "Now are you letting me into my own house, or should I plan on sleeping out on the street?"

Errance stepped aside with a wry smile, but the questions in his mind were far from satisfied. Even so, he couldn't pin which question he needed an answer to the most.

"I'm going out," Errance announced as he finished the evening meal prepared by the cook. It had probably been delicious; too bad he was too distracted to taste it.

"Thank you for actually telling me this time," Coren said, his mouth caught halfway between a smile and a scowl. "Where to?"

"The Grand Library."

"You do know that curfew is due in less than two hours? Unless you are planning to run the roofs again or skulk the streets or even, heaven forbid, ask Remrant for one of those convenient curfew passes he keeps about."

"No, I have no intention of asking Remrant," Errance said. "In fact, I am going out because of him. It is strange to you too, is it not, this influence he possesses? I want to know exactly how this bank came about and how it started controlling governments. Furthermore, I want to know the extent of that control. I doubt the library will have all those answers, but they should have something. It might drive me mad to exert energy over something other than Tryss, but I want to know exactly who I'm dealing with in this search for her."

"You want to know what he intends with this alliance he keeps pressing," Coren said, nodding to himself. "Let me come with you. With as little time as is left in the day, it would be better for both of us to search for information."

Errance nodded, shrugging into a coat. "Let's go."

There was one remarkable difference between libraries in Aselvia and libraries in Dormandy—here, it was dark. The tall, long, and closely-cramped shelves blocked out almost all illumination from the high windows and even the lamps on the walls. It was almost as if they wanted you to light a candle and bring it with you. Which seemed like a fire hazard, but Errance was doing it anyway.

"This is taking too long," he muttered as he returned yet another boring tome detailing the taxes and economy of some bygone year to the shelf. "We need to know if the books we're looking for even exist."

"We could ask the nice little old man up at the desk," Coren suggested, not looking up from whatever volume he paged through.

Errance glanced back the way they'd come. "You mean the one who hasn't acknowledged anybody from the moment they've arrived?"

"Yes, that one. It must be an awfully good book he's reading."

Stuffing back a sigh, Errance tucked the current book he held under his arm and walked back down the aisles to the circular wooden desk in the center of the floor. It was apparently bad form to speak loud in a library, but none of the other people passing by had gotten any attention from this attendant by whispering.

"Do you know anything about the Cole family who established the All Nations Bank?" he said, no suggestion of a whisper to be found.

The old man sniffed and turned the page of his book, the paper peeling away with a rasp.

Helpful. Very helpful. Errance cleared his throat, tone sharpening. "How about history of the bank in general?"

One scraggly brow lifted above the rim of spectacles.

"Perhaps even a record of laws passed in the last, oh, century or so?"

With an annoyed sigh, the man finally looked up at him. His brow folded into several wrinkles as he took him in. "What has you so insistent at this hour? Don't you know we are closing soon?"

Right, he had to remember he looked young to this fellow, so he attempted to adopt an innocent, bright-eyed expression and said, "I'm a university student. I'm doing a paper on the subject. I, um...." He paused, scrambling to remember what Leoren had said about the practices of the university here. "The deadline is approaching, and I'm running out of time."

Muttering something about the irresponsible youth of today, the man opened a drawer and pulled out a catalog, flipping through it with enough fire to burn the paper. "Door on the left, up the stair." He slammed the drawer shut and gave him a look. A look that said, *go away and stop bothering me, it's late at night, and I'm reading.*

Errance turned around to find Coren by his side, grinning of all things.

"What?" he hissed, as they started for the stairs.

"You know, most times, I would take point on things like talking to the librarian, but I'm learning it's much more fun to just sit back and see what you come up with."

The air smelled stale in the room through the door on the left, as if nobody had bothered to come inside for some time. The curtains were drawn, so Errance was forced to hold the candle dangerously close to the spines as he perused the titles.

"My word, it actually says *The All Nations Bank: History and Achievements*," Coren said from a shelf behind him.

"If it existed, why was it so hard for him to tell us?" Errance hurried over, irritation prickling his scalp.

"Like I said, must have been reading a good book. I'm sure he's had enough of irresponsible university students with imposing deadlines."

Rather than running downstairs to the chairs and tables, they sat on the floor and paged through the volume. It began with the account of how especially enormous goldmines were discovered.

"While the Great Western Cliffs spark debates between history, religion, and myth, early kingdoms of men soon discovered them to be a source of wealth," Coren read aloud.

"That's referring to the Celestial Cleft, is it not?" Errance said, wrinkling his nose. "What debate is there to be had about it? Are some humans unsure if the Celestials existed or not?" But why was he getting offended about that? It was better that the celestial elves were beyond the ambition of any mortal mind.

"Let's not lose focus," Coren said, tapping the book. "Anyway, it says here that while the cliff sides have never been scaled or mined, people could see many ore veins running through it, and mines were tunneled into the land at the foot of the cliffs. Wars and political upheaval changed the owners of the mines many times, but the largest mines today are owned by the Cole Family, whose line can be traced to one of the last successful warlords."

"Brights, how do you read so fast."

Ignoring him, Coren adjusted the book onto his knees and flipped through the pages more comfortably, calling out bits of information as he went. "Recent generations of the Cole family bear little resemblance to their ancestor warlords, and have been distinguished citizens and leaders in the city of Meece."

Meece was about as far north a human kingdom could get without officially being part of the North. Errance remembered his father telling him how its origins had been one of the greatest stands of faith in Ayeshune during the Dark Days, but that over the centuries that faith had soured to a strict religious society that all but deified the Celestial Elves, and as such, Rendar had broken contact with them.

"Remrant doesn't seem like he has any Meece influence in his thinking," Errance said aloud. "The closest to religion he seems to get is swearing 'by gods' and I don't think he means anything by it."

"Meece was the first government to invest in the Cole gold mine, but over time, the family broke their citizenship and position in Meece," Coren went on, holding up a finger, "to become an independent estate and bank. Its untold wealth and influence grew till Dormandy, Korince, and even Oolum had much of their investments backed by the riches of the mines."

"Does it talk about them having an influence over laws being made? And what does it say about the family?" Errance craned over Coren's shoulder, but couldn't pick up anything with how fast the pages turned. "What's in it for them that a family should work so many generations towards that goal?"

"I don't know that it was a goal from the beginning, though it may have shifted to that at some point. Anyway, hold on, I'm getting close to recent years. Ah, I bet these are Remrant's parents, Howett and Enathine Cole. Yes, let's see, they were extremely active in securing more investments and trust in their bank in a time when economy was at a low and smaller banks needed loans to prevent runs, blah, blah blah. They lived in luxury till the year 1179 when—oh."

"Oh?" Errance squinted at the page, trying to see what had startled him so. "What do you mean 'oh'?"

"On Mries 30th, 1179, the Cole Estate burned down to the ground with Howett and Enathine inside. This incident was later concluded to be arson, although the arsonist was never found nor was his motive determined."

Errance silently stared at the words, a shiver passing through him at the thought of such a death. "And you think these were Remrant's parents?"

"The Cole Family's remaining heir is Remrant Cole, who was schooled at Dormandy University when his parents' estate burned down," Coren read, closing the book with a soft thud. "And that's the end. There's a tiny bit more discussion on the bank's future, but this book was written before Remrant rose to power."

Errance sat back, sifting it all over.

"I'm not certain exactly what age he is now, but if I were to guess, he was still a youth when it happened. I imagine it would have been hard on a lad, even if he'd been boarding away for some time."

Every time someone's grief involved parents, Errance felt the sting. Whether it was the loss or the complete lack of loving parents, the hole in his own heart ached with the memory.

"I didn't see anything in there that sheds light on our situation," he said dully.

Coren shook his head. "I didn't either. Just a bank being a bank, albeit a very ambitious one." He set the book back on the shelf and blew out his candle. "We have to get back before the bells ring the curfew hour. I'd guess we don't have much time left."

Even so, Errance didn't stand, and Coren sat back down beside him.

"We'll be sweeping the first brothel house tomorrow," Coren murmured, rubbing a hand down his face. "You're ready for that?"

"I'm ready for anything if it helps me find her."

"I know that. I just meant…" He hesitated. "It's not easy going into those kinds of places. The atmosphere is thick with a presence of bondage and ill souls. I don't want you to feel alone in there. I'll be with you every step."

"Thanks." For all the shortness of his reply, hearing that really did steady his heart. If he was honest, he wondered what going to a place of imprisonment might do to him, even now. But he would face whatever shadow the future could bring.

25

Errance was still awake. That was hardly surprising, but it did surprise him that he'd stayed in the palace living quarters rather than retire to his own private rooms. He sat at a small tea table on a veranda overlooking the garden, but there was no tea, and he did not look much at anything. Just sort of stared off into space.

The clink of two glasses caught the edge of his hearing and he turned his head to find Leoren standing alongside him, holding a steaming teapot in one hand and two cups in the other.

"How about something hot to drink?" his uncle offered.

"It's not exactly cold out," Errance retorted. Which was true, but it was hardly the warmest of summer nights either.

"Then how about something delicious and comforting to drink instead?" he said, not skipping a beat as he poured the tea into the cups. Sitting down, he gazed off across the moonlit gardenscape, listening to the crickets and the midnight breeze.

Errance didn't say anything more, but he did sip at the tea, even if still preoccupied by whatever fixated his thoughts.

"I'm glad Coren came back to celebrate his wedding with everyone here," Leoren went on. *"I always hoped my son would marry, and while I never dreamed it would be someone from the outside world, I must admit I've rarely seen such a happy couple."*

"Mm."

"What's on your mind, Errance?"

Errance did look at him then, although it was a sideways, appraising look. "Your son once asked me something very similar, and I'm sure he regretted it."

"I'm sure he did not if you actually told him anything."

Heaving a sigh, Errance leaned back. "Did he inherit good listening from you?"

"I don't know about that, but I will listen the best that I can."

In answer, he only threw him another glance, eyes questioning and uncertain. Wondering if it was too soon to trust him yet to that degree. But of the men whom Errance had grown up closely acquainted with, Leoren was the only survivor. True, he'd been close with Casara and Ah'mava, but they weren't somebody he would burden with his troubles now. And while Leoren had not been a favorite in his childhood, unlike General Reyin, he'd still always been there.

"I'm ninety years old and I'm unused to and uncomfortable with seeing people kiss, how's that for starters?" Errance said abruptly.

Leoren's mouth opened and closed as if he debated how to respond or was attempting not to laugh. "Well, I don't suppose that is exactly surprising," he replied, the words drawn out. "It's not like you were around many married couples even when you were a child. There was of course the household staff of the palace, but most married elves weren't showing open affection in front of you, at least not as boldly as Coren and Zizain."

"Daava never told me much about marriage, considering most elves do not marry young and I never showed interest in romance."

Leoren waited, somehow sensing the thought was not complete.

"The Darkness gave me a different kind of education altogether."

Leoren set the tea cup down with the weight of a sinking heart. "Oh."

"Tell me to stop."

"No, go on." Go on, even if this spoiled the good mood of the happy day.

"I see Coren and Zizain's happiness," Errance said, staring off into nothing again. "I see the love you and Aunt Casara share. I've seen the sweetness with which Tellie and Kelm look at each other. I see all these things and I know they are good. I've studied passages of the wisemen and the words of Ayeshune on the matters of marriage and love, and they tell me it is good. And yet." He raised one hand, elbow braced against the table, fingers poised as if to grasp something. "And yet I cannot reconcile it all with the disgust and shame that I am acquainted with. I know the Darkness's favorite thing is to pervert that which is good, and that his shadows are not true depictions, but I...don't think I can undo the damage they've done on me. I don't think—" His hand slowly curled into a fist. "I don't think I could even kiss anyone or be kissed without feeling hurt."

Leoren did not answer right away. Instead he took another few sips of tea, watching the stray petals circle in the miniature lake within his cup. After a few minutes, he finally spoke again. "I never knew the man who conceived me."

Errance didn't respond.

"I never knew him because he was an unknown soldier in the Dark Days that hurt my mother."

At that, Errance did turn, full-on this time, and look at him, throat constricting. For some reason, it had never occurred to him that such things had happened in the Dark Days. Well, of course, it would not have occurred to him until now, he had not been told before, and it was still only a few months since his return from Tertorem. He hadn't spent that time dwelling on a past he had not lived in.

"Later, she married the man I now call father for both safety and for provision," Leoren went on. "And she came to love him and they had two other children together, my half siblings. They don't live close by; they enjoy the quiet of the mountains, but whenever I see them together, I feel comfort in knowing that she is happy."

He met him eye for eye, a soft, sad smile resting on his lips. "I don't know what you went through, and I leave it up to you to decide if you ever tell me, but I am saying this because I want you to know that although damage of the body and mind feels irreparable, there still can be a future and a hope where love is found and possible. It takes time and trust in both another person and in Ayeshune, but you need not endure your wounds forever. They will heal. Scars, they may remain, but someone who loves you will accept whatever scars you bear."

His uncle had not been wrong. It had not been easy to give over such trust, even to Tryss who was nothing if not gentle and caring. But slowly, they'd mended together. Or not so slowly, as he'd expected far more years to pass before he could fully be a husband, let alone a father. And for certain, he doubted his maturity and stability as both even now, but he'd taken the risk.

He'd chosen love over fear. And he would not go back.

Perhaps it was Ayeshune's prompting that had sent that memory so vividly into his mind as he sat in the rocking carriage, knowing it delved them deeper into the dregs of the city, where there was far more fear and shame than love.

The carriage that drove them was unmarked and tattered, but large enough for himself, Coren, Remrant, and the police captain. The larger force of the police entrusted to them for the raid would travel in a similarly unmarked storage wagon, enclosed on all sides with oiled, grunge-colored canvas like a box.

With a jarring stumble, the carriage came to a stop, and Errance peeked out the curtain to the street beyond at the reported brothel house.

It did not look like any establishment run by the corrupt elite, that was for certain. Merely a grey-planked, three-story tenant house like many others he'd passed through the lower rings of the city.

The pang of doubt that they would find out anything about Tryss's disappearance here twisted his stomach, but there was nothing for it, they were already here. These ears would be down to the ground; it was possible rumors had slithered through the shadows.

"It's just standing in town like this?" Errance glanced about at the people trudging down the street and then back to the boarded windows. While hardly a pleasing sight, it didn't look like a prison either. There were women actually sitting on the porch, taking a drink. "Why would they stay here?"

"Not easy getting out of slums, not when you've been raised in them," Coren replied. "Whether they came here or were dragged here, these girls are probably getting paid next to nothing, possibly not paid at all. But they have a roof over their heads and they're not dying, so they probably consider that enough. Slavery and prison isn't always as obvious as chains and bars, I hate to tell you."

He knew that. He did. Head knowledge and meeting it in person were two different things.

"And you really think these people might be able to direct us to who kidnapped Tryss?" He turned this next question to Remrant.

"Looks can be deceiving. I think you'll find the interior of this place far better funded than the outside. The elite are less likely to bump into anybody they know in this part of the city, and law enforcement is not as present here as it is in cleaner neighborhoods. Believe me, the owners of these establishments have connections. Which is why you're dressed like so."

Errance reached a hand to the collar of his shirt as he spoke, tugging again at the tightness. Again, Remrant had taken it upon himself to provide a wardrobe, and this one was dark from the top of his neck to the tip of his boot, but not in the manner of stealth as it had been the other night. No, this coat was of a very fine matte black cloth delicately trimmed with gold, and the entire interior was inlaid with shining gold. It was intimidating when closed and awe-inspiring when hung open.

Upon first seeing the brothel, he'd wondered at Remrant's sanity in choosing such an outfit, but now he saw the genius in its design—easy to overlook on the outside, secret wealth within.

"This is where we part ways, my friends," Remrant said, opening the door for them. "Briefly as it may be."

Errance stepped out, the thick heel of his boot clinking against the cobblestones. Coren followed behind him, dressed to look like hired protection rather than a client.

"This is going to sound crazy," Coren went on, his voice dropping to a hush as they approached the house stairs. "But this is an absolute dream come true."

He was right, that did sound crazy. "I'm sorry, what?" Errance hissed back.

"Back when I was a kid, I dreamed you were alive. And you know, my age, and we would be off getting into the wildest kinds of trouble. And then when I was an adult, and surprise, you were alive, I dreamed that there would be a day when we could fight injustice together. And here we are."

"Here we are. Is it as great as you were picturing?" Errance asked, raising his brows in a droll arch.

"Nearly. Although I never pictured His Lordship Moneybags as part of it." Coren nodded to the other side of the street. Remrant had left the coach and walked over to the storage wagon, carrying on a show of casual conversation with the undercover captain at the seat.

Errance smothered a snort with some difficulty.

There was no time to say anything more. They had arrived and were walking up the stairs, eyed by the women with undisguised interest.

The moment of amusement gone, Errance repressed the shudder that trickled down his spine as the door was opened for them by a young woman with a sultry greeting. Just inside, a man stood at a counter, polishing drinking glasses. There were a few other men drinking at the counter, some talking with the maids, but other than that, it seemed suspiciously empty.

"Welcome, welcome to the finest drinks in Dormandy." The man from behind the counter approached them, a brilliant grin curling his already curved mustache. "We have not had you visit before, have we?"

Remrant was right, the inside was far different than the outside. There were very few windows, and those that existed were small and high up. The room was cast in a low lighting by wall sconces, which only served to make the wooden panels of the counter darker and the red patterned wallpaper deeper.

Of course the walls would be red. Of course it would be warm in here, even if it was cool outside. He looked at the drinks set out on the counter, but even with the ice in them, he doubted they would be refreshing.

He knew how the worst places could take on a glamour of something rich and luxurious. Even then it couldn't quite hide its true nature. He stood there, and he could imagine it all again as if it were yesterday. Suffocating red and gold, colors of lust and heat. Lukewarm water reflected on red tiles so that he could only imagine blood.

He swallowed once, then twice, before he could manage a response. "I've heard your selection is unlike anything else in the city. I'm traveling back to Korince but was told to come here for refreshment."

He sat down at the bar, some distance from the other men, and took the folded menu handed him by one of the maids, immediately turning his attention to it before she could try to catch his eye.

Coren sat a few stools down, as a guard should. Close enough for protection, but not as a friend. It only took him a few seconds to give his order to the waiting maid.

The barman took his place in front of Errance, wiping the counter as if it could gleam any brighter. "What is your taste today?"

Errance cast one final glance over the menu and set it down with a firm flick. He reclined, his arm draped over the arch of the stool's back, letting his coat hang open. "I want your secret menu." It bothered him to no end that between Remrant and the Dormandy law force, there had been knowledge on what to say in this place and yet nobody had bothered to stop it.

The man's smile curved wider. "I should have known that someone like you would have come for only the best. Of course, of course, sir, if you only follow me this way."

He led Errance down a narrow hall deeper into the building, and as they went, he dropped pretense and spoke plainly. "We have girls here of every variety, and the ones currently available are in this parlor. You can take your time getting to know them before you choose. I assume money is no object?" He cast a glance at him, eyes taking in the golden interior of Errance's coat that glinted with each step he took.

Errance knew he had to say something, but the knot in his throat was so thick he hadn't the strength to push past it.

Commotion rose up behind them. The sound of the front door banging open, feet clattering, voices upraised in command and others in surprise.

"What's all that?" the man said, eloquent pleasantry vanishing from his face and tone. He turned back the way they'd come, pushing past Errance, and hurrying towards the bar. Errance followed a few steps behind him.

A small force of the police guard stood inside, hands on their swords, and the captain's palm resting on the butt of his flintlock. Remrant stood just behind them, hands folded on the top of his cane.

"What is all this?" the barman said again, this time nearly in a yell.

"Dormandy Police, sir. We've had sufficient leads to conduct a raid that will determine if your business is engaged in the illegal activity of human sale," the captain of the guard said, unflinching. "Your exits are guarded until the investigation is complete. Please cooperate in our search of the building."

"You can't just barge in here!" the man shouted. "And you can't make any accusations! I've nothing to hide here, but I won't be invaded by any—" He went dead silent as the tip of Errance's knife pressed into his back.

"How would you explain it to them?" Errance asked softly over his shoulder. "That all the ladies here are daughters, nieces, cousins, aunts? Perhaps you run an inn purely to put a roof over women? No excuses will work, scum, you've already told me more than enough to incriminate you."

The man turned his head to look at him, face registering such appalled betrayal that it was almost amusing.

"Now," Errance prodded him back down the hall to where they'd originally been headed. "How about we go and see those girls you were talking about? Since money is no object."

Feet leaden, the man led the way to the door at the hall's end, but before he had taken hold of the handle, he turned back to them. He licked his lips, looking not unlike a rat stroking his whiskers. "Now, lads, now let's just slow down a minute. I know you're doing your jobs, doing a fine example of it. But nobody needs to know you didn't let us off with a warning or maybe that…maybe that nothing was found. How about you just look the other way this time, and any time you're in need of some company, this house will board you free of charge, yes, how about—"

"Step out of the way before I step over you," Errance said, eyes narrowing.

The man's mouth snapped shut with an audible click. With one final grimace he stepped aside.

Errance swept past him, turned the doorknob, and entered in.

26

The inner chamber of the brothel parlor rose three stories high. A stair led up to a balcony on each floor, leading the way to several closed doors. A few women lingered on the stairs or by the railings, but most of them sat on the couches and chairs on the lower floor, chatting softly or busy over some distraction.

The chatter stopped when the door opened, and the silence deepened as Errance, the owner, and then the law enforcement stepped in one by one. Coren and Remrant came in last of all, but they were barely noticeable by that point.

The guard captain gave a sigh, jotted down some notes in a book he kept in his breast pocket. "You are under arrest, sir," he said to the man who was turning purple with rage. "Corporal, please cuff him and wait out in the bar. Sergeant, search for and seize any and all documents of transaction. Any client here is under arrest and investigation. Master Reyid, sir, you are free to begin your questions while we continue to sweep the building."

Errance nodded, blotting out the sounds of protest from the brothel owner as he was led away. He didn't want to talk to him, or at least not yet.

Instead he walked forward into the luxurious parlor, the thick carpet silent beneath his boots.

Neither Tryss nor Dahlya were here, but he hadn't expected them just to be out in the open at such a place anyway. Even so, he could almost imagine their faces here. He could imagine the face of any one of his people. He could imagine himself.

Most of the women in the room wore expressions of distrust, if not hostility and disgust. There were a few who simply looked afraid. A few who looked curious. And one whose face held a tiny glimmer of hope.

Errance's gaze turned to that one, and her hope was almost completely drowned out by the alarm that washed over her face as he took a few steps toward her. Very carefully, he knelt, arms loose over his knees, so that he was eye level with her from where she curled on a couch. She was a small thing with frizzy red hair, and while it was hard to guess her age with such large eyes and delicate features, he presumed she wasn't much older than Tellie had been the first time he'd met her.

"May I ask your name?" He kept his tone as gentle and kind as he could. The way Tryss had been to him when he was afraid.

"Alia," she answered, hope and that curious spark returning again.

"Alia. We came here looking for a very dear friend of mine. She is a little older than your friend over there, though not any taller, and she's with child. Her hair is flaxen yellow and she may be with another woman who is dark-haired and elf-kind. Have you seen or heard anything about them?"

"No, my lord." Her words quavered. "Though I wish I had."

His heart sank, but he'd known that finding news from places like this had been pure speculation. Still, he couldn't say it was a waste of time and effort, not with these women surrounding him.

"Thank you, Alia," he said quietly. "I'll keep looking for her. In the meantime, I want to help you and the rest of your friends here. We haven't come to harm you, we came to save you."

"Really?" The hope flared again, chasing away the shadows of fear.

"Save, my land," one woman scoffed. "This place is our business, pretty lad, we didn't need your goons coming in to bust it up or your fancy words trying to justify that."

"This business is illegal in the city of Dormandy, and your employers are under arrest," the captain of the guard said, tone almost bored with the whole affair. "You will remain in this room until told otherwise. Lord Reyid, a word if I may?"

They stepped out of the room, leaving the door guarded, and headed a ways down the hall till their words would be out of reach of hearing.

"The masters of this establishment will be thoroughly questioned," the captain said. "Most times, information takes a while to reach the surface, so there's still a chance they know something about your missing women. You'll be informed of any updates."

Somehow, he already knew the answers he was looking for would not be found here. Instead, another question gnawed at the corner of his mind, drawing his gaze over and over again to the room which held the women. "Where do the girls go after this?" he asked.

"Go?" The captain shot him an incredulous look. "We're arresting them. To the prisons is where they'll go, cramped even as they are."

"Arresting?" The word all but broke out in a shout. He spun to face him fully, fists curling. "We're here to rescue the victims, not arrest them!"

"Look here, I don't know what your business is beyond finding your missing citizens, but the governor's orders were to stop this brothel ring. I'd rather let them go, believe me, it's not as if I want to stuff more mouths to feed in our prisons. But you can't stop a ring by letting the wenches go. This life is all they know and they'll just go right back to it, maybe even start one of their own."

Pain shot through Errance's jaw from how hard he ground his teeth together. "I just told those girls that we were saving them." He stabbed a finger towards the door. "This is not ending in arrest."

The captain opened his mouth, but Remrant spoke instead. He stood looking at a painting on the wall, thin fingers folded behind his back, not shifting his contemplation. "Captain, I am in charge of this operation. You will let the women go."

At that, the captain's mouth snapped shut, and he stiffened in a slight salute. "As you say, sir." But his eyes clearly held doubts at the wisdom of the order.

"Where are the safe homes for women like this?" Errance demanded. "Don't they exist?"

"Citizens are willing to pay taxes for prisons because it makes them feel secure," the captain said. His tone was not cruel, but it did not care. He clearly had not cared for a long time, cynicism having taken root instead. "You see how that works? People pay for what benefits them, but they aren't just going to fund charity houses."

"Charity?" Errance threw up his hands, startling the man back a step. "Who said anything about charity? If places like this house women and have the audacity to call it a business, where are places that give women real jobs with real shelter?"

"If I may," Coren said.

Errance started, unsure of when he'd joined them or if he'd been there the entire time.

His cousin reached into the pocket of his coat and withdrew a few folded sheets of paper. "I've already compiled a list of businesses, inns and homes in this city and nearby that offer help to victims of this nature. There are not many, and it's possible this isn't a comprehensive list, but it's a beginning."

"Saints, Coren," Errance exclaimed, "why didn't you say something sooner?"

"Sorry, I liked everything you were saying, so I didn't want to interrupt."

The captain took the sheet with a dawning look of interest. "Hadn't heard of places like this," he remarked at last. "I'll look into it."

"I made a few copies. Do you mind if I pass them out to the women who are interested?"

"Go right ahead."

Coren turned to Errance and pressed one sheet into his hand. "You'd be best to talk to Alia," he said with a small, sad smile. "I'll see what I can do for the rest."

The police were still cleaning up by the time Remrant announced it was time for their departure. Errance sank into the carriage seat as they headed for Albine Avenue, feeling as if his body carried the weight of a hundred stones. Despite the promises from the captain to pass on any information gained through questioning, despite even the hope for a fresh start they'd given the women—he didn't feel like he'd accomplished anything.

When they finally reached Remrant's townhouse, he headed upstairs and collapsed on the bed without even bothering to take off his coat or boots. There was a low fire burning in the hearth and steam drifted out from the water closet, suggesting a bath had been recently prepared.

Coren came in a few minutes later and began taking off his own boots and mussed clothes without a word.

"Poor Alia." Errance's voice was muffled by the mattress he pressed his face against.

A small smile pursed Coren's mouth. "I didn't know it was even possible for you to speak so gently. No wonder Tryss agreed to marry you."

"Thanks for that," Errance muttered, turning his head to scowl at him.

"No, honestly, I was impressed how well you handled yourself in there, considering the various stages of undress."

He rolled his eyes. "Come on, Coren, it's not like Tertorem clothed its prisoners with dignity and grace."

"I know, I know, but comparing how you've acted in other situations…"

At that, Errance's mouth thinned. He couldn't deny that, but the explanation was simple. "I don't like feeling threatened," he said crisply. Then a shadow cast across his face. "But in that room, I felt like *I* was the threat."

Coren nodded, an all too knowing sadness lining his features. "I'll be washing up," he said, stepping into the water closet. "Won't take long."

It was only a few minutes later that a knock came at the bedroom door. By now, Errance could tell the difference between the maid and

Remrant, though both were soft raps against the wood. He forced himself onto his feet, pretending to be busy at the desk, before calling, "Come in."

Remrant entered, balancing a silver tea set on one arm which he set on the low table in the middle of the room. "I would have invited you down to the tea parlor, but you looked like you needed rest. Can't say you've gotten yourself very comfortable." He cast a disapproving look at Errance's mud-dried boots.

"Thank you." Maybe if he sat and started sipping the tea, Remrant would leave him be.

Instead, the man took it as an invitation to sit down across from him. Of course he did, he should have known by now the man wouldn't miss an opportunity to talk over tea. He also never missed an opportunity to bring along his pastime, a strategy card game called Feint. He seemed determined to teach it to Errance whenever they had to wait a period of time, and Errance complied if only for the distraction.

"We did a great thing today, at least be assured of that," Remrant said as he began dealing the cards.

"Did we?" Errance stared into the flickering coals in the hearth, his eyes dull despite the bright reflection. "Something great, but only for a moment. It is as the captain said…where will they go? What will they do now? Coren gave us a list of places to direct them, but it surely is not enough to help all of them…and who can say if they will actually take the chance?"

He knew a thing or two about weakness when facing a chance. He'd had his share of doubt. Escaping from Tertorem stood out as the most critical of these times, and had it not been for little Tellie and everyone's persistent loving-kindness, he'd probably be a skeleton at the bottom of a very tall cliff. Had it not been for Ayeshune confronting him in his lowest moment, he'd still be a slave of His Darkness even now.

Remrant sighed, shaking his head. "My focus has mainly been on restoring order to the world. All my life, I have studied how to structure a safe society, how to bring evil to justice, even how to prevent crime altogether. After seeing your passion today, I can envision how well we could work together. Myself to create law, you to provide healing. If it's more houses of rehabilitation you want, then we can easily accomplish that. And by gods, if we can shake the gutters of this city even a little, then that's something."

"I've noticed something," Errance interrupted, suddenly irritated in his exhaustion. "Are you a religious man, Remrant? You seem to swear by gods quite often."

Remrant paused and stared at him. "Religious," he repeated. "I can't say that I am."

"So you don't think he minds?"

"Minds what?"

"Invoking his title with no meaning."

"Oh, Reyid, what are you going on about? Nobody is listening, except you, apparently."

"You don't believe in God?"

"No, I do not," Remrant said evenly. "Do you know how many gods mankind has invented since we first came into being? Too many to count. Someone is right, someone is wrong, but I'd just as soon not bother with them at all. Inconvenient things, gods are."

"But many elves born in the beginning of creation are still alive. By our count, it was not long ago. Do you deny that they met him?"

"I haven't had the pleasure of talking with any elf until now," Remrant replied. "Should I take it you've met him?"

Errance hesitated. There was no reason for age to come up in a future conversation. But still he would have to tread carefully if he aged himself now. "Yes," he said at last. Not over a thousand years ago, but a mere seven. He didn't dare mention that detail. Remrant would be sharp enough to match the timeline to the crowning of the new king.

"Fascinating." Interest lit Remrant's eyes as if he would like to discuss it more despite himself, but he said instead, "Well, then let us say that it is not so much that I don't believe in his existence, but I don't believe that he much cares about whatever he created. Perhaps he only cares about the elves. Perhaps he is dead." He smiled, but it had the shine of a winter sun, all brightness, no warmth.

Errance opened his mouth, but found nothing to say. He could point out that that dawn and dusk still came and went, that the rain still poured, that the seasons still turned, and yes, these all were signs of a world still upheld, but had he not had his own doubts so many times? He'd seen Ayeshune for himself and continued to struggle in belief, so who was he to lecture?

"That is why I make my own way," Remrant said. "We must shape the world for ourselves."

Perhaps that was their very purpose. Perhaps that was the way God moved through the world. When those who believed in him reached out to those who were hurting around them. And how were they supposed to do that, if they were too focused on living in their own safe heaven on earth?

"There must be an absolute standard," Remrant went on, disrupting Errance's thoughts. "Or else there would be disaster. I'm sure you can agree on that. So we make laws to keep the world in order and then we must enforce them."

"And what makes you qualified for such a role?"

"Gold," Remrant said simply. "I have a lot of gold, my dear Reyid. "It is the closest thing to a god I have ever seen in how it can control the lives of men."

27

ASELVIA

According to reason, they were safe.

The chema spy Alludium was in captivity, locked in a prison at the borders of the palace city.

According to intuition, they were still in danger.

Even after the fresh *iisveth* had finally dismissed the poison from Leoren's body, leaving him weak but recovering, the unease did not waver. The fear she had cast hung like a spell over the royal household. Nobody could scrape the feeling of being watched by their own shadow or checking everything they touched for signs of tampering. By habit of self-preservation, they kept to doing everything in pairs. The queen mother and Casara were still under careful protection, unwilling to yet return to their regular lives.

Tellie and Kelm were gathered with Maril, Damarik, and a resting Leoren. The Daisha had joined them as well, for they were in one of the upper palace rooms that had a sloping roof below the tall windows.

Lying on the roof, The Daisha could peek her head through the open window and share in the conversation.

"I don't like it," Kelm said again, pacing back and forth. "She's too calm by half."

"I'd have to agree," Maril said softly, not moving from her silent contemplation out the window. "By all accounts, we've won, but she sits there in her cell and smiles softly. She seems to have no fear of death or punishment at all. As if she's a martyr. As if she has the victory."

"Not to mention she gave us the answer to Leoren's cure so easily. Maybe she thought The Daisha would have to be sent away to the North, I don't know, but if that was the only damage she caused, I doubt she would want to even give us a chance at reversing it."

"So what do we do?" Tellie asked, rubbing a hand down her face. She was surprised to find her skin still smooth, by now she assumed she had developed several wrinkles.

"I will track her scent as best as I can," The Daisha said. "If I can follow her trail, I can find where she went."

"Isn't it, you know, a bit late for that?"

"A chema's scent is seared into my life's beginning memories. I don't suppose I can track her movements well inside the palace, but you don't know that she stayed in the palace, now do you? I shall begin at once. I should have started the moment after I captured her. Fool that I was to think the problem was dealt with so easily." With that, The Daisha crawled back out of sight, and the buffet of her wings blew the veils about the windows a moment later.

They waited, continuing their restless discussions, and in less than an hour, The Daisha returned. Her noble head peeked through the window, pupils dilated with alarm.

"What is it?" Leoren asked, struggling to sit upright from the couch where he lay.

"She definitely left the palace," The Daisha said. "I tracked her scent outside the city to several of the springs and rivers in the hillsides where crops grow. I can smell something there. Faint, but unmistakably foul."

"More poison?" Tellie gasped.

"If it was direct poison, I'm sure we would have seen consequences by now. And it would surely take more poison than she could carry to taint that many water sources." Damarik pressed his knuckles to his mouth, face furrowed in thought. "…Seeds," he said after a prolonged silence.

"What?"

"A way for poison to take effect in the future. She could carry many seeds of a toxic plant on her person and sow them in select locations that will nurture their growth. In something like a spring, it would spread to the crops, the livestock, and then, of course, the people."

A stunned quiet followed his words, everyone taking measured breaths in an attempt to not panic.

"It is just a theory, of course," Damarik said. "I'll send for Ahspen and have The Daisha take us to these locations. Between his sharp eyes and her sharp nose, I'm sure we can find all the areas that have been tampered with, and maybe even locate the seeds themselves. Either way, we shall mark the areas of concern and watch them closely for any invasive plants so they can be rooted out before they have a chance to spread and cause damage."

"So…" Tellie managed faintly, "so you're saying it will be all right? We can stop this?"

"We can," Damarik said confidently. He laid a hand on Leoren's shoulder, jostling his fixated stare into nothingness. "I am a healer and an herbalist, and I will see to it that none of our people are sick from this attempt. We owe it to The Daisha for finding the problem before it could start."

"Good," Kelm growled. "I have a half a mind to go tell that vicious witch and see how smug she is then."

"I am also tempted," Leoren said slowly. "If only to see if it shakes her confidence or if she has yet another back-up strategy. It is hard to fathom how carefully she planned this infiltration. It has been poison from start to end."

"I have wondered how neither Ahspen nor I found it on her person when we were taking care of her," Damarik admitted, "but perhaps Taersidel carried it on him until he left. He certainly administered the antidote, so it was likely he gave her resources at the same time." He nodded with the emphasis of a seal stamped on paper. "Come then, The Daisha. I must first prepare gloves and a mask so that I am not poisoned in any way, and then you must take me to these areas and we shall weed it out."

Even as he left, stepping out the window to join The Daisha, Maril turned to Leoren. "With your permission, my Lord," she said, "I shall go and inform the chema spy of our progress. As you and Kelm suggested, I think it is possible that she might let something slip."

Leoren nodded, waving a weary hand.

Not long after Maril had left, the door slammed open, revealing her return with the countenance of a windswept storm. "She escaped," she snarled, voice savage with anger.

Tellie paused, heart skipping a beat. "Wait—what?"

"We're not talking about Alludium, right?" Kelm asked.

"We are," Maril said, dipping her head to the guard that stood just behind her. "Explain, soldier, as you explained to me."

The elvish soldier looked pale and unwell, and an impressive purple bruise blossomed on the side of his face. "It was right after the changing of the guard. My comrade noticed that the prisoner was lying curled up in the corner of the cell, unmoving, and…the colors were all wrong. Her hair was brown, and her clothes also appeared to be a different shade."

"But that's what chemas do," Kelm began, a note of frustration bleeding into his voice.

"Alludium was in manifix shackles," Maril reminded. "As far as we knew, she should not have been able to use her power."

"We were wary that it was a trick, even so," the guard said. "But we had to confirm that it was still her. I watched my partner's back as he approached, but…we were unprepared even so. She moved like lightning. She was on me before I knew what was happening, and I remember my face hitting the wall, and then everything went black. By the time I came back to, she was gone."

"Other guards gave chase but met similar fates or lost track of her," Maril said. "Shortly after, word came that one of the fastest horses was taken from the courier stables. Other riders have been sent in pursuit, but who can say if they'll catch her. We need The Daisha."

Tellie listened, but all the words seemed enveloped in a fog, difficult to look at clearly. She sorted out one part at a time, focusing on what could be addressed immediately. "Is your fellow guard all right?" she asked the shaken soldier.

"The injured were taken to medics, and this one is returning there for further check-up," Maril said with a nod. "We believe everyone will recover quickly."

"That's good," she said, wiping a hand down her brow. One question down. One question next. She could deal with this. "So, did she get rid of the shackles somehow?"

"We believe she is still wearing them," Maril admitted. "We had no previous record of chemas being able to overcome the interference of manifix ore. But chemas have always had a vast range of power, so perhaps we just never knew they could be strong enough. Or perhaps she built up a tolerance."

"The Daisha can't have gone far," Kelm said, running his hands through his hair till all the curls stood on end. "Does anyone besides Errance have that handy whistle she can hear?"

"No," Leoren groaned. "She was very particular about the whistle. She only allowed it for him."

"So we have to wait?" Tellie all but wailed. "We just have to wait until she gets back?"

"I'll send scouts out to chase after her," Maril said. "The Daisha said the poison seeds were all near living areas, and I do not believe Alludium traveled far from the city. We can surely catch The Daisha's attention before it's too late."

No. Tellie knew it in her bones.

It was too late already.

28

DORMANDY

It had worked.

Dahlya's unceasing request for a writing quill and paper, all under the lament that they were artists and dying of boredom, had finally worked. Honestly, it was almost a surprise it hadn't worked sooner considering how thoroughly Dahlya had wrapped their guards around her little finger. In other circumstances, Tryss would have been afraid for her friend, but so far the interactions between them and whoever held them under house arrest seemed to be ordered to the minimum.

Writing tools are not often thought great treasures until they are taken away. And after being deprived of them, having them back in hand was like receiving rain after a long drought.

Tryss held the quill, inkpot, and small blank journal in her trembling hands and tried to take deep breaths to calm herself enough to write anything beyond an unintelligible scrawl.

"I don't even know what to say," Tryss whispered, pressing an arm to her aching abdomen. "I don't feel like I can tell him anything helpful."

"Letting him know you are alive and healthy is sufficient for the moment," Dahlya said, sensible as ever, stirring tea into the hot water kettle just brought in with the paper and ink materials. "His last letter told you he already knows about your brother's treachery, so you don't need to explain that."

As if sensing his services would soon be needed, Flyfar appeared on the little desk beside her.

"If I only knew the reason we were taken in the first place, it might help him track us down." Her hand brushed over her belly in rhythmic strokes as if she could soothe the stirring child inside. "What if they're just waiting for me to give birth so they can take Baby away?" Her skin crawled as she voiced the haunting fear that swelled in her mind each day.

"They'd be fools to separate a newborn from their mother," Dayhla snapped. "Anyway, I wouldn't let them. You just go ahead and write."

Three more raids. More women set free and directed to a better life, but ultimately not given the support they deserved. There were some children, and they were sent to orphanages. Errance could only hope the orphanages were properly maintained. He remembered Tellie once said her experience had been decent enough, although the hope of adoption had always been present. But there had been little precaution against who could adopt her, and hence her life with the Nornes had turned so bleak. He feared the children taken in by anyone as awful as the Nornes—or worse.

And each time, nothing. Nothing about Tryss.

What was he *doing*? It wasn't enough, not to help his wife and not to help the victims they uncovered. None of this could have any lasting effect.

He sat at the desk, staring at the stacks of reports Remrant kept bringing in for him to look over, but none of them contained any useful information. The candle set in the desk's built-in stand was running low. He opened the drawer and exchanged it for a new one, discarding the old in a stack that would be melted down and poured all over again.

When he looked up, Flyfar was sitting at the top of the desk. He hadn't even heard the flutter of his wings. He just perched there as if he'd been present all along.

Errance held out his hand, both relieved and wearied. Another ribbon, another strand of tattered hope.

What Flyfar dropped into his palm was not a ribbon.

Errance's fingers all but crushed the small piece of paper as he drew it to his chest. A note? A note! She finally had found a way to write him! He unfolded it with shaking hands, blinking several times till the blurry letters cleared. Her script was tiny and neat to write as much as possible on the strip of paper.

Errance, we're all unharmed. Dahlya says the baby and I need to rest rather than focus on escape, so I trust in you. I don't know where we are or who took us after we escaped Taers. The house we're in now is comfortable, and we are not bothered by our captors. We're still in Dormandy, but that's all I know. I love you, I miss you. Please come soon.

His knuckles pressed against his mouth hard enough to leave imprints of teeth. After reading the letter a few more times, he stood and began pacing. On the fourth return to the desk, he pounced back onto the seat and started scribbling out a reply.

Tryss, we've been combing through the brothel rings of the city in case they were connected or knew someone connected to your disappearance. But your captors have said nothing to indicate the reason you're being held?

He resumed pacing once Flyfar took the note away, hardly faltering a step when the bird returned a moment later with Tryss's reply.

They have said I am to be unharmed, but that is all. I have the worst fear that this might be about our baby. I could give birth any day now, and I don't know what will happen after that.

Darkness above, he hadn't even considered that possibility. It had always been about Tryss or Tryss and the baby both, but just his heir? It was all too real a threat. Had it not been the reason for his capture? His claim to the throne and to the Moonscript? Could this really be the Darkness's second attempt to—

No, no, he was panicking and overlooking the obvious. His child would be heir to Aselvia, but he or she would not be able to read the Moonscript. Since Errance could not withdraw the Celestial light from his own body, he could not pass on the light to his wife or any of his children. This had always been both a lament and a relief.

Even so, The Darkness or any of his servants could find much worth in an Aselvian heir, especially one raised from birth.

The fear curled its fingers around his throat, pressing against each labored breath.

Calm down. Calm down. You don't know if that's what's happening here. You don't know for sure.

Forcing himself back to the seat, he wrote out his own self-consolation to her.

It could be just a ransom situation. They might be waiting for us to grow in panic before setting their price. In which case, it will be in their best interest to keep you and our little one healthy. Please don't be afraid, I know I'm close to finding you.

Maybe if he just believed that hard enough it would be true.

Flyfar disappeared, and he waited.

And waited.

The air shifted. A coldness passed across his skin, carried on some fresh current in the atmosphere. He glanced at the windows, but they were shut. At least they were shut *now*. Slowly, he dropped one hand to the blade at his thigh.

The inkwell at the table shifted.

Errance stiffened yet more, fingers tightening around the hilt of the knife. "Does that amuse you?"

"It does," Taers said, his smile appearing before the rest of him. "Though you're not quite as entertaining to watch as others have been. I prefer it when they jump and scream. Really, how does the world sleep at night? Do they trust that we all will stay up North and mind our manners? How lucky Aselvia is, secure inside their shielded borders. The rest of the world must just be fools."

Errance leaned back in his chair, raising one unimpressed brow. "Have you come with any other reason than to gloat?" He refused to let any fear show in his eyes that would give away the stutter in his heartbeat. He wondered if Taers had seen Flyfar bringing messages back and forth. He could only hope the bird would notice the unwelcome presence and not reveal itself upon return.

"We made an agreement, sister's husband," Taers said, voice as sticky and sweet as honey. "The question is whether either of us is going to honor it. For my part, I came to tell you, my search has remained fruitless, which is uncommon. Now, have you done any better?"

Tryss and I made contact, she's safe for now, and all our raids are to no avail.

He said none of that.

By now, Taersidel had to suspect the nature of Flyfar, but Errance wasn't about to explain the details of his kingdom's royal gift. And everything he and Tryss had spoken between each other was personal, not something that would actually help them find her. Besides, he had a feeling Taersidel would not bother coming to him with any useful information if he attained it, even with Alludium on the line, but instead chase after it immediately. The agreement they had made was a sham, he guessed.

"Nothing," he said coldly. "We're scouring the dregs, but there is no word to be found."

"Ever thought you're looking in the wrong place?" Taers said, sitting down on the surface of the table and picking up the quill pin to twirl it upon his fingers.

Yes. Errance stared at him until he had the curiosity to return the look.

"What?" Taers smiled. "You're surprised I'd bother to help your narrow little brain? You're so busy focusing on an obvious evil that you just overlook the cleverer one. Whoever hired me was not so shallow as to only be after your wife's prettiness or prestige. It's about power."

"I know that," Errance said, scowling. All right, so maybe he'd thought that back at the beginning. "Still, Remrant suggested that the criminal markets would be most likely to have heard of any underhanded plots."

"Ahhhhh yes, Master Remrant Cole." Taers rolled each word slowly off his tongue. "Quite an interesting friend you've found. Or he found you, from what I've gathered. Which is all the more eerie. He knows so much about you, save your true identity, but we can excuse him for that, given what a mystery the elf king is. But what do you know of him?"

"He's the head of the All Nations Bank. He is looking to establish a connection with Aselvia."

"Awful lot of trouble he is putting in."

"Wealth seems to be a powerful motivation for most."

Taers nodded, tilting his head. "I've been looking into him some myself. You've noticed the influence he wields over the cities that intrust in his bank, do you not? Many new laws, most to establish order, have appeared in the cities with the most investments in the bank throughout his lifetime. It could just be a coincidence, or it could not."

"And?" Errance said, unwilling to let him see the unease creeping into his heart. He doubted it was a coincidence. He'd seen firsthand just how much influence Remrant wielded.

"So impatient. I am merely suggesting, elf king, that wealth may not be the only thing this Master Cole is after. Call it chema intuition."

"Yes, and speaking of chemas, at least of your lot, they are prone to manipulation and lying," Errance said, folding his arms.

Taers shrugged and eased off the table. "It takes one to know one. Believe me or don't, I couldn't care less. I'll see you around. Whether you see me will be another matter." He took a few strides to the window, slid it open, and then vanished into the night air.

Errance stayed where he sat for a few moments, listening and watching to be sure it wasn't a trick or there wasn't another one lurking about before he got up and closed and locked the window. He was quite certain it had been locked before, so locking it again seemed ridiculously futile.

What *did* he know of Remrant? The man rarely discussed himself in their regular conversations over tea, always speaking instead of grand ambitions for the future.

He'd already tried to research his past in the libraries, but the tragic arson recounted there held little connection to anything happening now. And the history of his bank seemed to have nothing but glowing records of how it had improved the cities who invested in its gold.

The man was no doubt in his rooms, but if there was a moment he wasn't, perhaps it would be worth snooping around in. See what skeletons in the closet he might find. Or he could try the more polite method and simply ask him questions, but Taersidel had set him on edge, and he wasn't sure anything he'd be told would be the truth.

"He's trying to get under your skin," Errance muttered to himself. "He doesn't have any desire to help you, so he's just casting out snares."

Ill intentions or no, Taersidel's point remained.

A growl rippling in his throat, Errance ran his fingers through his hair and stood. He needed fresh air. A place to think. Clearly, this room was no safer than anywhere outdoors.

The water closet door creaked open and Coren walked in, scrubbing his still wet hair with a towel. "The bath is all yours," he yawned.

"You just missed Taers," Errance said.

Coren froze. "Wait—what?"

"He came to exchange information, as we discussed, but neither of us had anything useful. Anyway, I'm going out again."

"Going out—are you kidding me, when he's out there?"

"What does that matter when he was in here minutes ago? I need fresh air. A place to pray. And I want to be alone."

"You cannot possibly be serious."

"Yes, I possibly can!"

They glared at each other for a few moments before Coren sagged with a weary sigh. "Nothing I can say will stop you, will it? Fine. There is a church a few streets north, if you want, the one I was telling you about. The parson is a good man. But be careful, will you? The last thing I need is for someone else to go missing. Brights, I can't believe that skinblending snake came in here. Why is it people keep coming to talk to you when I'm in middle of a bath?"

"Maybe if you didn't wash, the smell would keep them away," Errance quipped, but with little humor.

The door clicked shut behind him and he started down the stairs. He paused in his tracks, noticing the light glowing under Remrant's door. Just before they'd retired to their rooms, he remembered the man telling his maid to heat water for his own bath. Which meant he would be in there a while because he didn't take them as fast as Coren.

He hesitated. Fresh air and a chance to think? Or just skip thinking now that he had a chance to act?

Remrant kept a study up in the turret tower. Errance had been there once or twice, invited by Remrant to discuss their next plan of action, as always over tea and a game of Feint. If Remrant had any evidence of secret dealings, it was most likely to be there.

Taking a deep breath, he headed up towards the tower, taking care to not let the carpeted steps creak.

The oak door at the top of the stairs was locked, which wasn't a terrible surprise.

Fortunately, he knew a thing or two about picking locks from his time in Tertorem. Even more fortunately, he had a few pins stabbed through the knot of hair at the back of his neck. He slid them out, letting his hair hang loose.

As he fiddled with the lock, a thousand warnings flickered through his mind. He probably should have told Coren his plans had changed. He should have an explanation for what he was doing if he was caught. But all those things would require time, which he did not have.

The knob clicked and turned. He slipped inside and softly pressed the door shut behind him.

The turret had three tall windows set together in the shape of an arch. They were of solid glass, not designed to be opened. The moon was in sight, shedding enough light to illuminate the surroundings. Just as he'd remembered, the room was such an ordinary looking study that his heart fell a bit in his chest.

But suspicious things could be hidden in plain view in ordinary places because nobody expected to find them there. He'd have to be careful to leave things as he found them if he hoped to escape this venture without notice.

There were certainly enough stacks of papers on the desk to hide something, but somehow Errance didn't think anything useful would be there. They looked like reports, bank reports probably. It looked like Leoren's desk, the kind of paperwork that gave Errance an instant headache.

A portrait on the desk caught his eye, and he lifted it up for better inspection. The artwork was finely done, even if the delicate lines had faded with age. It depicted a small family—a man, a woman, and a young man as their son. It startled him to recognize the young man as Remrant. Somehow, he hadn't ever pictured him at any age other than what he was now, but there was no mistaking the lad.

This must have been drawn shortly before the arson, he thought, feeling another stab of guilt for standing in a place he didn't belong.

Setting the portrait back, he shuffled through a few books on the desk, opened up a few drawers.

The bottom right drawer wouldn't open. There was no lock on it, it simply wouldn't budge. He pulled out the top drawer again, then tugged it free of its runners and set it down. When he reached down into the bottom drawer, his fingers brushed a metal box. He lifted it out and inspected it in the light. It was not much longer or wider than a hefty book, and from the sounds shifting inside, he guessed a book and perhaps some papers were exactly what it held. A safe lock secured it shut.

If Remrant had gone through the trouble to keep it hidden and locked then there had to be something incriminating here. Whether it would actually shed any useful information on Remrant's motivations and past would be another matter. It wasn't as if knowing could really help him find Tryss. Most likely it would just make working with the man even more uncomfortable.

Curse Taers and his poisonous words.

What was he even *doing* here?

Suppose Remrant walked in this very moment. What could he do but admit that he was searching for truths he was not being told? Perhaps the man would be good-natured enough to laugh about it and understand.

Enough stalling. He was here, and he'd take whatever consequence followed.

Even as his mind raced, his fingers worked at twisting the tumblers, ears tuned to the delicate clicking within.

There, finally, a click. He peered at the number, just in case he needed to get in at a later time.

3. He turned opposite, turning all the way back around till he reached *3* again. Then kept going to *0, 1,* another *1, 7,* and then *9.*

And then, just when he was beginning to wonder if the combination would ever end or if he was doing something wrong, he felt the final lock fall out of place.

Exhaling, he set the box down upon the desk and lifted the lid. Yes, just what he had guessed—a few letters, report sheets, and a journal. He passed over the reports, not able to make any more sense out of them than the others, and took a quick perusal of the letter. It appeared to be someone concerned about gold, not a huge surprise, but it did mention something about the latest mine effort still running dry.

Was it possible that the bank was having problems with the gold mines? He supposed that's why Remrant could be cozying up to Aselvia. He'd certainly made his stance on money very clear.

Slipping off the cord about the journal, he let it fall open to where it willed and read the entry there.

1232, Jal the 22nd

Aselvia maintains its distance. The young king's rule does not quaver, though this surely lies in the steady roots of their ancient and unchanging culture rather than the strength of his leadership. If there is any weakness within, the rest of the world cannot see it. But there must be. There always is.

29

E rrance stilled.

Weakness. If the man was interested in a strong alliance, why would he be seeking to exploit weakness…? He read on, breath shallow.

Rumor has it that the king took a queen from someone outside his people. A chema even, whose family sometimes travels to visit from the eastern side of Niar Strait. I have heard the chemas who live in eastern jungles are estranged from their northern brethren. It might be possible that the queen herself will visit her family home from time to time. And if she does not come out, it may be that her family could draw her out.

A queen's ransom would not be enough to fill the bank's coffers, but the gratitude a king might give in exchange for his queen's rescue would open up opportunity for a whole new source of wealth.

Errance closed the book and took a step back. His vision reeled, and only by bumping into the glass windows did he steady.

He should have known. He should have seen it sooner.

Did Taers know? He said the original person who hired him remained anonymous, but was that a lie? No, if Taers had known, he'd have already confronted Remrant or found some clue as to where Tryss was hidden.

What kind of twisted mind played both sides? No, he knew the type, he'd seen them in Tertorem, but Remrant was more convincing than most, more sincere.

What is he doing by dragging me around? Playing friends until our alliance is secure enough that he'll return the queen? Does he want us to secure the kingdom treasury in his bank? Something else?

There was no way that a man who had invested so much effort into such a complicated scheme would just let it be undone in a moment. He was not powerful in body, only in mind. If Errance confronted him now and threatened his life to give up the location, he was not likely to do it. Any answer might be a false one, and then who could say if Tryss would ever be found?

There was only one sure way that he'd see her again.

Footsteps. The faintest, lightest warning before the knob of the door began to turn.

No more time to think. If a game of deception was what Remrant wanted, then that was a game Errance knew how to play.

He set the book against his arm, thumbing through the pages, and turned to the window, letting the light cast him into shadow. Only after the door had opened and the figure had stepped inside did he slowly turn.

If there was one thing he knew from Tertorem, it was this—the only way you could control your enemy was to make *them* fear you.

"Remrant, Remrant," he said, still not looking up from the journal. "If you had only told me from the beginning, this would have been so much simpler."

After only a moment's consideration, Remrant resumed walking in, taking his chair by the ashen fireplace. "I thought I had locked that door," the man said, taking off his spectacles and rubbing them with a cloth. "But you know, old age, I thought it was simply my mistake. I certainly was not expecting to find you here."

"Late night reading is good for the soul, they say." Pressing the book shut, Errance set it upon the desk, fingers resting idly on the cover. "Although, I myself am a bit perturbed about the contents of this one."

"Is that so?" It must have taken many years to master such a look of innocence.

"Yes, call me sensitive, but I feel very lied to."

"And how," Remrant said, eyes fixed on the journal, "would the truth have helped my interests?"

"You seek to control the king, do you not? I could have helped you with that before this got so complicated."

"Reyid, I understand you don't like the man, but I didn't peg you a full-blooded traitor."

"How is it betrayal to serve the best interests of one's country and the world around him? You've proven what change we can make by working together, and world integration is something I have long sought. However—" Both palms came down flat upon the desk and he stared straight in the face of the man. "However, you chose to go about getting my attention by kidnapping the queen. I am not sure I can forgive that."

"Shall I call Beki for some tea?" Remrant said, beginning to rise.

"*NO.*"

Remrant sat back down with a sigh, rubbing at the wrinkles between his brows. "Well, it shouldn't surprise you that I have more than one reason. Everything I do, as you know, is meticulously planned for its effect. I shall start with the most rudimentary and embarrassing reason, of which you may have already guessed by looking through my things." He met Errance's stare eye to eye. "There is no more money, Reyid. The gold mines of my family dried up years ago. I've been running a sham show for some time, exchanging money between governments without acknowledging there really isn't enough gold backing them.

"And the fact is, Aselvia is very wealthy. I knew that this simply wasn't a story people dreamt up. I looked at the accounts of King Rendar's trades with the rest of Orim, and I noticed he accepted a great deal of gold. Now perhaps your roads are simply paved with it, but I believed that he was a man who prepared for the future, and that therefore he would have it locked away in some vault. But not just anybody can walk into Aselvia and even if one could, you can't expect to overthrow it and take the gold for yourself. So I wanted to establish friendship. I've been trying for a very long time, even before the new king came to the throne. That ambassador would always shut down whatever attempts Dormandy or other countries would make for a closer alliance. So clearly, other measures needed to be taken."

"You had Tryss kidnapped just so you could save her and present yourself the hero," Errance said, quiet, calm, cold.

"That is the truth. I know it seems wicked, but I assure you, she was never to be harmed in any of this."

"No harm?" he repeated, feeling the temperature of his blood rise. "No harm? She's late in pregnancy! How can you pretend this stress is not causing her harm?"

"To be fair, I was not aware that she was with child," Remrant said, adjusting his glasses. "You elves do keep your secrets close to your chest. I was only made aware of that detail once she was in my own custody. I assure you, her every need and desire has been met to make sure she and the baby are in good health. I would have provided her a midwife, but her own lady has kept close to her side throughout this whole venture."

Errance listened, even over the roaring in his ears. The man certainly had an endless stream of justification, as if such actions could be justified. "So you just dragged me around in search of her until we became lifelong friends, is that it?"

"Yes, exactly that. If I had just given her back at once, don't pretend you and your king wouldn't have said a brief thank-you and then slammed the door shut again. I needed to build a relationship. This may seem strange, Reyid, but I truly have enjoyed our time and our talks. And look at what we did together, look at all the people we rescued. Everything I do is for the greater good." He paused, and leaned forward. "I do hope that you can understand."

"I despise your methods," Errance spat.

Remrant waited.

"However."

The old's man mouth twitched.

"However," Errance said again, every word drawn out as if by a chain. He had to play along; he had to make the man believe him. "I do see your reasoning. And as I've said, I do believe Aselvia should be more involved in Orim than the king has previously allowed. So. More for the sake of the people we helped and the people like them, I am willing to consider our alliance further. I'm willing to talk to the king on your behalf and not mention your connection to the kidnapping. But I will only do this if I am given the queen back in complete health and safety. I must be taken to her now and she must be returned home, not missing a single hair from her head. No more games. No more tricks. None.”

“Of course, Reyid, of course. Tomorrow morning, then?”

What part of *now* had he not understood? Folding his arms to hide the tremor of his hands, Errance took a deep breath. “And why not this very moment?”

“Impossible.” Remrant shook his head as if this should be the most obvious thing in the world. “I’ve had plans on how I was to reveal myself the hero and another the villain eventually, but I was not prepared for the time table to be moved up so quickly. I must prepare for tomorrow to look convincing. At the very least, we have your red-headed friend to convince, do we not? Every report back to your king must be without question. At least have the confidence that since now you know my truth, I have nothing to gain from betraying you.”

In fact, his mind was trying to work out the different ways Remrant could use the delay to his advantage. But every single one set them as enemies, which was not the way to build an alliance. He had to trust that the wealth of Aselvia was indeed this man’s final goal.

But *stars,* he did not want to wait. She was so close. He couldn’t take losing her again.

“Very well,” he said. “I expect us to take the carriage the moment the curfew lifts.” Catching the journal back into his hand, he slapped it into Remrant’s open palm and strode from the room, not giving a glance back.

But once he made it to the door of his quarters, he hesitated. If he went in, Coren would surely be able to read from his expression that something else was wrong.

And he couldn't tell him. He knew he couldn't.

He knew he was being watched now. To accomplish all that he did, Remrant needed a plethora of spies and minions. Who could say if he had other chemas under his employ?

I think....I think I need that fresh air I talked about earlier.

30

He stood at the threshold of an old church, staring up at the brick building with its round glass window flickering with candlelight.

Coren had said he knew the parson. Earlier in their trip he'd suggested stopping by as it was one of his frequent shelters when he found himself in Dormandy, but they hadn't yet found the chance.

The friendly lamplighter who'd directed him here assured him the door would be open, that the old man who lived there always kept it unlocked. That seemed rather unsafe in Errance's opinion, and he still felt like an intruder when he turned the latch and stepped inside.

Candles in glass jars lined the walls, warming the dark room with a welcoming glow. Rows of empty benches led forward to the back of the room where there was a small wooden altar stacked with even more candles, a few bundles of dried flowers, and an open book. All the wood was quite old, but even in the candlelight Errance could see the place was faithfully kept clean. Taking care to not make a sound, he sat at the foremost bench and gazed at the little flickering flames on the altar.

It wasn't the breathtaking beauty of the woodland chapel, but it held its own peaceful sanctuary. He closed his eyes, letting the light and shadows dance only in his mind. The sounds on the street were muffled, fading by the moment, and the silence in the church sharpened until he could hear every slight detail. The hiss of the wicks, the drip of the wax, the skitter of a mouse's claws, and…the shuffle of slippers coming from the back room. He waited until the shuffle had drawn nearer and then he opened his eyes to stare at the old man just entering from a back door. The man paused when he saw him, and a slight smile curled his whiskered lips.

"Ah, I have a guest. Welcome, welcome, my friend." He once might have been a tall man, but he was stooped now and huddled in a thick brown robe with a yellow scarf draping down his shoulders. "Would you like some company or do you prefer the quiet?"

Errance glanced up at him and stiffened as a peculiar look came over the man's face. He raised his fingers to his cheek self-consciously, wondering if there was something to merit such a strange stare.

The man passed a hand over his eyes, looked again, and seemed no less troubled. "Your eyes," he murmured.

What about them? Yes, they were an unusual brilliance for humans, perhaps more so caught in candlelight, but he hadn't expected them to be so shocking. Perhaps he shouldn't have come here after all. "Sorry," he mumbled, beginning to stand.

The man waved his hands in protest. "Oh no, please, no, it is I who am sorry for disturbing you. Return to your rest; it is safe here."

He turned and began to walk away, but Errance couldn't shake the unease of seeing that expression. As if the man had known him. He couldn't leave it unquestioned. "There was something about my face," he said, a little harsher than he intended. "What was it?"

The old man paused, leaning over heavily. "I do not suspect there is anything the matter with your face, young man. I saw someone else's, I'm afraid, so I must go and pray about it."

"Where had you seen this face before?" His fingers curled against the wooden bench. Nobody should have recognized him, not here.

"A terrible place, I'm sorry to say. A place no man should ever be, and a place I am glad to have left long ago."

It couldn't be. It could mean anything. He might actually be right in saying he was seeing a face other than the one Errance wore. But what if…someone from long ago…from *that* terrible place. A guard? A slave?

It didn't matter. He had to get out of here.

He stood, starting for the door when the old man spoke again.

"Why does that trouble you?"

"If you're seeing a ghost, I don't need to hang around," he said briskly. It would take only a few steps to get him out of here, so why was he rooted in place?

The old parson came close again, this time holding a candle in his wrinkled hand. He squinted at Errance's face as if willing to see something different. "What is your name, young man?" he said.

Reyid. The name didn't slip off the tongue like it had before. An alarming urge to tell the truth hovered in his mind instead. "Doesn't matter," he said at last.

"My name is Ordan," the man said. "Does that mean anything to you?"

No. He'd heard many names over the course of his life, and few of them had mattered in the span of his imprisonment. "Why should it?" he rasped. "Where do you think you know me from?" He straightened and turned, narrowing his eyes in a challenge at the man. "As you said, I'm a young man, aren't I? Why would I remember you if it was a long time ago?"

"He was an elf," the man said. The uncertainty was gone from his voice, challenge rising to meet Errance's own. "He had the same defensive manner as you."

A small voice whispered in Errance's mind that a holy church wasn't the best scene for a confrontation and that smacking down an old man would be frowned upon, parson or not. He had to go now. Now. NOW. He was already five paces away, only a few more paces till the door—

"Errance."

He ground to a halt. No one in Tertorem had called him Errance. It was always the Prisoner or the Elf or a thousand names too cruel to repeat.

After a long silence, the man gave a thick cough. "I suppose you think I'm one of the guards who tormented you. That's fair. You're probably wondering why I am here as a parson in this old church if I came from that hellish place. But in truth, you were the one that set me on the right path, or at least warned me of the evils the wrong path would take one to. I don't expect to be welcomed, but I...I was the captain of the guard who pitied you and kept you at my quarters for a few days. You left on your own, back to the torture, rather than risk me being found out."

Errance's breath stilled. He did remember that. There had been a man who'd asked for his name. He'd forgotten. Strange, since it had been such a unique occurrence in his years of cruelty, but then it had been early on, at the end of the second decade, and the things that had happened afterwards had well and truly snuffed any hope the guard Ordan might have sparked. He couldn't speak, his mouth turned ashen.

"I don't expect you to thank me," the old man continued humbly. "I was no hero. I'd committed many crimes to reach such a place as there. I didn't go back and try to rescue you. I didn't even stay to see if I could abate your punishment when you returned to your overseers. I just left. I ran from Tertorem that day and never looked back. I hated myself for trying to help you and only going halfway. I'd assumed you'd died there. But here you are, if it is you, alive and not a ghost. I am glad to see you are free. You are free, are you not? Or have you come here seeking freedom?"

Errance sat down hard on the nearest bench. His legs were shaking, so he tucked them into the shadows. "Ayeshune saved me," he whispered. "Though I'm still figuring out what 'free' means."

"Your scars not fading, eh?"

Errance laughed shortly. "Please, isn't it obvious? Not a scar on me."

"Oh, I'm seeing quite a few," the old man said. "Some wounds sink in past the skin and stay there."

Burning tears pricked at the corners of his eyes. Blast. Blast it. Why did he have to encounter someone from *there*. Why now? He didn't need this. At least it was the *one* man who had shown him a bit of kindness as opposed to one who had done everything in his power to hurt him. The odds had been definitely stacked against meeting that *one*, so Oriah would call it Providence, but he didn't want this pain awakened right now. He had enough on his plate. To think he'd come here for peace.

"I never expected to see you again," the old man went on. "I should have tried taking you with me. It has always been one of my greatest regrets."

"How did you end up here?" Errance managed, throwing a vague hand about the chapel.

"Strange and long story that. I wandered for many years, seeking peace and some salvation. I finally did accept forgiveness in Ayeshune and I even found love. Marbil has been gone five years now."

"Sorry," he said. An automatic reply. But if he was honest, hearing it really did sting. The thought of lost love.

"No reason to be sorry for me. Death comes to all. The life I had with her was the greatest gift that could be found on this earth, I have no doubt of that. And we had a son who still lives nearby and helps take care of these old bones. What about you? What have you been doing?"

"Well." The words stuck in Errance's throat. He hadn't come here to have a conversation, least of all with someone from his past. How ludicrous could you get? But his soul was raw, and the words came out anyway, almost with a hysterical lilt in sharing them. "I got married."

"Oh, that is good," the parson said, genuinely delighted. "What is her name?"

"Tryss," Errance said, too tired to hold back, tired of lying. "Actually, that's why I'm here. She's missing."

"Missing? What do you mean?"

"She was kidnapped in Oolum some weeks ago. We tracked her here, but…"

"We? So you're not alone in this search?"

"I've got some help from the…" He didn't know why he was saying all this other than he was tired of keeping it all in. Coren he could talk to, but Coren already knew this. Maybe he'd gotten more used to speaking through his troubles with Leoren, Erran, and other wise men than he'd thought.

"Well, that's the funny thing. So I just found out that the very man who has been aiding my search," he breathed with a hoarse chuckle, "is the one behind the kidnapping."

Ordan stared at him for a long moment and then let out a low whistle. "That is some betrayal, that is. Somebody close to you? Trusted?"

"No, thank God. No, this is some political figure who has apparently been after an alliance with Aselvia for some time, and he's been working both sides of the game, playing me for a fool." He didn't know for sure if Ordan had ever known he was a prince and now a king, and he hoped he wouldn't ask for details now.

"Ahhh."

"The thing I cannot get over is how he seems absolutely convinced that he's in the right. I've met plenty of monsters who are well satisfied to be monsters, but I swear this man thinks all of his actions are justified and reasonable."

"That is true of most men."

"I'm not used to that," Errance said, jabbing a thumb at himself and then poking a finger back at the parson. "I'm used to Tertorem."

Ordan winced, then heaved a weary sigh. "Yes. Yes. Though a man can even find himself in Tertorem and justify his reasons for being there."

Errance let this lie for a few minutes while he stared at the flickering votives on the altar. "Do you speak of yourself?" he asked at last.

"As I said, I committed many crimes in my youth. After a childhood of violence and lawlessness, I took up a job as professional intimidation. The sort of muscle that rich men employ to get their way, a key element in political games. It was the nature of the world, and I was not ashamed of it. I was known to be a good shot with a crossbow, and soon enough I was hired as a hitman. I barely batted an eye at taking lives. It was not as if, I told myself, those lives didn't deserve to be taken. But living without mercy or remorse has a way of creeping up on a person. I may not have killed innocents, but the stain of blood reached further into me with every life I took. Contracts kept going higher up in the world until I heard whispers of an opportunity to work for the greatest power of all. I admit, going to Tertorem was the first time I truly questioned my decisions in life. But I surely would have given myself a reason to belong even there had I not been met with the brutal truth of its evil the day I met you."

After a few moments of quiet, Errance said, "I think that's what I find most terrifying about all of this. I was starting to think Remrant and I were so similar. That our goals aligned, that our alliance actually could make a difference in the world. But now that I know what lengths he's willing to go to and still call it good...I wonder if that same shadow resides in me."

"Shadow dwells in everyone. Accept that. And accept that you may abandon its lure and choose the right path. Accept that if you make mistakes, you can acknowledge it and correct what you've done. You don't have to figure out what is right and what is wrong by yourself. You've already been saved by the Light. Now just keep your eyes on that."

When Errance returned to his room at Remrant's house, he found Coren pacing a trail on the floor.

"There you are," Coren growled, coming to a halt. "I was just about to see if I could find you. Next time you go out, could you make the trip *a bit* shorter?"

"Sorry," he muttered.

The conversation with the parson had not continued after those heavy words were spoken, but he'd sat there a while more. The curfew bells had rung throughout the city long before he'd taken his leave, and fortunately he hadn't been stopped and questioned as he stole back to Albine Avenue.

"The fire went out and the bathwater is cold," Coren informed. "Not that you'd mind."

"Think I'll just go straight to bed. Probably another long day tomorrow." He headed to the water closet, changed into night attire, and threw himself under the bedcovers with as much haste as he could without raising any questions. Fortunately, Coren took the hint and turned out the lights.

He wasn't planning on sleeping. He honestly did not think he even could. And for hours he didn't, he only lay there, brain and body aching with unresolved tension, listening only to Coren's wheezing breaths and the creak of the house.

But as the night drew on, he sank into an unsettled sleep. At first it was only the darkness of dreams, and then it became dreams of darkness.

He could feel the oily caress slinking around his body. Somewhere, deep in the layers of shadows, voices whispered, reaching over impossible distances. He stood still, fearing even his own breath would betray his presence.

But they already knew he was here. They always knew.

Even now they drew near. He could feel them, if not see them. Each shade was distinct, and he knew them all by name.

He could try running, but that never worked—not in dreams, not in reality. In the end, they always caught him, like a cat with a mouse.

Sometimes it was almost better to submit rather than give oneself false hope. There wasn't much pride in that, but then there was no point to pride in dreams.

The world shuddered, a tremor from his physical body. He could feel consciousness so close, but they wouldn't let him go, not until they'd had their sport. These dreams could feel so real sometimes, and this one more than most.

"...Errance..."

He closed his eyes, but that could not prevent him from seeing the phantoms glide through edges of deeper darkness. One came closer than the rest, its features forming from the fog into delicate contours of beauty. Long, wavering fingers reached out for him. He jerked away at the last possible second. No, no, no, so long as he had strength, he would never submit, not even in nightmares.

As he flinched back, he felt another presence, strong and carnivorous, waiting for him to fall into its clutches. With a gasp, he stumbled to the side, reeling to catch his balance. A sudden sensation of plunging depths all around thrust his heart against his chest. He froze, terrified of one wrong step, and his desperate panting echoed in the mocking silence.

The wraith-like figures drifted on either side of him, their eyes aglow with hunger as wolves knowing their prey could not outlast their patience. "Come now," one whispered. "You know us so well, why so shy?"

A shadow suddenly darted from the rest, sharp teeth diving for his throat. He started to duck, but once again that sensation of standing on an edge pricked his mind, and he stiffened where he stood. The cage of teeth crashed shut before his face, and the purring laughter faded into disappointed growls. They continued pacing back and forth.

Struggling for air, Errance tried to watch them all from each corner of his eye. Their behavior made little sense. They never held back in his nightmares. The memories that haunted his sleep held no respect for his saved soul.

And yet they hung back as if a wall stood between them and their toy.

For the first time in any of his dreams, he realized that he could see his own body and surroundings in the darkness not because of the vision of dreams, but because there was light. Whether it had been there this entire time and he had only been blind or if it just now appeared, he did not know. But his gaze slowly dropped to his feet from where the light came.

He stood upon a thin path of white brilliance cutting through the night. The demons did not cross it and every time they drew near it, they darted away again.

Somehow knowing he was now aware of the path, the shadows twisted in grotesque patterns. "Come—come—come." Their rising voices rose from every side, growing more frantic and rough. They might as well have chanted, "Fall—fall—fall!"

The path went somewhere, perhaps to where horror could not follow. Squaring his shoulders, he began walking down the light, ignoring the reckless rage surrounding. There was a greater light ahead.

"Careful, dearest," a soft voice murmured in his ear. "This path is very narrow. Stray but a little…"

He could not suppress a shudder, but he kept walking.

"It is fragile, very fragile, like thin ice. Aren't you afraid it will break beneath your feet?" another voice rumbled. "Free to fall, straight to me?"

"It will not break," Errance said with more confidence than he felt. Even as he spoke, he fancied he felt it bend beneath him.

Fall—fall—fall.

"I did teach you well, didn't I? You can play the part of a traitor so convincingly. It comes so naturally to you, it's frightening."

They lie, Errance told himself. They always do. But it was often mixed with truth. And the narrowness of the path did unnerve him. Was he being careful enough to follow it in waking?

Darkness loomed in front of him. It stood on the path, a tall, terrible figure, drowning all light under its shadow.

The Voice spoke.

FALL.

Errance's knees buckled, and he collapsed to the floor. At the sound of that voice, everything rushed in tenfold. He could feel it again, the emptiness of his exposed soul with all Darkness rushing in. He could feel it now. Had his lack of faith bared him to their advances again?

"You struggle so to save your loved ones," the Voice mused. "Don't you know this world is mine? I master those in it as a puppeteer, and the One rarely stops me." His coiling figure swooped down to whisper at Errance's ear. "Don't you know I could kill your precious wife and child?"

The threat fell...and sounded strangely hollow. Perhaps it was because he had dreaded the idea so much already that it did not shock as intended. Or perhaps...

Errance lifted his head and stared at him. "You're afraid."

There was a dreadful silence. Then—

"What?"

"You're afraid of me." The painful grip on his chest loosened as he saw total confirmation in the Voice's confounded expression. "You've always feared what I could do if I was saved. And after I was saved, you've been nothing but *afraid of me."*

"I am the one holding the lives of your wife and child over your head," The Voice snapped, too obvious in getting back to the threat at hand.

"No, you aren't. They don't belong to you. Even if they did die—and I admit that thought terrifies me—it will only be a small separation in the end. Is that all you can threaten? Glorious eternity, beyond your stain, where I shall someday join them? A sliver of mortal time?" He drew in a hissing breath, his fingers curling against his palms. "That's some victory."

"You in glorious eternity?" The Voice jerked back, ribbons of darkness lashing out like a cat o' nine. "You have hardly enough faith to make it there."

"No," Errance snarled through his teeth, pushing himself off the ground. "No, I have been saved. I am redeemed by One, and no other may have me. I may stumble, but I will not fall. No prison can keep me."

Panting with the effort, he raised his head and looked straight at the Darkness, his eyes ablaze with the purest of fire. He saw it then, the path of light beyond him, shining and true as ever.

"Out. Of. My. Way." Errance surged to his feet and stalked forward, his hand slashing out like a sword.

With a shriek, the Darkness shredded before him, vanishing altogether and dragging the smaller shadows away with it.

Light shone softly around him, the bright path now spread as far as the eye could see. Here there was peaceful quiet, the kind that is not utterly silent, but aware of life—distant twinkling water, the flutes of bird song, and the whisper of trees unseen.

And another Presence was there, quietly waiting. Errance again dropped to his knees, but now as an act of a weary son in need of comfort and renewal. Some distant corner of his mind wondered why he did not demand all the answers to the questions that had tormented him of late. This very Presence was answer enough, even if he felt too small to understand why. It was power, it was wisdom, and it was love. It was enough.

"Be mindful of your steps in this journey, brave heart," *said the One. A warm, strong hand clasped Errance's shoulder, and for just a moment, he looked into eyes shining with galaxies.*

"Walk well."

31

He couldn't hide his tension in the morning, even with the excuse of a poor night's sleep, and when Coren questioned him about it, he told the truth concerning the parson and their shared past. It was enough to explain his mood, and it distracted Coren thoroughly.

He had come so close to sending Flyfar to Tryss with the message that they were on their way to rescue her. But he didn't dare. If her captors happened to catch the bird or if they had been intercepting messages all along—then his deception would be ruined and his chance to find her with it.

A bit of warmth began to color the light coming through the window. He kept glancing at it, wondering when it would be time to head out. Would Remrant come to them with his pretense or would he have to remind him of the urgency?

"Worried about Taers?" Coren followed his gaze to the window. "Brights, it's unnerving he can just slide in and out like that."

"Yeah." By the stars, he wished he could tell him the truth. Give him some clue that something else was wrong. But what could he say without endangering all of them?

The swish of footsteps sounded just outside their door, and then a rapid knock on the wood.

"Come in," Errance called.

"I have it," Remrant said triumphantly as he entered the room, waving a slip of paper in his hand. "A lead on who ordered the queen's kidnapping."

He said it with such conviction Errance began to start forward. Just in time, he remembered to go along with that sensation, rather than turn cold at knowing the truth. "Who?" he demanded, eyes burning hot enough to burn Remrant's own from his skull.

"A tip that the Chancellor of Korince had a secret bounty sent up North for undisclosed reasons. The timing is immaculate."

"The Chancellor of Korince!" Coren growled. "I've heard things about him. Honestly, my conscience has trouble bringing shipments in and out of that city. The city has its share of splendor and talent, but their leader has made himself fat upon it. I've heard slavers go in and out as if there was no law supposed to be keeping them away. The brothel houses are fully legal, which is part of the attraction for the rich, but nobody bothers to check under what rules or conditions."

"True enough," Remrant said with a sigh. "We have a bit of an understanding with so much of his wealth invested in my bank. As in, we understand not to like or trust each other."

"And what did he plan to do?" Errance said, trying not to feel so unsettled that Coren bought the news so easily. "Surely he did not think he could keep the Queen of Aselvia as his secret prize?"

"I wouldn't put it past him." Remrant gave an indelicate snort. "Even so, I'm sure his plans run deeper. He is a man who lives on blackmail, on secrets, and others' shame. I will do my best to investigate what he intends, but—" he leaned forward, fingers folded beneath his chin, eyes twinkling. "But I have better news than that. We found her. My spy brought news of her location just this morning."

"Brights!" Coren swore, leaping forward. But then he paused and looked back at Errance, questions and concern upon his face.

For Errance remained frozen in place. He didn't think it was the most unbelievable response to the news. After all this time, he could finally see the end, and it stole the strength from his body. But it was also so terrible, so ready to go wrong at any moment.

His cousin was sharp enough to sense that wrongness, even if he didn't know why.

His tongue had turned dry and sharp as paper in his mouth, making every breath or even thought of speaking difficult. "Where?" he managed to choke. "Where is she?"

"Right here in Dormandy. The Chancellor was not such a fool as to hide her in his own city. He's been very good about keeping himself anonymous in this plot; he might have had plans to blame it on someone else."

Exactly the thing that you are doing, you clever wretch.

"There have been rumors of a pregnant woman in one of the housing quarters, yet the house was not rented to anyone who spoke of having women there. When I had my spies inquire further, we found a witness who saw two women taken there late at night. Their descriptions match your missing queen and midwife."

Errance's hands slowly closed, tightening into fists. "All right," he said hoarsely. "Then take me there. Take me there now."

As Remrant hastened from the room, Coren took a step nearer to Errance. "Are you okay?" he whispered.

"I will be. After we save them."

"We will. We're going to save them."

"I know." His teeth ached with the pressure of his clenched jaw. "I know."

Now meant two very different things to Errance and Remrant.

For Remrant, it meant waiting another hour or two until his mercenaries had arrived in their carriages to accompany them on the incursion. In reality, it must have taken a great deal of money to persuade them to respond so quickly when the notice reached them that very morning, but Errance was not in the mood to appreciate their hasty arrival.

It was certainly a fine display of Remrant's intention to rescue the queen, but all it really meant was that Remrant not only had the men keeping Tryss captive at his disposal, but also these reinforcements. Whether they were all the same men as on the night of the chema ambush or not, who could say, but he thought he recognized at least a few.

It would not be an easy thing to spirit Tryss away to safety.

For a forgetful moment, he'd imagined playing along with the ruse until they were all safely returned to Aselvia, leaving Remrant hung out to dry. But that would never work.

When Tryss saw him, she would speak his name, and the game would be over.

Remrant would know he was the king, living a lie of his own.

A fight was inevitable.

He just couldn't see a way they all made it out.

Silence between the three of them stifled the atmosphere as the carriage took them along through the streets of Dormandy. It wasn't a far drive when they stopped, and Errance found himself looking out at houses only a little less classy than Albine Avenue. How maddening to know she'd been this close all along.

There were a few people walking down the street, looking curiously at the carriages parked in front of the house and the men piling out of them. Somehow, Errance didn't think the Governor had given them a license for this, but since Remrant no doubt owned the house, he'd find a way to brush the disturbance under the rug.

The man at the lead knocked on the door. Knocked again, and called out in a loud voice. After a moment, the door cracked open, and the mercenary took that as his opportunity to barrel right inside. There was some shouting as more of Remrant's men trooped in, Errance in their shadow.

He glanced about the house to see that the guards inside the house had all been taken captive. A bit of food was spread out on the table, suggesting they'd been interrupted in their midday meal. Their expressions and exclamations of outrage were so genuine that he guessed they really hadn't expected to be raided just then. There was even a chance they didn't know that the man who'd employed them was the man now walking over the threshold.

"Well done, gentlemen, efficient as always," Remrant said with a quaint clap of his hand against the top of his cane. He approached one of the captive house guards. "Now then, sir, yes, you. Stop struggling for a moment and don't pretend to be innocent. Where are the women you are keeping here?"

"What! Women? There are no women!"

"Yes, well, we shall see how long you keep that story up. Master Reyid, how about you check that room over there?"

Errance followed the direction of his point to a closed door at the far end of the house. His footsteps on the rug echoed the dull thud of his heartbeat. He could feel Coren's eyes on him, full of expectation, apprehension, and uncertainty.

He touched the brass knob and found it locked, but beyond the door, he could hear her. He could hear Tryss's voice, tense and worried, caught in some argument against Dahlya's mellow and reassuring tones.

By all the stars in the heavens, it was really her. She was really there in that room.

There was nothing he wanted more than to be the first one through that door, the first one that Tryss saw.

But he couldn't. He had to be the one who started the confusion and chaos. He had to be the one that controlled it, that steered it away from Tryss and Dahlya, giving Coren the chance to free them.

Coren was still looking at him, still trying to guess at things he knew he didn't dare ask aloud. Errance could not look back. He could only trust that his cousin would see this through.

He took a deep breath and turned around. "The key, if you please."

Remrant snapped a finger at a man holding one of the house guards captive, and they produced a key in a matter of moments.

"Thank you, Remrant," Errance said softly, as his fingers closed around the proffered key. "At least this wasn't another lie."

Remrant's spine went stiff, and his eyes narrowed in suspicion.

"Coren," Errance said, quiet and mild as he handed the key over to his cousin. "Please go in, explain things, lead them out, and take them somewhere safe."

"Reyid…" A warning hung in Remrant's tone as he lifted his hand, and the guards by his side tensed.

"I'm sorry, Remrant Cole," Errance said. "But our road ends here."

"Somehow that apology feels very insincere." Remrant's eyes turned cold. "Think this through, Reyid. There is so much we could accomplish together."

"I've thought it through."

A long, rigid moment of stillness stretched out between them. Then Remrant sighed. "In that case, Reyid, it is my turn to apologize. Only, I really do mean it." He flicked his hand to the men around him. "Take him, and do not let the others escape."

The truth dawned on Coren in the matter of a moment. He'd known all morning something was dreadfully wrong, that Errance's mood had not suited a man about to be reunited with his missing wife.

Their very helper was their enemy, and now they were surrounded. Couldn't Errance have waited until they were out of the house? No, he supposed the truth could not have waited till then. Nothing for it now.

He stabbed the key into the lock and twisted. Mercifully, it opened, which meant there would be no breaking door-knobs today. He closed it behind him with a firm click and braced himself against it as he faced the room.

Tryss and Dahlya stared back at him in shock. The queen lay on one of the couches, and the lines in her face and sweat on her skin said she was in pain. Dahlya knelt beside her, stiff with apprehension.

"Coren?" Tryss managed, sounding almost strangled. "Is that you?"

Coren hurried to them, hoping their voices wouldn't carry to the people outside. "Yes, yes, it's me. Errance is here too, we're here at last. Are you all right? What's wrong?"

"I'm in the middle of labor, is what's wrong!" Tryss snapped, struggling to push herself upright. "Where's Errance? Where is he?"

In the middle of labor—no, no, no, could the timing be any worse? "He's holding off your captors as we speak. I've got to get you both out of here now." He looked down at Dahlya's whitened face. "How far along is she?"

"We're still in fairly early stages," Dahlya said, rising to her feet. "I know we have no choice but to move her, but I hope you have somewhere nearby where we can finish."

"I do." In truth, he had no such place in mind, but he'd have to think of one as they went. "Okay. Okay, let's do this." He knelt down and scooped Tryss up into his arms. "Tryss, you will probably see him as we leave, but you can't call his name, all right? We're undercover; blowing his identity now would only make things worse."

Tryss spat something in response he was fairly certain was chemish swearing. Good lord, he'd never seen her sweet self this angry before. But he supposed birth pains, untimely rescues, and a husband in danger could do that to a girl.

Something crashed outside the door. Voices were now raised in shouts, and steel clanged together.

"Ah." Coren's shoulders drooped. He wouldn't be able to defend them at all while carrying Tryss. He only could hope to move fast while carrying a very pregnant woman. "I don't suppose you can do that chema thing now and hide us all?"

Tryss's glare and groan was answer enough.

"I thought not. Well, nothing for it. Dahlya, keep close. We're just going to have to run for it."

Remrant's men had let go of the house guards and now they were all facing him, waiting for the word to attack.

"Take him alive and do not harm him, if you can," Remrant said, stepping back towards the door. "And whatever you do, don't let the redhead escape with the women. Reinforcements are arriving, as I thought this might happen."

Errance could hear them now, the clatter of a wagon pulling up outside the house, and the mutter of many men. There was not much chance he could protect Coren's path out the front door, but there had to be another door, right? Or a window? Yes, he could see a large window and possibly a servant door in the kitchens down the wide hallway to his left.

The first man gave an attempt at a roar and charged. *Yes, yes, how about all of you attack one at a time, why don't you,* Errance thought as he ducked under the tackle. *It will make my job a lot easier.* He caught the leg of a nearby chair as he swung upright and brought it cracking down against the head of his first attacker. Another man was on him in the same moment, arms around his neck. He reached over his own shoulders and dug his fingers into the man's face until he felt the grip loosen just enough to twist around and knee him to the floor.

The door beyond him opened, and Coren stepped out, Tryss held in his arms and Dahlya close to his side.

Just for one breath, he let himself look at her. His wife.

There was pain in her face, though if that was from their situation or something else, he couldn't say, and he couldn't let himself wonder.

"Your left!" he shouted.

Coren didn't hesitate, immediately spotting the kitchen and way of exit. He bolted for it.

Several of the men leapt towards him to block the way, but Errance leapt first, meeting them halfway. He dropped low to the floor, jabbing into the flesh behind the knee and striking the kidney as he rose. When one man dropped, he went to the next. One of them slipped past him. As he caught another in a stranglehold, he reached to his belt, and flung out a knife that embedded into the leg of the man catching up to Coren. It didn't bring him down, but it slowed him. Slowed him enough. Errance grabbed another man's arm and spun him, letting him go crashing into his fellows while using the momentum to launch toward the one that got away. He felled him with a strike from the edge of his hand to the neck.

Coren was out the door, Tryss and Dahlya with him.

He would not be able to thank Leoren enough for insisting he keep training in combat these last seven years. It had seemed a terrible idea to him at the time, even if he had found some comfort in it later. But now it was priceless. His trainer had kept his speed and senses sharp, even honed them in ways that Tertorem's chaotic nature hadn't.

There were more men; the reinforcements Remrant promised had arrived. And now Errance had far too many tangents to cover. He couldn't let anyone out through the kitchen door in direct pursuit of Coren, but at the same time, he had to stop enemies from going out the front door and intercepting them on the street.

Remrant was calling orders, no doubt redirecting men to the outside exactly as Errance feared.

Remrant.

Dodging his next assailants, Errance leapt for the kitchen table and from that to the shelf lining the wall. He didn't stay anywhere long, just touched something solid enough to propel himself across the room like a leaf on the wind.

Remrant saw him coming, evading each and every brute that sought to stop him. The man started to retreat for his carriage, as he should have done in the first place.

But Errance was already there. He grabbed Remrant by the collar as the man turned to run and pulled him into a tight chokehold.

"Stop there, or your employer dies!" Errance shouted through the open door at the men who were outside on the street.

That halted them, sure enough.

He doubted they had any real loyalty to Remrant, but they were being paid for this job, and as Remrant dearly loved to say, gold was a god to man.

"You are certainly effective," Remrant managed to gasp out past the tight hold around his throat.

"Call them off," Errance growled. "Call them all off."

"And then you'll let me go?"

"I'm not letting you go until my friends have had sufficient chance to escape."

"Ah. Ah, I thought as much."

Bright red pain pierced into Errance's side.

For some reason, he hadn't pictured Remrant carrying a knife, much less using one.

Ridiculous that he hadn't considered it when he was used to thinking everyone a threat. He really had let this man pull the wool over his eyes.

Hissing in a breath, he found the knife with his free hand and twisted Remrant's fingers off of the hilt. He didn't pull it out because while it hadn't hit an artery, it was still bleeding. "At least you had the stomach to do it yourself," he growled. "But next time, try a longer knife if you want to kill me."

"Reyid. I've never had any intention of killing you."

Errance felt it then, felt the sudden sway in his head.

It wasn't poison.

His celestial light would combat poison.

But it couldn't identify a sleeping drug as a threat. And now in his bloodstream, it was spreading fast.

Errance took a stumbling step back and braced himself against the wall, still holding Remrant between him and the mercenaries. He didn't have long. He just hoped it was long enough to give Coren the time he needed.

Remrant was saying something again, but he couldn't hear him past the heavy weight that was dulling his senses.

The only thing he could see now was his memory of that brief glimpse of Tryss's face. Why were her beautiful features crumpled in pain? Why? Why....

The darkness enveloped him.

32

"Finally, you're waking up."

Errance heard those words before he was aware of anything else. What sign of waking he'd given, he couldn't guess. He peeled his eyes open and took in his surroundings.

He was back in Remrant Cole's apartment. He was tied to a chair in the middle of the parlor. The light outside the windows suggested a few hours had passed. The crick in his neck confirmed that. His senses were fuzzy, the drug clinging on for as long as it could. The pain in his side still ached.

"You'll be glad to know," Remrant went on, for it was he who had spoken, "that we haven't found the queen, her midwife, or your redheaded associate. They melted into the city, and my men have not come back with any report of where they went."

There were two other men standing in the room, close to where Errance sat bound. Large, unpleasant looking men. He recognized them vaguely as the ones Remrant had known by name among the hired muscle, mentioning that he'd worked with them before. They must have been employed by the bank for these sorts of jobs on the regular, since they looked comfortable and adjusted to the whole affair.

When he looked further into the corners of the house, he saw more figures. Remrant was taking precautions, as he should.

Errance cleared his throat, trying to prevent any chance of a voice crack when he spoke. "So I guess that means I won."

"It was really quite impressive, how you defeated so many of my men so quickly." He shook his head in disappointment. "Oh, Reyid. I had suspected this outcome, for certain—but I *had hoped* that you truly saw things my way. I hadn't wanted it to come to this."

"But now it has," Errance said grimly. "So what happens next?"

Remrant sighed, sitting in his own chair across the way and running a hand through his hair. "I have wondered that very thing. You see, until now, I have been very meticulous not to cause any permanent damage. You saw the queen a few moments ago; she was in perfect health. I have taken great care that this plan ultimately profits everyone. And even when you had to go snooping, I gave you the benefit of the doubt. Now the queen is gone, and while I would be willing to suffer that loss and wait for the next opportunity, you clearly are working against me. If I let you go, you will return to the king and paint me in a negative light, will you not? So you tell me, Reyid, what am I supposed to do?"

"What villains normally do, I suspect."

"Sticks and stones, Reyid. For now, I'll keep you locked away here. You told no one else our secret, fortunately. Or so you promised." His eyes narrowed. "You know, you seemed so sincere about joining me. It makes me wonder what else you've lied about." His mouth hardening, he gave a sharp nod to both the waiting brutes. They stepped forward, untying the rope that bound his torso to the chair, but not the one that bound his wrists together. "Take him to the basement for questioning and keep him there until I have decided on a course of action."

"Come and watch," Errance said sharply, forcing a step forward, dragging his captors with him. "The suffering of others is always intoxicating as wine to the likes of you."

"Don't mock me," Remrant said, rising to his feet and throwing him a look of disgust. "Sometimes, the hard thing is required in life. You have put me in an extremely difficult position, so don't shift the blame. And by gods, don't pretend to be so righteous. I have seen that you would do anything to save the woman you love. My motivation is just a bit broader, that's all. I am not the villain."

"No," Errance spat. "No, you're just a coward."

"We're done here. Garis, Ban." Remrant flicked a hand to the basement door. "If you please."

The men dragged him towards the door, now prepared for a fight after his first sign of resistance. Errance thought about trying to escape then and there, but the remnant of the drug still clung to the corners of his mind like dusty cobwebs, slowing his movement and ease of thought.

But when the door shut behind him, leaving the stairwell dark and yawning below, he wondered if he should have fought all the same. There were a few candles along the way to prevent anyone from tripping, but precious few. They passed wooden doors to pantries and storage rooms. And then the wallpaper and plaster that usually covered the house interior gave way to cold stone.

"Does Remrant often have you dragging people down here for questioning?" If it was an interrogation that was coming, he might as well get answers of his own.

"You'll be the one giving answers, not us," the one walking ahead of him said. "You gave a storm of a fight back there, and I owe you a few bruises."

"It was a fair fight. We could always try again if you want to be sporting about it."

"Enough of that." Pushing his elbow into the small of Errance's back, the man shoved him against the wall. Errance involuntarily flinched, waiting for some follow-up, but there was no strike, just rank breath against his neck. The moment stretched, and he could feel the contemplative study if not see it. "Garis," the man spoke again. "You ever heard of Brivan's gladiatorial theatre? Word is they pay a fortune for fine foreigners. How much do you figure he'd fetch?"

"Master Cole said to make him talk, not to get rid of him," the other man said, pausing on the stair and turning around to look at them.

"Oh, we can make him talk, I was just thinking about what happens after that. Cole will want him gone in some way since he knows too much. I'm just saying it would be a shame to dump this body in the river."

Good lord. Errance's eyes fluttered shut. Had Remrant's stance against trafficking also been a ruse or did he have no clue that the very men he employed were willing to supply the market for some extra coin?

Wrenching him off the wall, the man dragged him a bit further down the stairs and around the corner into the empty basement. Empty, except for a chair bolted down to the floor.

And a figure standing beside it.

He almost didn't notice them at first, for they were not quite material. Almost a hallucination. Except when he focused on it, they became clear, as opposed to flitting away.

Ajahliesh. One of the Red Three. Lord of wealth, mastery, and dominion. Just another way of saying the master of slaves.

"Fancy meeting you here," Errance said coldly, nodding to the stone walls and interrogation chair. "Given this setting, I would have expected Raduer."

"A little bird told me that profit is on the wind," Ajahliesh replied. "So I headed right over." His gold teeth flashed in a glittering smile. "After all, you have always been one of my favorites."

"Just one of them?"

A fist cuffed Errance's temple, scattering stars across his vision. "Enough of that!" the man named Garis said. "Who are you even talking to?"

When Errance's vision cleared, the room was empty. No demon. Just the chair.

"Come on then, fancy thing," Garis said, shoving him forward. "The sooner you talk, the less I have to mess up that face of yours."

He didn't have to listen to this. He didn't have to take it. He was *not* in Tertorem with no way out, no hope of a better tomorrow.

His tomorrow was today, and it was waiting for him just outside.

Drug or no drug, the brief glimpse of Ajahliesh was all the motivation he needed to leave now.

He threw himself backwards, smashing Garis against the wall and pinning him there with his shoulder blades. He'd already seen where the man kept his knife on his belt, and his bound wrists quickly found it. Pulling it partway out of the sheath, he caught the rope on the sharp edge and sawed once, twice. It was just enough for him to wrench his wrists apart, breaking the torn fibers.

The one called Ban was there now, seizing his freed hands before he had a chance to use them. They grappled for a moment, and then Errance found his face crushed against the wall again. His arm was twisted behind his back, forced upwards into an unnatural angle. The strain was less than seconds from rending tendons, the pain enough to drive any thought of escape from mortal man.

As if pain *mattered.*

Snarling, Errance forced his knee up between his chest and the wall, found a footing, and shoved backwards, toppling the man pressed against him. The hold on his arm broke, the pain flared, and then leveled.

Garis was on top of him before he could run, a thick arm wrapping around his neck, the other around his body. A tight, solid hold. Good. Throwing his weight fully against the man, he scythed out an arcing kick, catching Ban on the temple with the heel of his boot. The brute crumbled to the floor.

Garis's arm was still around his throat, and his arms were still pinned to his sides. But he hadn't set his feet down to the ground yet, so his weight hung entirely dependent on his captor's strength. The man was trying to regain balance from Errance's momentum. It was enough. Just enough to wiggle his body downwards till his chin was tucked underneath the arm, and he could bite.

Bite hard.

The fabric was thin enough to taste blood.

His captor yelled, releasing his grip, and Errance dropped to the floor and rolled forwards.

When he turned around, still on the tips of his hands and toes, Garis was lunging for him again. Errance tackled him at the knees, bringing him down with a crash. Before the man could recover yet another time, he grabbed him by the roots of his hair, yanked his head forward, and then cracked it back against the stone floor. Garis's eyes rolled up into his head and he went limp.

Errance wiped his mouth, fingers coming away bloody. Somewhere in the struggle, he'd bitten his lip, but even now, he couldn't feel it.

He staggered upright, limbs shaking. His attackers were stunned, but he knew that it might not last long. There were other guards in the house, but they weren't expecting trouble right now. He could run for it. Already, his mind was mapping out the floors above him and the nearest exit.

He started up the stairs, trying to keep his footsteps silent as they were swift.

Just as he reached the door at the top of the stair, he heard the creak of it opening from the other side.

A young man, Remrant's clerk, stood there, papers and pen in hand. The young man jolted backwards upon seeing Errance, his pupils terrified dots in the whites of his eyes.

In that brief moment, Errance knew. He was about to kill the boy. His body was already tensing for those quick, sharp movements ingrained into his limbs that would end a life in a few seconds flat.

No.

No. The boy was simply in his way. Perhaps he was here by accident, perhaps on purpose. Whatever his motivation or mindset, his backstory, his future, it didn't matter. He didn't need to die.

Shifting the strike of his hand, Errance grabbed the boy by the shoulder and threw him to the side. He heard him crash into the wall and stumble down the stairs with a startled cry, but he'd be fine. He closed the door behind him.

No one else appeared to be around just then, thank God, but someone would be guarding the front door, he was certain. The windows didn't open on the lower floor. So, the servant door it was then. Down that hall, past the kitchen, past the broom closet, and then—

He burst out the door, the free, fresh wind striking his face with fierce thrill.

He sprinted down the street with wild abandon, not caring if anyone looked his way. He was free, and no one, *no one*, could take that away from him.

Up in Master Cole's study, the teakettle was beginning to whistle. Gripping its handle with a mitt, Remrant poured it into the awaiting cups on the small table, set it aside, and then settled another log onto the fire. The clouds outside were growing darker and he would need the warmth to continue through the cold day. The only heat left in the room was from that fire and a single candle, but it was enough to drink tea by. He sat in the cushioned chair, taking sips in a rhythmic trance, his eyes fixed on the empty chair across from him and a game of Feint set up on the table.

A log in the fire shifted with a crunch, sending sparks up the chimney.

After a moment, Remrant stood, picked up the second teacup and placed it back in the cupboard.

33

That was the thing about large cities. They had so many buildings you could never find the one you were looking for.

There had been no time in the rescue to discuss a meeting point, and all the places they had stayed in Dormandy had been somewhere Remrant would be aware of. There was a chance that Coren would just take Tryss straight back to Aselvia, since that would be the safest. Yet he was certain that they were still somewhere here, somewhere Coren could be certain they'd be taken care of until they could know what had happened....

It was not a very crowded street, not like Oolum where you could barely move without bumping into anyone, but it was still busy enough that he felt both surrounded and exposed. Shoulders hunched, he kept his face turned down to the cobblestones while still managing to dodge the various gentlemen and women who busied themselves from building to building.

...the church.

The very moment the idea flitted through his mind, Errance knew it was true. Coren had been the first one to tell him about it; he'd been there before and considered it trustworthy. Remrant eventually might think to look in such a place, but it probably would not be his first thought that the God whom the elves called Lord was the same one that humans prayed to in a little brick building on a Dormandy curb. Anyway, even if they weren't there, it would give him a place to breathe and gather his composure. And it wasn't far.

He broke into a run again. Not as fast as he would have liked, since he still had to be careful of people and carriages, and at this point, he didn't want to look as if he was fleeing for his life. He didn't think anyone was after him yet, but if they were, it would do no good to lead them straight to the sanctuary.

The street where the old chapel stood was quieter than most, and he forced himself to slow down, pause, and be certain that nobody was looking his way before he hurried inside.

Freshly cut flowers spread across the altar at the front of the pews, and Ordan stood there, arranging them into little pewter vases. The old man's head lifted at the sound of the door opening, the remnant of a captain's sternness on his weathered features, but a look of relief replaced it a moment later. "There you are," he said. "I told the redhead you were sure to be along soon, but he was about to head out and look for you anyway."

"Where are they?" Errance managed, the words strained between his heaving breaths. He hadn't been running fast as all that, but this whole horrid experience left him quite winded.

"In my quarters," he answered, softening still more. "Through that door and up the stai—"

But Errance was already through the door and taking three steps up at a time. He burst through the final door barring the way to his wife, and there, at last, she was.

Fear struck a painful chord across his nerves, for she was lying in bed, eyes closed, as if in a faint rather than a restful sleep. Dahlya was nearby, folding blankets into a basket. He started forward, only to trip over a large tin bathtub that had been pulled to the center of the floor, of all blasted things. He very nearly fell into it, except Coren caught him by the arm. He had not even noticed Coren in the room, which must have been because he'd stood near the door when he'd burst in.

"Careful, careful," his cousin said, helping him regain balance.

Some vague part of Errance recognized that the water was a pink, bloody color, which sent an equally vague fright that someone had been injured rushing through him. But he hardly noticed any of these things, for he was now finally at the side of the bed.

His knees gave out from under him, and then his arms were wrapped around her, his face nestled against her neck. He could hear the sound of relief and joy in her voice, but he hardly understood what she said. After a few moments, the blurred reverberations formed themselves into words.

"Thank God you're here," she was saying. "You gave me such a fright, Errance, such a fright—"

He pulled back and cupped her face between his hands, pressing a kiss to her mouth as if she was the only air in his universe. She was more real than any lovely dream, more warm than any sunlight that had ever touched his skin. Her fingers wrapped around his in a fierce grip as she returned it with all the long frustration of their separation.

He pulled back after a few moments, everything in the room spinning but her. Her eyes were glowing with relief and happiness, but saints, she was looking so weary and ragged. What had been done to tire her so? Her hair was clinging to her face as if both had been damp, even though she was sponged dry now. And she seemed…smaller. When he'd been embracing her, something had felt different. Her belly was still large, but not as large as it had been, and—

His mind went blank.

Slowly, he looked over at Dahlya and the basket she'd been so busy over. She was holding a bundle of the blankets now, her arms nestled up close to her chest for support. When she saw Errance look at her and Tryss reach out a hand, she stepped forward.

Tryss struggled to sit up, Errance quick to assist, and reached out to accept the bundle that Dahlya offered. She tugged back the wrap of soft cloth, revealing the little rosy face within. "Rather…rather awkward timing, this one," she said with a breathy chuckle. "But I'm glad she didn't come any earlier or leaving that place could have been harder. I mean, it was hard enough, but at least I got to deliver her in safety. The parson here was so kind to lend us his room and bathtub."

She was talking so normally. How could she talk so normally?

She'd given birth. The baby that had been on the inside was on the outside, and it hadn't been that long since he'd seen her, a few hours at the most. He hadn't ever been at a birth, but from what he heard, they were supposed to be longer than that, weren't they? His mind wasn't functioning. Some distant part of him knew he'd stood and taken a few steps away, as if to reorient himself. Tryss was looking at him, head tilted.

Then his breath burst out in a windy rush, and he was back on his knees, peering at the tiny creature in his wife's arms. "I...I...I can't even...how even...are you both well? Is she all right?"

"Yes, yes, our baby is a she, and she is as healthy as can be. Dahlya says my body took it well, despite the stress, which is largely due to her quick work in helping me with a water birth. It was quite the fortunate thing, the old parson had just filled his tub for a bath when we arrived."

"The water had been boiled earlier and was about the right temperature when we came in, so, while it may not have had all the precaution I would have taken in Aselvia, I did need the tension in Tryss's body to ease," Dahlya said in a hurry, as if afraid Errance would question the safety of it all. "I had Coren drag it to the center of the room and it went on from there. In Aselvia, I would have cleaned it out a few times already, but circumstances—"

"You have served my queen beautifully and courageously, Dahlya," Errance said. "Nobody doubts your decisions as a midwife."

He raised his eyes from his child to his wife, still frightened over her wan complexion. "Your body is well, but how are you feeling? I can't imagine what you've been going through, I'm so sorry, I should have gotten to you sooner, I should have—"

Tryss lifted a tired hand and set it against his lips. "Shhh. None of that, My Majesty, none of that. It is enough," and a smile floated upon her mouth, "that you are here. That was the last thing weighing my heart down. I just need you here to see her. To hold her. Your princess, Cerenity."

"Should I hold her?" Errance stared down at the tiny, pink, and somewhat squishy elf maiden, certain that he was quite unqualified. Wasn't it safer for the mother to keep her close? Or if not the mother, then a trained professional like Dahlya? Wouldn't it be better to wait at least a few days, just to be sure that the child could not be damaged by mere touch—oh help, she was already handing her over, and he could do nothing but accept.

Oh, heaven.

Holding the child in the streets of Oolum had been an experience in and of itself, but this—

This baby was so small, so impossibly small and light. And it was the child that he and Tryss had created. A mystery that both thrilled and terrified him with the wonder of it all.

Cerenity.

She squirmed in his arms, rosebud mouth opening and closing with a soundless sigh. She seemed awfully calm for having been through such a drastic change in scenery. Her pale lashes lifted, revealing bright cyan eyes like his own. While her skin was still ruddy from birth, her hair had been cleaned. It lay upon her crown like wisps of morning mist, soft and silver-warm. While hard to be sure this early, he thought her features favored Tryss. But ah, she did have distinct elf ears. He had been a bit curious how the ears would turn out; wondering if there could be a hybrid of the two.

"I thought perhaps that her coloring might be all white and silver like your celestial kin," Tryss said faintly. "But it didn't quite catch, though her hair is paler than mine. Her eyes are just like yours. The color is always in my thoughts."

"Heavens, you mean you can influence that in the womb?"

"I was waiting for the right time to tell you. Then I thought it might make a nice surprise, and then things happened, as you know. She might have some skill of her own as she grows and can color herself how she likes."

"She's beautiful." It was really the only thing that could be said at this point. He sat next to Tryss and handed her their baby, and then nestled down on the bed beside them both. Normally, he wouldn't have gotten himself so comfortable with both Coren and Dahlya in the room, but he barely noticed their existence anymore. Anyway, they were busy cleaning, not staring.

Now that the adrenaline was wearing off, he could feel whatever strength left in his body draining away. While he wasn't about to mention it to a woman who had just delivered a baby, he felt more weak and tired than he had in a long time. There was a biting pain in his side, something more than a stich from running too hard. Ah yes, Remrant had knifed him to deliver that drug, hadn't he? It had been a shallow wound, and he hadn't noticed it in the chaos afterwards. Only now did its burning throb make itself known, but he was certain it was already healing, so he made no mention of it. Besides that, he could feel the tug of a bandage against his skin, suggesting Remrant had seen the wound tended while Errance was still unconscious. The blood on his shirt was under his coat, and nobody would notice it until he stood up, so he would just lie here and rest for now.

He may not have said anything, but the slight tremble in his body gave away his shock and exhaustion, and Tryss gave him a kiss on the cheek.

Coren and Dahlya were discussing something in quiet tones, concluding with them leaving the room with both the tub and the soiled cloths. Somewhere on the first floor, the voice of the parson could be heard hailing them.

"Are you sure you're all right?" Errance whispered. "I don't mean from birth, but everything…there isn't anything that happened that you didn't tell me in the letters?"

Tryss shook her head with a sigh. "Being held captive by my brother was the worst part of it. I was unharmed, but always angry. Somehow, being taken to the other confinement by literal strangers calmed me down. Or maybe it was just Dahlya who calmed me down. Either way, nobody did anything to hurt me. I just had to keep up my hope that we could escape or that you would come in the end."

She shifted Cerenity to nuzzle more comfortably against her breast. "And you did. And she's here now. And everything just feels like a bad dream. Or that this is a wonderful one. In which case, I will happily stay here, thank you. But what about you? How did you finally find me? And are we…" She hesitated, as if afraid this question would break the spell. "Are we still in danger from whoever took me?"

Errance dragged a hand down his face with a groan. "Remrant Cole. The man who was helping me search for you. He was behind it all."

"Wait—really? What for?"

"He apparently is some diabolical strategist. He planned on building a strong alliance with Aselvia to have access to our wealth and power while he continued some political game with the other city states."

"That's…that's ridiculous! Who would go through so much trouble?"

"Somebody desperate. He was out of funds and playing a very dangerous game of deception with the rest of the world leaders. I do not think he will be after you anymore; it is now pointless. I don't know if he will try anything else."

He allowed himself to silently contemplate what other moves Remrant might make. He could stir up the city states and attempt to make war on Aselvia, gaining their wealth through conquest, but that would likewise be pointless. You couldn't just lead an army into elf country with the shield up, and now that a few enemies had come in under pretense, security would be even tighter. He didn't suppose the man would waste the resources on that. So long as Errance let things lie quietly, he thought Remrant might do the same.

But he wasn't sure he wanted to let things lie quietly.

They said no more for a while after that. Cerenity had taken her fill of her first breakfast and was now fast asleep, both her parents nodding off as well.

The door opened without a sound and Errance glanced towards it, expecting to see Dahlya or Coren. Instead, there was no one at all.

And then the door closed, and Taersidel was leaning against it, his hands still clutching the latch behind him.

A strangled gasp of fear and rage broke from Tryss's throat, and she bolted upright in bed, worn as she was. But Errance already had his feet on the floor, one arm keeping Tryss and their baby at his back.

He'd just walked right in, audacious as he pleased. He might have gone through the window except the only windows in the church were built of solid, stained glass.

For one awful moment, Errance thought of Coren, Dahlya, and the parson lying dead downstairs, but no, he could still hear their muffled voices in casual conversation.

He thought about yelling, but he was not at all sure how Taersidel would react, and truthfully, he didn't know if he could protect Tryss and his baby if the chema *did* make a move.

"So here you are, at last," Taersidel said, sounding very petty and annoyed. "Of course your husband found you first. I realized that he would, which is why I just started following his trail."

"Taersidel," Errance said. "If you come one step closer, your life is forfeit."

"Save your threats for someone else," Taersidel said. "You won this time."

He didn't believe him, not for a second, but the chema went on, regardless of being believed or not.

"It would be far too much work to take her North now, since she's proved so unwilling and yourself so devoted. It's not the right season to start a war, after all." He didn't move, but his eyes did peer past Errance to look at the bundle Tryss clutched so fiercely to her chest.

"I see you delivered the baby. I must congratulate you about one thing, Tryss—not even the northern courts imagined the crown heir of Aselvia being half-chema."

"Get out," she snapped.

"I will," he said, eyes softening. "I only wanted to be sure you were safe. This is good-bye, sister."

"Don't," Tryss snarled. "Don't even start with that."

His gaze became cool, quiet even, as he regarded her a moment more before looking at Errance. "I will grant your husband this. He is a relentless opponent. But. He does leave loose ends."

And with that he vanished, even the shimmer in the air waning a moment later. The door opened and shut, and they could hear footsteps fading down the stairs. They could even hear the front door to the church close a few seconds later.

After a moment, footsteps came up the stairs again, and while Errance had not left his defensive posture and wasn't about to, he still recognized them as Coren's. Sure enough, Coren poked his head around the door's edge.

"So we just had a strange incid—hold on, what happened?" He stiffened as he took in their white expressions and tense posture.

"Nothing much, Taersidel just came in for a word or two," Errance said, a bit faintly.

"What? What! Brights! Brights! How did I not see him come in? I mean, I know how, but to let him sneak past—brights, I'm sorry, Errance!"

"Never mind." Errance eased back down to sit on the edge of the bed, exhaustion returning to his limbs. "Just…just stand at the door for now. I think he really left, but I can't be sure…"

It didn't seem right that he would just give up after all this trouble. After all, didn't the elves still have Alludium in their custody? Didn't he want to negotiate with the elves about that?

And what did he mean by loose ends?

34

Remrant stared at his flustered young clerk and at the purple bruise blossoming over the boy's face. The news he'd just been told slowly repeated itself in his mind. Even so, he needed a second confirmation. "I'm sorry," he said. "What?"

The clerk paled a shade further, thin fingers twisting together. "I went down to record the elf's confession, as you said, sir. He was on me in a flash the moment I started down the stairs, and I've been dazed from the attack for a while, I'm afraid. When I could stand up, I found Garis and Ban recovering in the basement. They've suffered injury, and the elf...the elf is gone, sir."

"Thank you, Irekson, you may go."

Without any hesitation, his clerk bobbed another bow and darted from the room.

Closing the book upon his desk, Remrant stood and faced the dwindling fire in his hearth, hands folding behind his back. Well. He should have seen it coming. He should have enforced more security. But Garis and Ban were not untested grunts; they'd always come through for him in the past. Reyid had to have fought incredibly well to have bested the both of them.

So then, that was that. What now?

There was no point in trying to catch Reyid or trying to spin a tale to the elvish king that could serve as an excuse. Aselvia was a loss at this point, but what he needed to make sure was that the loss stayed contained. Whatever accusations the elvish king hurled his way could be parried since the king's silent treatment to the rest of the city-states could hardly be considered as grounds for believing his words. The other rulers would side with Remrant's story, of that he had no doubt. He just needed to be prepared for any questions considering the rumor of bankruptcy that was sure to arise.

He sighed, rubbing at the ache that was beginning to pound between his brows. First things first, he'd need to invent his own counter to the king's accusations, and the reason for bad blood between them. Perhaps the king had attempted to bribe him into an exorbitant loan or perhaps—

"Spring, Mries the 30th, 1179."

The voice spoke from empty air, far above in the shadows of the ceiling.

What.

What.

Did he know the voice? He did not. Not that it mattered, any voice did not belong in his private office at this hour. It most certainly did not belong in the turret rafters.

But that *date*. That was the worst of it all.

Hand closing on the hidden knife in his vest pocket, Remrant drew a few steps backwards, drawing the poker from the fire with him. "Show yourself," he said, manner calm and crisp despite the pounding of his heart.

A crystal laugh rang out in response. "I think not," the stranger replied. "Why should I show myself to the one who kept himself hidden? You must think yourself very clever, Remrant Cole, to believe you could win in a battle of deception against the chemas of the North."

"Taersidel, is it?" Remrant said, listening hard for any indication of movement. "I have no quarrel with you or the North. I am sure you understand the importance of guile and false appearances. I would have preferred that I hired you face to face, but my business was with Aselvia, and our arrangement needed to be kept secret, even from you."

"You thought you could play me for the fool," the voice said, the sneer in his tone turning ugly. "That in itself is quarrel enough."

"What have you come for?" Remrant said, easing his knife and poker down. "Fair settlement? Aid in revenge against the king?"

"Alfreck Haverston," the chema continued, as if he hadn't heard him. "Just one of the many whose lives came crumbling down in financial ruin thanks to the machinations your parents wove during their golden rule of the bank. What made Alfreck different than the rest was that he acted upon his desire for vengeance. In the spring of Mries 1179, Alfreck Haverston followed the Master and Mistress Cole to their villa in Meece's countryside and burned it to the ground in the middle of the night. You were sixteen, studying at the university of Dormandy."

Remrant's jaw tightened, the muscles in his temple throbbing with each beat of his pulse.

"I think it is poetic, don't you?" The sneer in the voice had left, replaced with sing-song amusement. "A fitting end for Remrant Cole. As like your parents in life, so also in death. A legacy only of ash."

A shuffle from his left.

Remrant swung the poker with all his might, drawing the knife in the same movement to finish the job after the blow. But the blow struck nothing but air, and as he staggered, he saw his mistake. Of course, it was a ploy. Someone like himself should have known the art of a well-placed distraction.

Something pinched into his neck, his vision swam, and then the world blackened.

He couldn't have been unconscious for long, but when he awoke, he found himself strapped by the ankles and wrists to his desk chair. Just when he was wondering if the chema had already left, he noticed a book floating about in an invisible hand.

"Good, you're awake," Taersidel said. "It wouldn't do to have you asleep as you perished. Would miss the point entirely. Now I can move on. I thought about just starting the fire in here with all your books, but that would be too fast. Better to start on the lower floor and let it work its way up while you think about it."

Remrant swallowed, the prickles in his throat making it difficult to speak and the ache in his head difficult to think. Strangely, he found himself thinking less about his own approaching death and more about the members of his household. Irekson, his clerk, would still be doing paperwork in the rooms below. Beki, the housemaid, would be tending to the fires on such a cold day to be sure they didn't go out. His cook, Missus Olstout, might be coming up soon to knock on his door and deliver luncheon.

"Nobody else needs to die." The words scraped from his dry mouth. "They're not part of our quarrel."

"What a gentleman," Taersidel said, and if anybody could suggest a roll of the eyes without being seen, he could. "Yes, yes, I'm sure so long as no heroics are attempted, everyone else shall escape cleanly. And that includes no yelling on your part. Yell, and somebody might come to try to rescue you, and I cannot promise their life will continue after that. Anyway, that is all." The book he was holding snapped shut and returned neatly to the shelf, as if that mattered. "Good day, Remrant Cole. At least you won't die in the cold."

Loose ends.

The words still echoed in Errance's head, a more irritating distraction than any biting gnat. What had Taersidel meant by it? Perhaps the enemy that had taken Tryss to begin with? But he had never figured out Remrant's secret, he hadn't—

Or had he?

A delicate chill crept up the back of his neck. Taersidel had been among the first to plant seeds of doubt as to Remrant's intentions. He may not have known the full of it, but who could say if he'd searched deeper? If Errance had been able to sneak into Remrant's office and discover the evidence, a chema would have done the same with ten times the ease.

"He knows," he said, and to his dismay, he said it aloud.

Tryss shifted from her place on his arm, giving him a look. Tired as she was, she was content, but there was no mistaking the fact that her husband was far from at ease. "Who knows what?" she murmured.

"Your br—Taersidel. He knows who hired him now. The loose end. Remrant, the man I was working with to save you…the man who had you kidnapped to begin with."

"That is really the most backwards way to arrange an alliance that I have ever heard of," she said, forcing the words past a yawn. Almost funny, now that everything was as it should be again. "So what of it? Taersidel knows. He won't take kindly to anybody treating him as a pawn in a game. I suppose that is the last we shall have to worry about the man."

"He'll kill him," Errance said softly.

She could feel the strain in his chest under her ear as he spoke those words. She shifted again, this time leaning forward so she could look him in the eye. "You…" A bit of wonder touched her tone. "You don't want him to die."

Errance flinched, as if that was an accusation of the worst kind. "He deserves it," he said, though his voice lacked venom. "But…"

"You liked him," Tryss said, eyes widening. Her husband couldn't hide from her, especially not now. There was something so raw about this Errance who had been returned to her. So unrestrained, so real, so alive.

"I did not," Errance retorted, but when she gave him a look, he recanted a little. "Well. Maybe I liked parts of him, or agreed with some things he stood for, but his whole intention was a lie, Tryss. Even when I didn't know the truth, he was entitled and arrogant, and now knowing the truth, the man is the most manipulative and conniving of weasels, and I—"

"And you don't want him to die," Tryss repeated. "That is speaking of your own character; it has little to do with him." She sighed, easing back against the cushioned seat. She couldn't just let him go. Not now, not after she'd gotten him back for the second time.

But...but she did not want another regret added to his life. Had she not desired him to live freely, following the will of God? If there was any compassion in his soul for such a wretch, it could not be anything less than from God.

"All right," she said, burying her nose into his sleeve and inhaling his evergreen scent.

"All right, what?" he asked, startling.

"Go," she whispered. "Go and stop it, if you can. Do whatever you think needs to be done. On one condition. You come back. You come back to me."

"I..." His mouth hung open as a thousand emotions tangled across his face. "I promise."

Coren started as he burst out the door. "What! What now?"

"You stay here and guard them!" Errance said, flinging out a hand as he ran down the stairs. "I'll be back!"

The coach rattled and jerked over the cobblestones at the swift pace with which Errance had commanded. He gripped the edge of the seat, his feet braced against the floor. With every lurch, a question stabbed through his mind.

What did he think he could do? Did he plan to just run up to Remrant and warn him, and then run off again before getting caught for a second time? If Taersidel was already there, did he have a hope of winning against him?

"God, this is crazy, talk me out of it," he muttered under his breath, raking a hand through his hair.

What he wouldn't give to just be back in that parish room with Tryss.

There was shouting and commotion; he could hear it even above the clatter of the coach, which slowed to a halt. Errance flung the door open and swung himself out far enough to see the coachman. "What's going on?" he shouted.

"A fire," the man said, pointing to the wooden blockade set in front of Albine Avenue. People were scurrying on foot past the barriers, eager to see the excitement.

Fire. Of all threats, of course it would be fire.

The smell of wild smoke already was sending his stomach into coiled knots. Memories of agonized burning pulsed in his mind, trying to force themselves into his vision, but he thrust past the images savagely. He would not wish burning to death on his worst enemy, and Remrant...he was not sure what he considered him to be.

He hopped out of the coach, running down the street through the milling crowd.

Yes, the fire was coming from Remrant's house, exactly as he'd known it would be. Flames licked out of the lower windows, smoke billowing up from every crack it could find.

He could hear the nervous whinny of horses and saw that there was a fire brigade parked on the street. Many men stood in a line passing buckets back and forth from the buildings to the parked wagons filled with water barrels. They seemed to have given Remrant's building up as a loss, but they were working hard to keep the fire from spreading to the houses next door.

Nearby the wagons, a portly woman was sobbing into her apron, crying out things to an officer like, "It must 'ave been the pudding. The pudding must 'ave caught fire and sent the whole stove ablaze. I knew I shouldn't 'ave stepped out to talk to the cheese peddler, I knew I shouldn't 'ave! Poor Master Cole! Poor Master Cole!"

Even at the same time, the young housemaid, Beki declared her own certainty that the fire was her fault, tears streaming down her ash-dusted cheeks.

It was too late to enter the house from anywhere on the first floor. Perhaps too late even from the second floor. But the third and Remrant's tower study—that was still untouched.

He ripped off his outer coat and ran to the next-door house, springing off the edge of one of the window frames and catching a gap in the bricks. He pulled himself up from one narrow edge to the next crack before gaining the rail of the second story balcony.

"Eiy, what's he doing?" The shout came from somewhere below him, some stranger catching sight of him amid the chaos.

Wouldn't I love to know?

He stared over the distance at the house across from him, the stench of the smoke strong in his nostrils and the crack of the fire loud in his ears. It was destroying everything in that house, every woven rug, carved piece of furniture, painted piece of wall.

If there was one thing he could not stand to smell again, it was the smell of burning flesh.

Then jump.

If you jump, the burning flesh will be your own.

Brights, just jump.

He leapt from the rail, the cries of onlookers distant in his ears and immediately drowned out by the wild fever that roared to life in his head as hot as the flames below him. He could not fear. He could not hesitate. There was only time for action. If he paused, he would panic and then perish.

If there was one place he could guess Remrant to be right now, it was that tower study. But he couldn't hinge everything on a guess, not when he was this close to Remrant's room. He swung himself to the nearest window, clenched the ledge above it, and kicked through the glass with his boot. The smoke came out, but not as dense as from the windows below him. The fire hadn't gained the second floor, but it was about to, judging by the way the floors were glowing orange.

"Remrant!" His shout didn't seem like it reached any further past his own ears.

He wouldn't be able to search the second floor. If Remrant was still alive, he could only hope it was on the third.

Pulling back out, he kept climbing. If he gained the roof, it would be faster to make it out to the tower that way, but he remembered the glass in that room. It had been thick and without any latch to open. He doubted he could break his way in, at least without shredding his leg to the bone.

When he broke through the window on the third level, the heat inside was less formidable and the wooden floor looked stable. Even so, smoke was coming up from the stair and beginning to pile against the ceiling. He slid inside, the shards of glass catching on his clothes.

It might have been Beki's room, showing signs of cleanly living, but he barely noticed details. What he did see, from the corner of his eye, was a basin on a table nearly full of shining water. He caught the towel next to it, dragging it through the water so that the basin toppled to the floor, splashing across the wood with a steaming hiss.

Binding the wet cloth around his nose and mouth, he hurried out of the room, hunkered as low as he could without crawling. His boots protected him from the heat for now, but every time his hands brushed a surface, he could feel the warmth rising.

There, the door to the tower stair. The stairs would go down to the second floor near Remrant's room. He could only pray the fire hadn't broken through that lower door, because if it had, the stairwell would be filled with smoke and impossible to pass through.

But no, no, the stairwell was still clear. He leapt up it, bursting through the door at the top.

For one sickening moment, he thought the room was empty.

And then he saw him, sitting on the chair by the glowing hearth as if the room was not already warm enough. His head was bowed to his chest, although there did not seem to be enough smoke in this room yet to cause asphyxiation.

"Remrant!" Errance shouted, skidding down to his knees beside the chair. Ah, now he could see the ropes binding the man to the wooden arms and back.

Remrant's head lifted, peering at the elf beside him with as much confusion as a man woken from the dead of sleep. "What in Orim—what are you doing here, Reyid?"

"What does it look like?" He drew the knife at his belt, slitting the ropes with a few haggard jerks.

Remrant staggered upright, still staring at him as if he were a hallucination.

A groan, a crash, and a volcanic roar. As their foundation shook beneath their feet, Errance knew that the second floor had caved in. The heat changed in that very moment, all the flames and smoke free to burn directly beneath them, leaping up faster than ever before. Smoke was billowing out of the chimney shaft onto the floor and from under the door to the stairwell. There would be no escaping the way he'd come.

The window.

He couldn't have broken it from the outside, but he was inside now and there was furniture. He picked up the very chair Remrant had been bound to and swung it with all his might into the glass. It shattered into a thousand stars, glowing bright as embers in the light of the fire.

"Come on!" Errance turned to find Remrant fumbling at his desk. He grabbed him by the arms and bodily hauled him to the window. He shoved him through first, but the man almost fell headlong rather than turning to the outside wall. Errance climbed after him, pulling him to the windowsill and pressing his hands on the ridges that would keep him from falling if he held tight enough.

The smoke was high around them now, forcing a cough from his lungs through the damp rag around his mouth. He wrapped one arm around the old man, found his footing, and began climbing around the outside of the tower to the roofline of the house.

When they gained the ridge, he found he couldn't even see the outlines of the nearby houses through the heavy rising smoke and heat. Stray sparks from below had lit small fires in the shingles of the roof, coating the air with a stench of tar.

The one thing he could see in the smoke was the shape of the tower next to him. The lower edge of its coned steeple did not rise far above the roofline; he was just tall enough to reach it.

"Get up there." He could barely manage the words, and Remrant couldn't give a response through the violent coughing that was shaking his body. But the old man still grabbed the edge of the turret roof and pulled himself up with the shove and support of Errance beneath him. The moment he'd made it, Errance grabbed the edge himself and swung up onto the steep slope.

Higher. Higher. Find some way out of this smoke.

Whether that final climb made a difference or he finally looked the right way, he could now see the suggestion of the roof of the neighboring house.

He could leap for the far building. Even if he didn't make it, he was fairly certain he'd survive the fall. He'd survived much worse drops in Tertorem. Then again, back then his life had been bound to his body by dark magic until his inner light could reverse the damage.

But he hadn't come this far just to save himself.

If he carried Remrant with him, his chances of making the leap cut in half. And if he did fall, there was very little probability the man would survive.

The world crackled and burned as the fires below met the fires on the roof. It was hot, so hot. Embers stung against his skin and burned small holes through his clothes. Remrant was immobile on the shingles of the turret roof.

There was no other possibility but the leap.

Fighting past the waves of shadow and brightness blurring his vision, he pulled the man onto his back, tying him on with his jacket, and prayed that it would be enough. He crouched against the slope of the roof. If only he had a running start, but at least he had a bit of height to his advantage.

He threw himself out into the air, the rush of hot wind tearing through his hair and blinding his vision. As he plummeted downwards, he knew.

He hadn't made it.

Stars, Tryss, I'm sorry.

35

The hard impact punched all air from his lungs.

He flailed, struggling to draw another breath, as he felt the wind rush past him in the complete opposite direction of falling.

Rising? Yes, that was it, he was rising. He'd heard songs and poems of ascending into heaven, but hadn't supposed he'd physically feel it.

The rushing swells of wind drove the smoke away, lifting him above the fire and ash. He could see the burning building below him, growing smaller. Then he was gasping in breaths again, the rag fallen from his mouth.

And with clear air in his lungs, his mind cleared and he understood.

The Daisha.

How she was here, he could not guess. But he could feel her strong front paws grasped around his waist, if a little clumsily at the effort of holding both his and Remrant's bodies.

He couldn't speak and he didn't dare turn his head lest he pass out completely. So he only breathed, gulping in its fresh, crystal taste.

The city of Dormandy swept underneath him, the roofs of the neighborhoods giving way to the much larger roofs of university buildings. The Daisha circled, closing in on one roof that was wider and flatter than the majority. She hovered with huge flaps of her mighty wings, setting them down gently upon the roof and then bounding to the ridgeline above them.

Errance pressed against the steady surface, grateful for the returning sense of balance and the absence of any sound of fire. Pushing up on shaky limbs, he looked up at The Daisha's magnificent self staring down at him in concern.

"You have a habit of showing up when I most need you," Errance whispered, voice scratched from the smoke.

"Call me Timely, call me Fate, just never, ever, call me Late," The Daisha said in a sing-song manner. She stretched out her long neck to bump her nose against his cheek. "As it was, I was pursuing the skin-blender we had in captivity. She got away and she has managed to keep away, even if I'm catching hints of her trail. When I smelled the smoke, I figured you'd most likely be involved. While we are on the subject of *habits*, you have an affinity for attracting trouble."

Alludium had escaped? Well, that couldn't be good. Still, at least it was one less thing that would need his immediate attention upon returning home. Maybe Taersidel had caught wind of it somehow, and that was why he hadn't brought her up at his departure.

"What *were* you doing, Errance?"

"Trying to save him, though only God knows why."

"I suppose you mean that literally."

"Indeed I do."

"So who is he?"

Rather than answering, Errance crawled down to Remrant's side to see if the man was even still alive. Just as he reached him, Remrant Cole coughed violently and began inhaling wheezing gasps of air. He tried to say something, but it only came out as scratched croaks.

"Calm down," Errance said, pressing a hand to his shoulder to discourage any attempts at getting up. "Just focus on breathing for now."

Remrant obeyed, but his bloodshot eyes kept glancing between Errance and The Daisha as if he didn't know which sight was more unbelievable.

"So who is he?" The Daisha asked again, which drew another round of racking coughs from the man.

Errance leaned back, legs braced in front of him. "Remrant Cole, master of the All Nations Bank. He's the one who had Tryss kidnapped."

"Is he? Shall I bite off his head then?"

"Considering I just about burned my skin off to keep him alive, I'd rather you didn't."

She poked her nose in Remrant's direction, giving him a good look at the teeth beneath her curled lips. "Is there something useful about him living?"

"I daresay there is." Errance rubbed a hand down his face wearily. Now that he thought about it, revealing the truth of Remrant's collusion would change and rock the world. The rulers of the cities needed to know, and it would be far easier to prove with Remrant alive. But he hadn't been thinking of any of those things when he'd run to the fire.

"It's a daisha." These were Remrant's first words, never mind that The Daisha was contemplating his death as he spoke.

"You'll address me as The Daisha or forever hold your peace," she snapped, and that shut his mouth with an audible click.

She turned to look back at Errance, and her eyes, piercing as a diamond, softened to a wildflower blue. "Ah, my dear, my dear, you are hurt."

"It's nothing." In truth, he was beginning to feel it. While the desperation for survival had been in his blood, he'd barely noticed the pain. But now as he looked down at his blistered hands and singed clothes, he realized how many burns he'd taken for his efforts. Some part of him wondered if he should be sick to his stomach, if that was an appropriate response considering what he'd suffered in the past. But no, that was the past, this was now. It hurt, but it had not destroyed him.

Remrant was staring at him. Slowly, the man raised himself up onto his elbows.

"Why?" His voice croaked, sounding more like an old man's than it ever had. "Why did you save me?"

Errance lifted his chin, coolly looking down at him with all the power of a man who has spared the other's life.

"You're the king," Remrant muttered. "You're the bloody king."

"A little bloody, but mostly burnt, at least today," Errance replied. "Took you long enough to figure it out."

"I've been a blind fool."

"In so many ways."

"Does he know where Tryss is?" The Daisha demanded. "Is that why you kept him alive?"

"I know where Tryss is," Errance said. "And I should like to return to her as quickly as possible. But first we must do something about him. Could you fly us down to the street?"

"So long as I don't get shot at," The Daisha said dubiously. "There is a crowd gathering on the streets, so I assume we've been spotted up here.

I suppose I can't be mistaken for one of those hideous gargoyles they have up here."

"They shouldn't be able to scramble armed guards fast enough if we fly a little ways from here. I just need to be dropped off close enough to walk to the Governor's house."

"Very well." She sighed with a heave of her shoulders. "Get on."

Errance took Remrant by the arm and hauled him upright, pushing him over to The Daisha's side. She curled her lip at the man, again showing off her very shiny set of large, sharp teeth. The man's limbs were shaking, and Errance had to all but lift him up onto her back.

Once Errance was also astride, The Daisha plunged from the university's crown, causing much outcry from the street below. She swept over the rooftops, tilting a wing with Errance's direction till they were within sight of the governor's house, but not so near the crowded streets that they couldn't find a landing.

She dove down to the cobblestones, scattering pigeons and terrifying the stray pedestrians. Errance hopped off, pulling Remrant with him. "Take back to the sky," he commanded. "I'll call for you again once we're outside of Dormandy and ready to go home."

"Very well, very well, but I'll be keeping a close eye on you, young man. You'll be in trouble again before I know it."

A squad of the police guard was gathered outside the gates of the governor's home, no doubt having been called for extra security at the rumor of a winged beast flying about the city. Fortunately, Errance recognized the captain as the very one who had accompanied them on many of their forays.

The captain stepped forward as he saw them coming, his face wrinkling in bewilderment and alarm. They must have looked quite the sight covered in ash and sweat. "Lord Reyid...?"

Errance paused a few steps away, pinning Remrant's arms against the man's own back. "I am here to turn in Remrant Cole under the charge of kidnapping the Queen of Aselvia."

The captain's eyes roved back and forth between them, perhaps wondering if he'd somehow ended up on the wrong end of one of their scamming raids.

"And for fraud and collusion against the Dormandy government," Errance went on. "Therefore, I need to meet with Governor Dolfen this very moment."

"Just let us in, Captain, that's a good man," Remrant said.

Errance gave him a look of surprise as the captain hesitantly gestured for them to follow him through the gate.

"What?" Remrant shrugged his thin shoulders. "I'm an old man who's been nearly burned to death in my own house, took a short flight on a mythical creature, and been dragged about the city by an elvish king. I need to sit down."

Fortunately for them both, their soot-covered and ragged appearance hurried along their audience with the Governor. Even so, it was a painfully tense few minutes of waiting, Remrant on a chair, Errance right behind him, hand firmly on his shoulder. The maid who had shown them to the parlor had the presence of mind to cast a sheet over the chair before Remrant had sat in it, but the floor clearly would need cleaning later.

The Governor came in at last, a napkin still tucked into his collar from a meal. "Master Remrant Cole and Lord Reyid! Whatever is the matter! There is talk about burning buildings and flying monsters. I trust you can explain?"

"Yes," Errance said, adjusting his grip on Remrant's bony shoulder. "First of all, I am not Lord Reyid. I am His Majesty, Errance Celestrum, king of Aselvia, son of Rendar and Cerene, third in line from the Firstborn."

Governor Dolfen's expression shifted from confused and concerned to confused and alarmed. He took one step backward.

"And to think I thought the king was weak," Remrant muttered aloud, though more to himself than to anyone else.

"How can you prove that?" Governor Dolfen managed at last. "Who just comes in here claiming they're king?"

"A madman or a king." Remrant heaved a sigh. "Come now, Governor, he is not the deceptive one in this room— I am."

Errance's fingers bit into his shoulder as he looked down at the man in even greater surprise. "What are you doing?"

"Stop looking so bewildered," Remrant said, shrugging his shoulder in an attempt to loosen the painful grip. "Why should you be surprised that I'm confessing? A wise man sees his own end before it comes. I could fight you on this. I could deny and run and hide. But it will raise enough suspicion to cause an investigation, and at some point, I will be caught. Perhaps confession can earn some measure of mercy, even for what I've done."

The man turned back to the governor, rising from the chair with such determination that Errance's hand withdrew from restraint. "Governor, I am here to bear witness of my crimes. I have lied to your good self and your good city, and many other governments besides. The All Nations Bank has no gold to back your investments and loans. The gold mines dried up years ago, and I've been attempting to cover it up while trading fortunes back and forth. Effective, but deceptive, yes."

"What are you saying? Saints, what are you saying?" The poor governor took another few stumbling steps back, hit the edge of a chair, and collapsed into it with a thud. Sweat had broken out on his brow, and he swiped at it with trembling fingers. "Master Cole, what is this nonsense?"

"I have been using my influence to shape the world as I saw fit," Remrant went on, not pausing. "And to maintain my power and wealth, I took aim at Aselvia. As you well know, I used your alliance with them in an attempt to get closer, but when that failed, I took…drastic measures. I arranged for the Queen of Aselvia's kidnapping. That is the citizen who we've been searching for these past few weeks. Yes, I was helping search for the very person I hid, because I hoped that would build a relationship with Aselvia. And indeed, it was working, but Lord Reyid is, as you heard, none other than the king himself, and he has bested me."

"I'm turning him in to your custody, Governor Dolfen," Errance interrupted. "You may question and investigate him as you see fit. I suppose you might even let him go and lie about the circumstances; I don't know how deep his influence with you goes. Whatever the case, take him off my hands. I have a wife to return to."

He was already to the door before it seemed to hit the Governor that he was actually leaving.

"Wait!" the man cried. "Wait, you can't leave just like that! How am I supposed to know if any of what is said is true?"

"By investigating the All Nations Bank, like I said." Errance waved a hand. "I suppose it will take a while."

"If you are...if you are His Majesty...and if all Remrant said is true...then...then, there will have to be a council with the affected world leaders. Such a thing has not been called in this generation, and the elven king has not been part of it for a thousand years. How shall I contact you if we proceed?"

"You may send a letter to Aselvia's embassy if you wish to discuss things further once you've sorted this out. Good day."

And with that, he shut the doors behind him and showed himself out, scattering all the house servants who were not so surreptitiously eavesdropping in the hall.

He was out of breath by the time he'd returned to the old church. A carriage took him part of the way, but he'd run the rest of it on foot.

When he burst through the door, he nearly collided with the old parson.

"Ah, finally," Ordan said. "Your wife and friend have been working themselves into a frenzy imagining what might have happened to you. I just volunteered to go out and see if I could hear of anything. What kept you?"

"Arson was involved," was Errance's only reply as he dashed for the stairs. He swerved to miss Dahlya, who was carrying some rags down, and then just as he reached the door, it opened.

Coren stood in the entrance, one hand concealed as if it held a weapon just in case, but his face held all the expectation of seeing his cousin. "There you are!" he snapped. "Do you have any idea how long it's been?"

"Thanks for keeping watch," he panted. "Sorry."

"It's not me you should apologize to," Coren said, sheathing his knife and stepping past him to head downstairs.

He swallowed in an effort to relieve the tension in his throat as he entered the bedroom. In time only, it hadn't been that long, but in matters of the heart, he felt he'd aged eons since he'd seen her.

"Errance!" Tryss bolted upright in bed, the blood draining from her face as she saw him come in. "You're hurt, oh stars, oh stars, I should have known you'd get hurt!"

"I'm not that hurt." He hurried to her side, both for reassurance and to make sure she didn't leap up or any such drastic action.

"I've been going mad wondering why I let you go, wondering what happened—are those burn marks? You got burned?"

"There was a little fire," Errance said, brushing the strands of hair back from her cheeks. "Just a building fire, nobody held a torch to me, if that's what—"

"*Just* a building fire? Do you have any idea how ridiculous that sounds?"

"I…I suppose it sounds a little ridiculous. I am sorry for making you worry. I questioned myself the whole time too."

She sagged back against the pillows, some of the fear fading from her eyes. "I suppose if you weren't a bit crazy, you wouldn't be Errance. Did you do it then; did you save that horrid man?"

"I did. He's under Dormandy custody now. He appears to be pleading guilty to his crimes, and the Governor says there will be a world council called to pass judgment and decide the future."

"When?"

"Who knows? I can only imagine how chaotic it will be."

"And you'll be going, I assume?"

He hesitated. "With your blessing."

"Errance. *You're the king.* You don't need your wife's blessing to go to world-defining councils."

"I'd like to have it."

"Of course you have to be there. But don't ask for my blessing just now, I'm not ready to think about letting you go again." She held out her arms and he leaned into them, knowing she would take care to avoid his injuries. "Just now, I want to go home and be safe with you and Cerenity. That's all."

A sigh slipped from his lips as he rested his head atop hers. "That. That sounds perfect to me."

Over a thousand scents coated the streets of Dormandy. A myriad of meals baking, the smoke of factories rising, the reek of refuse, and many more that could not be named.

Alludium doubted that even The Daisha could catch a chema scent amid all of that, especially when she was covered in human odor. The heavy wool skirt, cloak, and hood were stifling to her athletic form, but it made her look like one of the many ladies shopping in the damp weather, and she smelled like it too, the musk of sheep not entirely absent from the material.

She completed her purchase of baked bread, tucked it into the basket on her arm, and weaved her way to the outer edges of the market. She brushed aside the brunette-shaded wisps of hair from her face and took a bite of the bread loaf to ease the gnawing of her stomach. While in

Aselvia, stealing food hadn't been difficult, but she'd eaten very little since escaping across the border.

It was fortunate the horses of Aselvia were known for their speed and stamina, or she would have never kept the lead she'd gained on The Daisha. As it was, she'd still barely escaped the creature. After leaving the horse behind, she'd covered herself in sludge from a nearby marsh to hide her scent and movement. After that it had been a tense run to a nearby village where she'd broken into a blacksmith's shop at night and finally rid herself of the manifix shackles. She'd wrapped them in cloth and stuffed them in a bag which was now tied to her waist. After that, she'd stolen another horse and made the final stretch to Dormandy.

"There you are." A voice of black silk slipped from the shadows behind her, and Alludium's mouth curved up at its sound.

She was always truly impressed that he could remain unseen even from her and that he could pick her out no matter the disguise. It was only a pity his goals were still so focused on the present world, because he surely would attain Glory with little effort once he put his mind to it. Ah well, once she ascended, he might be more compelled to follow.

"You sabotaged my goal," she said only, wiping the beginnings of her smile away along with a few breadcrumbs. "The king was gone before I could strike."

"I can't say that I'm sorry." Taersidel appeared by her side with a shrug of his shoulders. His hair was dark for now, so nobody would give them a second glance. "As it turns out, he's a little more interesting than I thought he would be. It will make the war ahead more fascinating to be sure."

"Domination is the aim, not fascination," she replied with a quirk of her brows. "You do get so side-tracked."

"And you got caught," he replied. "You know, for a few moments there, I was actually worried for your safety. But the more I thought about it, the more unlike you it seemed. I decided it must only have been part of your plan. So? Did you get what you were after?"

"I did," she said, withdrawing a letter from the wrap around her chest. "I wrote it all down in case something happened to me. Read for yourself."

Taersidel took the transparent sheet between his hands and swept a swift gaze over the scrawled words. A small hiss blew from his lips, a visible cloud in the cold air.

She watched him with narrowed eyes. "Yes. It is as we feared," she said.

Taersidel folded the note back up and tucked it into his own pocket with a whispered curse. "So then," he muttered. "The Wraith is yet alive."

"And unaccounted for. The elves seem to truly not know where he is."

"That could be a farce. But I wouldn't put it past him to be running solo either."

"It changes none of our plans," Alludium said firmly. "Not even the Wraith can stop what is coming next."

Taersidel nodded, blowing a breath out between clenched teeth. "I know. It's good to have you back, Allu. Come on. Let's go home."

36

Home.

What a remarkable thing it was to be coming home.

After resting for a day, Tryss and Errance bade their farewells to the kind parson and set out for Aselvia.

Coren had given his own farewell, but just for a time. He would return to Oolum first to reunite with Zizain and Zoren, and then he would bring them both to the elven kingdom to celebrate.

Dahlya had insisted she go with him under the excuse that she hadn't gotten to see Oolum properly the first time. It was a ridiculous but generous guise. There was really only one thing she could want more than to return home quickly—and that was to see that Tryss and the little princess returned even quicker. This way, Errance and Tryss could travel by The Daisha and arrive home in a short period.

Familiar scents of evergreen woods and autumn leaves drifted up on the wind as The Daisha flew in for a landing on the wide palace dais. There were small figures below, growing gradually larger until Tryss could make out the smiles of Tellie, Kelm, Leoren, and Casara.

"Let me hold Cerenity when we land," Errance said, voice at her ear above the wing-stirred wind. "They'll want to see you safe and sound after all this, and then we can move on to celebrating the newest member of our family."

"They'll want to see you too."

"I suspect I'm at the bottom of the list in comparison to a kidnapped friend and a brand-new baby. Besides, whenever Leoren gets around to noticing me, it will probably be to scold me for not consulting him in my reckless actions."

"As king and husband, I don't think you needed to consult him about anything."

"That was my conclusion as well, and he'll probably agree, at least to the husband bit."

The Daisha's landing was especially soft, as had been the flight. The whole way to Aselvia, she'd been extremely conscious of the baby. From the moment she'd met her, blue diamond eyes shining, she had become a very protective aunt of sorts.

No sooner had Tryss's feet touched the ground, her hand gripping Errance's for support, did she find herself surrounded on all sides.

"Oh Tryss! Oh Tryss!" Tellie's arms were around her nearly before she could turn around. Her embrace was strong but gentle, holding back in consideration of her soreness. Tryss returned the hug with a tight squeeze of her own, feeling the sting of tears in her eyes.

It was so good to be back. So, so good.

Each one waiting for her took their turn to give her a hug and a word of thankfulness for her return, and then she could finally turn back to Errance who still perched atop The Daisha's back, the precious bundle nestled in his arms.

He handed the little one to Tryss, then swung down to her side so they could present their child together.

"Oh," Tellie said, her voice as soft and gentle as a dandelion wisp. "Oh, she's so tiny. She's so beautiful."

Tryss had seen her enough of her share of births to know this was always said about babies, but really, the more babies she saw, the truer she found it to be. And now that it was her very own in her arms, she could agree nothing was more absolute.

Both Tellie and Casara had crowded in so close that neither Leoren or Kelm could get a proper look, but Tryss was vaguely aware that they were congratulating Errance in some way, Leoren's eyes warm and shining like a summer sun.

"All of you giggling like a flock of pigeons," The Daisha complained loudly with a ruffle of her wings. "I'm exhausted, and I'm sure this pair is too! Not including the baby, she slept nearly the whole trip, bless her little soul. Carry on your cooing somewhere more comfortable, will you?"

Their laughter carried across the dais to the palace, where the household servants appeared in windows and doors, ready to welcome their returning king and queen and the newest member of their family.

Errance sat at his desk, staring at the reflective, smooth surface and the neat stack of books and papers. The morning sun was shining in through the window, proving every rim and corner to be impeccably clean. It had only been a little over a week since he'd returned home, but the ease with which he'd returned to his quiet, comfortable life was almost frightening. It was as if he'd never left. As if everything was right with the world.

He knew better.

"Knock, knock," Coren said aloud only after he'd already opened the door and strolled into the room.

"You could just actually knock," Errance said, raising a brow at his redheaded cousin. "Like a normal person would when a door is shut."

"Yes, well, since you summoned me, I figured you wouldn't be startled by my sudden entrance."

Yesterday, Coren, his family, and Dahlya had finally arrived in Aselvia, and the celebratory reunions continued. Everyone in the palace collectively could release their pent-up breath since the ordeal began. Everyone was safe and home; everything was as it should be.

But only here in his hidden little kingdom.

"I wanted to thank you for all your help," Errance began.

"Oh, is that it?" Coren said. "T'was the least I could do since I take responsibility for it happening in the first place; no, don't argue with me."

"It wasn't just that," Errance protested. "Not only helping me find her, but also…helping. Talking me down when I felt crazy, giving me fresh perspective. Honestly, I really do feel like the younger cousin."

"You can come for advice from your world-experienced senior anytime," Coren said with a smirk.

"I want to lend you full support in your work in Oolum. But I don't know if I can do that without casting suspicion on your true identity and breaking your cover as a simple merchant."

Coren's mouth opened and closed as he considered this, leaning so far back in the chair that it tipped. "Hmm. I admit, I've always wondered if I could keep up the secret forever. I've even wondered if I could do more if I was just honest about who I am. But still, it would paint an even bigger target on my back."

"But also a shield," Errance said. "Anybody who crossed you would not be dealing simply with a vigilante, but someone backed by the Aselvian royalty."

"What if...." Coren stroked his chin, ruffling the little patch of red beard there. "What if you began a very public agency backed by your government and you can partner with my charity work? It will already be spreading that I've worked with the elves before, so you can both support and protect me in that regard. As for my more secretive work, well, we can help each other in the shadows. As king, you need to work a bit more by the book. And if there's something you need done under the table, you can always send me."

Errance leaned back in his chair and considered. "Very well."

The rustling sound of many feet coming down the hall announced the arrival of his next guests before they ever reached the door. It had been left open, so they came in one after another—Tryss, Tellie, Kelm, Casara, and Leoren. Earlier that morning, Errance had dragged an empty chair behind the desk next to him, and Tryss took it now, her fingers resting lightly on his arm. Coren rose from his chair, offering it to his mother, but when she only shook her head, everyone else remained standing.

"This is exciting," Tellie said, "A family gathering in your study. It's much more spacious than Leoren's. What's this about?"

"Well, first of all," Errance began, running his hand over his knuckles. "I plan on leading a far more active life than I've been living, and I have so many ideas I'm not sure where to begin. I want a great deal more involvement with Orim than we had before, but I can't do it all on my own. To start, one thing I very much would like to do is create a home here for orphans and rescued children."

"Oh!" Tellie looked as if she wanted to say more, but pressed her mouth shut and let him continue, eyes shining.

"And I was wondering," Errance went on, mouth turning up at her expression, "if you two would be interested in running such a home."

"I say!" Kelm exclaimed. "I have often wondered the same thing!"

"Why didn't you ever talk to me about it then?" he asked, brow furrowing.

"Oh, come on, Errance, you've been stressed enough about your own child, I wasn't sure how to approach the subject."

"I want to do it," Tellie said, squeezing Kelm's arm. "Please, Kelm, we can do it, can't we?"

"I would have to take fewer jobs in Orim," Kelm said thoughtfully. "But I have been getting rather tired of traipsing about anyway."

"You wouldn't be running the home alone, of course," Errance said. "I'm not asking you to give up your woodworking, Kelm. I would have to find more volunteers, but—"

"You have one already," Casara said. "Tellie and I can manage if Kelm has a few jobs away. Tell us more, Errance."

"The idea is to give them the best care and education, while hopefully finding them safe families either in Aselvia or the rest of Orim, so that after adoption, we can bring in more children, and so on."

"I believe there are a great many families here in Aselvia who would adopt if given the opportunity and guidance," Casara mused. "I had so many questions regarding Tellie when we brought her home."

"All right then," Errance said, opening up his book and writing down a few notes. "If the three of you are interested, that's a start for that idea."

"And the rest?" Leoren had remained quiet throughout the talk so far, both in word and in expression, but through the glass windows veiling his eyes, one could glimpse the ever-analyzing shrewdness of his mind.

"The rest…" Errance hesitated. "The rest will be decided after this world council. But I will tell you my hopes regarding it now…"

The last light of day was beginning to fade from the sky, casting the nursery into dark lavender shadows. Tryss could barely keep her eyes open under the heavy weight of exhaustion. She lay upon a couch, propped against pillows, holding the small princess who snoozed with a full stomach.

Flyfar slept on his nearby roost, head tucked under his wing. Even if he was not an ordinary creature, he seemed to follow ordinary customs such as eating and sleeping. It was hard to say if all the back and forth had truly worn him out, but he seemed very content to finally be home.

Dahlya finished lighting the candles and stirring the fire before she gathered up her healing satchel and headed for the door.

"Dahlya…" Tryss's voice slurred as she tried to hold off sleep just long enough to speak her heart.

Her friend paused, glancing back over her shoulder. "Yes?"

Tryss's mouth trembled, and she pressed Cerenity tighter against her chest. "I can't…I can't thank you enough. You kept me sane. You kept me and the baby healthy. I don't know what I would have done in that situation without you. I wish there was some way I could repay you."

"Your husband already thanked me and my family and gave us tribute," Dahlya said, looking somewhat amused. "And I'll accept that as service to my king. But there is nothing you need to do to repay me, Tryss, because you are my friend."

"I…I still think of what you told me. About the one you loved. If there is some way I can help you find someone else…I don't want you to be lonely…"

"Lonely?" She shook her head, lips pressed together in a soft smile. "With friends like you, how could I be lonely? You don't need to fear me feeling unhappy, Tryss, because I'm not. It's funny, I don't feel old, yet I have lived many years. Even so, I can't say I've had friends as dear as you. It makes me excited for the future ahead. I have no idea what will happen. With you and Errance as queen and king, I am sure it will not be boring."

And with that and a final bell-like laugh, she swept from the room, leaving the scent of chamomile behind her.

Lord Leoren was a wise and gracious man.

Errance knew this, but he knew better once he realized his uncle had no intention of mentioning the suddenness of his departure from Aselvia.

He did detail the trouble that had come from Alludium after that, but there wasn't any hint of blame in his tone for Errance's absence.

Even so, Errance felt a sting of regret that he hadn't been there to play his part as king in the first breach of Aselvian security since…well, centuries? Perhaps ever since his own father had been king?

But Tryss's safety had come first; there had been no way for him to be in two places at once.

The effect it had on the citizens of Aselvia had been minimal. The elven palace kept the matter contained until the threat was gone. There was no doubt that with loose elven tongues, word of the threat would get out sooner rather than later, but hopefully there would be no panic since peace was restored.

"I suppose all of this might make them question my leadership," Errance muttered, and to his dismay, he said it out loud.

"Everyone's concern was for you and your queen," Leoren went on. "There was no way to keep that a secret, not when you went after her. I assured them you and Prince Coren would bring her back safely. And you have, so if anything, you have enforced their confidence that you are effective in your endeavors."

"Yes, I suppose that's good." Errance's finger tapped against his mouth with restless abandon as he stared at the books stacked upon his desk. "Hopefully, my plans for the future don't crush whatever confidence they have in me."

"Your plans are worthy." Even so, there was hesitance in his uncle's tone.

Errance fixed him with a direct look. "What?"

"Just…" Leoren hesitated, fingers curling into his palms. "Are you sure you want to go down this path? Confronting the wickedness in this world comes with a price. There will be no going back."

"Going back?" Errance echoed. "Going back, I remember when Ajahliesh would gather the lords of the crime-world and present me before them, promising the profit they could make off of Aselvia. I had to stand there and take it, and the only thing I could do was promise myself that it would never, ever, happen to any of my people. And these past years maybe I thought just staying in Aselvia and ignoring everything out there was enough. But it isn't. It doesn't matter if they're my people or not, I can't stand that he's ruining lives. And if you want a reason I should do this as king, then know that he hasn't given up his elvish ambition. So I'll take the fight to him before he brings it to us."

When he ran out of breath, Leoren stared back at him, mouth tight and eyes red with unshed tears. "I am sorry," his uncle said after a long moment, voice wavering. "I know…should've known…you have thought it all out. I only…"

Errance sagged, running a hand across his brow. Leoren *did* know, more than most, thanks to late night talks. "And I know you only ask because you don't want me to get hurt anymore. Maybe the nightmares will never end. Maybe they'll get worse. But I believe this is what I must do."

A soft swish against the tile drew his attention back up and he found Leoren bending into a deep bow, arm catching his tunic aside.

"You are my king, your majesty," Leoren said, raising his face with a quiet and proud smile. "And I will follow you wherever you lead."

"Uncle…" Errance held out a hand to raise him up, but Leoren waved him off.

"Come with me," Leoren said. "I want to show you something."

He led him down several flights of stairs into the depths of the palace, taking up a lit torch from its bracket on the wall when the lights became more scarce.

Errance recognized where they were going, although he had only been there a few times in his whole life. The royal treasury.

Leoren produced a few keys from his robes and undid the locks and bolts one by one as Errance held the torch aloft.

The doors slowly swung open with a guttural groan, and they descended the final stair into the darkness. The light of the torch awoke thousands of glittering stars in the gold bricks and coins, turning the whole chamber into something warm and alive.

Errance turned in a steady circle in the midst of it, mouth pursed thoughtfully. Gold had never held much value to him, although the sheer amount of it here was a staggering sight.

"Do you know what Daava's plans were with this gold?" he asked as Leoren came down behind him.

"Precaution, I believe. In case of times that we were involved in world affairs." He paused, then added, "It was mainly the desire of Queen Cerene and the people to cut Aselvia off from the rest of Orim and be as little involved with the politics of other kingdoms. We helped out the aliths and the daishas as we could, but that also stopped after the daisha massacre. Your father was focused on raising you, and then later, grieving you.

"But you should know…he always had a heart for the outside world. He focused instead on the peace and prosperity of his own people, but as a youth, he loved to wander. How do you think he ended up with the earth elves instead of his own kind? And in the Dark Days, he was involved in other kingdoms' conflicts. I think he was looking to the day when the scars of Aselvia would fade and the people might find their courage to reach out again."

"Yet he didn't want me to leave home," Errance said softly.

"You were his son. You were young." Leoren heaved a sigh. "Parents can sometimes hold on a little too tightly. As I did with Coren. As I wanted to do with you. But eventually, the young grow up. And they can become greater than their fathers even imagined."

Leoren was not the only uncle that Errance had to speak with. Except for the prolonged silence, Erran surely had not known what trouble his nephew was experiencing down in the Lower World, unless a Celestial from the Unseen had informed him.

Errance sat before the Moonscript now, twirling the pen in hand as he tried to imagine some way to begin to explain everything that had happened. In so short a time, his entire life had changed, and he knew now it would go on changing at a pace perhaps too rapid to explain.

"Well," he breathed, scratching the words down onto the page. "I'm back."

37

What a storm had stirred the currents that swept between the politics and press of the Mid Orim governments. No matter how the world leaders tried to hide it, the news of the collapse of the All Nations Bank was on every tongue. And every eye was locked on their city's leader to see how they might prevent ruin.

The taverns of Dormandy were a popular haunt for anybody looking for the latest gab, so long as one could tolerate the noise of several conversations buzzing at once, the rubbing of elbows, and the smell of ale. For the regulars, not only was that not a problem, but a desired expectation.

"Oi, isn't this a day you usually guard the gates for the Governor?" the bartender called out as two men squeezed into the seats at his counter.

"Usually, usually," one of the men said, doffing his cap and setting it on the table to twist between his hands. "But I'll have you know we were deemed *unsuitable* for the events today. They have the police guards at every corner of the estate, and blimey, if they didn't even close the streets nearby."

The bartender tsked. "And here I was relying on you to give me the inside scoop! Can you imagine it? All the world leaders called together in one place! All for the punishment of that…that banker, what's his name, Cole, that's it, Remrant Cole."

"Forget Cole," the other guard said with a wave of his hand. "And forget the big coats and powdered wigs. They called in the King of Aselvia. The King of Aselvia himself!"

Financial ruin of governments was all dour and unsettling, but nothing stirred the imagination like hearing that the King of Aselvia was finally making an appearance. He was all but myth to them, and it did not matter if he was a different king than the one that had been ruling the last several centuries.

It was said that he'd had a hand in exposing the villainous Remrant Cole, although stories were very unclear as to if he'd done it himself or had sent a skilled spy on the job.

"You saw the elf with Remrant Cole, didn't you? Did he look like he could be a king to you?"

"Yes, yes, I saw him. And I'll be trying to make sure that my wife doesn't. If he is the king, we're in for a world of hurt. The women are going to be insufferable when they find out that the Almighty made a man who can look like *that*."

"What about his flying beast? You see that?"

"No, no, that I didn't see, though my wife said that her cousin's neighbor saw it flying about. Haven't heard if it came this time. They said the elvish envoy came without it. I suppose they could have hid it, but I don't know how you hide a giant flying animal."

Despite whatever claims belonging to the neighbor of the cousin of one's wife, very few saw the elves arrive.

And once the elves came, they kept out of sight until the day of the council.

The Governor had promised a meeting and luncheon in his own house beforehand, and the most distinguished of the city's citizens, the most affluent of envoys, and the most privileged of reporters were invited to join the foreign leadership for refreshment. The streets around the house were closed to the public, guards stationed on every corner.

The Chancellor of Korince was the first to make an entrance, settling himself very comfortably amid the luxuries provided. Soon after came the Elect of Oolum, richly hued robes fluttering with every movement. And one by one, the other guests arrived.

The grand parlor of the Dormandy estate had never been filled with such distinguished guests all at once, nor had it ever been so crowded with all the tables and couches and plants and lamps and the servants who bustled about to keep said guests pleased.

Everyone was gossiping amongst themselves, taking note that the elves had not arrived yet, when the doors opened and the king of Aselvia walked in.

No eye had seen such a magnificent sight in the city of Dormandy, something so extravagant and elegant at once, so foreign and yet so familiar as if from a dream.

Clad in sharp contrasts of white, black, and gold he was, the fabric both fitting to and flowing from his form in turns. The black coat, crossing diagonally across the chest and high collared about his neck, was trimmed in hard edges of engraved gold, the sleeves tight down the muscles of his arms. Gold clasps encircled his biceps, from which hung sheer white fabric that billowed like wings in the wake of his approach. The coat split in several panels about his legs, all different lengths but none longer than his mid calves, leaving plenty of room for mobility. The black leather of his boots came up to his knees and shone brighter than the silk of his coat, and they struck the floor in small claps of thunder.

But perhaps only a few people bothered to take in such detail about what he wore. Perhaps there were those who only noticed how beautiful and proud his features were. Perhaps some whispered over the length of his hair, quite uncommon for most Dormandy men, and yet not unwelcome.

Most of all, for the room was full of politicians, there were those who saw everything at once and summed it up in a single thought—he was a rich and powerful ruler.

"His Majesty of Aselvia, King Errance Celestrum," the doorkeeper announced, as if nobody could guess. A heavy silence followed, accompanied by a few bows by those who remembered to be polite as well as awestruck.

With formal introduction out of the way, Errance headed towards a somewhat quiet corner of the room where an empty tea table and chairs stood. His guards remained nearby the entrance, at a civil distance so as not to come across paranoid. A servant came by his table with water and asked if any other service was required, but Errance declined. Presenting the water alone seemed to give the servant a thrill, as he apparently had never served a king before, much less an elven one.

No one else came over to speak, though there was an empty chair across from him and plenty of stares or side-glances were cast his way. He didn't mind, but coolly looked back at each one of them, and he found much to observe. Observations had always lent him a great advantage. The Governor of Dormandy was heartily engaged in a story with the Duke of Meece, and they at least seemed to harbor sincere good feelings towards one another. The Elect of Oolum seemed more interested in sampling the food, inspecting the ornaments, and ogling the serving maids than in engaging in conversation. And there were more people of varying importance attached to each party.

Somewhere in his musing, he had taken his eyes from his surroundings to stare at the design on the table, and the voice that addressed him came unexpected.

"Your Majesty, is this chair taken?" The voice was thickly accented and rumbling, and it came from a mountain of a man. He wasn't all that tall as he was wide, and he took a seat in the chair without waiting for an answer. The seat did not have arms, so he fit, but it creaked ominously.

The Chancellor of Korince. Errance eyed him silently, revising the assessment of what he'd heard with personal experience. No one else here was more elaborately dressed, but that was not a compliment. Who knew so many frills, ruffles, and jewels could be fit onto one heavily embroidered outfit? And who needed so many gold pocket-watches and chains? But it was the man's face that bothered him. It had nothing to do with the fluffy beard trimming his jowls or even the permanent stain of red on his nose from overdrinking. It had to do with his eyes. They might have been jolly so brightly did they sparkle, but they were cruel instead. Cruel and cunning.

Errance had seen such eyes before; he remembered Ajahliesh's most favored men had possessed them. Men of power and affluence and riches. And no moral center.

This was the man whom Remrant had planned to blame for Tryss's kidnapping. While there were many things he did not trust about

Remrant, he did trust that he must have chosen this man in particular for a reason.

Errance blinked, realizing the chancellor had been speaking to him and he hadn't heard the last several sentences.

"…ever been to Korince, Your Majesty?"

"No, I haven't."

"A pity, you really must come by, I would be honored to give you a personal tour. The greatest art in the bloody world is collected there." He raised a brow as if daring Errance to contradict him.

Errance opted for cool silence instead. With the right impassive expression, silence was an intimidating and graceful tool.

With a loud harrumph, the chancellor dug into one of his many pockets and pulled out a deck of cards. "You look as if you are in need of a distraction, young king. Do you play Feint?"

"I'm a beginner." Despite Remrant's best efforts in their time together, Errance doubted he'd paid much attention to the card game to consider himself proficient.

"A popular game among politicians, passes the bloated time well enough. Here, I'll be glad to give you some guidance."

He passed twelve cards over to him, and after a pause, Errance took them. "I learn quickly," he said smoothly.

The chancellor flashed a slick smile. "I'm sure you do. But careful, your youthful boldness may not be enough against seasoned players."

Youthful. Errance pressed back a tight smile and listened to the rules explained again. The man had a forked tongue, there was no doubt about that. Every word he said seemed to contain a double meaning.

"Now, most men play with a small wager involved, but, of course, I wouldn't ask you to risk anything yet since you're only a beginner."

"Hm," Errance said only and reached for another card.

The chancellor reached out suddenly and caught his wrist. "I heard you suffered some nasty burns, Your Kingship. Have they healed already?"

Errance stiffened. His burns had healed, but if they hadn't, taking someone by the arm would have been a poor move. It was bold enough to grab anyone like that, much less a king, and this grip felt like a shackle. It hurt. He did not assume that was by accident.

Holding a flinch behind gritted teeth, Errance twisted his hand around and pinched the tender flesh of the chancellor's wrist.

The man let go and sat back with a look of amusement. "I hope you'll be more careful with fire in the future, Your Majesty. It gets out of hand so quickly."

"Thank you for your concern," Errance bit out. He glanced at the cards he held again but could hardly see them. The man's guise of goodwill was vanishing by the second and there was little hiding the predator now. The last thing he wanted was to sit here a moment longer, and yet he couldn't think of a way to excuse himself without letting the chancellor know his tactics had won.

"Pardon me, gentleman, but I do believe this was my promised game."

Errance looked up…and up… to find someone entirely new beside them. He did not match any of the Orim dignitaries Leoren had described. This man seemed youthful, but there was a sense of experience to him as there was a sense of strength to his slimness. His golden hair had slight curl and his blue eyes held snap. His smile was the most powerful—wide, white, and full of mischief.

"Ambassador d'Argon," he said with a slight bow to Errance, even though his attention was fixed on the chancellor. "Chance, you said we would have a rematch of Feint, and here I find you playing with a newcomer. Lost your nerve?"

"I've never played Feint with you," the chancellor growled, leaning back with a scowl.

"He doesn't like to admit I won off his left leg and an arm," the other man said, flashing a quick smirk at Errance. "Mind if I cut in and show you how it's done?"

"Actually," Errance managed to stand smoothly without knocking the table over in his desire to flee. "I believe my steward wished a word with me before this council commences. Good luck on the game." He inclined his head, ignoring the chancellor's glare, and stole away.

He went first to refill his glass of water, needing something for his dry throat. A glance back showed him that the strange ambassador had folded himself into the chair, long legs extended to the side, and was already well into the game. The chancellor's face was nearly purple like a storm cloud and looked completely unsettled.

Hmm. Errance swallowed a smile and went to look for Leoren. He would have to find a way to thank that d'Argon later. Nothing too obvious of course. It seemed politics were spoken in another language entirely.

The council itself was not to be held in the governor's estate. For a trial of such magnitude, the grand courtroom of Dormandy itself was the host, all other trials cleared for that day. There would be no jury to decide the matter of guilt or innocence—that evidence had already been accepted, and the only matter at hand was to decide the punishment. A judge would preside over the council of leaders, but simply to maintain order and to deliver the sentence.

The largest courtroom reached up three stories high from the floor to the ceiling, and the three-tiered seats spread out in a crescent around the judgment square. The judge's chair rose at the head. It was a bright room, painted white walls reflecting the light coming in from the high windows and glass dome above.

Errance took his seat on the third tier, glad that each world leader sat some distance apart. His robes swept across the smooth wood on either side of him, panels of the outer coat and trails of the sleeves draping down the steps below him. If there was one thing sitting in a throne had taught him these past seven years, it was how to sit well.

There were scribes at desks in each corner of the room, pens poised to record every word that would be spoken.

The Governor of Dormandy stood first, his hands clasped in front of his chest in gratitude. "I thank you all for agreeing to meet here and coming with such haste. There has been little precedent to gather like this, but we have shared in a violation against our trust and our welfare. It was thanks to the elven king that Remrant Cole's treachery was discovered, and while we must decide that man's proper punishment, I would also hope that we can work together to face the economic crisis we each will be facing in the coming years."

One of Oolum's Elect cleared her throat and stood. "Our cities have been benefiting one another for generations. Just because the gold that was supposedly backing the bank ran dry doesn't mean that the gold going back and forth between us was a lie. We can continue loans as we did before. Oolum is willing to extend its riches even further than before with the promise of fair trade in return."

"It won't be enough," the Duke of Meece protested. "Many things were spent and many plans were made in the name of gold that did not exist. Loans between our countries will not cover the damages, not when we're all facing the same problem. Maybe in the future, but not now. You cannot pretend nothing has changed."

A few murmurs of concern spread around the room, before the Chancellor coughed. "There is at least one change for the better, my friends. A new player has come onto the board. Aselvia is one of the last true kingdoms on this earth, and it has long been rumored to be filled with unimaginable wealth. This kingdom also was never in debt to the All Nations Bank or to anyone here." He turned, seat creaking, to look across at Errance, a strange smile curling his mouth. "So, Elven King, would you be willing to treat with us? And I don't mean a few exports across your closed border. I daresay there might be enough gold in your vaults to replace everything Remrant had promised us. If you have no other plans for it, you could consider starting a bank of your own."

Dead silence fell, even the scribes at their desks stopped scratching pens across the page. It was as if everyone held their breath as every eye looked to Errance in expectation.

Errance held his tongue, prolonging the moment. It was almost amazing how the Chancellor had spoken aloud some of the very same thoughts that had been stewing in his mind. There was no doubt that if he held the gold, if he held the power, he could wield an influence over all the cities same as Remrant had done.

Same as Remrant had done.

In many ways, he understood Remrant's intention from where it had begun. Who didn't want to see a sense of stability and morality applied to the world? And yes, Remrant had failed to keep himself free of corruption, but couldn't he, an elven king, do better? Couldn't he—

He was no longer seeing the courtroom. He felt himself standing on it again, that terribly narrow little path in his dream, the endless darkness yawning on either side. His fingers tightened on the side of the chair, returning him to his sense of balance and setting.

"No," he said.

The exhaled breath around the room was audible, and several leaned back in their seats with frustrated frowns.

"I will not be acting as any kind of bank. But." He paused, taking a deep breath. He had talked it over with Leoren for many nights. Debated might have been a better word. The decision he had come to pained him in a way. It felt too terribly close to taking the power he feared. But as Leoren said, that was politics for you. A desperate game of give and take. "But, I am willing to offer loans. So that your cities, and more importantly, your people, can weather this particular crisis. I cannot say now if I will continue offering loans in the future or not. It must be paid back, but rather than interest on the loan, I ask this—that you grant Aselvia permission to aid in restoring civility within your cities. Do your people suffer from poverty? Allow me to lend support with direct offerings to those who need food or medicine. Are your orphanages and hospitals overrun? Allow me to build establishments within and without my borders to meet that need. I am willing to extend embassies to other cities besides Dormandy for heading up this purpose."

"So you're saying," the governor of Dormandy said carefully, as if he was trying to solve a riddle, "that not only are you offering gold, but instead of charging us for it, you just want our permission for you to help us *more*?"

"I smell a rat." The duke leaned back in his chair. "What are you not saying? There must be something in it for you."

"Oh, there is," Errance agreed with a flick of a sunless smile. He rose, the drapes of his robes cascading behind him. "I am utterly against the slave trade, especially that which pertains to sensual desires. If you are misusing Aselvia's gold to support this instead of keeping your country from collapse, I will hear of it, and you will never have a drop of that gold again."

Every single member of Oolum's Elect stiffened in offense, while Dormandy and Meece's leaders only gave half nervous, half smug glances their way. Only the Chancellor's expression did not sway from its steady smirk.

"I will be making a stand against it," Errance continued. "If any of you are willing to fight against it within your own borders, then I would ask you to allow Aselvia to come alongside you in the effort."

"Yes, yes, but those in the West already have laws against it," the Chancellor said, sneer still in place. "It is unfair of you to target Oolum in this. Just because the Elect shares this council does not mean they share the same culture or beliefs. You cannot expect every city to have the same moral code as yours."

"I am not talking to Oolum alone," Errance said, meeting his gaze without waver. "Just because Korince has laws does not mean they're being followed. Perhaps it would set a better standard if you listened to the law yourself."

The tension in the room tripled, and the sound of scratching pens increased its vigor.

The Chancellor's mouth opened and shut as a few people cast knowing glances his way. "What exactly are you accusing me of, Your Majesty?"

"You say there is a law against slave trade, yet Korince boasts of its many brothels."

A belly laugh burst from the man at that. "You call that slave trade? Ah, my dear boy, these establishments are respectable places of employment, not slavery. You, in your elvish innocence, may not understand the concept, but there are people who actually wish for such an occupation."

"Yes, I imagine so," Errance said crisply. "I have heard you are a regular, so thank you for assuring us that you have personally made sure every member is there by pure choice rather than any kind of force, coercion, or lack of alternatives for survival."

The smile faded, a scowl darkening the man's brow like an oncoming thunderstorm. "If you make that argument, you might as well say that anyone with a job they don't desire is a slave. Are you really that naïve?"

A brightness as sharp as lightning flashed in Errance's eyes. "If you make that argument, you might as well say that sensual employment does no more damage to the spirit than ordinary labor. Are you really that corrupt?"

"Order, gentlemen." The judge spoke for the first time in the proceeding, his brow furrowing.

"If I may," the Governor of Dormandy interrupted, a suggestion of panic in his voice, "redirect this debate back to the topic at hand. Perhaps later we can decide what paths we will take moving forward, but the purpose of the council today is to determine Remrant's sentence."

"Hang him," one of the Oolum ministers muttered.

"Hanging is too good for his sort," another replied.

"I am sure none of us," the Chancellor said, very magnanimously, as if he hadn't been glowering only seconds ago, "have been wronged by Remrant to the same degree as this young king and his lovely little bride. Therefore, I propose that this council waives Remrant Cole's fate to the jurisdiction of Aselvia."

How anyone could manage to be so insulting while sounding so generous, Errance couldn't guess. Had it taken practice or had the man simply been born with the ability?

There was a heavy pause throughout the court, and Errance felt a prickle run down his spine as he realized the other council members were actually considering it. But it was a joke, wasn't it? A mockery?

When the Chancellor did not withdraw his suggestion, the Governor of Dormandy cleared his throat. "I second that decision." He did not look altogether comfortable saying it, not as if he disagreed with the notion, but that he couldn't understand why the Chancellor had put it on the table.

One by one, the other leaders looked at one another, gauging the reasoning and result.

"So long as he is being punished, I care not who decides what is to be done," the Duke of Meece said with a shrug.

"The Elect of Oolum will not disagree," came the next answer.

Even now, they are trying to curry my favor. Errance stifled an annoyed groan. Even after he'd offended more than a few of them. *They're hardly angry at Remrant at all. They're just angry they lost money, and they want it back. They look at me, and they see money. Power. Influence. Just as Leoren said they would. Saints, I hate it.*

He had half a mind to refuse them. But now that it had been said—even if it came out of the mouth of that slimy Chancellor—he wanted it. He wanted the fate of Remrant in his hands. So, whatever their reason, whatever their motivation….

He gave a short, clipped nod of his head.

"Very well," the judge said. "Name your decision, and we shall have Remrant Cole brought in to hear his sentence."

Four guards brought Remrant in, shackled at the wrists. Purely ceremony. Purely ridiculous.

In only a few weeks, Remrant had felt himself age by several years. When he'd looked in the small mirror inside his solitary confinement that morning, he'd found his face thinner and his wrinkles drooping in more pronounced folds. A tired, resigned look clouded the eyes of his reflection, but now he could feel a bit of life returning to him as he took center stage in the room and looked up at those gathered to judge him.

His gaze flickered briefly over each member of the council before settling on Errance. He felt his mouth purse in something almost like amusement, though it was amusement at himself for all those times he'd failed to recognize the king. There was no mistaking the power and presence of a ruler now, and he'd been a fool not to see it sooner.

"Remrant Cole." The judge spoke, forcing him to reluctantly look his way. Look his way and listen to his fate. There would be no wasting of time. Just the delivery of his just due.

"The charges against you are as follows: collusion against world government, embezzlement of government funds, misappropriation of government funds, coercion of government leadership, kidnapping, and injury. Further charges are too numerous to name. For these charges, this court has found you guilty beyond reasonable doubt. You have been sentenced to permanent exile from the human world."

Remrant's eyes closed. So it was prison, then. He almost would have preferred death, it would have been quicker. Prison meant living out the rest of his days in isolation. If it was a decent prison, maybe they would give him books or some sort of distraction, but nothing was a substitute for company and chatter—but what was he going on about? What right had he to take issue with his sentence? He had done all that they had named, and if another man had done it, he would have condemned him the same.

The judge lifted the gavel in his hand. "I hereby deliver you to the jurisdiction of the King of Aselvia. Court adjourned." The gavel thudded against the block with a resounding, declarative toll.

Remrant blinked. Blinked again as the room blurred into vague shapes of figures standing, the sound of robes and shoes shuffling. The hands of the guards took his arms and guided him back the way he'd come. He barely even noticed when outside the door, they handed him over to another set of guards, these ones fair and foreign from humankind.

Why. Why?

In what world was exile to Aselvia a *punishment?*

Perhaps Errance wanted to kill him on his own terms? Perhaps they had their own form of capital punishment that they'd rather keep quiet within their own borders?

But that didn't match with the man who'd run into a fire to save his enemy's sorry life.

Confusion and questions continued to clatter inside his mind like a crowd of chaotic pigeons. He didn't even realize he'd been led from the courtroom and out of the building until he found the cold wind buffeting his face. A carriage was waiting for them, and the elf guards on either side nudged him inside. He numbly obeyed and they climbed in with him. The carriage clattered off, and he folded his hands, waiting. There would be no answers until he could meet with the king. If they planned to let him meet with the king. He wouldn't blame him if they didn't.

The elvish embassy was kept safe behind walls, a solid iron gate, and guards so that none of the crowd hoping to see a glimpse of their foreign visitors could cause trouble. Even so, Remrant could hear the murmur of the curious throng outside the stone walls when the carriage came to a stop outside the doors of the embassy building.

The elves led him through the door, past a few more guards, and then into a clean, orderly room full of books and a few seating arrangements. There was a low fire burning in the hearth. The guards took their leave, and silence fell with the closing of the door.

He stood there in blank contemplation for a few moments, straining to hear the distant commotion, but all he could hear was the crackle of burning wood, the thud of his own heartbeat, and the jangle of the cuffs still around his wrists.

The doors opened again, startling him. He hadn't heard any footsteps. Errance shut the doors behind him.

Remrant stared, trying to reconcile in his mind what king would come into a room with a convicted criminal without any guards. In the end, his only answer was the same king who would run around the world under a false pretext with only a pirate as his backup.

"Why?"

It took a moment before Remrant realized he'd voiced the question aloud.

Errance quirked a brow in response.

"Why did you spare me?" Remrant forced the thought to form in entirety.

A small scoff slipped from Errance's lips. "Let me make this clear," he said. "You are not pardoned. You may be in Aselvia, but you will be living in a home separate from the palace city, and you will be kept under exchanging guard at all times. You are to not come near or even look at my wife and daughter."

Remrant nodded slowly. Even now, even in acknowledgement of his wrongs, he hadn't been sure he was sorry for all of it. But the thought of the frightened, pregnant queen did send a rush of self-loathing through his bones. How had he ever managed to justify that in his mind?

Errance walked away from the door and took a seat next to the fire. "That being said, you will not be left to die of boredom; that would be much too dangerous. You'll have books, a garden, and will be taught an honest trade. You will not discuss any politics with me, but you may be asked questions by Lord Leoren, my steward, if he deems it necessary to deal with world affairs. Don't think about trying to deceive him, he's far older and wilier than you'll ever be."

"Lord Leoren parried communication attempts from my family for years," Remrant said. "So believe me, I know." He shook his head, as if still trying to wake up. "How did you end up with the power to name my sentence anyway?"

"The Chancellor of Korince convinced the council to give me the authority."

"Oh, good gods, you should have refused it," he huffed. "He is setting you up; there is no doubt about that. When he wishes, he can plant seeds of distrust by suggesting you only wanted me in your custody so that we can work together in new deceptions. While I was waiting outside the courtyard, there were already rumors he'd asked you about starting a new bank. No doubt he was already planning to someday say it was part of a plan you made with me. You would have been better off ordering me executed, though I'm sure he would have found a way to twist that against you too."

"You're really advocating your execution?" Errance asked, brows raising higher.

Remrant coughed into his hand. "I cannot say that I am unhappy to be spared such a decision, but it is the most logical for the harm I have caused you." He glanced up above the rim of his glasses. "Unless..."

"Unless?" Errance leaned back in the chair, arms folded across his chest.

"Unless you truly did understand my vision. You could do it. You have the power, the charm, the intelligence, most of all, the long life. You could do all that I set out to do and better. You could—"

"Remrant."

The man paused, the energy building within him slowly deflating as he folded his hands and returned Errance's level stare.

"There is only one ruler of this world. May I ever serve him and never attempt to sit on his throne."

"Yes, but—"

"I won't deny there are similarities in what we desire," Errance continued, "and I won't deny that I perhaps would have taken such a path as yours if left to the shadows of my soul. But there is one major difference between us, Remrant. You seem to have a hope that this world can be fixed. That if you just teach, train, enforce law, and throw enough money at it, humanity will eventually evolve into a noble race. But I? I believe that this world will burn into ashes, same as your house and your dreams."

Remrant's mouth opened, then shut again.

"The least I can do," Errance said, folding his arms, "is try to stop poor fools from burning along with it. And that doesn't happen by law. Law can threaten with all the punishment it likes, but the heart loves to break rules and risk consequence. Therefore, the change we want must be within the heart itself."

"That doesn't work," Remrant muttered, before he could stop himself from arguing with a king. "You can't change the heart."

"I won't deny that," Errance said with a small sigh. "Only God can do that."

"Ah, yes." Remrant made a serious attempt not to roll his eyes, but he wasn't sure he succeeded. "I forgot who I was speaking to." He turned away, staring at the patterns on the papered wall as if it would give some guidance for his unraveling mind.

He didn't for a second believe in a good god. But just maybe, he could believe in a good king. And if delusions kept Errance on the right path, then who was he to scoff at that? Perhaps if he'd had a similar compass, he wouldn't have ended up where he was today.

"Beware the Chancellor," he said at length. "I did not pick him as the perpetrator of the kidnapping just by the roll of the dice. You've seen it by now. He is an odious, terrifying man. His manipulation and control of his city rivals mine, but he puppets it entirely for his own selfishness. I do not think there is a politician, businessman, or idol in that city who does not live in fear of his shadow or who does not leap to his beck and call. He always gets exactly what he wants. Blackmail, bribery, force.

We worked out a deal when it came to the bank and to my suggestions of reform for his city, but he was never one I could control."

"Yes, I did see he was that sort of man," Errance said, sounding worn at the mere thought of the encounter. "And I remembered you planned to blame Tryss's kidnapping on him."

"I was going to set him up to blame for the queen's disappearance because then I could bring similar crimes of his to light. With the elf king casting blame on him and myself to support you, the other powers of the world could no longer ignore his lewd presence. I might have at last brought him down from his porcelain throne, long has he sat on it. There is little hope of that now, of course, but I thought you should know."

"In other words, you are telling me to be afraid of him?"

A bitter, wry smile twisted Remrant's mouth as he turned back around. "You will threaten his wealth with your conviction and your influence. So he will attempt to frighten you. With his newspapers, with his letters, with his self-satisfied speeches. But I am telling you, Your Majesty, to never once let that stop you."

38

At no point had Errance actually stopped breathing throughout the council, but nevertheless, his chest felt tight and low on air by the time he left it. That discomfort remained throughout the return to the embassy and his confrontation with Remrant. Only when he had returned to the room set aside for him and his wife did he exhale his pent-up tension and inhale fresh and free.

Tryss wrapped him up in her arms, burying her face in his chest. He nuzzled his nose into the sun-bright wisps of her hair, relaxing in the honey scent.

It had not been part of his plans to bring her and Cerenity with him to Dormandy. He'd been quite sure she would both want and need to rest after her ordeal, but she'd insisted he could not leave her sight so soon. And while Aselvia was certainly the safer harbor, he could not deny that he wanted her nearby. Both her presence and the sight of their sleeping child in the nearby crib did more to soothe his soul than any medicine.

"It's over now," he murmured.

"Home?" she said, tilting her face up to look him in the eyes.

Errance hesitated, a smile playing on the corners of his mouth. "Yes," he said. "And by that, I mean our other home."

Her brow wrinkled in confusion. "Other home...we don't have...another?"

"Really, because I'm pretty sure you spent most of your life there."

Lips slowly opening to form an astonished 'O,' she leaned back to get a better view of him. "Are you saying you're coming with me to visit my family? In the jungle?"

"I assume it's in the jungle unless they moved without telling me. I'm sure they've sent messages to Aselvia by now, demanding updates on your delivery. Since you never sent word when you were coming ahead, I guess they don't know how terribly late you are about visiting them."

"It's not my fault for being late!" she exclaimed, poking him in the chest. The bright humor died in her face a moment later, replaced by weary dread as she sagged against him. "I'll have to tell them about Taers. They're going to be..." Her words faded, too weary to finish.

"You won't have to tell them alone," he said, arms tightening around her. "I'll be there, and I can explain whatever you need me to."

"I thought you were terrified of my family," she said, words a bit muffled as she pressed her cheek into the folds of his tunic.

"Terrified is an extremely strong word. I would say that I was more aware of their intense disapproval of me, and I did not blame them a whit." He sighed, the puff of breath stirring the top of her hair. "I doubt they will approve of me any more when they learn I lost you to such danger."

"I think they will be a little too angry and heartbroken about Taers to blame you much in the matter," she replied, a hard edge lining her voice before softening again. "And I know they will approve of you coming with me to show off our child. Are we flying there on The Daisha?"

"I don't trust any other method of travel."

"Which is ironic considering how high we are in the sky, but I agree. I hope she won't mind the baby screaming. I'll have to wrap up little Cerenity very warmly to keep her safe from the cold winds up there." She shivered just thinking about it. "But it will all be worth it when I finally get one of those natural hot spring baths again."

"Was that a thing there?"

"I guess you were unconscious when we took care of you," she said, raising a brow. "You'll remember it much better this time, I am sure."

"I am sure."

"And then of course, there is the ultimate luxury, the milthi moth milk bath."

"When you say "milk" you are referring to that thing Kelm refers to as "moth spit-up," are you not?"

"That is a very unappetizing way to describe it."

"Considering the milthi milk is one of your most valuable food and export sources, making a bath out of it sounds incredibly wasteful."

"It is only for very special occasions," she said. "Such as for newly-weds."

"We've been married for three years now."

"You're not getting out of this."

Heaving out another sigh, Errance relented with a soft smile. "All right," he whispered. "Milthi moth milk baths and all that makes you happy."

———————— ☾ ————————

The problem with jungles, The Daisha had oh-so-thoroughly explained on the way to Tryss's home, was that there were never enough clearings to land in.

And indeed, Errance had begun to lose hope of them finding any clearing within reasonable walking distance of the chema village when one finally appeared.

Leaving The Daisha to sulk about the heat and the incessant bugs, they headed into the depths of the trees, taking care not to tangle themselves in the thick vines and foliage that carpeted the floor. Both Tryss's hands remained free, the baby bound securely to her chest, but he kept a hand hovering about her just in case she lost balance or tripped. Which was unlikely, given that she'd grown up in these parts, but at this point he couldn't be too careful.

Why in Orim hadn't he done this sooner?

The green and yellow of her eyes shone so vividly, reflecting the brightness of the broad, waxy leaves, her pale hair as warm and sylphlike as the veils of sunlight casting down to the forest floor. Her laughter bubbled with the same depth as the small rivers that trailed through the trees.

But perhaps if he had come sooner, he wouldn't have seen it the same way. He would have been too busy looking inwards. When all the time, this world had been around him. Both its beauty and its brokenness.

Invisible scouts in the jungle must have seen them as they'd come, because when they approached the village borders, people were already running out to meet them. Mainly curious children who'd heard of the chema maiden who had gone far away to marry the elf king. The children whom Tryss had helped raise were either gangly youths or adults with children of their own, and they came too, eager to see what had brought her back.

Soon, Errance and Tryss were surrounded by chattering children of various ages, all with a hundred different questions and comments. If moving in the jungle was hard, moving in such a crowd was next to impossible. But in a few moments, more adults arrived and the children scattered to make way.

At the head came Tryss's father, his spear still in hand as if he'd grabbed it upon first hearing of the intruders and had not believed the news that it was his daughter and her husband. When he saw them, the spear dropped to the turf and he ran forward to gather Tryss into his arms. He saw the baby just in time and gave her a very careful, loose embrace to avoid squishing the child. Just behind him came Tryss's mother, openly weeping and laughing, her slit skirt dragging along several small grandchildren.

Errance took a step back, giving the various milling family members space to be reunited. Hardly anyone gave him a glance. His presence accepted, but not welcomed. That was all right. So long as Tryss was happy.

But then amid the sea of faces, he saw Tryss's eyes searching for him and saw her hand stretch out across the shoulders of those surrounding her. He caught her reaching fingers and pulled himself to her side.

"Take us to the Ancient," Tryss said, unwrapping her child from her bosom to hold in her arms instead. "We have much to share."

The Ancient was a very old man. He was old even by chema standards. He'd seen several generations of grandchildren grow up around his feet and become responsible leaders in his village or else set out to find their own way in the world. Even so, with all those memories, loves, and heartbreaks, he held a special unique affection for each grandchild that came and knew them well.

Tryss, he'd always suspected, was going to have some sort of extraordinary future, so it had been no surprise to him when she had chosen to up and move to Aselvia and then later announce her plans to accept the elven king's proposal. The whole thing rather upset the village, who thought her a favorite even though they usually meant that as their favorite to dump their own responsibilities upon. The news had neither upset nor shocked the Ancient. On the contrary, it pleased him very much, which nobody could understand since their brief encounters with Errance had been unfriendly, to say the least.

He'd only hoped that they would not take too long to have children, because he very much wanted to see such little ones.

A child of elf and chema blood.

Such marriages had happened in the beginning of days, or so he had heard, but those were happier times. Before the two races had named themselves enemies and secluded themselves behind impassable walls—the elves, the shield of their Celestial king, and the chemas, a shield of ice-covered mountains and terrible blizzards.

To say that Errance and Tryss's children would be remarkable was an understatement.

And now, today, this very fine late autumn day, his wish came true.

"Well now," he said, carefully adjusting the softly wrapped bundle in his papery arms. "Well now, little princess. I meet you at last."

"Her name is Cerenity," Tryss said. She had already said this a dozen times to a dozen different family members, but didn't seem too sure if her many-times-great-grandfather had heard her or not. Dear girl, he was old and feeble, but he still had the hearing of the great moths that covered the jungle canopy.

Cerenity blinked up at her elder with those bright blue-green eyes, soft fingers curling open and closed, small mouth working as if already trying to figure out how to manage something other than wails and mewls.

"Wen," the Ancient said.

"Eh?" Tryss blinked, tilting her head.

"Cerenity is a very queenly name, my dear, but she won't be able to pronounce it properly at first. She will say Cewenity, and thus you will decide to shorten it to Wen as a pet name. This is not my suggestion, merely my prediction for the future. I am very good at predictions when it comes to things like this."

"O-oh," Tryss said, eyes widening. "Well, I can see…I can see where that might happen."

"Wen," Errance repeated thoughtfully, testing it out. He reached a finger down to his little baby, tapping her nose. "Wen. Yes, I could definitely see that happening. It's better than what they call me."

"Oh?" The Ancient's wispy eyebrows shot up. "And what do they call you?"

"You can hardly expect me to own to it in front of this many people."

The Ancient wheezed a small laugh. "I suppose not." He squinted at Errance with a smile. Yes, yes, the boy had grown up very well. No longer was he the caged, wild thing they'd found in the jungle. He was a man and a king, through and through, carrying the weight of the world on his shoulders and yet not broken.

"There is something troubling the two of you," he said. "Something you want to tell us."

"Not here," Tryss replied quickly. "I want a private audience with you and my parents."

"Very well." The Ancient handed Cerenity to one of Tryss's sisters and rose to his feet with the help of his cane. "Follow me inside my hut and you can share. Best to clear the air now, so we can celebrate in full later."

Tryss took one breath in after another, the rhythm as calming as the lap of an ocean tide. It was over. The moment she'd been dreading— telling her parents about Taersidel's betrayal—was past.

They were still absorbing the news, the hurt on their faces too painful to look at directly. They hadn't wanted to accept it, but there was no denying it either. Equal to that horror was the news that they'd almost lost her in a different way, and now her father was finally looking at Errance with something resembling respect.

The Ancient was unruffled. Sad, to be sure, but not surprised. "I feared something like this might happen," he said. "When Taers left, I knew his skill would be too great for the Northern powers to leave him alone. I just did not realize they would radicalize him to this degree."

"Grandfather," Tryss began hesitantly. "While I was prisoner, Taers said some frightening things. He seemed to believe that by kidnapping me he was saving me from some terrible doom. He hinted that terrible things were coming. Do you think the North might attack the elves?"

"It is possible," the old man said, looking older than he had ever looked. "The Northern chemas are supremacists. I led my people away from them because of this belief—that they were greater than any of the other races and should rule as gods above all else. They killed the daishas in that belief, and while they have not had the strength to make war on other races, they may be climbing to that goal."

A puff of air escaped his weathered lips. "I have tried to ignore them all this time. Perhaps it is better that I send spies of my own to try to learn their secrets." Looking up at Errance, he said, "Great king, if you have any assets left in the North, I would learn all that you can from them. He who the chemas call the Wraith was your father's greatest weapon and spy, but nothing has been heard from him for decades. Rumors have spread about whether he died or became even more invisible."

Tryss shivered a little at the name, although she hardly knew why. It wasn't as if the Wraith had been a frightening bedtime story in her childhood. She'd heard a few rumors of him at the elf palace, but there he had simply been called Cerand, Errance's lost uncle.

"The throne has likewise heard nothing from him," Errance said softly so that no ears outside the room might hear him.

"That is a heavy loss indeed." The Ancient's shoulders slumped. "Well. Then, if I may advise you, when you have a chance, rebuild the alliances your father made in the North. There are tribes of aliths and men who still respect the Celestrum name."

Errance bowed his head in respect. "Thank you, Ancient. I will." His hand tightened on Tryss's shoulder. "Now then, I must excuse the both of us to rest. We're still recovering from the last couple of weeks."

"Of course, elf king, of course. I will tell everyone to give you some privacy in the hot springs and prepare a hut for you tonight."

Tryss hugged her parents and the Ancient both, and then took Errance's arm as he led her back out.

Part of her wondered if she should be in mourning with her family over Taersidel, but the rest of her was quite finished with him. Now that they'd shared the truth of his allegiance, it felt as if a heavy weight had been lifted from her shoulders. All she really wanted to do now was rest and marvel over Cerenity.

The first wish was answered when she and Errance were sent to relax in the hot springs, while Cerenity was fussed over by her grandmother and aunts. In Aselvia, the elves provided warm baths, but there was nothing quite like these bubbling hot waters to wash away a multitude of strains.

She submerged into the green pool with a thankful sigh, dipping up and down with the simmering surge. She was just starting to undo her tight braid when Errance plunged in, splashing her with the wave of his entrance.

It was hard to believe that the same elf she'd found broken in this jungle was now her husband. Back then he had been deathly pale, bones running ridges across his ravaged skin—nothing like this bronzed and sculpted creature with a mane of dark silk.

"Look at you," Tryss said softly.

"I know, I'm beautiful, or so they say."

She laughed aloud. "You're listening to *them* now, are you?"

"The only opinion that matters is yours," he replied with a smirk, pulling his wet hair back from his face to rest in a sheet over his shoulder.

Amazed to have been derailed from her original topic so thoroughly, Tryss shook her head in amused exasperation. "You are exactly that, but that isn't what I meant. I just can't believe that…well, I honestly thought with everything that happened, you would be more reclusive and fearful than ever." She folded her arms on the mossy bank and settled her chin upon them. "How are you this changed?"

He settled next to her with his back against the bank and considered. "Is it strange to say that despite the absolute panic of the last few weeks, I've felt more grounded than I have in years? I don't know how to explain it. I found myself noticing my blessings more, and looking for ways I could use them to help others. And even…even my burdens seem less heavy when they give me a better chance to help people I couldn't understand otherwise."

She slid a bit closer, leaning her cheek against his shoulder. "I don't think that sounds so very strange."

"My fears haven't gone away. But I'm finding they control me less. I'd lost faith while sitting stagnant, falling right back into my own self-reliance. I think trust in God might be easier to remember when it's being tested. So I'm not slowing down. I've just begun." He paused, leaning down beside her. "But…I want to make sure you are at peace with this. You gave me your blessing, but I didn't give you much time to think about it. I just started making plans and it all started rushing together and—"

"You talk as fast as you think and then both are jumbled," Tryss said, tapping his mouth shut with a finger. "Didn't I tell you back when you proposed? I wanted to see what God would do with you. I've known you were meant for something extraordinary."

"More extraordinary than hiding in my rooms?"

"Yes, I rather think you were meant for more than that. Just…" she hesitated, "just please promise me that you won't commit to anything too dangerous while Cerenity is still young. I will be proud she has a hero for a father, I just don't want…"

"A dead hero," he finished softly. "I promise. Don't worry, Tryss. I will be here for you and our girl."

She nestled against him, closing her eyes and relaxing in the warmth of his breath against her hair. She would be lying to herself if she didn't find the future as frightening as it was thrilling.

But they would face it together. And that promise was all she needed.

39

Aselvia could always be counted on to give this—a sense of peace, quiet, and stability.

Errance found he loved it more every time he returned to its fields and forests after an absence. All the more reason for him to go back and forth in the world now.

After returning home from the southern jungle, he'd thrown himself into studies for the future with a blazing drive. There were languages to learn, economies to study, threats to consider. He had so many changes to make within his own walls, not just outside the borders. First would be the proposal and building of safe houses within Aselvia for victims. Once he knew he had the proper support and foundation, he could present actual aid to Coren and the cities who'd welcome him.

But amid all that gale of planning, he forced himself to take moments of rest and relaxation, whether with his wife, family, friends, or by himself.

Now and then, he'd find himself taking a horse on a ride into the forest hills just north of the castle where a small house and a smaller garden stood in a cliff-sheared clearing.

There were other houses within walking distance, but not to be seen by eye. It was both a lonely and lovely little place, fit only to house one person.

Errance greeted the guard who sat in a large tree overlooking the house, then left his horse to graze as he took the stair up the balcony that bordered the southern side.

Remrant sat upon a chair on the terrace overlooking the forest slope, golden patterns of light dancing on the wood below his feet. The chair, built to swing with the sway of the body, creaked underneath him as he paged through folded sheets of paper.

"Kind of you to visit an old man," he said without looking up from whatever he was reading.

"I have to make sure you're not getting into trouble when I'm not looking," Errance retorted, leaning against the rail. "Though my guards say you're more boring to watch than a dead cicada."

Remrant snorted. "I do believe you are the one getting into trouble. The Korince Affair paper is filled to bursting with scandals against you already." He waved the paper in his hand. "Apparently you rescue slave girls only to add them to your harem, and you're still intimate with a sorceress from Tertorem."

"WHAT."

"I did tell you this would be coming."

"I know. I know. I knew before you said anything. Just hearing it is another thing." He scowled, then flung his hand through the air. "Ah, what do I care? Let them spin their lies. The people can decide for themselves based on my actions.”

“From what I can hear, many are deciding in your favor already. I haven't seen such support for a good cause in all my life. Must be your ‘astounding, rare beauty’ as this article calls it.”

“Glad it’s good for something,” Errance muttered.

“Ah, and the Dormandy Times declares you a romantic, tragic hero out to save the slaves because you share their past. This of course has launched cheaper articles of sordid, if sympathetic, speculation on your background.”

“Where did you even get these papers?”

“Your steward brought them to discuss any viable threat against you. And he allowed me to keep the pieces he thought safe to share.”

“I’m glad the scandals are deemed appropriate reading material,” Errance muttered.

“I took a walk the other day,” Remrant went on. “Shadowed, of course, by your dutiful guards. Found my nearest neighbor, who was surprisingly a fellow human. A worn man who said he’d been a fellow prisoner with you in the Tertorem mines. I was surprised he lived out here instead of the city considering how fragile he appeared, but he said he appreciated the quiet peace out in the forest.”

“I suppose the two of you can drink tea over a game of Feint or something like that,” Errance said.

“How nice of you to plan out my retirement so thoroughly. Korince papers would be disappointed to discover you actually collect old men instead of pretty girls.”

Errance rolled his eyes and pushed off the side of the rail. “Ha, ha. I think I’ll go and see how he’s getting on since I’m out here.”

"I've bored you already, I see. Didn't even have time for a cup of tea."

"Not sure I can trust the tea not to be poisoned, Remrant."

"Heavens, as if I'd do that and forfeit my chance to read all about the future uproar you'll be creating."

Shaking his head to hide a growing chuckle, Errance started down the stair.

"Errance."

He paused and looked back.

The clever quips were gone from Remrat's eyes, a shadow of regret and acceptance flickering across his face as visibly as the dappled light. "You may have your clever reasons and your solid justifications for bringing me here, and I will accept them accordingly. Just so long as we both know that anyone *but* a man of mercy would have let me burn down to the ground."

Errance looked back at him, gaze unwavering. Just when it seemed he would not reply, he spoke. "Why am I a man of mercy, Remrant?"

Remrant opened his mouth, sensed a trap, and shut it again.

"It is because, someday, I hope you will know the answer to that question." And without further explanation, Errance took the first step down the stairs and walked away, the leaves dancing in the wake of the wind behind him.

EPILOGUE

Errance was not certain what woke him, noise or dream, but he found himself lying in bed with tense muscles and held breath. He was in Aselvia. He was in his own room. And Tryss lay beside him, warm and softly breathing.

Tryss.

They were together again. He exhaled softly, heartbeat calming down. Together again.

Since everything that had transpired, he'd found his response to dreams had changed. The nightmares were not exactly decreasing in intensity, but when he woke from them, he felt more grounded, more controlled. The pain and fear remained, but he wasn't ready to lash out. Allowing the dream to stay just a dream, and he could be thankful for the present waking moment.

The slight crackle of embers in the hearth told him he had not been sleeping long. Well into winter, they kept a fire in the deep hearth at the far side of the room to keep away the night's cold.

A small mewling sound murmured from the foot of the bed.

Cerenity.

Their little girl.

Very carefully, so as not to awaken Tryss, he slid out from under the covers and padded down to the cradle where she lay nestled in her blankets.

She had already grown so much these past three months. Her hair was silkier, her features a bit more pronounced.

It had taken some time to coax her to sleep before they'd retired to bed themselves, and now here she was awake again. By now, he was used to this. Tryss had been feeding her several times a night, and he'd been glad to sit up with them. Recently, Wen's hunger through the night had become less frequent, but she still seemed reluctant to rest alone.

"Who is going to wake up more at night, you or me?" he whispered, kneeling beside the cradle and resting his chin on the rail. "Well, at least we can keep each other company."

He hesitated, afraid to cause any disturbance and wake Tryss, before reaching down and gathering her into his arms. To his relief, she made very little sound, only small, grunting noises as she looked up at him with her large, shining eyes. He moved closer to the window to better see her, marveling at the bright interest in her expression.

"I would have thought you'd at least be a little sleepy," he whispered. "Were you dreaming? You have only good dreams, I hope, though I imagine you've found this whole experience very strange."

With a small yawn, she wrinkled her eyes shut and tucked her head against his chest, falling back asleep within moments. He hardly dared breathe, but as the minutes ticked by and his arms began to ache, he decided to take a seat near the hearth to better support her weight.

What a thing it was to be so trusted.

The minutes turned to hours, and while he caught himself yawning then and again, he still could not bear to set her back inside her crib. Maybe some other night.

Before he knew it, the veil at the window started to color with a pale honey glow. He could hardly believe she'd slept the entire night in his arms without crying for Tryss.

"Do you see that, little one?" he whispered, rising and pulling aside the veil. Cerenity slept on. "Do you see that light on the horizon? It always brings me great comfort."

As if that last bit caught her attention, the princess opened her cyan eyes and peeked towards the window, rubbing her small, chubby fist against her cheek with a sigh.

"The night is over," Errance said, a soft smile brushing his lips. "The sun is rising."

ACKNOWLEDGEMENTS

Story is a marvelous thing. It is both simple and complex, at times easy to tell and at times impossible to share. Some days I am frustrated that I am a slow writer, and at others I am grateful to take my time.

But a story is nothing without its audience, and I am grateful to each and every one of readers who loved Moonscript and were willing to wait so patiently for the continuation.

My family is always there to support and encourage me in each step of the story. Mom and Grammie, you heard and loved the story first, and Dad, you were a champ for listening to the whole thing on a nine-hour drive down and a nine-hour drive back. I'm still not sure how I read aloud that long without talking your ear off.

Thank to my alpha readers, Bryn, Wyn, and Tara! Bryn, you always help me keep the lore of the story straight and my focus on the journey ahead. Wyn, for being an absolute cheerleader on all the new developments, and Tara for speaking in all things retaining to a Hot Elf Male Lead.

Thank you to my beta/proof team Merie, Rose, Hannah, Jessica, Bethany, Misty, Rachel, Faith, Olivia, and Natalie.

Thank you to Kateryna for the beautiful cover, and for working with me on every detail. Thank you to Noverantale for the gorgeous map. And thank you to Hannah Rogers for creating such perfect art titles for part one, two, and three.

Here is to the stories ahead!

From the beginning, H. S. J. Williams has loved stories and all the forms they take. Whether with word, art, or costume, she has always been fascinated with the magic of imagination. She lives in a real fantastical kingdom, the beautiful Pacific Northwest, with her very own array of animal friends and royally loving family. Williams taught Fantasy Illustration at MSOA. She may also be a part-time elf.

FAIREST SON was her first venture into the publishing world, a novella to teach her the ropes.

She is also an artist and has long dreamed of illustrating her own books, a dream realized today. You can check out and follow William's art page over at hsjwilliams.wordpress.com

SIGN UP FOR H.S.J. WILLIAMS'S NEWSLETTER
hsjwilliams.com

Follow her for writing updates and art at
Facebook: @hsjwilliams
Instagram: @h.s.j._williams

THE ARTISTS

Cover Art by Kateryna Vitkovska
@morgana0anagrom

Map Art by Noverantale
@noverantale

Interior Illustrations by Hannah S.J. Williams
@h.s.j._williams

Part I, II, III Art by Hannah Rogers
@inscape.studio

KINGS OF ASELVIA

CELESTIAL

Currently in Development

www.ingramcontent.com/pod-product-compliance
Lightning Source LLC
Chambersburg PA
CBHW072035190726
48294CB00005B/1273